SILENT WE STOOD

SILENT WE STOOD

A NOVEL

Henry Chappell

Texas Tech University Press

This book is typeset in Amasis. The paper used in this book meets the minimum requirements of ANSI/NISO Z39.48-1992 (R1997). ∞

Designed by Kasey McBeath
Cover illustration by Tiffany Naylor

Library of Congress Cataloging-in-Publication Data
Chappell, Henry.
    Silent We Stood / Henry Chappell.
        pages cm
    ISBN 978-0-89672-832-5 (hardback) — ISBN 978-0-89672-833-2 (e-book)
1. Abolitionists—Texas—Fiction. 2. Slavery--Texas—Fiction. 3. Texas--Race relations—Fiction. 4. Texas—History--1846–1950—Fiction. I. Title.
    PS3603.H376S55 2013
    813'.6—dc23   2013028361

13 14 15 16 17 18 19 20 21 / 9 8 7 6 5 4 3 2 1

Texas Tech University Press
Box 41037 | Lubbock, Texas 79409-1037 USA
800.832.4042 | ttup@ttu.edu | www.ttupress.org

For Linda Chappell Ingle

I was at hand, silent I stood with teeth shut close, I watch'd . . .

WALT WHITMAN, "Year of Meteors"

Caution, caution, sir. I am eternally tired of hearing the word caution. It is nothing but the word of cowardice.

JOHN BROWN

PREFACE

On Sunday, July 8, 1860, Dallas, Texas, burned. At about 2 p.m., a fire started in a kindling box in front of W. W. Peak & Sons Drug Store, on the courthouse square. Within minutes, the flames, fanned by a gusting southwesterly wind, spread to adjacent buildings. By late afternoon, twenty-five establishments had burned. Only the brick courthouse at the center of the square survived. Townspeople with buckets and shovels saved homes beyond the square.

Given the summer heat, wind, aridity, wooden buildings, prevalence of cigar smoking among men, and the dependence on wood fires for cooking, blacksmithing, and steam generation, disastrous fires seem, in hindsight, inevitable. Lacking evidence to the contrary, most historians consider the Dallas fire the result of spontaneous combustion of highly unstable phosphorous matches, called "prairie matches," in common use at the time.

But in the summer of 1860, fear of slave rebellion gripped farmers and businessmen in Dallas County. The previous October, federal troops put down John Brown's maniacal raid on the arsenal at Harper's Ferry, Virginia. Abraham Lincoln's election, secession, and war loomed. North Texas newspapers urged vigilance against shadowy seditionists and abolitionists who wished to lead slaves in a murderous insurrection.

The ashen remains of Dallas's square had barely cooled when Charles Pryor, editor of the *Dallas Herald*, wrote that abolitionist preachers had fomented a "deep laid scheme of villainy" to terrorize North Texas by fire and assassination. After interrogating dozens of slaves, Dallas's vigilance committee charged three alleged ringleaders. On July 23, after a closed-door meeting, city leaders sentenced three slaves to death by hanging, and every other slave in the county to disciplinary beating. The next afternoon, the three slaves were hanged on the banks of the Trinity River.

The leadership class in antebellum Texas consisted largely of slave owners from the Deep South, while most yeomen came from the Upper

South, especially the border states. Certainly, some of these smallholders were ambivalent about slavery if not resentful toward prosperous slaveholders. In 1860, only 27 percent of Texans owned slaves while 68 percent of state officeholders were slave owners. At that time, the population in Dallas County stood at 1,074 slaves and 8,665 whites. About 775 whites and 100 slaves lived in the town of Dallas.

Violence between unionists and secessionists in the Sulphur Forks region north of Dallas in the months leading up to the Civil War contradicts the popular perception of Texas as a unified proslavery, prosecession state. During the Civil War, Confederate deserters and ideological opponents of slavery and secession sought refuge in the region's dense thickets, as did miscreants of every stripe.

Historians have uncovered scant evidence of Underground Railroad activity in Texas. However, newspaper articles and advertisements from the period suggest runaway slaves were common in the state. Chroniclers such as Frederick Law Olmsted wrote that runaways sometimes sought refuge in Mexico.

Although accused of fomenting the alleged insurrection and arson, Parson Solomon McKinney and Parson William Blount had been arrested, severely beaten, and expelled the previous summer, and they were reported in the Midwest in 1860. Once back in the North, both men denied all accusations of abolitionism. Their characterizations in this novel are purely products of my imagination, as are those of other historical figures, such as John McCoy, Judge Nat Burford, and Alan Huitt. Marshal James Moore and his deputies are fictional characters. Their words and actions should not be attributed to any of the lawmen serving in Dallas during the period in which the novel is set.

All newspaper articles attributed to the *Dallas Herald* are works of fiction save for the Associated Press report of John Brown's raid at Harper's Ferry, which I've edited for brevity and punctuation.

I offer no theories about what happened in Dallas during those hot, violent weeks in 1860, only a story that suggests something could have been afoot, and that a few well-placed people might have been happy to attribute the fire to carelessness, the insurrection stories to collective hysteria.

H.C.
Parker, Texas, 2012

ACKNOWLEDGMENTS

Silent We Stood could not have been completed without the help and support of my family, friends, and colleagues.

My wife, Jane, proofread every draft and encouraged me through many rough patches. My ever patient editor, Judith Keeling, guided me through the tentative early chapters and directed me to much needed scholarly help. Her advice and sure editorial touch greatly improved this book. Dr. Alwyn Barr carefully read the manuscript and steered me clear of numerous historical blunders. Anonymous reader number 2 provided the most thorough and helpful critique I've ever seen. I am eternally grateful.

I found several books essential to establishing the novel's historical and cultural background: T. R. Fehrenbach, *Lone Star: A History of Texas and the Texans* (1983); Randolph B. Campbell, *Gone to Texas: A History of the Lone Star State* (2003); Michael V. Hazel, *Dallas: A History of "Big D"* (1997); G. P. Gallaway, editor, *Texas: The Dark Corner of the Confederacy* (1994); David Pickering and Judy Falls, *Brush Men and Vigilantes: Civil War Dissent in Texas* (2000); Michael V. Hazel, editor, *Dallas Reconsidered: Essays in Local History* (1995); Michael Phillips, *White Metropolis: Race, Ethnicity, and Religion in Dallas, 1841–2001* (2006); Stephen B. Oates, *To Purge This Land with Blood; A Biography of John Brown* (1984); Edward J. Renehan, Jr., *The Secret Six: The True Tale of the Men Who Conspired with John Brown* (1997); Fergus M. Bordewich, *Bound for Canaan: The Underground Railroad and the War for the Soul of America* (2005); Donald E. Reynolds, *Texas Terror: The Slave Insurrection Panic of 1860 and the Secession of the Lower South* (2007); and Eugene D. Genovese, *Roll Jordan Roll: The World the Slaves Made* (1974).

I am also indebted to the staff of the Texas/Dallas History and Archives section of the J. Erik Jonsson Central Library, who were never too busy to help me locate a journal article or load rolls of microfilm of 1859–60 issues of The *Dallas Herald* onto the viewer.

Any historical error or misinterpretation is mine alone.

Principals

Reverend Ignatius Bodeker—Rotund, melancholic minister from western Virginia. Settled in Dallas after years of antislavery work in Kansas. Rachel Bodeker's husband.

Rachel Bodeker—Fierce, erudite abolitionist from Maryland. Ignatius Bodeker's wife. Joseph Shaw's lover.

*Nat Burford—Judge of the Sixteenth Judicial District, which included Dallas County. Known and respected for fairness and moderation.

*Cato—A slave in Dallas accused of inciting insurrection.

Parson Jonah Chambers—Radical abolitionist minister and close friend of Parson Zephaniah Newton.

Brother Sid Claggett—Slave preacher owned by Sarah Cockrell.

Stephen Conklin—Southern abolitionist who, along with his friend Levin McGregor, guided many slaves out of the South.

Ebenezer Euler—"Professor Euler," a secret abolitionist and teacher in the La Reunion commune.

*Al Huitt—Beloved and trusted local slave and skilled blacksmith. Secretly worked with local crypto-abolitionists.

*Patrick Jennings—A slave in Dallas accused of inciting insurrection.

William Keller—Recently arrived land speculator. Charismatic, rakish, and shrewd, he quickly maneuvered into a position of local influence. Vocal about the dangers of slave and abolitionist sedition. Claimed to have lost his right hand in the war with Mexico. Brandished a hook in its place.

*John McCoy—Prominent Dallas attorney much respected for his generosity, competence, and honesty. Often addressed as "Major McCoy."

Levin McGregor—aka David Singlearm, escaped slave, who, along with Stephen Conklin, guided many slaves from the Deep South north to freedom. Operating in North Texas, he achieved near-mythical status as a slave stealer.

Malachi Meade—Dallas attorney and secret member of the local abolitionist movement. Met Joseph Shaw and the Bodekers in Kansas.

Parson Zephaniah Newton—Firebrand abolitionist preacher from Iowa, much feared by local slave owners. Works closely with Parson Jonah Chambers.

Pig Nuchols—Frontier abolitionist from eastern Tennessee. Veteran of the war with Mexico. Often served as Ig Bodeker's bodyguard.

*Charles Pryor—Publisher of the *Dallas Herald*, slave owner.

Rebekah (Bekah)—Indomitable runaway slave from Alabama purchased and secretly freed by Samuel Smith. Two of her children, Timothy and Mary, were sold to distant plantations. A third, Flora, died of diphtheria after being carried on Rebekah's back during an unsuccessful escape attempt. Her husband, Robert, was killed during an escape attempt. Her brother James escaped to Philadelphia, where, with the help of the Philadelphia Anti-Slavery Society, he tried to buy her freedom.

Joseph Shaw—Carpenter and undertaker in Dallas. Veteran of Underground Railroad in Kentucky, southern Ohio, Kansas, and Missouri. Ig Bodeker's closest friend. Rachel Bodeker's lover.

Winfred Skaggs—Dallas-area traveling salesman burned to death for his antislavery views.

*Samuel Smith—Young crypto-freedman and apprentice carpenter posing as Joseph Shaw's slave.

Ben Thigpen—Slave catcher.

Richard Van Huss—Owner of a Dallas butcher shop. Longtime member of circle of abolitionists from Kansas.

SILENT WE STOOD

Father's Reminiscence
Transcribed July 24, 1911

If after all that I am about to tell you—or admit—you think I'm a coward, imagine standing amid a mob, watching as three condemned men are kicked off a bluff above the Trinity River. They roll and careen off of roots and stumps, tumble out onto the cracked mud below the river bank. One of them cries out; his shoulder has been torn from its socket. All have been stripped of their shirts. Filth clings to their bloody backs.

Above them, on Commerce Street, workmen resurrect a vile, venal town that burned sixteen days prior. A cloud of ash still hangs in the air. The hammering and sawing never stop—even for public murder.

Someone had to pay.

Try to imagine it.

For fifty-one years, I've been unable to forget.

That day on the riverbank I looked into the eyes of one of those three men an instant before a mail clerk named Randolph Spurge kicked a barrel from beneath his feet and left him dangling. The next two in line watched as ropes were slung over other limbs.

I've seen his eyes every day since he sought mine in those last seconds, but I sleep with a clear conscience. I saw no accusation there, only sorrow and resolve, love, and a measure of relief when he knew I would hold my tongue and let him hang.

CHAPTER I

Dallas, Texas
May 1859

Rev. Ignatius Bodeker was sweating from exertion and poor tent location.

Five rows back, Joseph Shaw, sitting on a rough bench and perspiring himself, suspected the black woolen suit hugging Brother Ig's 280 pounds contributed also. To the congregation's back, the ancient pecan trees that cast inviting shade along the creek blocked the breeze that soughed in the little bluestem on the surrounding prairie. Gnats swarmed in the still air beneath the canvas.

Brother Ig stepped before his chestnut lectern and smiled at his flock. His turgid jowls and sandy-red muttonchops drooped. For a moment, his eyes settled on Rachel, his winsome blonde wife sitting in the center of the first row. The front-row matrons beamed. The good reverend's darling bride. Beloved Rachel, thirty-one, childless and despairing, who recently confided in her closest friend, Rosemary Meade—who in strictest confidence told Hilda Van Huss, who passed the morsel along to her husband, Richard, who, despite Hilda's threats, downed one too many shots of whiskey and told Joseph, who feigned disinterest—that Brother Ig, faithful and affectionate as he was, and despite his frequent and best efforts, rarely succeeded in his primary conjugal role.

But there was nothing impotent about his preaching.

"The enemy—sin—must be met on the battleground of our souls and our soil. We must be ruthless in this purging. None shall be allowed to remain therein!" Brother Ig paced back and forth, gesturing, wetting his hems in the ankle-high grass. "And Joshua said unto them, 'Fear not, nor be dismayed, be strong and of good courage!'" He waved and blew at a swarm of gnats hovering about his face.

"And then what did he and the army of Israel do at Eglon? 'They took it on that day and smote it with the edge of the sword, and all of the souls therein he utterly destroyed that day, according to all that he had done at Lachish.' Chapter ten, verse thirty-five." He glared at his congregation as if confronting them with irrefutable evidence and awaiting the obvious reply. "Surely you see it!"

On the front row, sitting next to her husband, Malachi, Rosemary Meade quietly said, "Amen."

Brother Ig smiled again and clasped his hands behind him. "Now, of course, I speak metaphorically. For while we must be ruthless against sin, we must never raise the edge of the sword against our enemies among God's children as did the great old patriarchs. Our Lord has shown us another way through Jesus Christ. But humanity toward our enemies does not preclude courage, nor absolve us of our quest for justice and godly living."

The redness in his face deepened as his volume rose. "Nor, in outwitting evil, does it preclude utter ruthlessness, cunning, and ultimate sacrifice. Nor can we tolerate meekness in the face of barbarism, cowardice in the face of injustice, the tiniest compromise in the presence of sin!"

Horses nickered in the rope corral back in the woods. A mule brayed. Brother Ig looked up for a second, then continued. "And Joshua passed from Libnah and all Israel with him, unto Lachish, and encamped against it and fought against it. He encamped against it. . . ." Brother Ig looked up as Pig Nuchols led his sorrel gelding in among the wagons and headed toward the woods. A few in the congregation turned to look. "And," Brother Ig continued. The four Nuchols boys, seated with their mother, Cathlyn, two on each side, looked out the back of the tent.

"And, and, beloved. And!" The boys turned back toward Brother Ig. "And, they fought against it. They laid siege against it."

For an instant, Ig's eyes caught Cathlyn's. Joseph thought he saw a brief nod—or a blink—of acknowledgment.

Brother Ig continued his sermon on the necessity of tireless battle against iniquity. A few people turned to watch Pig return from the woods and squat on his heels at the rear of the tent. The benches were packed. Several men were standing. Pig chewed on a blade of grass, waiting for Brother Ig to finish. He'd be waiting for a while yet.

In spite of himself, Joseph let his attention wander to Rachel's graceful neck, grateful, for the moment, that it wasn't covered by her hair, though he often imagined her hair draped about her shoulders, such as it might be of a night just before bedtime, or mornings before she gathered and pinned it.

Lately, he'd realized Brother Ig had only one sermon, a message of vigilance against sin and injustice, terms he used interchangeably. Brother Ig was a practical man of this world. He spent little time on abstractions such as salvation and grace or hell. His attacks on sin appealed to his congregation's sense of rightness or what he thought their sense of rightness should be. Smite sin with the Old Testament; appeal for justice and peace and love with the New Testament. Perhaps, in the end, that was the only sermon.

The clearing of throats and the rustle of cotton and wool nudged Joseph from his reverie, and he stood with the rest of the congregation. Brother Ig led them through "Come Thou Fount of Every Blessing" and "How Firm a Foundation," then closed with an unusually short prayer. As they adjourned, Joseph realized there had been no invitation to come forward and accept salvation, even though there were new faces in the congregation.

The women gathered around Brother Ig and Rachel as the men crowded out the tied-back door of the tent, most groping in pockets for tobacco. Though Brother Ig generally practiced temperance, Joseph could recall no sermon against tobacco or drink.

Already Pig Nuchols was walking out beyond the horses, into the open meadow. Joseph, Richard Van Huss, and Malachi Meade worked their way toward him, speaking to the other men, shaking hands, commenting on last night's rain. Back in the tent, Cathlyn Nuchols would be wending through the crowd of men, keeping her boys close with threats and tugs, smiling, greeting.

Pig stopped on a gentle rise fifty yards from the tent. Grinning, looking in the distance as if taking in the horizon, he knelt and snatched a handful of grass and tossed it. Joseph slowed, waiting for Brother Ig's flock of women to scatter. Malachi had stopped, was leaning against a wagon, nodding and talking to some new people, a young couple named Squires.

Joseph watched Rachel holding an elderly woman's hands and fussing over Ig, who kept glancing up the hill. The crowd of women thinned, and directly Ig bent to say something in Rachel's ear. She nodded. He patted Rosemary Meade's hand and headed up the rise. Joseph eased on toward Nuchols. Richard and Malachi took his lead. Halfway up the hill, Brother Ig yelled, "Pig, I'll take you tardy over absent."

"I'm much relieved, preacher," Pig yelled back. "If my mare hadn't foaled when she did, you'd have had to settle for absent."

Ig unbuttoned his jacket as he strode up the gentle rise. "If you're square with the Lord, you're square with me. And I trust God has a keener appreciation for horseflesh than he does for my preaching."

People catching horses and milling about wagons laughed. Ig's smile vanished. Joseph could hear his breathing as he strode up the hill.

Joseph, Richard, and Malachi greeted Nuchols, then said nothing as they waited for Brother Ig, who trudged up. The air smelled clean and fecund, bracing after the close air in the tent. Their open jackets flapped in the gusts. Brother Ig coughed and spat. "Well, Pig, why not just walk on up to McKinney?"

Pig said, "I wanted to get out of earshot. They'll think we're discussing church matters."

Ig looked back down the rise. People were leaving, most heading south. "Well. So. Did you deliver word?"

"I did. They have some concerns. Nothing that can't be sorted out, though."

"Excellent." Ig took off his hat and wiped his brow with his sleeve.

Joseph said, "You look awful forlorn for a man bearing good news."

Pig rubbed the three-day growth on his jaws. He was normally clean-shaven. "They got Winfred Skaggs up at Breckinridge. Somebody did."

Malachi said, "Got him?"

"Caught him on his way down from Sherman, looked like. You can't tell."

"Wait. You've seen him?" Ig asked.

"Afraid so."

Richard Van Huss said, "What do you mean they caught him?"

Pig looked at him, shook his head.

Richard said, "I told him about carrying those books around in his wagon. He promised he'd quit. Now he's got caught, and it's liable to be the death of us all."

Winfred always carried copies of *Impending Crisis in the South* in his wagon, hidden among the Dutch ovens and elixirs and dry goods he peddled. He'd shown Joseph his hidden stash and said he gave them out to sympathizers and men and women of goodwill. "Caught him coming or going?"

"I can't say. We'll have to send somebody else to make sure."

"I thought you saw him," Brother Ig said.

"He wasn't in no shape to talk. They'd hung him by his wrists over his wagon, killed his team, poured kerosene all over it and lit it."

Brother Ig said, "Beloved Lord."

Richard and Malachi swallowed and nodded. Joseph pictured the little salesman holding forth on the evils of slavery while his killers bound his wrists, his tirade growing shriller as he watched the wagon being pushed beneath him and doused in kerosene.

"I pray he went quick," Brother Ig said. "Or the Lord took him quick, before the flames got him." The color had left his jowls.

Malachi glanced down the hill toward the tent. "Any law been notified?"

Pig said, "Somebody went after Moore."

Everyone snorted.

"I think Winfred has a sister in Missouri," Joseph said. "What about remains?"

Pig said, "Uh, Joe, I guess the fire finally burned the rope in two. We had to run hogs off."

Joseph nodded. He'd worked with less. Don't think about it. Close the casket. Put it in the ground. Then you could imagine him whole again.

They walked down the hill to catch their horses. A new man, a bachelor named William Keller, met them and said, "Brother Ig and Brother Pig."

Joseph laughed at the stale joke, more out of courtesy than humor.

Keller extended his left hand. A metal hook protruded from the right sleeve of his coat. He'd lost his hand in the Mexican War. "A moving sermon, Reverend. How are you?"

Ignatius grinned and clasped Keller's hand. "Thank you, Bill. Good to see you again. I'm very well indeed."

CHAPTER 2

In the weak light of the bedside candle, Joseph Shaw noted with affection the shadows beneath Rachel's blue eyes. The skin on her cheekbones seemed tauter, thinner than he remembered from just three weeks before. He traced each dark half-circle with his finger. She smiled and closed her eyes. He kissed her eyelids. She was two years older than he.

"I'm afraid my youth left me some years ago," she said.

"You seemed plenty vigorous."

She smiled again, scooted down in the bed, and laid her face on his chest. She lacked only an inch being as tall as Joseph. He could feel her feet beyond his. Her toes probably were off the end of the bed.

"I've been hoarding my ardor," she said and laughed into his chest. "I've had little choice, though Ig and I did manage the night before he left. He seems more able right after he rises from a melancholic spell. Suffering seems to purge him."

Joseph stroked her hair. She'd taken it down after they'd eaten their late supper. She held his gaze as she pulled out the pins and ran her fingers through her hair as it spread about her shoulders—her signal they'd dallied over their meal long enough.

"Then he goes back out and feels the world's suffering," she said. "No wonder he falls into despair."

"Yet here we lay." He kissed the top of her head.

"Our reckoning awaits us," she said. "Ig would say so."

Her breath was warm on his chest. He felt her lips moving when she spoke.

"And you?"

She said, "When you're here, judgment seems impossible. But after you've gone, and I'm lying here alone in the dark, it seems certain. And certain to be harsh."

They lay in silence. He stroked her hair, kissed her shoulder. Down the road, a dog barked. A coyote answered from the river bottom. After a while, he said, "Seems to me Ig's momentary virility could be fortuitous."

"It was pleasant. I recognized the signs and was laying for him."

He laughed, felt her grin.

She said, "I feel wretched saying things like that."

"You're a plain-spoken woman."

"Only in your company."

"I mean it could be fortuitous if you conceived tonight."

"Yes, or tomorrow night or the following night. Or perhaps even on those nights last month." She scooted up and lay back on her pillow. "But what if the child has dark hair and eyes and tends toward gauntness?"

"You're not the fleshiest woman I've seen. Any gauntness could be your fault."

"Yes, but dark hair and eyes? Who could I blame that on?"

"Any swarthy cousins? Aunts or uncles?"

"One great uncle. Otherwise, all fair."

"Well. Ig's people?"

"Perhaps. I've met only a few of his kin. His sister has red hair. His brother was nearly a towhead when he had hair." She clasped her hands behind her head. "Ig would celebrate any child he could claim. So would I." She turned to him. "And you?"

He placed his hand on her belly. Still firm. "Any child of yours." Something turned over in his chest. The thought of giving her a child, making a child with her, stirred him, brought a fierce tenderness that sharpened his arousal.

She closed her eyes and smiled. He spread his fingers on her belly. She drew a breath, put her hand on his. Her skin seemed to warm. He felt the slight rising of her hips. She rolled on top of him. Her breath and hair fell on his face. "Well then," she said, and kissed him.

He brushed her hair back. "But how will I see you with children climbing your legs?"

She smiled, studied him. "There's always a way, as long as the flesh is willing."

"Or weak," he said.

She kissed him. "I suppose. Yours seems to be firming up again. I had hoped it would."

―――

Just after three in the morning, he left Rachel and walked footpaths and hog trails through the cedars and briar thickets on the southern end of town. A waning moon lighted his way. Despite the early May coolness, mosquitoes waited in every eddy of still air. He lived less than a mile from the Bodekers; normally he'd have ridden, but he couldn't risk someone seeing his horse at their house—a tiny, low, log box in the middle of two acres that the previous owners hacked out of the cedar break.

Ig and Rachel lived on what the congregation could provide, which wasn't much. Their place had no barn, no henhouse. Their chickens roosted in the trees or on the roof. The birds thrived, though Rachel could rarely catch them or find their eggs. She joked that she'd spend less effort shooting quail or prairie chickens than gathering a meal from her own flock. She kept a kitchen garden, but deer and rabbits ate from it at least as much as she and Ig did.

Their fathers and grandfathers had been ministers; in turn for spiritual care, they had always been cared for by church members. As they moved southwest, from western Virginia to Ohio, Kansas, and farther into the frontier, the comforts of congregational care became fewer and fewer. Texas tested them in ways they'd never imagined. Joseph did not consider them practical people.

Nor were they timid people. The prior morning Brother Ig, with Pig Nuchols along for help and protection, left with two wagons loaded with his tent, lectern, and a few benches, to ride up to Breckinridge to preach to families from the border states—Tennessee and Kentucky, primarily—some of whom owned slaves. Some perhaps who'd bound Winfred Skaggs's arms and hands and set his wagon ablaze.

Ig would be away at least a week. Neither Joseph nor Rachel knew the preacher's travel plans beyond that. For the next five nights, he and Rachel would take as much from each other as they could. Then they would wait again.

Hogs and other night things rustled and started in the brush and tall grass. He barely heard them. By the time he emerged at Lamar Street, his house and shop in sight, his desire had returned, though his eyes ached from lack of sleep. He'd scarcely dozed in the Bodekers' bed.

Samuel, his Negro apprentice, would be at work before sunrise. His cabin sat next to Joseph's. Weak light shone beneath the door.

He thought again of Rachel's scent and hunger, caught himself thinking of life without Ignatius Bodeker, the likelihood of paranoid slavers made suspicious by his sermons. Then the image of Ig's charred, withered body in a coffin. "Disgusting," he whispered. "You vile pig. He's the best man you've known." He walked into his yard. "Forgive me," he said. He decided his fatigue had made him weepy.

—

When Joseph stepped out his back door, the sun had cleared the horizon, and Samuel was already unloading a wagonful of lumber from Sarah Cockrell's sawmill. The sight and scent of the wood cheered him. He'd always be a carpenter at heart. If the trade were as lucrative as undertaking, he'd be a full-time carpenter.

"Good morning, Samuel. You're up and at it early."

"I'm late and you know it. But not as late as you." Samuel pulled a board from the wagon and stacked it against the side of the shop, beneath the overhang where they did most of their work.

Joseph smiled and began helping with the unloading.

"So, Mister Joseph. I suppose you called on Miss Ellen last night and lost track of time."

"I haven't called on Ellen in months. Anyway she's seeing Ben Holt."

"That's right. Moved on to older and steadier. I forgot. Miss Ann Renner then."

"Far too pious for me." He'd grown tired of her prudishness. Since that afternoon at the Bodeker place, he'd not given Ann Renner a thought.

"Ran you off for caddish behavior, I 'magine. You never told me about that." Samuel wiped the sweat from his eyes and picked up another plank.

"You misjudge me, my friend." Over the past three years, Samuel had come to know him better than anyone.

"Oh, I might be wrong about what happened with Miss Ann, but I ain't wrong about caddish behavior. If she didn't run you off for that, she should've, because I know very well you gave her reason."

"You'd blame me."

"Not one bit."

"Careful where you say things like that, my friend."

Samuel walked back after stacking a board and put his forearms on the wagon rail. "Always." He studied Joseph. "That leaves checking in on Miz Rachel Bodeker. She must've had some work for you. I know Brother Ig can't drive a nail. Doors fallin' off, were they? Roof blowed off?"

Joseph laughed, mostly out of exasperation. "Samuel. Now hell. I did a few little things around the place and came home. Just like I promised Brother Ig. Rachel is about as helpless as he is. I believe some of the women are checking in on her this afternoon or tomorrow." All very well, so long as they left before dark. Maybe he'd take a short nap after dinner and another right after supper.

They worked through the morning, measuring and sawing the makings for three adult-sized caskets. Joseph liked to keep five on hand at all times. Working together, they could build one in a long day, but they'd started too late today, and Joseph certainly wouldn't work after supper, even though the days were getting longer. Not for the next few nights anyway. He preferred to work outside in good light, though winters some-time drove him inside where they worked mostly from candlelight and light from oil lamps. His head ached from lack of sleep, but he slipped into the comfort of work he enjoyed.

He had trained Samuel in carpentry, so their work habits and methods rarely clashed. They could converse, as they did most days, and measure and saw and plane and finish with no loss of efficiency. This day, though, they worked mostly in silence, which suited Joseph. It seemed to suit Samuel as well, although the young man seemed in fine spirits. Think-ing about women, or a woman, Joseph suspected. Thoughts of lips and loins made a day pass quick and pleasant. But if the yearning was fierce enough, you could grind your teeth to dust. He'd known both ways.

Joseph owned a slave, a fact that deviled him, no matter his inten-tions. He'd bought Samuel two years prior from W. B. Mitchell, a prom-inent Dallas farmer and stockman. He'd met Samuel during the funeral and burial of Aunt Anne, one of Mitchell's elderly house slaves, and had been at once impressed by the young man's wit and energy. He'd needed an assistant and talked Mitchell into hiring Samuel out for three months. The arrangement worked so well that Joseph offered five hundred dol-lars for Samuel with the intention of giving him his freedom. He hoped the young man would be grateful enough to stay on as an apprentice. To his surprise, Mitchell accepted the offer without dickering, saying that Samuel was a bright boy and ought to have a chance to make something of himself.

When Joseph explained his plans—after the purchase—Samuel be-came anxious to the point of panic. How would he—a black man—ride freely in Dallas County? Should he be caught on the roads, especially at night, he would be hanged or worse. In many ways, a free Negro was less free than a slave in Dallas County. An unattended slave who could prove he was traveling on his master's business would be left alone. Slaves had value, and only a fool or desperate criminal tampered with the property of those prosperous enough to own slaves.

But a free Negro belonged to no one except himself, which was to say that in the eyes of many white Texans, especially those prone to violence, he belonged to no one and was therefore worthless chattel. Worse yet, he might have pretensions. He might want to own land or put ideas in the heads of other Negroes, those who had value because they belonged to someone.

So they dropped the talk of legal if not practical freedom for Samuel. Joseph merely said they'd talk about it some other time. Samuel seemed relieved and set about learning carpentry, for which he had talent, and undertaking, for which he had more ability than affinity.

Then one day as they were trimming a child's casket—scarlet fever had passed through that spring—about a year after he had come into Joseph's ownership, Samuel brought up his freedom. Maybe he could continue to work for Joseph, save enough to own a small house, tools, a horse. He'd keep quiet about it. Stay in town. People would see he was no threat.

They talked on this for several days. The idea seemed reasonable. Joseph complimented Samuel on his good sense. He'd see what he could do. Next Sunday he'd speak to Malachi Meade, who handled his legal affairs, about drafting the documents.

Two days later, a preacher was dragged from his room in Cedar Hill and nearly beaten to death. Most of his teeth were kicked out. Rumor had it, he had abolitionist leanings. The marshal questioned members of the preacher's congregation. No one had heard any seditious preaching. Eleven different interviewees gave the same description of his sermons. No arrests were made, no suspects named. During the wee hours the following Saturday morning in Lancaster, Clyde Hill's inn burned to the ground. He'd granted two of his slaves—a cook and her fifteen-year-old daughter—their freedom the week before. They'd stayed on as employees. Both died in the fire. Samuel and Joseph gathered their remains from the ashes and buried them in the Negro cemetery.

Samuel worked on. No documents of freedom were drawn. Joseph told him to consider himself an employee. His wages—the going rate for an apprentice carpenter—would be accounted for and dispensed discreetly or set aside as he chose. Samuel chose the latter. Both men understood they were saving to buy a woman.

—

Joseph lay with Rachel that night and the two following. The last night, a Thursday, though she'd been as desirous as ever, she seemed distracted afterward. But her ardor rose again, then they slept instead of talking into the wee hours. He shook his head at the pink horizon as he walked into his yard. Later that morning, as he and Samuel adjusted the hinges on a casket, he looked up and saw Ignatius Bodeker taking up two-thirds of a wagon seat as he drove his team down Lamar Street.

CHAPTER 3

Brother Ig whoaed his team along the edge of Joseph's yard. He kept his seat, exchanged waves with Samuel. Joseph said through his smile, too softly for Ig to hear, "That's right. Keep your big ass right where it is, Reverend. I'll come to you."

"Somebody didn't get his sleep out," Samuel said. "I reckon you can catch up now, though."

"Good morning, sir." Joseph walked over to Ig. "I trust you found the hinterland rife with open and agreeable hearts."

"As always. How goes the cadaver business?"

"Slow, but we're patient men. The fevers and infections will pick up soon enough. An undertaker soon learns to spend cautiously lest he be ruined by health, peace, and general prosperity."

"The Lord will occasionally test a man with a mild, healthful spring."

"What'd you do with Pig?"

"Released him to Cathlyn. She'll be happy with him for a day or two. Then she'll be ready to get him out from under foot again. A man of God strives to strengthen the bonds of matrimony."

"Well." Joseph leaned against the wagon. "Hear anything?"

"Just a little. Seems Winfred got the word to Sherman and McKinney. I didn't make it up to Preston, though. If he told his murderers anything, they're keeping it to themselves. Nobody's talking."

"Scared."

"I had a good crowd in Breckinridge the first night. Second night, I preached to eight people. About the same thing in Plano. I don't know who to talk to."

"Don't think they won't kill a preacher."

Ig seemed to ignore the comment. "We have our network to the south."

"One family? We still haven't talked to the Germans. I don't see how it'll work, Ig."

"The communists might be sympathetic."

"We keep saying that, but nobody's approached them."

"Surely one of them will approach their Bavarian neighbors."

"That's not what I mean. It's the distance between here and the border. Hell, the distance between here and the Germans. We've got one family, thirty miles south of here, willing to help. It's a long damn way from there to Fredericksburg."

"That again. Faith, my friend."

"And most of it in Comancheria."

"The Germans have learned to negotiate with the Comanches."

"Apaches, too? We're nowhere near ready. We're a good two years away."

"You think Dallas County is crowded with slavers now? In two years, we won't be able to move. Kentucky and Tennessee are emptying into Texas."

"I say we look north in the short term."

"And how many miles between here and the Ohio?"

"We have people in place along most of the routes."

"Except for the four hundred miles between here and Lawrence," Ig said. A gust blew his muttonchops forward.

Joseph imagined Rachel lying beneath Ig, then shook off the thought.

"Courage," Ig said.

"Yes, and practicality. A man will risk anything for freedom, but only if there's some hope. And there's none between here and Mexico. Or in Mexico. We've only the faintest connections there. Hearsay."

"We have to trust."

"Winfred trusted, and his poor judgment got him burned alive. If we do no better we may as well be murderers. Risk is unavoidable, but there has to be at least some hope."

"God's plan is unknowable. He shows us only a bit at a time. Just enough for us to carry out our portion. Winfred carried out his portion, maybe unbeknownst to him." Ig sighed. "I think we need to get everyone together again and talk."

"Sunday after the sermon again?"

Brother Ig studied the reins in his hands. "I'm seeing too many new faces in the congregation. And of the familiar faces, I'm not entirely sure who we can trust."

"Our usual spot, then."

Ig nodded. "Let's not set a time yet. I need a meal and a night in my own bed. I trust you checked in on my Rachel."

"As always. I found her very well, though a bit haggard from worry." He held Ig's gaze as long as he could.

Ig smiled and shook his head. "How can a man be so blessed?"

He rode away. Joseph left the casket work to Samuel and went inside to his office to update his ledgers and attend to business correspondence. His conversation with Ig had drained him of hope. The beliefs that had driven him to risk his life and the lives of others along the Ohio River now seemed impractical in this violent frontier town. In Ohio, there had always been friends, even on the Kentucky side of the river. From there, you could look across and see the lamps in the windows, hope within sight.

Here there were no lamps and few windows. On the south bank of the Red River, you could look across and see only more wilderness. To the south, there were few friends and scores of hateful towns and trackless wastes, the Rio Grande only a vague concept, and Mexico vaguer still. In Ohio, freedom seekers could find community. In Mexico? Slavery was illegal there, but what awaited a runaway slave if he made it that far?

And Rachel. In Ohio and Kansas and during his first years in Texas, he had felt a purity, a worthiness, but that passed when he began to sense her need, began to plan ways to exploit it, and found himself checking in on her when Ig was away, just to catch her eye as he drank his coffee or sat talking with her. As he spoke of his work or the weather or some improvement that should be made to her home, he sensed she was not so much listening to him as she was imagining him. Then he would hold her gaze until she looked away, and he could see both her shame and her brazenness.

He'd caught her eyes on Sundays, before and after her husband's sermons. Already, they were unfaithful. They held a secret they had not discussed but had acknowledged nonetheless. Early on, when Joseph would leave her, she would thank him for his help and for checking on her. Then she began saying, "You'll come back tomorrow?"

Then Ig came down with melancholia and fever and stayed home for three weeks. Joseph visited often. Brother Ig stayed in his bed, talked only briefly about his work. Joseph felt Rachel's eyes and her fear and disgust for her husband. "He won't die. He does this," she said to Joseph. "Then he'll be up and frantic to get to everything he's ignored."

Ig recovered and returned to his preaching. Rachel clung to his arm as members welcomed him back to church. Joseph saw the brittleness in her smile.

Then Ig left for three days. Joseph went to her that first night. She watched him eat, sitting across the table. They said little. Did she see the unsteadiness in his hands? When he finished and leaned back, she undid her hair, and it fell about her shoulders. She laid the pins on the table one by one. He heard his pulse. "Will you be staying?" she said.

He nodded, couldn't hold her gaze.

"Well then." She got up and walked to her bed. He followed on weak legs, his hands clammy despite the cabin's warmth. She sat on the bed, reached for his hand. She smiled. "Like ice." She rubbed his hand between hers. He touched her hair with his other hand. She laid her head against his chest, and he felt the heat of her breath through his thin cotton shirt. He'd never felt a woman's hair loose and soft before. The warmth surprised him. Her grip tightened and she lay back, pulling him to her.

Next morning, he noticed tooth marks on his chest. That afternoon, as he buttoned a clean shirt before returning to her, he looked in wonder at the bruises. Some were beginning to yellow.

For nine months he'd gone to her at every opportunity. He saw no end to it, and though he occasionally courted other women, he looked with contempt upon their piety and manners and passivity.

He thought less and less of the movement. He avoided Ig, hated Sundays, went about his days away from her with jaws clenched not from the injustices that had always outraged him but from desire. He felt unworthy of righteous anger.

He woke in darkness, his face in his ledger. He had no idea of the time and hoped he didn't have ink all over his face.

Father's Reminiscence
Transcribed July 25, 1911

Record my words exactly. Stop me if you find yourself lagging. I am not senile. Trust me, as you always have trusted me. Have I not earned that much? I am quite lucid. I have churned these thoughts and memories for fifty years. Now, this is what I know.

Apostle Paul was a wise man. He understood the destructive power of fleshly desire. The ecstasy of mutual desire. The knowledge that you have incited desire in another. Does your father shock you? You barely raise your eyes to me as you record my words. But I know the meaning in my words doesn't shock you. Only my candor. You have always been my daughter. I know that you know. But decorum. You must keep the truth about some matters to yourself. Leave utter frankness to harmless, decrepit old men.

I am sure you would prefer to hear this story in order, from start to finish, but I must qualify, explain from the outset, so that the reader's initial impression, and yours, most importantly, is at least fair. I cannot hope to avoid harsh judgment in the end. I've earned it. But I can bear only so much piety and self-righteous indignation. I ask only for fairness. Please indulge me. These are not mere asides.

Paul, a far better man than I, wrote, "It is good for a man not to touch a woman." Of course. Romans or Corinthians, I can never remember. It matters not at all. Good advice for either the Romans or the Corinthians. Or Timothy or Philemon or the Galatians. Good advice and impossible. Absurd, except for those as strong, allegedly, or as flawed as Paul or those pedants who would sacrifice every gift to be Paul. "For I would that all men were even as I myself."

Forgive me. Surely my laughter strikes you as odd. Or heretical.

To be desired by a woman is the great mystery, a man's greatest gift, my addiction. Tell me of the quiet satisfactions and comforts of family and honor and prosperity, and faith, or eternity in paradise, and I will tell you, still, at the age of ninety-one, that they pale, as do the seductiveness and euphoria of drink and laudanum and powders, beside the heat and mystery of a woman's desire. Ideology is nothing beside it. Morality bends to it.

Paul knew. He feared it and responded, "Nevertheless, to avoid fornication, let every man have his own wife, and let every woman have her own husband."

Very well. And necessary, I say. Faithfulness, affection, tenderness, endurance. But is this love any finer than maddening, euphoric yearning for another? Not merely the flesh as we know it but the soul. All of it. Call it lust, label it base, but if it is mutual and sustained, it is no less fine and real, even if taboo makes it all the fiercer.

Paul again: "But if they cannot contain, let them marry: for it is better to marry than to burn." How this delights the pious! Marry or burn! Abstain or burn! Deny or burn!

Idiots. In their certainty, their self-loathing and haste to judge, their fear, their lust for violence, they misinterpret. The apostle understood mankind, if not marriage. Can a creator blame his creation? Hold it accountable for its traits? Its faults? If you are blessed, if you have lived, you will burn. The heat comes not from the fires of hell, for it not only burns, it consumes.

Write all of it down. Every word. Omit nothing.

CHAPTER 4

There was no moon. Joseph felt his way down the hog trail through the oaks and elms. He could hear and smell the creek. He carried a shotgun in his left hand and steadied himself by grabbing the trees and vines with his right. He heard no one below. The trail was damp and slick in places, but he could move quietly. Gnats and mosquitoes deviled him. Across the creek, the bank rose and merged seamlessly with the sky. Night creatures skittered. Something crashed away down the ridge and splashed across the creek. He stopped to listen. A slight breeze brought a scent of carrion. Bear. Hopefully a boar. Sows would be with cubs.

He preferred the creek because it was within walking distance of home. He wanted no nickering horse, like the one that nearly exposed him six years earlier along the Ohio, just before a bullet tore off most of a girl's hand as she clawed her way up the north bank. He'd left the horse and lay in briars, listening to the girl and her family screaming and the balls hitting the water and timber on the far shore. But they all made it, and he slipped back to his uncle's farm. The horse showed up the next afternoon. He'd known the girl afterward, in Cincinnati. She never begrudged the lost fingers. She bore twin boys before Joseph left for Kansas.

At the foot of the trail he stopped to listen. The night sky, black as it seemed, reflected on the water. He waited, caught a whiff of tobacco smoke, and pictured Allan Huitt, always early, squatting on his heels, hand shielding the bowl of his pipe.

Joseph rested the butt of the shotgun on his thigh, thumbed one hammer, whispered too loud for comfort, "Al."

"Mister Joe. I'm here."

Joseph lowered the gun and walked up the bank toward Huitt. He glimpsed the glow of his pipe. "Any trouble getting away?"

"None at all." Al slapped at a mosquito. "I despise a creek bottom in hot weather."

"Well, hell then. Why don't we just all drop by your shop once a week and talk things over."

"I despise that shop more than I despise this creek bottom," Al said. "When you gonna start bringin' Samuel? He's a grown man now."

"He's a bit flighty yet," Joseph said.

"Don't trust him, what it is."

"He can't be held accountable for what he doesn't know."

"Joseph, you know better than that. Whip him 'til he talks or whip him 'til he dies. If he dies, well, there hangs one tough, hardheaded nigger."

"You'd die. I don't worry about you." Joseph heard him spit.

"I would. But I don't aim to. You ain't got that twin-bore pointed at me, do you?"

"Love of God. Al, what's wrong with you?"

Silence, save for their breathing and the tree frogs. "Al?"

"My apologies. Mister Winfred and all. You know you can trust me. You know that. There ain't nothing they could ever do to me."

Did he hear the *snick* of a revolver hammer eased down, mixed among the words? "Al, look. Come on. It's me."

"I know. It's just the others ain't here yet. I'd expect them by now."

"Where'd you get the hog leg?"

More silence. Then a soft, nasal laugh. "An undertaker, huh?"

"I've stood on a few creek banks of a night."

"Well. And I've trusted a few white men." He cleared his throat. "It took me six years. People bring things in to be worked on. Leave things. You know. A hammer, a spring. Cracked cylinder. I saw how triggers are made. Some can't be fixed to suit them. I don't know if this thing will even shoot. Might blow my hand off."

Rustling of limbs and scraping up the trail. They waited, listening to the slapping of cheeks and necks, soft cussing. Joseph said. "I don't hear any wheezing. Where's Ig?"

At least two men walked out onto the muddy bank. Pig Nuchols said, "I took Ig back home. He met me south of the graveyard and had already got peaked on me. Clammy as a damn bullfrog. Cold sweat. Said his back hurt. I don't know. Rachel put him to bed."

Richard Van Huss said, "Damn women have got to quit feeding him so much."

"They ain't making him eat everything they put out, Richard," Pig said. "I swear, this ain't work for a man with a weak heart."

"We were just talking about that," Joseph said.

Pig said, "About Brother Ig's heart?"

"About our work making a man a little jumpy."

Pig said, "Al, you heard anything?"

"Nobody's talking. I mean they're talking same as always, just not about what happened to Mister Winfred. Only person I've heard mention it was Mister Bill Keller, and he said to Marster George he thought we'd see more of it if the preachers and seditionists kept at it."

"Who started all this talk anyways?" Pig said. "A year ago, nobody was worried about it."

"Those two preachers from Iowa are about to get us all hung," Joseph said. "I wish Ig could talk to them, but they're firebrands. Both have had the hell whipped out of them a half dozen times. I don't want Ig seen with them."

Pig said, "They say that one, Chambers, has burns all over him. Tar and feathers. Somewhere in Arkansas, I heard."

"Gainesville, I heard," Van Huss said. "It could be worse. We could be there."

"I don't know," Joseph said. "You keeping up with the *Herald*?"

Van Huss said, "That beacon of liberty?"

"Goddamn these bugs!" Pig jerked off his hat and scratched his head. "Look, now we're fixing to miss breakfast."

"And Ig called the damn meeting," Van Huss said.

Just talk. Voices on a dark creek bank. Nothing solid. Two years and they'd done nothing but plan toward some unlikely future when they would have enough sympathizers strung along routes to the Ohio, and if Ig had his way, Mexico.

There had been no trackless wilderness in northern Kentucky and none in the rest of the South. Word could spread. People found you. Here, you were isolated with a few thousand border state ruffians and a hundred or more effete European communists who wanted to garden and make music and art in the middle of a violent backwater.

"I don't believe Ig understands how far we have to go," Joseph said. "I've done this. It takes people."

Al spat. "Nobody here's done nothing, though, and this country is as-warm with men looking for somebody to burn or hang. How's it gonna be if we ever sneak two or three out of here? Won't nobody be able to move. They'll hang me just to be on the safe side."

"Thousands have made it, Al," Joseph said. "You think slavers in Mississippi and Louisiana aren't doing what they can to stop it? It can't be stopped. Men will find a way." How many times had he said this? Perhaps he still believed it. Maybe he'd do more good back in Kentucky or Ohio, with the river always in sight.

Al said, "These two crazy preachers. I expect they know people. You

got to be crazy to prod somebody hard enough to find out what they believe. Ain't many goes around saying they don't believe men ought to be
owned. Not in this country. If a man would come to hear an abolitionist
preacher, he might be willing to hide a man running for freedom. That's
who we need to know."

"Well, Al, there's another bunch of people comes to these preachers'
meetings," Pig said. "They're the ones watching to see who else comes,
so they can keep an eye on 'em. Everybody's watching everybody. And
how do you tell one from the other?"

CHAPTER 5

June 14, 1859

Joseph lay in the dark, listening for what woke him. He always slept through the night until five. It wasn't yet four. He didn't need to check his watch. A soft rapping at the back door. He got up and felt his way out of the bedroom, down the hall, and through the kitchen to the back room. More knocking. He didn't go to the door. "Who is it?"

No answer. He felt the two throw rugs as he crossed the room, barefooted, to the fireplace and took the shotgun from pegs over the mantel. Weak light from a newly waxing moon filtered through curtains and shutters. He stood for a few seconds, orienting himself. There was his desk and lamp. His chair. He found the edge of one of the rugs, stayed just to the left of it. His door wouldn't stop a .40-caliber ball. He found the latch and knob, eased the door open a crack, led with his barrels, and peered into the empty yard. The singing of crickets and tree frogs poured into the room. Across the yard, his curing lumber and the half-finished caskets were black shapes beneath the overhang. A sliver of light shone beneath the door of Samuel's cabin. Coals in his fireplace.

His temples thumped. Who knew what Winfred Skaggs had told his captors? Maybe he gave away the entire movement, gave every name. And they burned him alive anyway. More likely, they burned him slowly, laughing, drinking for courage, goading him to talk. Probably they got only screamed curses and oaths. Still.

He knelt, keeping his body out of the doorway. There was no light behind him. A sniper wouldn't be able to see his head in the door crack. He'd wait him out. He wouldn't be stepping into the yard before he could see. But then what? An assassin could be anywhere out in brush along the river. Why else would someone knock and run? And if no one showed, how would he go about his days? Always, he'd be expecting a bullet or the blaze that would burn him out. And now Samuel would be stepping outside any time to relieve himself on the salty patch beside the shop.

Perhaps he—Joseph—could toss something against Samuel's window to get his attention.

A hoarse, hesitant whisper over by the lumber. He held his breath, heard nothing more. He trained the gun with one hand. He'd be lucky to hit the building. The recoil would sprain his wrist. He reached across his body to hold the stock with his left hand. Maybe the killer was trying to draw movement, flush him out. Sweat dripped from his chin. His knees hurt. He could feel a hint of breeze through the door crack, but it provided little relief against the dead air inside the house. He could think of no reason for anyone to be hiding among his lumber and caskets after knocking at his door in the wee hours. If he yelled a warning he might expose himself. He drew back a hammer. The click nearly took his breath.

From the blackness, haltingly, "Thou shalt not deliver to his marster—please don't shoot. I ain't armed. They said I could come here."

A black man. Joseph aimed at the voice. "Who said?"

"You Mister Shaw?"

"The same. Stand up and walk out where I can see you. Hands up." He sensed movement behind Samuel's door. A crack appeared. "Don't shoot, Samuel. Stay there."

"Silas Hemby said."

"Walk on out."

A slight man walked out of the shadows. No hat. Joseph stayed in his crouch. He smelled fresh sweat, someone else's. He eased the door open and stood. He doubted the man could make him out. "Come ahead."

Samuel sprang out his door and disappeared into the darkness behind the man. Joseph imagined him in the shadows, his shotgun trained on the visitor's back. "Come ahead. Come on in. Slowly, please." The figure moved toward him. Joseph could hear the man's shallow breathing, heard him swallow. As he neared the door, Joseph realized how short the man was. Maybe five and a half feet. Samuel stepped out of the shadows and into the moonlight behind him. He stood nearly a head taller.

"Marster Hemby said you might help me."

"Hush."

"Dear Lord."

"Get in here."

"Yes, sir."

"Love of God. Shut the door behind you, Sam." Joseph groped around, closing all the shutters in the front room, then lit a candle. Samuel stood before the closed door, his gun still trained on the man's back. Joseph motioned for him to lower the barrels, then showed the man a chair at the kitchen table. He looked about twenty-five, wore woolen pants and homespun shirt, galluses, brogans. "What's your name?"

The man looked again at Samuel, who propped his gun in the corner by the door.

"Peter." He watched Samuel. "I never seen a nigger with a gun before." The sweat on his face glistened in the candlelight.

Samuel said, "I ain't seen one neither."

Joseph pulled a chair away from the table and sat down facing Peter. "I'm sorry for the gruff treatment. We weren't expecting anyone."

Peter nodded. "I've knowed rougher treatment." He seemed to have relaxed a bit.

Joseph said, "What brings you to us?"

"I don't have no place to go. I never knowed of no place south of Breckinridge."

"He means why in the devil are you runnin' around loose?" Samuel said. "That's a fool thing to do in this country, because there ain't no place to go to yet."

Peter studied Samuel's face, looked back at Joseph, and let out a breath.

"Done something, ain't you?" Samuel said. "Had to run."

"Marster caught me with his favorite girl. Told me he'd kill me if he caught me again. I believed him."

"Caught you again," Samuel said.

"He come in late and drunk. We never expected him. I had to run right over top of him to get out the door. I might've hurt him. I never looked back."

"There are things a man will risk his life for," Joseph said. "That's one."

Peter nodded slightly. "I'd call it worth the trouble."

Samuel crossed his arms on his chest and leaned back against the wall. "I keep hearing that. Your girl might not think so."

"Marster sets store by her. He won't want to mark her up. If you seen her, you wouldn't either."

"You mentioned Silas Hemby."

"I took off. I don't even know which way I went. Ran all night. Hid out in the woods, up in trees in the daytime. Tried to figure what to do. I almost went back and begged. Then I'd run at night. Three days, I reckon. Stole some eggs out from under some hens. Snatched up a man's goose. Then I come over a hill and looked out and damned if I wasn't looking right down on Marster Reynolds's farm. I'd done run in a big circle."

"I reckon you'd eat a bite of cornbread," Samuel said.

"Reckon I would."

Samuel stepped past them and took a plate from the shelf next to the stove, unwrapped half a skillet of cornbread, and brought it along with a can of molasses. Peter watched him. Joseph watched Peter.

Peter took the plate in one hand and snatched a hunk of cornbread with the other and bit off a mouthful, then another before spooning molasses onto the plate. His hands trembled. Joseph heard him swallow. Samuel went back to the kitchen and returned with the water bucket, ladle, and a cup. Peter broke off another piece of cornbread, raked it through the dark molasses, and shoved it into his mouth. He'd broken off another when he stopped and looked at Joseph. "I beg your pardon, Marster. I thank you."

"Joseph is the name."

"Oh. I beg your pardon. Marster Joseph."

"No. Just Joseph. Or Mister Shaw, if you insist. That's Samuel, my friend and apprentice."

Peter studied him as he chewed, more slowly now. "Oh." He nodded. "Beg your pardon."

Joseph said, "Back to Silas Hemby."

"Word got out," Peter said. He ladled out a cup of water, started to drink from the ladle, then remembered the cup. "Somebody set dogs on me. I heard 'em barking off in the direction I come from. I knowed right then I was good as caught. I took off anyhow, them dogs gettin' closer. I was stumbling and fallin' down ridges and banks and running through briars. I thought about looking for a cliff to jump off, just end it all right then. But you know that country up there. You can't find a good bluff to jump off."

Joseph noted the scratches on Peter's face and the backs of his hands, his frayed shirt and suspenders. A rooster crowed down the lane. Samuel pulled the shutter back with his finger and peered outside into the work yard.

Peter stopped talking and watched him. Joseph said, "You're safe for now. Let's hear about Hemby." He could keep Peter inside for a few days, but then what?

Peter said, "About dark, I'd run up and jumped over every creek I could find. Sometimes it seemed like I gained a little and them dogs would quiet down some and then here they'd come. I don't know how they done it, but you know you can't throw a real nigger dog.

"I come clawing up this bank and there stood Mister Silas, only I didn't know he was Mister Silas until after we got back to his barn and he told me. He had old horse blankets rolled up under his arm. I thought I'd been caught and he was gonna roll me up in the blankets after he killed me. There is a lotta niggers put in the ground without nothing but a blanket around them. I just came on up out of that creek and just about died right there. I was trying to decide whether to just give it up or roll back down that bank and take off up the creek when he said, "Boy, I'll hide you. Drape these blankets over you so them dogs can't smell you.'"

Samuel said, "That wouldn't do no good. You wouldn't be throwing off no air scent, but them dogs would just follow your foot scent."

"Mister Silas carried me on his back a good half mile up and down them hills to his wagon. I don't believe he's no bigger than I am, and he's got grown daughters, but he never put me down 'til he plunked me in the bed of that wagon. I laid back there sweatin' under them nasty blankets while he drove on to his farm. It was getting toward midnight when Miz Hemby let us in."

"Then you came twenty miles south."

"Mister Silas said to. Said you might help me."

"And what does he expect me to do? We're not ready to help runaways. We're months from it."

"He never said nothing about that. He just said you'd help."

"That's all very well. Now he's rid of the problem."

"Mister Silas carried me on his back."

"Do you know how far it is to the Rio Grande River?"

"I understand it's a ways."

"If you covered twenty miles a day, you might make it in fifty days."

"Well."

"How long since your escape?"

"I've lost count." Peter moved his lips as he counted his fingers. "I believe thirteen days, counting two days with Mister Silas."

"So eleven days to go thirty miles."

"I ain't got nowhere else to go."

"I don't see how we can help you."

Samuel said, "We gonna give him back?"

"Only way I'm goin' back is dead," Peter said.

"That's not unlikely." Joseph caught Samuel's eyes and regretted his words, true as they were. He barely knew Silas Hemby—a friend of Winfred Skaggs. Hemby had likely gotten word of a runaway slave and had heard the dogs running. No doubt Winfred had given him an overly optimistic description of their network. But that was the nature of this business. Get them to the next station and hope. Turn them over and wait for the next one. He'd forgotten that. It'd been four and a half years since he'd sent that last slave north toward Iowa, a man named Jacob Brooks, taken on a raid out of southern Missouri. He'd hidden Brooks under the false bottom in his wagon and driven him seventeen miles north of Lawrence to hand him to a family of free soilers from Massachusetts. Then he'd returned to await the next one, who never came before he'd moved south to Texas. He'd never heard the man's fate.

The odds weren't good. All those miles across Iowa, then on to Michigan, the runaway's chances improving with every mile northward, even with slave catchers prowling all along the route. But there were contacts. Experienced station masters. Multiple routes to choose from. Negro communities into which a runaway could disappear for a while. And money from back east.

Still you never knew and rarely heard. But there was Chatham just across the border in Canada. He knew men who'd seen it. Over three thousand former slaves, some from as far down river as Louisiana, had made it, maybe some he'd eaten with and hidden and helped seventeen or thirty miles along to people who were friends only in that they shared a cause. A few words of thanks and good luck. Then back down the road to be home before daylight. Get up and go to work again. Wait for the knock. Most often a lone young man. But sometimes entire families. Or a mother with children. Aged parents who couldn't possibly survive the trip. Yet some did. Some made it to Canada or spent their lives avoiding slave catchers in Cincinnati or Detroit or Syracuse or Philadelphia. And he'd never known the details of the routes beyond the next station. Send them and hope. Now there were rumors of free blacks in Piedras Negras.

Gray light leaked around the edges of the shutters. A half-dozen roosters were crowing. A few blocks north, along the edge of the square, dogs barked at the day's first stirrings: shopkeepers opening their doors, drunks crawling out of ditches, women emptying chamber pots and slop jars. Samuel had taken a chair at the end of the table and sat with his chin in his hands. The shotguns had been forgotten. Peter gathered crumbs of cornbread on his plate and ran his finger through what was left of the molasses.

Samuel said, "I'm about a gallon behind on my coffee drinking," and went to the kindling box. Peter licked his fingers and watched him.

Joseph said, "I suppose a little bacon would go very well."

"I imagine so," Samuel said.

Peter swallowed.

Joseph said, "Maybe we can get you twelve miles down the road. Pig Nuchols has people down around Cedar Hill. After that, I can't say. I'm told there are Germans who might help, but I don't know which Germans, and I can't say anything about what or who lies between Austin and Castroville or Fredericksburg."

Peter shook his head. "I don't know nothing about no Germans or them places you said. I don't even know where I want to get to."

"You've heard of Mexico?"

"Where Mexicans live."

"We know there are Negroes living there in freedom. We think we know anyway. We have it on good authority."

"Well. That's where I need to get to, I reckon."

Joseph decided not to elaborate on what lay between Dallas and Mexico. Peter would find out soon enough, if he made it out of Dallas County. "It might take a week or more to prepare the way. We'll alert Pig, and then he'll have to tell his people. We can't just show up at his door with no warning. You can stay here, inside. Keep quiet. If you're found here, we're finished. Do you understand?"

"I reckon it won't be good."

"You'll be whipped; I'll be jailed if I'm not strung up beforehand. God only knows Samuel's fate."

"I'm obliged, if that's what you're gettin' at."

Samuel laid a piece of bacon in a cast-iron skillet. "He means keep quiet and keep hid. We reckon you're obliged. You the first one we're taking south. We don't aim for you to be the last one. Anybody comes around here, you keep your mouth shut and your ass hid."

"I done heard all this at Mister Silas's house. Miz Hemby said it four or five times." Peter eyed the coffeepot and ran his finger around his plate again. "What makes a free man want to help a runaway nigger?"

Joseph leaned back in his chair and laced his fingers behind his head. "Sam, where's the tape? We need to measure our friend Peter."

Peter stopped licking his fingers and dried them on his pant leg. "What for?"

CHAPTER 6

Ig Bodeker's lower back hurt and his stomach had gone sour, but Rachel pointed out that neither of these discomforts had affected his appetite. She still kneaded his back every few hours, but the last few massages had gone unaccompanied by conversation. She hadn't kissed him, even on the cheek, for two days. Her last kiss, a peck on the lips, had been so stiff he half expected her to turn away and spit.

Thursday came and he hadn't started work on his sermon, despite Rachel's goading. He assured her he didn't need to prepare every week. He'd been doing this for a while, after all, and sometimes you had to simply trust the Lord and stand up before your flock and deliver. Never mind that the last few times he'd taken this approach, he stammered and repeated himself and spent as much mental energy measuring the time between words as finding his next point. Rachel had never criticized his sermons until the last few months, although he supposed her remarks had been less criticism than observation and gentle suggestion.

That afternoon, after he finished the last of the cold chicken Rosemary had dropped by the morning before, he went back to bed complaining that even sitting at the table had been nearly unbearable, so Rachel suggested that she sit at his bedside and help him prepare. After all, these were grim times and the faithful—especially those core few in the movement who continued to believe despite having harbored not one fugitive—needed a message, not another warmed-over sermon. He'd turned his back to her. They hadn't spoken since.

Late afternoon, he lay facing the wall, listening to her supper preparations. Occasionally, she turned the page of the book she'd borrowed from Rosemary—something by Mr. Shelley. He loved her habit of reading a paragraph here and there as she worked about the house. Now, hearing her hands on the pages, imagining her finger lingering at the end of a sentence as she turned back to the stove, he swallowed a sob and imagined a blade plunged into his chest. Anything to purge the ache.

He'd pulled her out of Kansas and ruined her life. No wonder she hated him. How could he take her back there now? And what would he say to Al, Samuel, and the other Negroes in their confidence? *Well, I thought I could do some good, but I was wrong. Good luck to you.* No place here for a woman of sensitivity. *I suppose I had to see it for myself. I never would have believed the hopelessness of it all otherwise. Please understand I did my best. You're not alone. The Lord loves you. This life is only a wink measured against eternity. Remember that; it will help you endure. A better life awaits you. You have God's promise. And Joseph might stay. He has no wife to worry over, after all. I envy him in some ways. I'd stay, if not for Rachel. I know you understand. I'd expect—indeed I would insist—that you do the same, were our situations reversed. Please don't hate me, pitiful fool that I am. Fat, weepy, impotent, ridiculous. Embarrassment to my patient, indulgent, suffering wife, who surely wonders how she missed the obvious early signs of her impending humiliation and misery.*

Two years. They'd not moved one slave toward freedom. Now Rachel seemed distracted when he talked of his plans. Yet how could you fight injustice in a place entirely bereft of justice? You couldn't build an army from a population of enemies. What did slaves in the border states fear most? Being sold downriver to the Deep South, the heart of slave country, so far from support, so far from freedom that freedom was unthinkable. Not Missouri, or Kentucky or Virginia or Maryland, or even Tennessee, border states where freedom could at least be imagined beyond the horizon or even seen across a river. But in Louisiana or South Carolina or Mississippi, there was no hope, no imaginable boundary between bondage and freedom. Just mile after mile of slave country and slavers and sympathizers and apologists of slavery. And what was Texas if not farther "downriver" than even Louisiana?

His pride had gotten the best of him. He'd come to a place where he could do nothing but endanger others instead of staying where he might do some good.

He was no Moses or Paul or Gideon. Just a preacher with a gift for motivating the gullible on days he wasn't laid up with gout, ague, or despair. A man of forty-one who could no longer satisfy his wife or give her the child she needed. A ridiculous man, who, should his congregation abandon him, couldn't hope to keep her fed with a roof over her head. A man who could barely drive a nail, a sentimentalist who could not bring himself to wring a chicken's neck (he left that job to Rachel), let alone slaughter a steer or butcher a hog. Of course, his empathy with God's creatures didn't keep him from eating them after someone else had done the bloody work.

Perhaps he should devote himself purely to saving souls and forget this dangerous sedition. Life would be so much simpler, and he might in the end accomplish far more. When had he last preached on salvation? Back in Lawrence. He had that luxury there because his community didn't need constant reminders of the evils of slavery and injustice. It was taken as fact. There he could attend to other evils such as drunkenness and adultery. But not here in this cruel backwater. His sermons here had been thinly veiled—or timid—attacks against human bondage. All of his flock had to know his beliefs, yet only his core friends discussed it among themselves and with him. Did others suspect him of seditious design? Probably not. Only seditious sympathies. That was one advantage of being ridiculous. Few believed you capable of anything more than bluster.

And what had been the effect of his sermons so far? He couldn't say. Joseph, the Nucholses, the Meades, and Van Husses had been active in the movement for years. The Negroes all had a direct interest. He'd simply brought them all together. He could claim that, at least. But the others, those faces he saw Sunday mornings and during the week at tent meetings. Had he moved any of them? His tent had grown more crowded. People wanted to hear him. What did they say among themselves afterward? Many told him, "Fine sermon, Reverend," or occasionally, "Damn fine preaching," but no one ever commented on or asked about his message: the fight against injustice. Christ's love for all men, Paul's exhortation of Philemon. Talking openly against slavery here was suicidal, treasonous—unlike Ohio or Philadelphia, where treason and radicalism in the interest of a righteous cause were considered honorable among abolitionist men of God.

Then again, for all he knew, half of these illiterate border-state emigrants interpreted his sermons as a diatribe against those who opposed states' rights. Did injustice to them mean breaking current law or challenging accepted order? He didn't know because it was too dangerous to inquire. Or he was too cowardly. At least Rev. Jonah Chambers had his burn scars. Call him crazy and dangerous, but don't call him a coward. Do not accuse him of being anything but Christlike in his zeal and conviction. But you might call him impractical, because he could preach nowhere in Texas now without endangering his congregation. Yet sometimes tragedy, bloodshed, and persecution galvanized a movement. Great men have been willing to endure torture and imprisonment and death. Paul. Peter. John the Baptist. Jesus Christ. Who was he, then, to claim prudence and practicality in the face of the purest evil?

Yet not everyone was up to this kind of work. There had always been the quiet but important work of lesser men. At some point you had to recognize your limitations and get on with your work, the task you were meant for. Not all men could be physicians or engineers or statesmen. Some would be bakers, masons, or carpenters. Likewise, how many men were equal to Moses and the apostle Paul? And these men had epiphanies. God spoke directly to them. He—Ig Bodeker—had experienced no such encounter. He'd felt only the inertia of his father's ministry and then, in young manhood, a quiet sense of the rightness of his own work. There had been no radicalizing experience that had raised his ire at slavery, just the steadily growing conviction of its evil—and then rising courage and outrage as he met like-minded people with whom he could plan and converse in safety.

Now he faced the pharaoh's army or the Roman authorities; the metaphor didn't matter. He lacked courage, genius, and explicit direction. Yet had not Moses and Gideon felt unworthy and incapable of executing God's plan for them? Perhaps, then, until he received clearer direction, some obvious sign that risking his life and the lives of others to help slaves out of bondage—as opposed to worsening their oppression—he should simply do the humble work God had set down for most ministers. He'd preach to the Negroes when allowed, help them endure their earthly pain until they were called home to their heavenly rewards. After all, should he and his little group be compromised, the vigilance and the brutality of the slavers would only increase. Al Huitt and men like him, long trusted and even beloved by their oppressors, would no longer be able to move about. They might even be beaten or sold to the big plantations along the Brazos.

As a minister he'd been a leader, though Joseph was the only true, experienced guerrilla, the only member of the group who'd risked his life for his belief. Joseph would willingly spill blood for the cause. He—Ig Bodeker—on the other hand, would keep to his Garrisonian pacifism. Why? Because thou shalt not kill? Because Christ said turn the other cheek? Or because such a tack was less likely to put him in harm's way? Perhaps that was pacifism's true appeal. You could avoid a fight by claiming conviction.

And what would he tell Rachel? *I'm sorry, my darling. I'm just a gentle preacher, old and fat and afraid, no longer suited for daring work. I lead, still, but only hearts to Christ. I no longer lead men against tyranny. Having come up against the limits of my ability and courage, I now leave this noble, dangerous, and manly work to younger, abler, more virile men.*

A horse nickered out in the stalls. A hog grunted. Hoofbeats and voices along the road. Rachel parted the curtains. Ig shut his eyes against the afternoon light. "Visitors," she said.

"Rachel, I'm not up to company. Give them my regrets."

She hesitated. He felt her eyes. "It's Joseph and Mr. Nuchols."

"I just can't. I'm sorry."

"Ig, please get up. I know you don't feel well, but—"

"But?"

She closed the bed curtains. He heard her walk to the door. "Well, good afternoon, gentlemen."

Joseph's voice in the yard. Then Pig's drawl. He pictured them doffing their hats, stepping inside. Now Rachel's whispers. More low talk. The door shut. He felt the men in the kitchen. Rachel's soft steps. Now she'd stopped, her eyes on the bed curtain. *He's in there; has been there for most of three days. I don't know what to do. Perhaps you men could speak to him. He loves you two like brothers. He'll listen to you. Black bile again, but it's getting worse. And more frequent. I'm worried. The church. His work.* He felt them, felt Rachel, arms crossed, looking alternately at the curtain and the visitors.

A clearing throat. Joseph, of course. "Ig, you're not fixing to up and die on us, are you? We'd hate to have to put Pig in the pulpit this Sunday. They won't allow a spittoon up front, will they?"

Pig laughed. "I reckon I'd better get busy on my sermon." Rachel would be smiling hopefully, her arms still crossed.

"Good afternoon, boys. Awfully kind of you to check on me. I'm just a little down in my back. And a touch of sciatica and gout. I'll be about soon enough. You can't keep an old Virginia preacher down."

"I'm glad to hear that, Ig," Joseph said. "But I'm gettin' a little tired of talking to this bed curtain. Reckon we could peel it back? I don't care if you've shaved or not. I can surely stand to look at you if Rachel can."

"I'm sorry, boys, the light does my headache no good at all. I apologize. And you came all the way down here to see me."

Pig said, "Preacher, we have a bit of news."

Ig kept his back to the curtain. He sighed and worried that it sounded like a sob. Perhaps it was a sob. He cleared his throat. "Oh?"

The curtains flew open. Light hit the white plaster wall. He squinted, jerked the covers up under his chin, and pulled in his knees. "Boys—"

Pig said, "Good lord, Preacher, ain't you burning up under all them covers? I'm sweatin' just standing here."

Ig peeked back over his shoulder. "Well, I've been a little chilled. And of course you boys have just been walking." Helpless. Short of throwing them out, there was nothing he could do. Just bear them. Maybe they'd leave shortly. Surely Rachel wouldn't invite them for supper, knowing his condition. If he could just go to sleep for a while, his strength might return and he'd be able to face the unending, impossible trials that waited beyond the curtains. Couldn't they see his sickness and exhaustion? Of course not. All coarseness and practicality. What dreary task needs to be done next? No looking within. No considering. No sensitivity to suffering. They couldn't see it in him or in rest of the world. It all fell on him.

Rachel pushed two chairs beside the bed. The men sat, hats between their knees. Now they'd never leave. Rachel was behind this. She meant well, but she was just as coarse and simple as all the others. Pure and good, but simple.

Joseph said, "Ig, I do apologize, but, as I said, we have some news."

Ig faced the wall. "I suppose I'll hear it then."

"We have a passenger."

Another impossible problem. Why had he ever wished for this? "Well, we should be able to conduct him safely as far as Pig's place. I don't know about the next twelve hundred miles. Of course, the entire state is out looking for him."

"Just about. We're working on it, though."

"Keep me informed then. I'll be fairly recovered in a day or two."

"We have some time. He's hid at my place," Joseph said. "Sam is up with him."

Pig said, "Preacher, we need you in on this. You ought to get up there and say something to this boy. He's all to pieces. He ain't got nowhere to go and nobody else to help him."

"As soon as possible. He'll be in my prayers, of course. You all will be. I trust you will reciprocate."

"Why sure," Pig said.

"We'll get out of here and let you rest," Joseph said. "You get well now, Ig."

"I thank you boys."

The two men rose. Someone closed the curtain. A few seconds of silence. Ig imagined them looking at each other, shrugging and shaking their heads. The curtain opened. Joseph again, of course. "Something else. Knowing this might help you with your prayers. This boy came from clear up to McKinney. They set the dogs on him. He got away because Silas Hemby carried him on his back. Just something for us all to be thankful for. Something we ought to remember while we're sending up our gratitude." He closed the curtain.

Ig listened to them walking away, the swish of their clothes and boot soles on the floor. Then the door opened, and the sounds from the yard and street poured in, and the afternoon light, muted by the curtains. He heard talk but made out only a few words. Boy. Hemby. Coffin. Ig said. That bridge. Pig. River.

He stared at the wall but saw and felt himself lying on his back, in his nightshirt on white sheets. The voices faded. A pistol barrel against his left temple. He felt the handle and trigger in his left hand. Now, from above, he watched himself squeeze the trigger, heard the click of the hammer, saw the gun bucking in his hand, saw his head and face shuddering, his eyes bulging from the discharge of energy into his skull and then particles of bone and brains and blood and the ball blowing out the right side of his head, spattering the white sheets, the pillowcase, and the curtain, the ball flying out into the room to lodge in the far wall. Then Rachel in the front yard turning at the gunshot.

His eyes fell back into his emptied head. Again, the barrel against his temple. Again he looked down at himself. Again the click and stream of gore. Rachel must be out of the room, so the ball can't hit her. But she would come in and find him. Joseph would strip the sheets and change the curtains. He'd seen worse, the undertaker. Thank God he and Rachel had no children.

Now the muzzle was on his sternum, cold through his nightshirt. His eyes fluttered. Then the gun blast, and his head lurched from his pillow as the blast drove his chest back into the bed and the ball bored through his breastbone, his heart, his spine, out his back, through the mattress and out the bottom of the bed, driving skin and hair and meat and bone, cloth and feather into the floor.

Which would be best? In the head? Would he feel anything? Would he hear the shot? See a bright flash? But the aftermath would be horrible for Rachel. Would the chest shot be instant death? Would it feel like a sledgehammer on his sternum? At least it wouldn't destroy his face. And ruin the curtains.

And then?

What? Know ye not that your body is the temple of the Holy Ghost which is in you, which ye have of God, and ye are not your own?

But would God cast off this flawed thing he made? Would he doom a weak child to eternal damnation? One can repent of murder and larceny and idolatry, but not suicide. If God's truly there to accept repentance. If he's there. If he's there.

Charred flesh in a smoking heap, beneath a burned length of fluttering, unraveling rope. Limbs stiff, twisted. Teeth. Blackened barrel hoops and wheel rims, staves and spokes burned to ash. Hogs.

Outside in the yard, Rachel laughed. He heard his own breathing. The stiff red hairs on the back of his hand glowed in a shaft of light. Just stop. He rolled onto his back and looked at the blanket draped over his great belly.

Of course he will cast off his flawed creations.

Fifteen cubits upward did the waters prevail; and the mountains were cov-

ered.

And all flesh died that moved upon the earth, both of fowl, and of cattle, and of beast, and of every creeping thing that creepeth upon the earth, and every man:

All in whose nostrils was the breath of life, of all that was in the dry land, died.

All but the strong and obedient. Noah and his wife and his sons and the wives of his sons. And the beasts and fowl in his ark.

Noah and his sons. Shem and Ham and Japheth.

Ham, saved to be cursed. Saved so that his son and his son's descendants can be cursed. Because Ham looked under the tent and saw his drunken father's nakedness.

Of course. Hear now the Word of God.

And Noah awoke from his wine, and knew what his younger son had done unto him.

And he said, Cursed be Canaan; a servant of servants shall he be unto his brethren.

Yes. Because Noah got drunk and let his garment fall away.

An entire people cursed.

The Word of God.

Rubbish. Hogwash. If one verse is tripe it could all be tripe.

Stop. *Forgive me, Father.*

He heard his pulse, felt his heart. Sweat ran down his sides. The front door scraped the floor as it opened and closed. Rachel slammed it three times before latching it. Something else for Joseph to repair. Perhaps he could look at it himself. Just sagging on the hinges, probably. Should he plane the bottom of the door or relocate the hinges? He had no tools other than a hammer and pry bar. He knew nothing about the practical world. He'd devoted his life to preaching the gospel. He'd taken a great risk. He'd stood before countless congregations and held up the book he called the Word of God in which it was written that a people had been cursed because a man had looked upon his drunken father's nakedness. He'd staked his life on that.

He'd seen his own father's nakedness. He'd seen his mother's nakedness unbeknownst to her. Were his unborn and undoubtedly yet unconceived progeny cursed into servitude?

A man's wife turned into a pillar of salt because she looked back against God's command?

Of course. Hear now the word of God. He'd dedicated his life to this. A civilization and morality had been built on this. A people's bondage justified by this.

Stop. He'd been here before. Just sleep. If only Rachel were here. Then he could sleep. But he disgusted her. She'd wait until she was exhausted before slipping into bed, as far from him as she could manage. Or she'd sleep sitting at the kitchen table, her head on her forearms, her lovely hair spilled over on the table. He wept.

———

He woke before dawn to the sound of soft rain on the roof. He lay on his side, very still, facing the curtain, listening. Warmth between his shoulder blades. Her forehead. And breath. With his hand, he felt behind him, found her hip and leg. She scooted against him. He turned his ear toward her, heard her soft snoring.

He wished for a pot of coffee, but doubted he could get out of bed without waking her. Yet he wanted to be up. He'd had enough of the bed, but he needed to feel her. He'd lie there a while longer.

Friday morning already. He'd write his sermon today. Half a day should be enough. Run through it a few times tomorrow. First he'd ride up and see Joseph and their passenger. He had no idea how they'd help him. Joseph would argue for sending him north. He'd never gotten over Kansas. But they had no contacts in Indian Territory. Everyone else in the group believed their best hope lay southward in Mexico. Get him down among the Germans. Then the Tejanos. Then on to Mexico. They needed to talk to the Fourierists again, the communists. One of them might know someone in the German settlements. In any case, they had to do something. The time for talk and fretting was over. Maybe this was what they'd been needing all along. They'd do something. A man had come to them because he had nowhere else to go. He wished Rachel were awake to talk with him about it.

CHAPTER 7

Not long after sunrise, Brother Ig found Samuel and Joseph arguing over the proper design of a coffin lid. When he drove his team into the yard, the two stood under the shop porch overhang, with the lid laid across three sawhorses. Samuel shook his head and rolled his eyes while Joseph jabbed his finger at the lid. The slackened rain left only occasional dimples in the puddles, but the sky remained morose, which suited him. He could do without a bright, clear day.

Rachel had gotten up rested and undoubtedly relieved. He'd verbally outlined his sermon for her evaluation, and their ensuing cheerful argument had left him in fine spirits. They'd continue when he returned for dinner. Ig suspected she was refining her points while she did the milking and dug a few potatoes, which made him think of sweet potatoes, which reminded him of butter, biscuits, brown sugar, and ham, which they were nearly out of and would be until hog killing time in late October or early November, which dampened his spirits a bit. In the meantime, they were eating their way through flocks of chickens and turkeys, eggs, roasting ears, and sacks of cornmeal—theirs and their congregation's—and venison, beef, and wildfowl donated by members handy with shotgun and rifle. Pig and Cathlyn could often be counted on for fresh wild pork, bear, and other game.

He stopped his team and hailed the undertakers. They didn't walk out to meet him. Joseph looked up from his work. "Praise the Lord! We won't have to hear Pig preach."

"Faith, gentlemen, faith. Nevertheless, Brother Pig would have preached very well in my stead."

Samuel said, "There's room under here."

"I find the rain bracing."

Joseph said, "I find it wet. Get down and get over here."

"If you insist." Ig dropped the reins, set the brake, and climbed down, grunting. He straightened his hat and coat as he walked toward his friends. "So what are you artisans debating so fiercely? I had assumed casket-building methods were well-settled by now."

"Sam wants to bore peepholes in the lid."

"Whatever for?"

"So he can see out," Samuel said.

"You can't be serious." What heathenish superstition could this be? He should have insisted that Samuel attend Sunday morning services with Joseph. Unlettered slave preachers, no matter how pure of heart, were too tolerant of paganism.

"He asked for peepholes, so I say he ought to have peepholes." Samuel pointed at the center of the lid with a large wood bit.

"Who asked for peepholes?"

"Peter did," Samuel said.

"Peter-" Ig tried to recall a Peter. A minister ought to be one of the first persons notified whenever a member of the community passed on to glory. This could be a member of his own burgeoning congregation. Just because he'd been bedridden didn't mean Rachel couldn't pass the news on to him. "I'm afraid my memory fails me. Not one of ours, I hope."

The two undertakers looked at Ig. "Our *passenger*, Preacher," Joseph said.

"I beg your pardon." Surely the poor fellow hadn't died before he could be shepherded south.

Samuel said. "Peter. He's in the house. We aim to haul him down to Mister Pig's in-laws in this coffin, so nobody won't suspect nothing."

Joseph shook his head, exasperated. "Well, hell, Samuel," he said quietly. "Anybody that didn't suspect anything before doesn't have to wonder now. Why don't you just get up on the roof and announce our plans to the whole damn town?"

"I don't know what to think of a man that would swear right in front of a preacher," Samuel said.

Ig laughed. "I long ago stopped being offended, Samuel. I'm confident the merciful Almighty won't punish a man for a congenital flaw."

"We ought to take this discussion inside," Joseph said. "Anyway, Ig needs to meet Peter."

Samuel studied the lid. With his finger, he traced a circle about where a man's head would be. "We could bore just one hole to give him a little light. If anybody was coming, you could reach back and rap on the lid or whistle a little tune and he would know to stick a plug in his peephole."

They started across the yard to Joseph's office. "That's a lot of risk for a little light," Joseph said.

"That's a lot of miles to go in the dark," Samuel said. "And I imagine it might get to smelling pretty sour in a closed-up coffin."

Joseph snorted. "Not half as sour as we'd all get to smelling hanging from a limb."

"Gentlemen," Ig said, "I had been making excellent progress on my dinner appetite."

They walked through the office and back into the house. The windows were all closed and shuttered. The air felt damp and close. Ig dabbed his forehead.

Joseph said, "Back here." He led them to a small room in the front corner of the house. He rapped. "Peter."

A short, wiry black man opened the door. He nodded, looked at Ig. "Good morning, Marster. Joseph has me keep the door shut." He laughed nervously. "I expect he's about ready to get shed of me."

Joseph smiled. "Oh, soon enough. This is Reverend Ig Bodeker."

Ig extended a hand. Peter took it. "Pleased, Marst-"

"'Brother Ig' to you, sir."

"I thank you, Brother Ig."

Joseph stepped back up the short hallway and looked out into the living area, glancing again at the door and windows. "I believe we can sit out here. Just keep the talk low."

Ig and Samuel sat in the two easy chairs. Joseph and Peter brought chairs from the kitchen table. Ig leaned forward. "So. I gather now that Peter will travel the first leg in the coffin. Strikes me as a sound plan. But why not just make a run at night, like we used to?"

Samuel said, "News is out. They've already had the dogs on him."

"Which is why Hemby had to tote him, I imagine."

"Toted me a ways," Peter said.

Joseph said, "Notice in the *Herald*, too." He looked at Peter. "Old Reynolds is offering six hundred dollars."

"It ain't because he thinks I'm worth it," Peter said. "He'd be buying the chance to take every inch of hide off of me."

"The first leg," Ig said. He wanted to change the subject.

"Down to Pig's sister's," Samuel said. "That's only fourteen miles. But it'll get us across the river. Our story is we're goin' down to Cedar Hill with this casket. There's an old man down there working on his last row, and his family wants to be ready when he finishes. They aim to hide the coffin in the barn until they need it. That's our story. I hope we won't have to tell it." He wiped his palms on his thighs. "Anyway, we'll get to the Buttses' place—that's Mister Pig's sister and husband—and stay there the night. Peter can stomp around a little and get the feeling back in every-thing, empty out whatever needs emptying, and get his constitution in or-der. Next night or so, the Buttses will take him on down the road a piece."

"On the Mountain Highway," Ig said. "Busiest road in Dallas County."

"Well, Ig. We could've used a few good ideas three days ago, but you didn't seem too interested. Don't worry, though. We won't bring up your name if they catch us."

Ig raised his palms. "I'm just trying to understand our plan, Joseph." He'd grown used to the undertaker's irascibility and bluntness. If anything, he'd mellowed since their Kansas days. And he was as loyal and reliable a friend as a man could have.

"Won't say a word," Peter said.

"You won't be put to the test, my friend. Believe that. Trust the Lord." Ig wondered if his voice belied his constricted throat. He swallowed and smiled at Peter, who solemnly nodded.

"After that, we don't know yet," Joseph said. "Pig and his people are working on it. He's being careful."

Ig nodded, all the while remembering the way Pig had marched up after that first sermon and asked him his position on slavery.

"There ain't no reason to be hasty," Samuel said. "We've got time. We don't want to send him on before we've got somebody waiting on him. Anyways, I don't believe they'll be looking for him this far south, much less south of Horde's Ridge." He looked at Peter who looked at Joseph who nodded to Ig who suspected they'd already talked this through a dozen times.

"We ought to have a man down in Castroville or Fredericksburg already," Joseph said. "But who can leave a business long enough to go all the way down there? Pig, maybe. Can't you see him down there palavering with the Germans? And if he didn't get hung or locked up there, why then he could just head right on and lay things out with the Tejanos and Mexicans. Of course now, if we were going north, we wouldn't be having to worry about Germans and Mexicans, but I've learned to just let that drop."

"I don't know," Ig said. "If you want to go up and smooth things out between the Red and Kaw Rivers, I don't think any of us would object. We'll just sit right here and await your return."

Joseph leaned back, looked at the ceiling and shook his head. Ig knew this wasn't the last time he'd hear the case for sending runaways to Kansas. They'd often talked about smuggling runaways northward in wagons to the Red River. Once across, in Indian Territory, the runaways could walk alongside the wagons like slaves and could be treated like slaves in front of suspicious slave catchers or proslavery travelers. Just emigrants heading north. But how many times could a man cross the river without raising suspicion? Who could make the trip from Dallas County to Lawrence more than once a year? And Negroes headed north always raised suspicion, since slaveholding emigrants were nearly always headed into Texas, not out. What they needed was a string of stations—homes of willing abolitionists—along multiple routes north and south. That way no one had to be exposed for long. A passenger could be moved quickly, at night or by day if the means—abolitionist undertakers, say—were there. At present, in Ig's view, and in the view of every one of their inner circle except Joseph, south toward Mexico looked more promising than north across Indian Territory. The mutual distrust between Indians and whites—and Indians and Negroes—made for precarious arrangements. Worse yet, members of some of the civilized tribes traded in slavery.

Peter sat stiffly, rubbing his palms on his thighs. Joseph smiled gently at him. "You might be a year getting to Mexico. You're the first from here I know of."

Peter leaned back, crossed his arms, and sighed. Ig said, "Faith, my friend."

Samuel said, "Missin' that girl."

Peter didn't smile. "You'd miss her, too, if you knowed her like I do."

CHAPTER 8

From the *Dallas Herald*, May 26, 1859

$600 REWARD

Will be given for the apprehension of my boy PETER who ran away from my farm east of McKinney on May 2. Peter is a farmhand by trade but also knows the rudiments of blacksmithing and horse breaking. He is about 25 years of age, short, wiry, dark, and very smart, and when interrogated will tell a very plausible story. He is somewhat acquainted with the Central Highway and Preston Road. He may remain in the area as he is fond of one of my girls or he may attempt to make his way northward to take refuge among the freesoilers in the vicinity of the Sulphur and Red Rivers. The above reward will be given if Peter is apprehended and lodged in jail or for such information as will lead to his recovery.

ALEXANDER REYNOLDS

McKinney, May 21, 1859

CHAPTER 9

Ig paced back and forth behind his writing desk, mouthing the words to his sermon. He looked across the room at Rachel. She'd stayed awake as long as she could. Now she lay asleep in bed. He started to walk over and close the curtains. Instead, he sat down at his desk, plucked his pen from the well, scratched through the word "before" and overwrote "in the presence of." He mouthed his new sentence. No, he needed to hear his voice to gauge the real impact. "To sit idle in the presence of evil is to invite damnation," he said quietly.

He glanced at Rachel. Still snoring. She needed to hear this. Yes, it was the middle of the night. Around two, he estimated without checking his watch. But desperate times called for vigilance and stamina. He was up and working and had been since mid-afternoon the day before. Joseph and Samuel earned a living during the day and plotted Peter's escape all hours of the night. They both looked exhausted. The strain showed on their faces.

As it did in Rachel's, in the flickering candlelight. Her hair spilled over her neck and cheek. Her lips were barely parted. Even her snoring sounded delicate. He repeated his new phrase. Was it truly as powerful as it seemed? Or was it just late? Ideas often lost luster after a night's sleep. He needed to know. He'd be preaching in a few hours. He padded across the floor and nudged Rachel's shoulder. "Darling, I hate to wake you, but I need your opinion."

She sucked in a breath and opened her eyes, then lay still as if gathering her energy to speak. He waited. "I'm sorry," she said. "I just dropped off."

"And who wouldn't? But listen to this."

She bunched the pillow beneath her chin and brushed her hair off her face. Her eyelids drooped, but she blinked them open again.

Ig straightened and held his sermon at almost arm's length. "Now then. Yes. Where is it? Yes. This is toward the end. Are you awake?"

"Yes."

He cleared his throat. "To sit idle in the presence of evil is to invite damnation!" He looked at her.

She scratched her nose. "Again?"

He repeated the sentence.

"I would say 'ensure.'"

"I beg your pardon."

"'Ensure damnation.'"

He looked at his sermon. "Ensure damnation. Ensure damnation. Invite damnation. To sit idle in the presence of evil is to ensure damnation," he said at preaching volume. He walked away from her. "To sit idle . . ." He spun around to face her again. "I thank you. I believe I'll keep it as I have it."

"Well then."

"I'm sorry I woke you." He stroked her cheek with the back of his hand. She smiled and closed her eyes. He pulled the bed curtains together and walked back to his desk. "To ignore evil . . . out of fear . . . or self-interest . . ." He laid the sermon on his desk, took off his spectacles, and listened to the silence, studied his shadow thrown on the far wall. He wondered about his recent melancholy. How could one not love life when there was so much absorbing work to be done? The battlefront was here. He was here. Let Garrison, Parker, and Beecher preach from their New England sanctuary. Let Thomas Wentworth Higginson, supposedly a minister, a man of God, stump for armed confrontation in Kansas, in direct violation of the teachings of the Gospels.

Here in Texas, he had no *Liberator*, no North Star. The *Dallas Herald* would not be publishing his maxims. He, Ignatius Rowland Bodeker, *called to be an apostle of Jesus Christ through the will of God*, would take his message directly to the people, peacefully, behind enemy lines, or not at all. *And they went forth and preached everywhere.* He couldn't count on crowds of sympathetic locals to protect him from arrest or to storm the jail should he be imprisoned. Here, there was no Frederick Douglass or Josiah Henson to raise outrage and funds. Here, a man of God could travel the dusty roads and put his faith to the test, could risk martyrdom. Risk? No, could be granted martyrdom. What more could one wish for? He would succeed or suffer or die trying. There was glory in any outcome. There was glory in any route save not trying at all. Let the New Englanders risk reputation and solvency and comfort. He would risk flesh and heart. Here was reason to live. Here was reason to die. There could be no bad outcome. Here was a man blessed by a loving God. *What man is he that desireth life and loveth many days, that he may see good?*

And yet . . .

For thy sake we are killed all the day long: we are accounted as sheep for the slaughter.

He dabbed the corners of his eyes. He had to be careful. Rachel might fear he'd slipped back into despair. He wouldn't wake her to tell her of his joy. Rather he would show her. Show her why she'd married him and stood by him and assisted him and bolstered him. Beloved Rachel. *Whoso findeth a wife findeth a good thing and obtaineth favor of the Lord.*

He laid his spectacles on his sermon and wiped his eyes. There would be no sleep. He would savor this time. The despair would come again soon enough. Joy armed him against the pain, allowed him to survive it. He let it wash over him, inhaled it. It went to his fingertips, to the roots of his teeth. He felt it on his skin. Pure joy. He could imagine nothing else. Evil existed to be defeated. Out of suffering and battle came ecstasy.

He glanced again at the sermon and the spectacles on his desk. He loved the sight of his accumulated pages in the candlelight, his words, strike-throughs, marginalia, and smudges, his palimpsest, much, he suspected, as Samuel and Joseph loved the sight of their work. He often saw Samuel running a finger over a sound joint or stroking fine lumber. He supposed the drafts of his sermons were careful handwork of sorts, lovingly wrought.

He put on his spectacles and spread the four pages like a poker hand. Perhaps he should ask Rachel to save his drafts for posterity. Have them collected and bound, even. The busiest paragraph on the last page caught his eye again. Invite. Ensure. He marked through the former and replaced it with the latter. "To sit idle in the presence of evil, out of fear or apathy or self-interest, is to ensure damnation," he said, a little louder than he'd intended.

"Brazen," came the reply from behind the bed curtain.

"I beg your pardon."

"'Brazen evil.' 'To sit idle in the presence of brazen evil.'"

He picked up his pen and bent over his pages. "Perfect!"

CHAPTER 10

Mill Creek Fork of the Red River, Near Preston, Eighty Miles North of Dallas

Amos Potts knew they'd catch the boy before sunrise. His two lead hounds—a bitch named Josephine and a dog named Hook, both bloodhound—mountain cur crosses out of the same litter, were in full tongue. They probably were within a few hundred yards of their quarry. The other four dogs, assorted hound mixes he probably should've shot by now, were in the chase, but well back and probably following the two leaders as much as the boy. A real houndsman wouldn't hesitate to cull his pack, but Amos could never bring himself to shoot a dog, so he always had one or two good ones and half a dozen just one or two notches above useless. In his experience, maybe two out of twenty dogs were worth feeding, so if a man just had to have a really fine pack, he'd better be ready to buy and breed and shoot a few hundred dogs.

"Sounds like Josie'll be tearin' the seat out of his britches directly," Amos said. He and his son-in-law Marcus Fink were still on horseback, but the country had grown steeper as they neared the river. They'd have to dismount and follow on foot shortly. Amos usually didn't like to run a slave at night, but a nearly full moon lighted their way. Even under the oak canopy, enough moonlight filtered through that he could see the tangles of grapevine and the narrow, snakish forks of the creek. Mostly, they just let the horses pick their way in the general direction of the dogs.

He hoped the boy didn't break a leg or run off a bluff. He'd hate to take back damaged property. Sometimes the owners accused him of rough work and balked at paying the full reward. Then, of course, as soon as Amos left, probably underpaid, the owner would beat the poor runaway to within an inch of his life.

They sat their horses and listened to the hounds. "She's got a mouth on her, don't she?" Marcus said. "Hook, now, he sounds like you just scalded his ass. It hurts me to listen to him. I keep thinking something's chewin' him up."

"Long as I can hear him, that's the thing. Nothing wrong with his nose. I'd say he might be a little keener than Josie. Anyways, I don't know what would be big and mean enough to chew on old Hook." They'd had this conversation dozens of times, but Amos never tired of talking about his pack. He did wish Hook had a little mellower voice, but you rarely got everything you wanted in a dog.

The dogs' haying faded as they dropped off in a bottom. The men started their horses again, winding around trunks and through openings in the curtains of vines. Amos would have preferred more open ground—pastures or prairie like he'd seen down around Dallas—but he'd seen far worse than this up in Arkansas.

Marcus said, "If it was me, now, I'd throw them two in the corncrib together next time she comes in heat. You know good and well one of them pups will be good as mama and daddy."

"That's right. Have to drown or shoot or brain eight or ten crazy sumbitches just to get one good one." If they applied the same ruthlessness to the breeding and culling of people as they did hounds, Marcus would be in a weighted-down tow sack on the bottom of the river.

"That bastard has bent around to the west," Marcus said.

"Well. Lost, I reckon. Or just runnin'. You know he don't mean to end up over there in that damn thicket." They had assumed the runaway would head for the river. This time of year, the Red ran pretty slow, and a decent swimmer could get to the far side by resting on sandbars. What a runaway would do once he got to the far side was anyone's guess. Usually he'd end up caught by the Cherokees or Choctaws who had learned to be hard bargainers. But that would be a problem for the boy's owner. Amos couldn't swim, and he wouldn't be leaving his dogs to go up to Preston to take the ferry across.

"You don't reckon the dogs have crittered off, do you?"

"Nah. That sumbitch is just runnin' scared. Probably can't swim." He wasn't so sure. His hounds would ignore deer, rabbits, cougars, and bobcats. But sometimes hogs and especially bears could tempt them. And it would be just like a hog or a bear to head for Hagerman's Thicket. A bear could run around in there forever. He'd never get his dogs out of there. Even worse, there were said to be packs of wolves in there that would eat a man's dogs. He didn't know for sure. He'd never seen a wolf in these parts, and he'd been there since forty-eight. You were always hearing rumors about who or what might be living in the various thickets. Jernigan's, Wildcat, Mustang, Black Cat, Hagerman's. All thickets of hundreds or thousands of acres that no one but the most desperate ventured into.

And he wasn't desperate in the least. Sure, he'd like to catch this slave and collect the reward, but not badly enough to spend the next year wandering around lost in some hellish island of briars and cane and brush so thick you couldn't stab it with a butcher knife. And Hagerman's was one of the worst.

For that matter, he disliked slave owners in general, especially the pompous prigs from Virginia and Carolina or Mississippi or Louisiana, who showed up with an army of Negroes, bought up all the best bottomland, planted it in cotton, then expected everyone to bow down and kiss their asses. Thought they were back in Virginia, he guessed. Well, Mr. R. H. Blair, formerly of Biloxi, Mississippi, was about to lose a piece of property. And he, Amos Potts—formerly of southern Missouri and Arkansas—was about to call in his dogs and slow-witted son-in-law and head back to his cattle and goats and corn patches. Slave catching was just a side venture, sometimes profitable, sometimes not. If Blair didn't like it, he could saddle up one of his fine Kentucky mares and head into Hagerman's Thicket himself.

"Whatever they're runnin' has turned back away from the river," Marcus said.

"Sure enough? I swear." Marcus was good about telling you which direction your dogs were running.

"Sounds to me like."

"Sounds to me like they're close. We'd better get on up there."

They rode northwest along game trails, up the wooded slope, topped the ridge and looked out over the river bottom at the long silver pools and narrow runs marked here and there by sandbars, and the woods of oak and elm and cottonwood running unbroken for miles to the west. It felt good to be up on the spine of the ridge where the breeze dried their sweat and kept back the mosquitoes and clouds of gnats.

The dogs had turned again and now headed toward them and at a southwesterly angle that would take them into Hagerman's Thicket. Their baying had grown more frantic. They probably had already entered the outer fringe. But listening to their barking, Amos expected they would bring the boy to bay anytime. "Let's get on down there."

They angled down the western side of the ridge, holding their hats against the clinging mid-story. Amos hoped to intercept his dogs and their quarry before they got too deep into the thicket. Once in there, the runaway was gone but probably not to freedom. More likely death by starvation or infection. He'd never find his way out. Even Indians avoided the place, so the story went.

The dogs closed in, as did the slave catchers. Amos heard his hounds rustling in the brush. He stared into the blackness. No moonlight reached the forest floor ahead. The horses balked. He felt briars on his shins. He expected to hear the cries of the boy—or the squeal of a hog or growl of a bear. The dogs would rush a beast, but not a man. But this boy wouldn't know that. He wouldn't know they would corner him and howl bloody murder and bristle and maybe nip at him, but they wouldn't bite a man, these dogs who would lie on the porch and sigh and thump their tails while his grandchildren scratched their bellies. It was all a game to them. If the boy just knew to talk to them. Yell at them and tell them to shut the hell up. Just stride out and kick at them or grab them by the scruff. They'd cow down. Josie probably would roll over on her back and wag her tail between her legs. Amos had no use for biting dogs. Just hunting hounds trained from puppies to trail runaway slaves. Trained on neighbors' boys who made a game of it. But this one was probably about to shit in his britches. He'd just lay down directly or crawl back in the brush, cover his hands and face, sob and kick at the dogs. Amos always felt a little sorry for them. He'd hold his rifle on him. Tell him to stand up slow. *If you run, I'll set the dogs on you. They'll eat your black ass up.* Don't you goddamn try anything. He'd never lost one brought to bay.

They dismounted and tied the horses as best they could. Where the hell was the moon now? The dogs were maybe seventy yards ahead and moving deeper into the thicket. Amos clawed his way through the brush. Marcus shouted, "Lost my goddamn hat!" The dogs ran deeper into the thicket. Amos hit a wall of briars. "Shit! I'm hung up. This boy is gone! Hell with him." He called to his dogs. "Whooo, Hook! Whoooo, Josie!" If he could turn them the others would follow. But they sounded more distant. He couldn't move. He called again. He couldn't hear anything for all the flailing in the brush. "Marcus! Goddamn it, get still. Hush! Marcus!"

The young man stopped struggling. Amos looked up and saw only blackness. He didn't know if there were trees overhead or cane or a ceiling of vines. "You hear anything?"

Marcus coughed, cleared his throat. He was breathing hard. "I can't hear nothing."

In the distance, Josie barked. Two hundred yards? Half a mile? He couldn't tell. A dog could be underfoot in here and you couldn't hear him. They listened. Another bark. This one sounded closer. He called. Nothing. They called and waited, expecting to hear the dogs struggling through the brush toward them. Amos thought it ought to be getting on toward dawn, but he still couldn't see his hands. Was that a whiff of smoke? Surely not. Not in here. He smelled it no more. Sweat stung the briar scratches on his face. A mosquito whined in his ear. He'd lost all sense of direction.

A horse nickered ahead, much to his surprise. He'd been sure the horses were behind him. Thank God they hadn't gone in any deeper.

His dogs were gone. He'd followed hounds since he was child. He thought nothing of a dog working a mile or more away; always he'd felt connected to them. Felt them even when they'd gone silent. He'd find them or they'd find him. They'd pick up the trail and he'd hear them again. Or they'd swing around and pick up his back trail, come running in all aquiver, tongues lolling, happy to see him, but unconcerned. He'd never lost a hound. But these were gone. He couldn't feel them out there anymore. He was already wondering what he might tell his grandchildren.

CHAPTER II

Peter stayed on Samuel's mind.

Yes, the little man was a slave, and he faced a thirty-mile coffin ride in late summer, then another thousand miles to Mexico. He wouldn't make it. But at least, at least, he'd go back to irons or rack or collar, certainly to the whip, and maybe on to noose and grave having known a woman, the girl he'd told them about, the reason he'd been forced to run. And he'd fled with no regret except that he might never see this girl again. There was at least one thing in life worth knowing.

Conversely, he—Samuel—was free. He didn't call his employer, the white man on whose property he dwelled, "master." He needn't worry about being whipped or humiliated so long as he stayed within Joseph's protection and didn't overstep in his dealings with white townspeople who, save for Brother Ig and Rachel, and the Van Husses, Pig and Cathlyn, and the Meades, assumed he was Joseph's slave.

And legally he was. Yes, Joseph had assured him that, from a practical standpoint, he was as free as a black man could be in the South. But on paper he remained the property of Joseph Shaw, undertaker, carpenter, and secret abolitionist. All talk of legal freedom had ceased after Clyde Hill's hotel and former slaves had burned, which made you wonder: When it came right down to it, when Joseph was faced with capture or death or imprisonment, where would his loyalties lie? Would he sacrifice himself for his cause and friends? Would he hold his tongue? Would he ensure that Samuel wouldn't be sold back into slavery? And should the time become right, would Joseph really set him free or would he keep him to help with the cause? He'd often told Samuel how much he needed him, Samuel, his indispensable friend.

During times of stress or disagreement, he could argue. He could even argue loudly and swear and storm off to his cabin for a while—something he could never have done in his prior life—but in the end, he had no choice but to return and do things Joseph's way, if sullenly. Sometimes

Joseph took his sullenness with good humor and sometimes not. At times he seemed to view it as ungratefulness. He wanted Samuel beholding. And he was, generally, when he stopped to think about it, sometimes just before dark as he sat at his table eating, looking out the open front door and windows while the evening draft cooled him. He'd look out at the piles of cured lumber and the finished coffins and cabinets and tables and the works in progress and think of his money accruing under Joseph's care, and would lift up a quick prayer of thanks for useful and engaging work and bacon, biscuits, and milk, a breeze, a day's work, and twelve hours of his own. If he chose, he could walk down to visit Al Huitt or sort through scrap lumber and work at projects of his own, a little nightstand, perhaps, or a table, a stool, a shelf, a drawered box for his small tools. He had lots of these things already, but there was a solid feeling in making something for himself.

He could walk along the streets, trying to read the storefront signs. Peak & Sons Drugs, Van Huss Meats, Meador Street, Main Street, Elm Street, Huitt's Blacksmithing. He knew these words because Joseph had pointed them out, and he had memorized them. But there seemed an impossible number of words to know. Joseph assured him that there were methods that kept you from having to memorize the spelling of every word. A system that made sense of it all so you might guess the spelling of an unfamiliar word or be able to read and say a new word. In less than two years, he'd learned his letters and to print his name and to recognize a few dozen words. From his carpentry he'd learned arithmetic. He could measure, add, and subtract. But there were bigger numbers to be dealt with. He'd seen Joseph working in his ledgers. Figuring at such a scale looked impossible, but at least he could master it as far as his desire and abilities allowed.

Cursive writing. There was another thing to learn. Everyone's looked different. It looked nothing like print. All those loops. Why? What was wrong with print? He recognized *i* and *f* and *t* and *z*. Joseph assured him there was nothing to it, but Joseph took that attitude with everything, as if Samuel should pick up in a few years what Joseph had learned over nearly thirty years.

Some nights he'd look through issues of the *Dallas Herald* and pick out words he knew. But so far, they were just that—words. He rarely recognized a complete thought. A "sentence," Joseph called it. Samuel just called it a thought. Occasionally, he'd notice big, dark words that made a thought. River Up. Man Shot. Hogs Loose. And he recognized "slave." Joseph had pointed the word out. And "escaped." And "runaway." He looked for these. Usually he found them beside childish drawings of a black man with a bundle slung over his shoulder. There he'd also find "boy" or "girl," "light" or "dark," and "reward." Sometimes only one word made a thought. And some number. $25 or $50. But never $600, the amount Alexander Reynolds was offering for Peter's capture. Here was a man willing to pay for the pleasure of beating another man to death.

A miracle: Samuel could see a time when he would be a better carpenter, if not a better undertaker, than Joseph Shaw. Perhaps Joseph had been more careful as a young man and now, preoccupied with other concerns, he often hurried through his work, seemingly taking no pleasure in it. He always did sound work, but rarely loving work, even with cabinets and furniture. Casket making took little skill, but Samuel took pleasure in even simple work. A sound joint was a sound joint. A fine fit was a fine fit, no matter how rough or fine the wood. There was great pleasure in making something sturdy and serviceable from rough materials.

This knowledge of his superior skills and instincts he held to himself as sustenance. Samuel Smith, a quadroon, son of a house girl and a field hand, grandson of a Louisiana planter named Edward Smith and a girl named Louise, whom he'd never met, could do work superior to that of a white craftsman. What else might he be able to do better than a white man? Here was something worth considering with pleasure.

But undertaking. The decomposing corpses, watched over by grieving family. They'd sit with the rotting flesh until they no longer smelled it. If he ever left Joseph he would be a carpenter and nothing else.

Peter again. Why distrust and resent a man with whom he shared a bond—a shared bondage? They'd talked little. Neither seemed comfortable in the presence of the other, though both spoke freely and at length to Joseph and Ig. Could it be his own embarrassment at his good fortune compared to Peter's desperation and daring? After all, what had he done other than play up to Joseph? He'd always been vain about his work, his looks, his cleverness. And finally the right man noticed, and next thing he knew he'd changed masters and this new one was earnestly trying to tell him of the evils of slavery—as if he needed telling—and trying to work out some arrangement for his freedom, a safe arrangement that would keep the two of them from dangling from a limb. "After all," Joseph had told him, "you might be a free man in my eyes and in the Lord's eyes, and most importantly in your own eyes, but you can't be running around loose in Texas. Somebody will get you for sure."

Peter sensed this. And he probably thought Samuel somehow felt superior because of it, when in fact, in Peter's presence, he felt undeserving. Yet he could not find a way to tell him. Whenever he found himself alone with Peter, which happened only rarely, when he checked in on him or brought him some bit of news, he felt an odd annoyance, a repugnance even, as if he were afraid this man's poor fortune would somehow rub off on him. Or perhaps Peter represented a reality that, despite his carpentry skills and blossoming literacy, Samuel could never escape no matter how many airs he put on.

Look at you. You can point a gun at me, walk in and out of Joseph's front door at will, eat with him, speak freely to him and a few others, but you can't walk down the street without avoiding white people's eyes. And God knows you'd better walk a mile around a white woman. You still ain't got the nerve for anything but a quick look at Rachel Bodeker or Cathlyn Nuchols even when they're just asking how your day is shaping up or telling you what good work you do. You'll argue some fine carpentry point with Joseph, but if things get touchy enough with another white man, you'll resort to the same old skittering and head scratching and grinning and clowning and toeing around in the dirt and, "Oh yes, Marster," as the most degraded cotton picker or chamber-pot slinger, and Joseph Shaw would stand right there and let you do it to save face and hide. His face and hide.

Peter couldn't know these details, but he saw it all, this man who'd lain with his owner's favorite girl. A man whose hide alone was worth six hundred dollars to a farmer who, every time he lusted for his comely chattel, would know she'd accepted him because she had to accept him, or tolerate him, but she'd chosen Peter. Now every time he pried apart her thighs and tried to kiss her lush cheeks, he'd know who she wanted. And maybe, if she gave up and accepted him at last, resigned, and even rose to him, it was Peter she imagined. Alexander Reynolds could whip Peter until his flesh hung in tatters, until he begged for his life or begged for his death, but he couldn't strip him of this power. Samuel had lived enough to know that among men, though they might not speak of it, this was the highest power, above money and property and station.

And so he spoke to Peter. "We fixin' to cut you some peepholes, but you'd best plug 'em if somebody comes along."

"Well."

"And you'd best empty out good. They ain't gonna be much stopping."

"What'll I do for water?"

"We'll give you a jug. But remember what I said. There ain't gonna a bunch of stopping to let you out to piss. Maybe I ought to give you two jugs."

Peter laughed. Samuel didn't. "It ain't gonna be too funny in that casket. Be hot and rank."

Peter nodded. "Well. You be thinking about me while you're sittin' home with all your windows open, eatin' cornbread and side meat."

"I'll be driving the wagon, probably. I don't aim to get hung or hauled down to no cotton fields in chains."

Peter laughed in exasperation. "Well. I hate I come in here and upset everything. I'll be gone soon enough, and you can get back to sawing and hammering in peace."

"I got to get back to sawing and hammering right now." He left him, sorrowful and angry.

Samuel needed a woman.

CHAPTER 12

Often, when Joseph slid a casket into the back of his hearse, he considered the irony in the fact that his life's work—as opposed to what he did for a living—had been set in motion by a man named Coffin. He thought of the old man again as he and Samuel loaded a cedar box built to Peter's dimensions. Although Joseph had long since lost track of the number of coffins he'd built, this one was a first. In addition to a bit of extra room for Peter's comfort, they'd bored discreet ventilation holes into the sides and a silver dollar–sized airhole in the lid, directly above where Peter's nose would be. A well-fitted plug, which pivoted on a small screw, could be moved in and out of place from the inside of the coffin. Rather than being cut from a single piece of lumber, the lid had been made from three boards fitted together with an eighth of an inch gap between each. They wanted as much light and ventilation as possible. It would be hellishly hot by mid-morning, and it wouldn't do for Peter to come undone if trouble arose. Once, in Missouri, Joseph and a man named Jason Brown put a young slave in a false-bottom wagon and drove him fifteen miles out of Missouri and across the border into free Kansas. As they drove through the night, they had no idea that the young, severely claustrophobic runaway was clawing his face and chewing his tongue and cheeks to shreds and fouling the compartment.

Peter had said he wouldn't have a problem in the tight confines, but Joseph suspected the young man had never been put to the test.

Word had come from Pig Nuchols that his sister and her husband, who lived just north of Cedar Hill, were waiting for Peter and had arranged a connection another dozen miles to the south. After that, things were uncertain. The ad regarding Peter's escape was still running in the *Herald*. Word had come from Silas Hemby that things had quieted, but that a team of slave hunters was still working between Breckinridge and the Red River. South of Cedar Hill, Peter would draw less suspicion, especially if he had a plausible story. Joseph knew very well the dangers of keeping a runaway for too long. Peter hadn't been out of the house in three weeks, but things could happen.

Two hours until dawn. They needed to be on their way, before it got hot and the day's traffic picked up. The horses were hitched and the casket was loaded.

"Let's get a body in here," Samuel said.

"I wonder if we should've let him lay in it awhile already just to let him get used to it."

"A man might feel a little queer layin' in a coffin for practice."

"He might get to feeling a little queer not being able to breathe and clawing his eyes out and pissing in his pants, too."

"I reckon we could've give him a pillow and let him sleep in it a few nights." They started for the back door. Samuel said, "Poor old boy might get to wishing he'd picked somebody besides an undertaker to ask for help. I don't imagine he'd thought things all the way through."

Inside, they found Peter sitting at the table with Ig, who was buttering a piece of cold cornbread. The molasses jar sat on the table between them. Peter had barely touched his food. Joseph thought he looked shaken.

"Time for that long, one-way ride in a cedar box, my friend. I trust your affairs are in order."

Peter smiled weakly. "I reckon my affairs is pretty simple."

"Fear not. We've spared no expense in ensuring your comfort on your trip across the River Trinity."

Ig laughed. Peter didn't. Joseph regretted the remark. "Just trying to keep things light, my friend."

Ig swallowed a bite of cornbread, leaned across the table, and laid a hand on Peter's forearm. "Faith, my friend. It'll see you to Cedar Hill, and it'll see you on to the Rio Grande. The Almighty wants no man in bondage."

Peter nodded, swallowed.

Ig said, "Have you a common prayer you can repeat? The words will comfort you and make the time pass."

"I'll be prayin' the whole time."

"Speaking of passing time," Joseph said.

Peter exhaled. Ig squeezed and shook his forearm. "You won't be praying alone. Know that."

"We'll be right up front," Samuel said. "Once we get going you'll get to feeling better."

Joseph nodded toward the back door. "Peter, get your water. We've given you enough room that you can turn and sip if you need to."

Peter picked up his hat and followed Joseph and Samuel out the door. He took deep breaths, smelling fresh air for the first time in three weeks. The predawn sky was clear, and the firmament seemed dense and close. A waning moon sat well above the horizon. The light breeze felt cool, but Peter would quickly heat the still air in the coffin.

"Better go one more time," Joseph said.

Peter stepped into the darkness off the end of the shop.

Joseph said, "Preacher, it was good of you to get up and visit with us at such an ungentlemanly hour. If you'll hurry back home, your bride will still have a warm spot for you."

"I'd much prefer a warm breakfast to a warm place in bed. I'm afraid I'm up for the day."

"I expect Samuel would move over and make room for you."

Ig laughed. "No, thank you. I would say your team is burdened enough as is."

Peter stepped back into the moonlight, buttoning his pants. Joseph gestured toward the back of the wagon. "Your coach awaits." Peter shook Ig's hand and climbed into the coffin. He sat up for a moment, looking up into the night sky, holding the small water jug. Then he lay back.

"A fine fit, I trust," Joseph said.

"Suits me very well," Peter said.

Joseph laughed. "I wish all my customers were so effusive in their praise."

Samuel said, "Here we go," and they picked up the lid and set it in place. He rapped on the lid. "Just a short ride, my friend."

Came a rap from inside and the muffled reply: "Just wake me up when we get there."

Samuel climbed into the driver's seat and took the reins. Joseph climbed up beside him, and they drove out of the yard and onto Lamar Street and up to the corner of Lamar and Polk. They turned west on Polk Street and headed toward the river.

Joseph had been able to purchase two lots at the corner of Lamar and Polk because land was cheap so far from the courthouse square, which held nearly all of Dallas's business and most of the homes of its prominent citizens. Out here, a half mile south of the square, the streets were mostly sandy or muddy paths through briar and cedar. There were no homes or businesses on the adjacent lots. The Simon Peak family, his nearest neighbors, lived two blocks to the north. Ig and Rachel were his next nearest neighbors a half mile to the south between Columbia Street and the edge of town, near the burial grounds. You could stand in their front yard and look southward and see the one tall monument, a crude five-foot limestone tower topped by a cross above the grave of Charles Chirac, an avowed atheist and the first of the communists to die in Dallas County. The cross had been his wife's idea.

They rode west along Polk Street. Joseph sensed the pink horizon behind him, saw the darkness of the river bottom and smelled its rankness, wet and fecund, mixed with the dust from the street. To their right, across the tops of the cedar and bois d'arc and the occasional elm or cottonwood along the creeks, he could barely make out the roofs of houses and beyond them the dark two-story buildings of the courthouse square. When he'd arrived in Dallas three years before, the town population stood at four hundred. It had since doubled.

The horse pulled them across thirty feet of hard ruts known as Broadway, and they drove to Water Street and turned right. Back to the east, a hand's width of corona had edged above the dark hills, but the bottomland rolling away to the Trinity remained black. As they rode north toward the intersection with Commerce Street, the river bent toward town, and you could hear the croak of herons and cormorants, flushing ducks, and loud, hollow-sounding splashes that could be beaver tails or rolling gar or something coming out of the depths to take a duckling or a water snake. Joseph had heard these same sounds along the Ohio, and even on this muddy, narrow river, they soothed him. If only free soil lay across those mere sixty feet of shallow, muddy water.

They had met no fellow travelers, but now a few lights began to show in the cabins and houses along Water Street. He looked north toward the square. Two lamps were on in the courthouse and another on the second floor of Peak's Drug Store, and beyond that, one in a third-story window of the Crutchfield House at about the right location to be Malachi Meade's law office. Malachi was an early riser, probably already at work, sipping coffee and looking over a deed or will. He'd have had breakfast an hour ago. Rosemary often complained that he needed only three or four hours of nightly rest.

Roosters crowed. Two dogs barked. A pack of coyotes yowled out in the bottom. Something scuttled across the road in front of them, heading for the river bottom. An armadillo or possum, probably. Peter cleared his throat and shifted in his coffin. Samuel shot an annoyed look over his shoulder as if Peter should ride all the way to Cedar Springs without drawing a breath.

"You're a stern deliverer," Joseph said.

"We ain't delivered yet."

Joseph chuckled. He felt oddly at ease. He'd made these sorts of runs many times, leaving in the wee hours with an empty casket, heading to the outlying home of some solid citizen who wanted a proper burial for a loved one. You didn't have long. He'd often entered homes and smelled the early stages of decay. Winter was better. He'd picked up some swollen corpses. Twice Samuel and one of the deceased's family members had to sit on the casket lid while Joseph latched it. He'd also fetched the body of a five-year-old girl out of a spring house, where she'd been stored, and an elderly woman weighted down in a creek in winter. Another time, during an especially hot spell, a family had stored the body in a deep pool in Mountain Creek while they waited for Joseph to arrive. They hadn't counted on the turtles.

He smelled smoke from the fires heating the boilers at Sarah Cockrell's sawmill, a sure sign they were nearing Commerce Street. Alex Cockrell. Once the most powerful man in Dallas County. Gunned down in the street by Marshal James Moore in front of numerous witnesses. Moore was acquitted as Cockrell had been years earlier, after he'd murdered another man. Power doesn't buy friends, especially after you're dead. His wife, Sarah, now owned most of Dallas. Owned most of the river bottom. Owned the steam sawmill where Joseph had to buy his lumber. Owned St. Nicholas, the biggest hotel in town. You knew when Cockrell built it that it would be bigger than the Crutchfield House, with more office space, none of which Malachi would be leasing, despite the favorable rate. The Cockrells owned several slaves, and Alex Cockrell had been a slave trader.

An hour after Cockrell's murder, Joseph stitched his eyes open for the making of a tintype supervised by the demanding Sarah, who fussed over every detail while the photographer, Amos Reed, kowtowed and sweated. Joseph had sewn many sets of eyes shut, but only one pair open. After the tintype had been taken, he snipped out the two stitches from each eye and sewed them shut. He added two dollars to the funeral bill.

Two days later Sarah strode through the door of his shop, brandishing the bill, and accused him of taking advantage of a grieving widow. He marked through the two-dollar item and retabulated the bill. She paid him on the spot, turned and left without a word. He supposed he'd made a good business decision, as she'd since used his services after the deaths of two of her elderly slaves.

Dead slaves were often simply wrapped up and chucked in the Negro section of the burial ground. Area farmers usually buried their slaves on their property, though a few buried them in their own well-kept family cemeteries and sometimes purchased caskets from Joseph. Inevitably, these were the same families that hired preachers and put on weddings whenever their slaves married, even though Texas law didn't recognize slave unions. These people obviously recognized the humanity of their slaves, but he'd known none who questioned the ownership of human property. They wept when their slaves died. They would endure pecuniary hardship to avoid selling a beloved slave or separating a family. They worked side by side with men and women they owned under the law of the land. They laughed and grieved with them. Did they ever confront themselves during the dark, still hours? Did they ever pray for forgiveness for this practice they knew to be evil but lacked the strength to cast off? Were there legions of potential abolitionists in the South who wanted nothing more than relief from this moral burden, but who didn't dare act? Or couldn't afford to act? You never knew when you might find a sympathetic ear. You also never knew when you might raise suspicions.

Sarah Cockrell's whitewashed, two-story frame house, by far the biggest in Dallas County, sat at the intersection of Commerce and Water, overlooking her river bottom holdings, her bridge, and her sawmill. Every room was lit. Like her late husband, Sarah was not one to be abed. She was only a few years older than Joseph. He didn't expect to bury her.

They turned left onto the Commerce Street Bridge, Alex Cockrell's covered bridge over the Trinity. The sudden darkness made Joseph realize how light the morning had grown. Things flitted about in the rafters above. He hoped to get through unsplattered. For a while, a barn owl had taken up residence, but it hadn't been seen for a few weeks. It was stifling under the roof, smelling of dust and mud dauber nests and bird shit and old lumber. Joseph wondered why Cockrell had insisted on putting a roof over the bridge. But then few people would have told Alex Cockrell of the idiocy of one of his ideas. The ferry must've been more pleasant. At least the Trinity was narrow. He tried to imagine a bridge across the Ohio River. He didn't suppose it could be done.

They drove out the other side, and morning seemed to have lightened twice again during the seconds they'd spent on the bridge. He could see the white bluffs, rose-colored in the new light, and the stone houses and trellises and fallow plots in what was left of La Reunion, the commune. They rode through Hord's Ridge, past Judge Hord's modest, gray frame house and a few scattered cabins. Cliff swallows hunted above the river, and women returning from milking, a pail in each hand, helloed them.

Joseph realized he'd forgotten about Peter. He'd check on him after they got through the village and out onto Mountain Road. They met two boys on mules and then a man driving a wagonload of produce into Dallas, perhaps to barter at Peak's or Shriek's. Eggs and wheat for cloth and medicines or liquors, or even jewelry or perfume for young farm wives who, five years ago, couldn't have imagined such luxuries. There seemed to be little that humans couldn't work up a desire for. Then again, most of these people had never paid for a casket and burial. Now prosperous townspeople considered it part of civilized dying. Increasingly, Christian burial meant a casket and trip from home to a prepared grave and a headstone. How long before the poorest country people were offering eggs and wheat and chickens in exchange for funerary services? To know of was to desire.

Joseph took off his coat, lay it folded just behind him in the wagon, and rolled up his sleeves. They needed to be making time. He was sweating already. He tried not to think about Peter's misery.

Once through Hord's Ridge, they took the west fork, toward Cedar Hill. Already the country seemed to be rising cedar-green before them. The Mountain Creek country suited Joseph. It reminded him much of the northern Kentucky hills of his boyhood, except that those hills were covered with oak and beech and hickory instead of cedar. No one wanted for fence posts in this part of the county. The creeks here ran colder and faster than the ones around Dallas, and the hills held numerous springs. Flinty hill farmers from Kentucky, Tennessee, and Missouri preferred the area.

The sun was well above the horizon, and the cedars crowded about the narrow, winding road. Pairs of doves flushed from the roadsides and cedars, wings whistling. A horsefly deviled them until Samuel swiped and caught it off his thigh and, with obvious relish, crushed it between his thumb and forefinger. A horsefly's bite would have little effect on Samuel's work-hardened hands. Might as well have been drilling into bois d'arc.

"We'd best be looking for a little draw," Joseph said.

"I've been lookin'. This cedar's so rank you can't find a spot wide enough to spit through, much less drive a horse through. We might have to wait until we get to that little creek."

"That's three miles yet." He looked around. They'd met no one along the road. "Peter, how are you?"

There was a rustle within, and the lid opened slightly. "I can't hardly breathe." He sounded weak.

"Why in hell didn't you say something?"

The lid came up farther. Peter gasped. "I's afraid to."

"We'll get up top of this hill where we can see," Samuel said.

They rode up the hill, stopped, and looked out over the hills and draws. A quarter mile to the south, another wagon approached. They said nothing. Samuel started the horses down the hill. "Be just a little spell," Samuel said. Slide the lid off a little farther so you can breathe. We'll tell you when to put it back on."

"Well," Peter said weakly. "I spilled my water tryin' to drink it. I didn't even get a mouthful."

"We should've started in the middle of the night," Joseph said. "And why didn't we let him keep the lid off once we got on this road?"

"Now we know," Samuel said.

They rode down the hill, rounded several bends. Joseph began to wonder if the other wagon had stopped or turned off. "I don't recall any turnoffs," he said.

"There ain't any."

They rounded a sharp bend and met the oncoming wagon. A middle-aged man and a boy sat up front. Two young black men sat in the back. A pair of black mules pulled the wagon. The hearse was turned, coming around the curve and beginning to climb a slight rise. The driver of the other wagon could look right into the casket.

"Uh—," Samuel said.

Joseph said, "Morning!" He turned and eased the lid shut. Surely Peter froze.

"Mornin'," the man said. He eased his wagon to the right and stopped. Samuel stopped before pulling alongside. The man wore black wool breeches, a starched white shirt buttoned at his neck, and a new gray wool hat. His armpits were dark with sweat. The boy was dressed identically, save for a black hat. "Dead nigger?" the man said. "Where you headed with him?"

"South of Cedar Hill," Joseph said. "The man that owns him had hired him out to a family up in Breckinridge."

"What killed him?"

"A mule kick in the belly. Broke his insides up, I reckon."

"Long way to haul him," the younger boy said. His accent suggested the Deep South. Louisiana, maybe.

"His marster sets store by his wife," Samuel said. "She wants to see him before we bury him. That's why we ain't latched the lid down." He looked back over his shoulder. "We been smelling him the last little bit, though. We have to hurry if we aim to get him there before he blows up on us. I don't reckon that's the way his woman wants to remember him."

The man studied Samuel. "Talky, ain't he? Sounds right clever."

At that moment, Joseph thought Samuel the cleverest man he'd ever known. "He is for a fact. His thinking gets him in trouble sometimes, though." He hoped Peter didn't get delirious and push the lid off again. He'd seen heat make men crazy.

"Whoo, I believe I caught a whiff," one of the black men in the wagon said. He crinkled his nose and took another loud sniff. "I did for a fact." The other two tested the air.

The driver shook his head slowly as if, once again, he had to endure the rankest stupidity. "I wish your mind was half as keen as your nose. I'll know who to turn to next time I need a corpse sniffed out."

"Gentlemen, a good day to you. We'd best be getting on," Joseph said.

"I wouldn't keep a man from such grim work." He tugged at his hat brim and nodded. "Go put him in the ground."

Samuel flipped the reins and they started up the rise. The two black men watched Samuel and Joseph as they passed. Did the one who'd spoken give a slight nod?

They topped the rise and rode around another bend. Joseph said, "Surely, we're the two biggest bumbling fools who ever lived. You think they suspected anything?"

"I's afraid he'd want to know which family the body belonged to."

"Newcomer, I suppose." He looked back at the casket. "Peter?"

No answer. Samuel slapped the reins, and the horse hurried up another rise, down the other side, around a bend. They looked for a place to pull off the road, but found only thick cedar and hills. Finally, Joseph said, "Just stop."

"Top of this next hill."

Samuel ran the two horses up a quarter-mile rise and stopped in the road. They saw no one in either direction. He set the brake and they pulled the lid off. Peter squinted and tried to sit up but seemed only able to raise his head. His eyes were glassy. They clambered back and helped him sit up.

"He ain't sweating," Samuel said. He pulled the water jar from beneath the seat and dipped a cup of water and brought it around to Peter who reached for it unsteadily, unable to focus on it and grasp it. "I'll hold it," Samuel said. He held the cup as Peter took a swallow then grasped the cup with both hands and drained it. He wiped his mouth with a slack hand while Samuel dipped another cup. "I'm tingly all over. My face is tingly."

"You're out of sweat," Joseph said.

Peter drank another cup and started to lie back. "I'm feeling sick."

Joseph kept him up. "Stay up in the air, what little there is. Let's find some shade."

"There ain't gonna be no air moving back in them cedars," Samuel said. "Get him down on the shady side of the wagon."

They helped him up and off the back of the wagon. His legs wobbled as they led him into the small patch of shade. He sat. "I'm fixin' to be sick."

Joseph reached into the back of the wagon and set the casket lid back in place. "Anybody comes along, I guess we can say that old Peter here is mine and he just got peaked on us."

"He made it all the way down to Dallas ahead of them dogs, and we've liked to have killed him in one morning," Samuel said.

Peter bent over and vomited water. He wiped his mouth with his sleeve. "Beg your pardon." He laid his head back on the wheel with a thump. "Lawd."

Samuel dipped another cup of water and handed it to Peter. "Little sips, now. We got to get this to stay down."

Joseph said, "A fine pair of Samaritans we are."

"A good six miles to go, and it ain't doing nothing but warming up," Samuel said.

Peter held up the empty cup. His eyes were closed. "That little breeze feels good. I believe this might stay down."

He drank two more cups while Joseph and Samuel watched the road in both directions. After a few minutes, he seemed to be asleep.

Joseph looked up at the sun. "The shade will be leaving him shortly. Let's get him down to that creek. We put him back in that coffin, we'll kill him."

They helped him up and into the wagon. He sat groggily sipping another cup of water as they rode on, the sun beating down.

After a few minutes, Peter said, "I hate y'all done all that work on that casket and I can't lay in it."

Samuel shook his head. "A man killed by good intentions ain't no less dead. I hope you find somebody with some sense to help you next time."

"Aw, now," Peter said. He seemed to be feeling better.

Nearly an hour later, they turned right, up a two-track along a creek shaded by elm. The creek ran low and sluggish in late summer, but green and clear now. They found a shaded pool. Peter stripped to his long johns and sat chest deep and poured water on his head. Samuel and Joseph stripped and lay on their backs in the shallow riffles.

"A fine band of radicals," Joseph said. "Somebody shows up, I trust you two can act convincingly servile."

Neither man answered.

"It's past noon," Samuel said. They dressed. Peter seemed much improved, although weak. He buttoned his shirt with difficulty. "My head feels heavy as an anvil. My neck can't hardly hold it up."

"Sit back there and sip," Joseph said.

They rode on for another three miles, then turned southeast down a wagon track. Half a mile along, they forded another creek, came up the bank, and were beset by three howling mongrels. A dogtrot cabin sat in a clearing hacked out in the cedars. The surrounding stumps still looked raw, and the air smelled of resin.

A barefooted boy of about ten stood up on the porch roof. He wore no shirt, and his suspenders hung about his legs. He yelled for his mama, then looked at Peter. "He's the one we're keepin' a few days, I reckon."

"I hope you do better by him than we have," Joseph said. "Where's your mama and daddy?" The dogs, evidently satisfied that they'd alerted the authorities, now sniffed quietly around the wagon. A big, shaggy, black hound-shepherd mix reared up so that Samuel could scratch his ears.

"A mama cow's off calving somewhere. Daddy's huntin' her. Mama's down at the creek washing." The boy looked back up the creek. "She does her washing up the creek a ways. The ford stays muddy."

"Catching a breeze, are you?"

The boy stood, held his arms out, and turned around to let the air wash over him. "You get up out of them cedars, and you can find some air," he said. "You're Uncle Pig's friends."

"And better men because of it," Samuel said. "How'd you get up there?"

He pointed down at the propped-open window. There were no glass panes. "I step up in the window there, and then I can find enough footholds where the chinking has fell out."

"A reg'lar little squirrel," Peter said. He smiled, but still looked weak and waxy.

"Here comes Mama."

The dogs ran toward the head of a little path leading from the creek. A tall, skinny woman carrying a cotton sack over her shoulders strode up the path. She wore her black hair pinned up, a faded yellow cotton dress, and no shoes. From forty feet away, Joseph noticed the big hands, dark eyes, and narrow face. Pig Nuchols's older sister. "You'll be Joseph Shaw," she said, just as Pig would have said it.

"Mrs. Butts. This is Samuel, and this is Peter."

"What's got Peter peaked?" She walked up to the wagon and dropped the sack to her side. The wet clothes inside had darkened the bag, which looked stained by the creek water.

"We hit on an ingenious method of transporting fugitives," Joseph said. "Extremely clever and potentially lethal, at least this time of year."

"Hauled him in that casket." She was missing a bottom front tooth.

"It seemed like the surest method."

"Cooked him."

"Just shy of done."

She studied the casket. "Well." She felt Peter's forehead. "We won't do you that way. Lord, you're about as cuddly as a catfish." Peter was obviously discomfited by the touch of a white woman, no matter how plain and direct. Creek water dripped from her sleeve. Joseph noticed that her dress was soaking wet.

"I wouldn't lay in no casket," the boy said from the porch roof. He was sitting now, his feet dangling over the edge.

His mother glanced up at him. "You never had a pack of hounds after you, neither," she said.

"I understand you've made arrangements further south," Joseph said.

"We'll haul him around past Cedar Hill of a night. Martin has people nine miles southwest of there. Good Methodists. They can get him on south where there's a big farm with a bunch of darkies livin' out in the woods. They'll put him up there for a while. After that, I ain't saying. I hear Mexicans will help a nigger, but you've got to get south of Austin to find one, I reckon."

Peter said, "I don't have no idea where Austin's at."

Joseph patted his back. "There's many a free Negro in Canada sent north by people who knew only a single family who'd take in a fugitive. But that family knew another. And the next knew another." He listened to his own absurd words, powerless to stop. Well-meant, useless words spoken by a white man about to drive away.

Peter nodded.

"He'd feel better up here," the boy said.

"Well, come get him then, Georgie," Mrs. Butts said.

Georgie looked at Peter and then down at the cabin walls.

Mrs. Butts said, "Be staying on for dinner?"

Joseph said, "We'd best be off. We've a cadaver waiting on us in Cedar Hill. We'd prefer it to be no more impressive than necessary." Peter seemed lost in thought. He looked across the creek. Samuel did the same.

Joseph reached for Peter's hand. "Well, my friend . . ." Peter took it. "I thank you, Joseph." His grip was firm. Despite the heat sickness in his eyes, his voice was steady. He turned and shook hands with Samuel. Both men nodded but exchanged no words.

"We'll see him on from here," Mrs. Butts said. She looked Peter over as if deciding how to repair him. "May be a few days before we can haul you south."

They all waved good-bye. Joseph and Samuel pulled away toward the creek crossing, leaving Peter and Mrs. Butts in the yard, and Georgie on the porch roof. The ford had started to clear when they muddied it again. They pulled out on the main road and headed south toward Cedar Hill, six miles away. Though the sun beat down on them, a thunderhead had risen to the west.

CHAPTER 13

"Y ou could about drink the air," Samuel said.

"We'll be drinking what's falling before we get to Cedar Hill."

Two miles farther on, the first fat drops hit the dust. They rode into a deluge. By the time they reached the cabins on the north edge of town, the rain had slackened to a soft shower, and pale blue sky shone through the clouds south and west. A Negro boy of about fourteen crossed the road in front of them. A small, skinny hound nosed just ahead of him. Joseph spoke to the boy, who stopped and touched a heavy staff—a bludgeon, probably—to his forehead in salute. "Marster," he said. The hound raised her head and sniffed.

"Heading for the creek, I reckon."

"Things be movin' right after this rain."

"I'd wait 'til late this afternoon. Or tonight," Samuel said.

"Won't have time this afternoon. Snakes bad of a night."

Joseph asked him how to get to the Rayfield Montgomery farm. The boy told him.

"Mean-lookin' stick you got there," Samuel said.

The boy nodded to his little hound who caught the gesture and wagged her tail. "I shake a boar coon out, she might need a little help with him. A sow or a possum won't give her no trouble."

They left the boy to his hunting and drove down Main Street, past cabins, a few frame houses, a dry goods store, blacksmith shop, and two drugstores. Just south of town, they turned west, rode down into a creek bottom, crossed swollen Mountain Creek on a narrow timber bridge, then rode into the uplands where they took a wagon trail to a two-story white frame house in a pasture where sheep and few cattle grazed. There was a pole barn and a corral with four horses and a buggy shed. The house looked immaculate—white with green shutters, a shaded porch with a swing and cane chairs. Several large elms shaded house and yard.

"I'd say the lawyering is going just fine in Cedar Hill," Joseph said.

They drove into the yard. Samuel kept his seat while Joseph got down, stepped up on the porch, and knocked at the door to no avail.

He helloed. From behind the house a woman said, "Around here."

"Nigger," Samuel said. He got down. They both walked around behind the house to find a black woman hanging clothes on a line stretched between the trunks of an elm and a post oak. Beyond the clothesline was a half-acre vegetable garden. Joseph noted the rows of neatly stuck, but sere bean vines. The rain would help.

"I'm bettin' you're rehanging those garments," Joseph said. "Get 'em off the line in time, did you?"

The woman was barely five feet tall but looked strongly built in a thin, light blue cotton dress. She was barefooted and wore her hair pulled tight into a bun. Her face looked younger than the strands of gray in her hair suggested. Joseph guessed her to be in her thirties.

She draped a pair of wool pants over the line. "You might be early."

"This is the Montgomery farm, I take it."

"You the undertaker, I take it." She pulled another pair of pants from the basket. A white shirt came out with them and fell into the mud. She tossed the pants onto the line and picked up the shirt and shook it, looked it over, then dropped it back into the basket.

"Mr. Gabehart is still with us then?"

"Last time I looked." She glanced at the basket of clothes, then plucked out the newly soiled shirt, shook it again, and hung it next to the pants. She scratched at the mud flecks with her index finger while she held the shirt taut with her left hand. Joseph noticed two outside digits had been cut off at the knuckles. *She must've been right handed*, he thought.

She added, "Just barely with us, though. You want to go in and look?"

"I'd better."

They followed her onto a small back porch. She opened the door, stepped in, and held the door for Joseph. Samuel started to follow him in. She said, "Where you think you're goin'?"

Samuel stopped, sighed, and looked at Joseph, who shrugged. The woman nodded toward a cane chair on the porch. "That one sits very well." She shut the door in his face.

Inside, the house was close and dark. The windows had been shut against the rain. Joseph smelled approaching death. The woman opened two windows, then led him through the anteroom and down a hallway into a sitting room at the front of the house. There was a sofa and green loveseats with gold fringe and a dark leather wingback chair and a view of the lane outside two front windows. A staircase immediately inside the door led to the second floor. She disappeared down the hall. Shortly she returned with a plump, middle-aged woman with puffy eyes. The woman said, "My apologies, Mr. Shaw. I seem to have dozed off."

"No need for apologies, Mrs. Montgomery. I'm at your service."

"We thought he would be gone by now. I hope we haven't called you out for naught." She realized what she'd said and covered her face with her hands. "I mean . . . I didn't mean. . . ."

"I know precisely what you mean. There comes a time when there's nothing to hope for but a quiet passing."

She wiped her hazel eyes. He would have expected blue, given her red hair and freckles. She said, "Will you have something? Water? I believe we have buttermilk, still. We've had many visitors. My father is beloved in this county. Bekah could brew coffee."

"I'm fine. My helper out back might like a drink of water, though."

"Of course. Bekah."

Bekah left without a word.

"I apologize for our girl," Mrs. Montgomery said. "She's far more trouble than she's worth. Rayfield got her at what he thought was a good price. I'm afraid the seller was less than forthcoming about her history. She's worse than an obstinate child, and we're far too lax to own Negroes. Bekah is our first, and I'm certain she'll be our last." She sniffled. "My husband had some business in town. He should be back anytime."

They stood in silence. A clock ticked above the mantel. "I really should be with my father. Please make yourself at home." The words brought her to tears again. She sobbed and disappeared down the hall. Joseph sat for a while, listening to the clock. At times, the scent of failing breath came to him, and he thought he heard labored breathing or perhaps the rustle of dresses. After a while he stepped out the front door and walked around back where he found Samuel leaning against the hearse while Bekah, having finished her duties indoors, was hanging the rest of the wash.

Samuel, who looked to be in deep thought, probably trying to think of something to say to Bekah, seemed relieved to see him. Bekah petulantly flopped a sheet over the line, which now sagged to the point that some of the sheets and pants were only an inch or two above the mud. But they'd dry and the line would rise a bit.

"Samuel being lively company?"

Bekah didn't look up from her work. "Who?"

"Why, Sam, you haven't introduced yourself. I'm sure I've taught you better. I apologize for my young friend's behavior, Bekah."

The remark mortified Samuel. "Huh? I was just thinking about what all needed doing."

"I wasn't paying no attention to him," she said.

"Very little remains to be done. They've already prepared a grave, so we can't charge them for digging," Joseph said quietly. He leaned back beside Samuel. Perhaps they'd get a good meal out of this anyway. The neighbors would bring food. He suspected the kitchen was full of ham and pies. And Mrs. Montgomery had mentioned buttermilk. If the old man lingered, this would be one expensive casket and hearse ride. He glanced at the coffin. "I'll be goddamned."

"What?"

"We forgot to plug the hole," Joseph said under his breath.

Samuel turned and raised the lid. The casket held an inch of water. "It ain't like we're used to having to worry about holes in a coffin lid," he whispered.

They pulled it out of the hearse, one man on each end, and dumped the water. Bekah watched without a word, a smile, or change of expression.

"I suppose we'd better hope he lingers long enough for this thing to dry out a bit," Joseph said.

Bekah left and went in the back door.

"You don't think she went in there to tell on us, do you?" Samuel said.

"She doesn't seem like one to care. She probably thinks we didn't have the lid on good."

Bekah came back out with two stained, threadbare towels. "Y'all can dry it out some with these," she said. She tossed them in the coffin and went back to her clothesline. They thanked her and began swabbing. She didn't answer, just looked at what she'd already hung up and at what remained, then stared into the distance.

A horse and buggy came down the lane. Bekah sighed and bent to pull another garment from the basket. A man in a gray suit stopped the buggy beside the house and walked out back to greet them. He was as portly as his wife, maybe an inch taller, and clean-shaven. "Gentlemen, I trust you've made Bekah's acquaintance. Such a pleasant, ebullient creature, wouldn't you say?"

"And efficient," Joseph said. Bekah eyed him. He wondered if she thought he'd insulted her.

Rayfield Montgomery introduced himself, shook hands with Joseph, and nodded cordially at Samuel when Joseph introduced him.

"Good-looking boy," Montgomery said. "I'm betting you don't put up with the nonsense I do."

"Samuel's a good hand. He's about to be too fine a carpenter to call an apprentice."

Samuel leaned back against the wagon. "I thank you, Marster."

Joseph was relieved Samuel hadn't called him by his name, as he normally did.

Montgomery turned to Bekah. "This one has pretty well ruined me on the whole nigger business. It appears we just aren't suited for it. I'd take a hundred and a half and get out of it right now if I could find someone so gullible. Unfortunately, you've already made her acquaintance."

Joseph was trying to think of a reply when Montgomery said, "Since you're standing out here, I take it my father-in-law has yet to require your services."

"Mrs. Montgomery feels her father won't have to endure much longer. Let's hope for his sake and hers."

"And mine," Montgomery said. "I know a businessman when I meet one. I would try to negotiate a price this instant, but I know you'd cover yourself against a long wait and then, sure as hell, old John would die within the hour."

"You'll find me quite reasonable."

"For the only undertaker in Dallas County. A little competition would liven things a bit, I'd say." He laughed and slapped Joseph's back. "Excuse me, gentlemen. I had better go in and see where we stand." He started for the house and said to no one in particular, "Time was, you'd just beat together a box and dig a hole. Not now, by God. A man can't get to heaven without somebody being paid. Pay the preacher, pay the undertaker, pay the gravediggers. A man will eat up his estate just by dying. Just pitch me in a hole when I'm done. Save the money for a young man who can use it." He was still talking when he disappeared into the house.

The sky cleared. They moved into the shade of an elm where they sat dozing. After a while, Samuel got up and checked on the coffin. It would be dry before dark. Late afternoon, a nice breeze cooled them and relieved them of the gnats and mosquitoes, and a persistent biting fly. The garden and shade, the distant line of woods along the creek and the wooded hills, and the neatness of the Montgomery place soothed Joseph, put him in mind of Rachel, whom he hadn't held in over a month. They'd been too busy preparing Peter, and Ig had stayed around home. The few times Joseph saw the couple together, Rachel seemed very pleased with Ig. She'd seemed happy with him since he'd gotten through his last bout of melancholia. For that matter, Ig had seemed pleased with himself, which in turn pleased Joseph. You couldn't help but love Ig Bodeker.

And it wasn't as if Ig didn't please Rachel in general. She'd said as much many times. She loved him, was devoted to him in her way. And Ig was devoted to her completely. And dependent on her completely. Unless her affair with Joseph was discovered and Ig drove her away, she would stay with him for life, more or less content except for one thing, which, for now, Joseph provided.

At times he thought he loved her—now, for instance—but he told himself he couldn't know for sure. He hadn't known her long enough, and their encounters had been few enough that they still were fueled mostly by desire and excitement. Then again, he always felt tender toward her after he was sated. He thought of her foibles, the ones she'd revealed to him, with affection and humor. Certainly she possessed others he might not look upon with affection.

When they lay together she seemed focused only on her pleasure with him at the moment. Nothing else. At times he felt sure she forgot him the instant he left. When she was with Ig, her gaze never lingered on Joseph. There were no glances in acknowledgment of their secret. She was polite and friendly and solicitous, as she'd been before their affair, but nothing more. The preacher's wife.

He leaned back against the trunk and closed his eyes. Her scent came to him, and the warmth of her hair falling about his face. While he tried to remedy the bind in his pants, Samuel said, "A hundred and a half. Ain't that what he'd take? Old Man Montgomery."

"My God, man, she's a dozen years older than you are."

"And right handsome."

"And sour as a March apple."

"I reckon she'd sweeten up."

Joseph laughed. "I suppose the right sweetener might bring her around. I don't suspect she's regularly sweetened as it is."

"Not by that fat little toad."

"She might improve your demeanor."

"I 'spect she might."

"You could easily afford her."

Samuel nodded. "What else am I gonna do with money?"

"You'd be buying her freedom. She might choose not to stay."

Samuel nodded. After a few seconds, he said, "Of course now, we get things going good between here and Mexico, a few hundred dollars might help a man along."

"It would. I would advise against it right now, but I'd never try to stop you. Likewise, we couldn't stop her. I'd help either of you. So would Ig and Pig and Malachi and Richard."

"Well, I need to see how this all goes."

Bekah came out the back door and walked up to them. "Missy said to ask if you wanted to come in and eat a bite."

"We would. I thank you."

"Thank her." She looked at Samuel. "I can't let you in. Come on up to the porch and I'll bring you a plate." She turned and started for the back door. Joseph got up and dusted the seat of his pants. "Clearly, she's taken with you."

Samuel shrugged and watched her walk away. Joseph chuckled and said, "I say come in low and see what he says. He might take a hundred."

The old man hung on. Joseph expected the Montgomerys to ask for his assessment. He'd seen many near death, especially since coming to Texas. But Mrs. Montgomery stayed with her father and didn't invite Joseph into the sick room. A few friends and neighbors came and left. Some brought more food. Joseph thought half the food in the kitchen would spoil before it could be eaten. Rayfield Montgomery retired to his small office, a copy of the *Dallas Herald* folded under his arm. He looked back at Joseph standing in the kitchen. "You think about how well we're feeding you when you tally up your fee."

Bekah came through and said, "Just get what you want. They won't know a bit of difference." He ate two fried pies. Rhubarb. His favorite. He chased them with buttermilk, then took two pies out to Samuel.

That night, Joseph went to bed in the back bedroom. Bekah brought out two quilts and a blanket for Samuel. He set the casket on the ground and made a pallet in the hearse. Joseph awakened during the middle of the night to the sound of low voices and scurrying in the hallway. Someone knocked at the door.

"Yes?"

The door opened a crack. Bekah said, "He might've passed. Missy wants you to come see."

He lit a candle and dressed, then knocked at the old man's door, stepped in, and found the Montgomerys standing at the foot of the bed. Mr. Gabehart lay still. He was tall and thin and had a full head of white hair and several days' growth of beard. His wife must have been short. Mrs. Montgomery looked up. Her eyes were dry now, but red. The room was stifling, but the women had kept it and her father clean. Joseph smelled no bedpan, no soiled sheets. Still, there was the familiar scent.

Mrs. Montgomery said, "We've summoned the doctor."

John Gabehart was gray. His fingernails were purple. He was stiff already. Joseph didn't need to check but did anyway, for the sake of procedure and the family's comfort.

"He's been gone awhile."

"I fell asleep." She sobbed. Her husband sniffled and put his arm around her.

Joseph said, "I'm here to assist you in any way."

"We'll prepare him, get him into his suit," she said.

"I'll be glad to take care of that for you. You've had a difficult wait."

"Thank you, no."

"Of course." He paused. "I don't advise a long sitting. The heat. We've a few hours at best. I'm sorry." In the doorway, behind him, Bekah turned and walked up the hall toward the kitchen. The light from the bedside candle flickered on the dead man's face.

Father's Reminiscence
Transcribed July 26, 1911

E ven after all that I have done and risked and supported, I remain suspicious of social movements, despite the good they sometimes accomplish. I doubt the purity of motive of the those who embrace and carry out causes. Yes, some are driven by outrage at injustice. Others, equally efficient, are motivated by resentment of privilege. Still others seek to carry out religious imperatives. If their interpretation of the Scriptures condemns slavery, then slavery must end. What the religious feel toward the enslaved seems to matter little. Others love the pain of those with whom they hold stark ideological differences. Some take more pleasure in revenge against perpetrators of injustice than in aiding the oppressed. A good many seem natural Jacobins, born to disaffection. They chafe against any perceived power, any state of affairs.

My own motives shifted and melded. Fifty years have provided little clarity. I could claim that in the end I demonstrated absolute fealty to our cause, that I did what the situation required. It could also be said that I saved my own skin. I cannot fully accept or deny either.

Yet since that day on the riverbank, I have understood how great men hurl ten thousand lightly armed boys at artillery emplacements. Don't think, gentle daughter, that you are incapable of terrible resolve.

Word traveled. Slave to slave. Runaways found sanctuary and succor in slave quarters. They passed on directions and names, while we so-called abolitionists cowered in our uncertainty, afraid to inquire, for who knew whom to trust? All the while the tracks were laid, the branches and spurs formed, mostly by those for whom failure meant torture or death or permanent separation from family, and loss of all hope.

They would find us. We'd send them on. Twenty miles maybe, north or south, depending on situation or rumor. Some were recaptured. We rarely knew. Send them or deliver them, then wait for the next desperate man or family or mother and bedraggled children. Send them and forget them. That was the only way. Take pleasure in the cunning. You took little pleasure in helping, for you could be sending someone to his doom.

And take pleasure in the slavers' discomfort. Now that was something to hold onto. You could see it in the newspaper editorials, the pamphlets, the public meetings in the Masons' lodge where earlier in the week Ignatius Bodeker had preached. The paranoia. Men galled by any perceived slight to their honor. Their arrogance a ruse to cover their fear. Think of it. Ride through your fields and catch your Negroes talking. What were they saying? Why do they hush at your approach? All the laughter and grinning, and head scratching, and yes-bossing. What is it? And what do they know? Down the road, a boy ran, then escaped the dogs. Someone had to have helped him. But who, among these Southerners? No one is talking. There are rumors, though. Preachers. Agitators from the north. Agents of John Brown. Now there was something to worry a man. Down in Waxahachie, three barns burned—and right after several slaves ran off, mind you. And word is, quantities of arsenic turned up missing from drugstores in Denton and Paris. And that girl that does the cooking and looks after the babies? She's showing a little attitude lately. What's gotten into her? The wife stays worried. Sell her. Sell them all. But then how do you run this place?

I used to imagine them looking at their food, taking that first bite. Undoubtedly, some were thick enough or arrogant enough to believe their slaves were too loyal or too cowed for subversion. Some, perhaps, believed gentle treatment bought loyalty. Others, no doubt, trusted in the basic goodness of those whom they held in bondage. Surely most understood human nature and knew full well the humanity of those they brutalized. Given that knowledge, how could a slaver not fear? Perhaps venial sinners slept well, if there were any. Do tyrants face themselves alone in the dark?

You see? It was a fine time to walk the streets and listen. To read the papers. Those were among my few solid pleasures. I had grudges, yes, and admirable motives, certainly. There were other motivations, too, which I will get to in time.

I beg your patience. I tire quickly these days, as you know. I give you my thoughts as they come to me. I leave it to you to bring order to these ramblings after I'm gone.

Chapter 14

A mile up the road, north of Cedar Hill, Samuel wondered what he'd gotten himself into.

Bekah sat morose and silent on the back of the hearse. And he was now responsible for her. Buying her had been his idea, one that seemed perfect until it became clear that Montgomery was serious about his desire to sell her at a good price. As soon as Samuel realized this, the weight of his decision and the manifold problems and responsibilities became startlingly clear. Now there she sat, sullen as a toad, her bag in her lap, the afternoon sun beating down on her. Still, she looked fine. Joseph, of course, was in splendid spirits, no doubt enjoying Samuel's self-inflicted vexation.

"A noble use of your wealth," Joseph said. "Money provides many opportunities. It's a fine thing." He turned in his seat to study Samuel, who refused to smile. "Now how much did I tell Montgomery I wanted for those funerary services? I'll need to debit your account as soon as we get home. So as not to forget, you understand. Good business and all."

"I thought you said twenty-five dollars." Old Montgomery had jumped at the chance to sell Bekah in exchange for the casket and trip to the cemetery. When Joseph had asked Bekah what she thought about going with them, she shrugged and said, "I don't have nothing to say about it."

"No, I'm sure I said a thousand. We've got two days in it plus the extra refinements we made to the casket. The insufficient length was unfortunate. I don't suppose a dead man minds lying with his knees bent, though." He leaned back and laced his hands behind his head. "Just figuring here. A thousand. That'll wipe your account clean and put you four hundred dollars in debt to me. You'll work it off soon enough."

"I reckon you can make sport over this."

Joseph had been about to say something but caught himself. He looked straight up the road, his head rocking to the motion of the wagon. "Did you ever laugh before, Samuel?"

"When something was funny."

"I see." They rounded a bend and started up a hill. The cedars still held the scent of yesterday's rain. Near the top of a tall elm, a mockingbird deviled a hawk. The big bird flapped away. The mocker lit at the top of the bare snag abandoned by the hawk and preened. Joseph said, "Sometimes a thick, hard callus is the only thing that allows the work to continue."

Samuel didn't answer. He'd made his point. And he didn't need Joseph Shaw telling him about calluses.

CHAPTER 15

On the third Sunday in July 1859, Parson Zephaniah Newton—
formerly of Oelwein, Iowa, and more recently of Bonham,
Gainesville, Denton, Sherman, Paris, Preston, Honey Grove,
and Ladonia, Texas—suspected Northern agitator, friend of notorious
abolitionist Jonah Chambers, alleged disciple of Parsons Solomon McK-
inney and William Blount, accused Ig Bodeker of cowardice. That the
parson made his accusation in Rachel's presence further confirmed Ig's
theories about inborn Northern brusqueness.

Ig was already annoyed with himself for preaching a tepid sermon,
from the tenth chapter of Matthew, on standing up to wickedness and
overcoming adversity. After he'd greeted the congregation and accepted
a dinner invitation to the Van Husses, Rachel took his arm and gave him
a sympathetic look that said, "Yes, you were off today, and I know that
you know it and feel badly." She'd offer detailed commentary after dinner
had revived him.

The men had already taken down the tent and loaded it in the wagon.
The creekside meadow was nearly empty save for some skinny cattle
grazing near the top of the rise. Ig was about to help Rachel into the wagon when a short, slight, freckled, blond-bearded man who'd sat near the
front called to him. Clearly, he was not a Southerner.

Ig stopped. The man strode toward them. He wore a dusty gray suit
and no hat. His white shirt was buttoned at the neck. No tie. Filthy.

"Reverend, I want a word with you," he said. Ig held out his hand,
warily. He was used to warm greetings, not a stranger wanting a word
with him. They shook hands. "Zephaniah Newton," the man said.

Ig glanced around. "Ah, Parson. Your reputation precedes you. Honored to make your acquaintance." And nervous. Fortunately there seemed
to be no one else around. Perhaps no one in the congregation recognized
the little troublemaker.

"I'll be direct, sir," Newton said. "Your vagueness appalls me. Say what
you mean or step aside for a stouter man of God."

"Your imprudence appalls me," Rachel said. "Where's your congregation? Your reckless behavior has gotten you run out of every town where you might have done some good."

"Precisely," Ig said. Newton was in for it now. Rachel's neck was flushed. He'd just get out of the way and watch.

"Do you suppose the apostle Paul concerned himself with prudence?" Newton said. "Do you think Christ allowed himself one second of intimidation before he laid righteous siege to the venal temple?"

"You vainglorious little troll." She was smiling now, lips taut over her teeth. "Has it occurred to you that we are not in Syracuse or Boston or Philadelphia?"

"A man might have to suffer the law of the land, but he needn't obey it if it is in opposition to God's law. To do so is to condone it. At least that's what I thought I heard your husband say this morning." Newton's blue eyes were wild, gleaming. He'd found a worthy opponent.

Ig began to feel left out. "While I admire your forthrightness, I'll thank you for not endangering our work here."

Newton laughed. "Your work. Your work or your hides? Which do you fear I'll endanger, Reverend? Which do you hold most dear? Why do you keep looking about? The important discourse is right here. Are you late for an appointment? Don't let me detain you."

Rachel said, "You are a dangerous man. A danger to the Negroes you claim to help and a danger to all people of goodwill. No different than that absurd Captain Brown who kept the slavers in Missouri and Kansas in such a state of agitation that no one could safely move passengers along the roads, all the while disparaging responsible work. It's perfectly obvious you're of the same ilk. Why don't you go back up to the border counties? I'm sure they'll write about you in the newspapers up there. Perhaps someone will even honor you with a daguerreotype."

"You misjudge me."

"I judge you rightly, sir, and I'm tiring of your company. Surely you have business elsewhere. Emmaus, perhaps. Or Corinth or Rome. Surely I'm not overestimating your aspiration. Why, I doubt a man of your godliness need bother with the ferry."

"Deflect the truth, then. But I'll ask this. Your *work*, as you call it— what does it consist of, and what have you accomplished? Do you think your tremulous queries to the north have escaped me? The hills up there are rife with free soilers, but our kin to the south, in Dallas County, are all too timid to ask for help. Oh! Word might get out. We might approach the wrong man. So years pass, and the evil continues unabated."

"We've recently moved our first passenger," Ig said.

"Yes—Peter. I've spoken with Brother Silas Hemby, who, I understand, sent him to you and your people Who else do you know between here and the Red River?"

Ig said, "We're concentrating our efforts southward, with considerable progress, thank you."

"Southward. How many miles to Mexico? But oh, to the north. Winfred Skaggs's murder has you spooked. Afraid of burning, are you, Reverend? There are many ways to burn. Some more lengthy than others."

Rachel said, "Do you have any idea of the work we did in Kansas and Missouri? What were you doing then? I don't recall hearing your name, little righteous man."

"Well, you wouldn't have, not there in free Lawrence. Yes, sir, there in the great *free* territory of Kansas, they'll have no slavery. They'll see it abolished, for it interferes with a white man's wage. As for Negroes, free or fugitive, well, they'll have none of those either. Get them on to Iowa or Detroit or Chatham as fast as you can. New England Emigrant Aid Company? More like White Emigrant Aid Company. I couldn't stomach it."

Ig suddenly felt dirty. "Let's not be reduced to comparing virtuous acts."

Newton said nothing for a moment. He seemed to be considering Ig's comment. "Well then. Know that you'll be tested very soon. I say that with utter certainty."

Rachel rolled her eyes. "Oh listen, Ignatius. He's prophesying now. I am truly awed and humbled."

Zephaniah Newton said, "I had best be getting back to the woods. I'm anticipating a productive association with my Dallas kindred. You'll be hearing from me soon, Mrs. Bodeker." He bowed slightly and walked away toward the creek. His pants below the knees were stiff with red mud.

"Dear God," Rachel said. "What an insufferable little bantam. And the last thing we need."

Ig watched him walk away. "Brother Zeph wasn't prophesying. I think he meant to prepare us. He seemed awfully pleased."

"With himself, no doubt," Rachel said. She shook her head in disgust as she watched him leave. "God forgive me. I know. I know."

CHAPTER 16
September 10, 1859

I n 1852, slavers in Missouri branded an *A*, for abolitionist, in Reverend Jonah Chambers's right palm. They'd caught him trying to slip into Kansas with four fugitive slaves, only because one of the runaways, a girl about ten years old, stepped on a copperhead. Her leg swelled to three times its normal size. Fever set in. She slowed them down, then became delirious. She cried out, fought. Her mother gagged her at times. They had to quit the woods and travel the roads at night. Outriders cornered them a few hundred yards from the Kansas border. That was the story. Nobody knew what became of the girl, her mother, or the other fugitives. After his branding, Jonah Chambers spent two years in a Missouri prison.

Jonah Chambers rumors had been rife in North Texas for most of a year: He was preaching in the Sulfur Forks country. He was hiding out in the thickets, gathering up area slaves. He'd been caught and jailed in Bonham but had escaped the first night. Way up the creeks he preached before bonfires to Negroes and whites alike, firing them into a seditious frenzy. He'd been seen skulking around slave quarters in Fannin, Lamar, and Grayson Counties and was said to be a spiritual brother to John Brown. He had congregants all over drainages of the Sulfur and Red, mostly ignorant hill people from the border states, men bitter about their sorry lot in life and looking for ways to undermine the prosperous. He was a man of fire and brimstone. Fire mostly. Barns had burned all over that country for two summers. If anyone had actually seen Jonah Chambers, they weren't saying. That's how it was: If you were against him, you never saw him. You saw only his work or work attributed to him. If you were with him, you kept quiet.

Now they had him. The rumors had been true. He'd been there all along. He ought to be coming down either Jefferson or Houston Street anytime. They'd caught him the night before with two slaves he'd coaxed off a farm on White Rock Creek. Heading north for his thickets for sure. Probably had agents in Indian Territory and certainly in Kansas. The two slaves would have been in Iowa before the end of the year.

Ig and Rachel had gotten the news from Joseph and Samuel, who'd heard from Pig, who'd actually seen Chambers—or the man purported to be Reverend Chambers—shackled to two Negroes, walking down Preston Road toward Dallas. Pig had raced ahead with the news.

It had been a rough year for Northern Methodists in Texas. In March their conference meeting on Timber Creek, in Collin County, had been broken up by proslavery leaders from Bonham. In August, a Dallas committee accused Parson Solomon McKinney of spreading antislavery views after he allegedly mentioned in a sermon that a few masters had been cruel to their servants. McKinney and his friend, Rev. William Blount, who spoke out in his favor, were arrested and jailed. Within hours a mob broke them out, whipped them bloody, and ran them out of the county. Yet McKinney-Blount rumors persisted.

Parson Chambers, if he made it to town alive, would be very fortunate to get off with just a whipping.

Ig and Rachel, Samuel, Bekah, and Joseph gathered just above the square, north of the intersection of Main and Jefferson, along with half of the citizens of Dallas. The other half milled around on the other side of the square just north of Commerce and Jefferson—blacksmiths, teamsters, bankers, merchants wearing armbands, women in cotton and wool, a few carrying parasols, and barefooted children.

The courthouse lawn had been vacant most of the summer due to an outbreak of fleas. If you had business inside, you hurried up the walkway to the front door. Word was, area attorneys seemed to be finding little business that couldn't be handled from their offices. Judge Nat Burford had temporarily moved his quarters to the second floor of Peak & Sons, spurring much speculation about how much the town of Dallas was paying Peak for use of his space.

Pig said the man who might be Jonah Chambers didn't look like much. He stood looking northward up the muddy road through the grassy hills and cedar breaks at the outskirts of town. In his excitement Pig had forgotten about Cathlyn and the boys. His three hounds had followed him to town. People had come out of their cabins, houses, and shops. Some brought chairs. Doors were open. Boys chased each other between houses. Dogs were barking. Ig was sweating, both from the heat and from the vague feeling that Rachel expected him to do something. Like everyone else, she seemed transfixed by the possibility of actually seeing this legendary, fearless, and perhaps crazy and violent abolitionist preacher.

What did one owe a fellow man of God? More than any other fellow man? And what if this man had acted recklessly, if bravely, thus endangering the larger movement? Now the various vigilance committees—every town had one—would be swarming the county. Every Negro would be stopped and interrogated or arrested and then beaten until he told his captors what they wanted to hear, then beaten again for his admission. No road would be safe. If Jonah Chambers was here, then what else was afoot?

Prudence. Patience. Why were these virtues so rare? Let the hotheads in New England safely shout from their lecterns and newspapers. There was quiet work to be done here, and he'd do it if it weren't for agitators like Parson Chambers. He might be a hero among open abolitionists, but his latest indiscretion would set them back six months and probably get Peter caught.

Ig had been looking forward to talking with Bekah, though he'd been warned she had little to say. She stood along the street in front of Samuel and Joseph, her arms crossed on her chest. There were dozens of slaves in the crowd. These days, slavers were eager to show Negroes what happened to runaways and their abettors. Across the street, Charles Pryor, editor of the *Dallas Herald*, was scribbling in his notebook as he watched the street and talked with his boss, publisher James Latimer, and attorney John McCoy, whose white beard hung to his waist and made Ig feel even hotter. Ig caught a whiff of bread baking at Bell's Bakery. He noted the time—mid-afternoon. This batch would be going to the hotels for the evening meals. It occurred to him, too, Rachel would normally be starting supper about now. But they were more than a mile from home and only a block from the Meades'. He didn't see Rosemary. Perhaps she was at home making preparations. This sort of calamity called for a good meal and grave postprandial musing.

"I never saw his hand," Pig said to Samuel.

"How close did you get?"

"Hundred feet, I s'pose."

"How you know it was him, then?"

"Everybody I seen said it was. I wasn't about to ride up and ask the deputies who they had."

"Probably not even him," Joseph said.

Pig said, "You think all these people would be standin' out here bakin' at three o'clock in the afternoon for somebody that ain't Jonah Chambers?"

"We are, and we don't have no idea except what somebody told you," Samuel said. "Anyway, you said he didn't look like much."

"I don't know," Pig said. "What's he supposed to look like?"

"I never heard," Samuel said. "Nobody's ever seen him that I know of. Whoever heard of a preacher that nobody ever sees?"

"Well, I believe I seen him," Pig said.

"Where's he at, then? We been standing out here for an hour."

"I had a good jump, and the prisoners were afoot. They didn't look too fresh."

Rachel said, "You don't suppose they'll hang him?"

"If they don't show soon, that's exactly what I'll be inclined to think," Joseph said.

Rachel shaded her eyes with her hand. "Surely they wouldn't hang a minister. He hasn't killed anyone or stole a horse."

"Marster Winfred never killed nobody or stole a horse neither," Samuel said.

"He makes it to jail, he probably won't get hung," Pig said. "Unless they break him out and string him up somewhere. Judge Burford won't abide it." He looked toward the courthouse. "I want you to look." His three hounds and two town mongrels were sniffing about the courthouse lawn. "Hey! Hey!" He stepped into the street and whistled. "Margie! Hank! Zack! Get up here!" The hounds jerked up their heads, pricked their long ears, then bolted up the street. The two mongrels followed. People laughed. Pig stepped out of the street shaking his head. "I just salted them three down for fleas. They're probably eat up again. Cathlyn won't let 'em in the house now."

Across the street, Dr. Sam Pryor yelled, "Pig, I admire a man who keeps a strong hand on his family." More laughter. Pig shook his head and praised the three dogs as they crowded around his legs, tongues lolling and tails whipping. He shooed them. "Y'all go find a drink of water. You got the whole damn river."

"I'm about to have to go find one myself," Ig said.

Samuel shook his head. "I reckon they stopped and hung him. Look— people are giving up and going home."

Bekah sighed, sat down in the dust, and rested her chin in her hand. Just then Ig noticed her two missing fingers. Still, she was a handsome woman. He wondered what she thought of her arrangement, assuming Samuel or Joseph had discussed it with her. He wondered, too, about Samuel's expectations. Joseph really didn't need the extra help, though he'd welcome whatever help Bekah was willing to provide. Joseph had often commented on Samuel's frustration. Ig had never given much thought to Negro marriages—or conjugal arrangements. Surely Joseph wouldn't allow fornication, though given Bekah's apparent disposition, she'd probably stay in a spare room, or the men would build her a cabin. Joseph had the space on his lot. Then, again, she might be the next southbound passenger.

"Somebody'll be wantin' them two boys back," Pig said. "They might hang old Jonah, but they won't hang them boys. Probably just whip the livin' hell out of 'em."

Wind kicked up dust in the street, bending John McCoy's beard and ruffling dresses and little girls' hair. People turned their faces away from it. When the wind laid, Rachel stepped into the street and looked north, one hand shading her eyes, the other on her hip. Now how many men were looking at her? Ig couldn't blame them. "I see a rider," she said. The men stepped into the street, squinting in the direction she pointed.

Rachel said, "One man, I believe."

Ig cleaned his spectacles and put them back on, pulled his hat brim lower. "I can't see a thing. If we'd settled west of Bird's Fort, I'd have been scalped right off."

"Too much reading and writing by candlelight," Rachel said. "He won't listen to me."

"My most grievous failing."

"There's one," Pig said. "Another one behind him." Others had noticed the riders, and now people stepped farther out into the street, pointing and looking back to comment. A few fathers held up small children. A little girl sat on her father's shoulders. Bekah pushed away one of Pig's hounds, rose, and dusted her thighs and backside. She seemed to look at no one. Ig noticed Samuel's furtive glances in her direction. He remembered that tension with envy and pity. The young man knew hope and despair and lust and little else.

Now he saw the two riders coming south on Houston, still north of cabins and businesses, two hundred yards out where the road became a rutted path through the cedars. And behind them, something else he couldn't make out. The riders came on at a trot into town. The first to arrive was a man Ig recognized but didn't know. He wore a filthy homespun shirt and galluses, knee-high moccasins, and had a wispy black beard. Long, sweaty hair hung from beneath his hat. Behind him rode a boy of about twelve.

"That's Odell Johnson," Pig said.

Johnson reined his horse and yelled, "They got him all right."

"You seen his hand?" someone yelled.

"Nawsir. But them deputies has. And he's spittin' venom the whole way." The boy nodded in agreement and looked back up the street.

More riders now. And a wagon and team and a jumble of men on foot. Ig's tongue felt like a file on the roof of his mouth.

"There they are," Pig said. "That's him in the middle."

Between an empty wagon in front and two horsemen in the rear walked a thin white man shackled between two Negroes. None of the men wore a hat. All staggered. People crowded into the street. "By God, they got his ass now," somebody said. "Hang the thieving bastard!"

They came on. The crowed pressed into the street. Others stood on their toes. "Look there, his goddamn bald head is blistered."

"Mouth still goin' though."

"Shut his ass up soon enough."

The two black men looked to be about Samuel's age. One taller and one shorter than the white man. Chambers stumbled; the two black men staggered under his weight, then stopped to help him up. The crowd hooted and laughed. A few looked away. Charles Pryor wrote in his notebook. John McCoy was pointing at the wagon and yelling something at the deputies who were leaning toward him, cupping their fingers about their ears. Jonah Chambers regained his balance and turned, jerking the man on his left, to yell at a gaggle of men who were pointing and shouting. His mouth moved; his sun-blistered face was tight, contorted. The crowd pressed closer, grew louder. Ig looked over hats and bonnets. Rachel bobbed on her toes. He caught some of Chambers's hoarse words: "You sir . . . before God . . . strike ye. . . ." A deputy goaded him with a rifle barrel. He swung his shoulders; the two men at his sides lurched but kept their feet. The crowd drowned his words. A deputy moved ahead of the wagon to clear the way. A horse apple flew out of the crowd across the street, missed the prisoners, and bounced into the crowd in front of Ig. The prisoners swayed. A boy ran between the prisoners and the wagon and punched Jonah Chambers in the chest in passing.

"Little beast!" Rachel yelled.

The deputies pushed back the crowd. Judge Burford stepped into the opening and motioned for Marshal Moore, who eased his horse over and bent to the red-faced judge, who pointed furiously at the wagon. The marshal yelled to his men. The two deputies dismounted and led the prisoners to the wagon. The three clambered in, falling on their shoulders and faces, rooting, squirming, gathering their knees beneath them. People lined the streets all the way to the courthouse square and to the jail on the east side of the square. The prisoners sat up. The wagon eased on, the deputies clearing the way.

The exhausted prisoners spoke among themselves and nodded. The two Negroes stood and helped Chambers to his feet. The mob roared; a horse turd, hurled from the crowd, missed the prisoners and hit the driver's neck. The wagon lurched. The three staggered and fell forward, heads and shoulders striking the sideboard. People surged in to slap and punch. As Ig stepped out of the way of the horses, he saw a slender, three-fingered hand reach out and touch the prisoners as they passed by.

He gripped Rachel's arm. He'd lost Pig, Joseph, and Samuel. The air smelled of hair, sweaty wool, dust, and horses.

The prisoners were standing again, bracing each other, their feet set wide for balance. Had someone pushed them up? The two black men looked out over the crowd, seemingly calm, no longer dazed, and Jonah Chambers, filth from the wagon bed on his face and lips, preached to the throng. As the wagon passed, Ig, standing three deep in the crowd, heard, "Others among you . . . burn . . . not alone!"

CHAPTER 17

At about half past ten, Bekah heard Joseph shut his bedroom door for the night. Though she'd closed her own door an hour earlier, her sense of solitude deepened after the men went to bed. She snuffed her candle and sat in the rocker next to the open window. Soft moonlight revealed the summer-burned front yard and empty street. The gray shop cat sat on a front path stepping-stone, watching for rabbits and cotton rats along the brushy margin across the road.

Night was hers. You could be yourself while white folks slept. *Early to bed and early to rise . . .* Just like something a white woman would say. Why, yes, ma'am, she'd be healthy and wealthy sure enough if she'd just get in the bed at a decent hour.

On the McCutcheon place, late spring had been best, before the summer heat. Plenty warm, but you didn't sweat as long as you moved along easy, which she and her brother, James, and her cousins had rarely managed until she turned thirteen and noticed that, overnight, James's best friend—quiet, skinny Robert—had grown from half a head shorter than she to a head taller, and his quietness and shyness now seemed like seriousness, especially when he leaned toward her, arms crossed, one hand stroking new chin whiskers, which drew attention to his jawline and the size of his fingers and that great thumb, and he'd listen, unblinking, turning each of your words over and over as if he were studying and admiring a keen blade or a mad stone or a fine carving.

Cicadas and crickets and tree frogs. Owls. Eleven cabins scattered amid giant oaks and hickories and beeches throwing shadows across the log walls, and the big house out of sight across the bottom and over the hill above the branch. Comforting voices from the darkness. You didn't remember the words, just the voice and laughter or singing or foot stomping off down the trail to Uncle Jeff's cabin or Miz Gwen's or Brother Thomas's. You'd see their cook fires and light from their candles and lanterns. Their voices and tiny lights, their presence, made the dark woods welcoming as long as you didn't stray too far beyond the glow. Even out in the darkness, her back against some massive trunk and Robert pressing against her, she'd look past him, through the leaves, branches, vines, and boles, at the fires. The voices and laughter, admonishments, whining dogs, crying babies, clanging cast iron, thwacking of kindling axes would rise above their breathing and the scraping of cotton against shagbark, the shifting of feet on forest duff, and the vernal hum.

Further back. Not yet seven years old. Daddy and Grandpap still alive. Firelight on their faces. Slipping drinks of brandy when they had it. They always thought it was funny. Marster McCutcheon was an awfully generous man. He didn't have no idea just how generous he was. Wouldn't break up a family. Neither would his daddy. Praise the Lord for that anyway. "Where's Bekah at? Child, you better get on to bed. Where you been? Get on now. James be along after while." Dying firelight on the ceiling timbers. Those voices outside. The jug tipping again. Almost empty. Grandpap says, "Ah! Lord!" He'd be wiping his mouth with the back of his hand. That James still out there and only a year older. Stay awake. Stay awake. Listen. Think about Daddy's rough hands holding something. Morning will come, and they'll all be cross and in a hurry, and threatening to cut a switch. Smell of cold ashes. Long old days. Hot. Marster Boyd squalling and carrying on, and Daddy mad, and one of the aunts crying before it's over with. Stay awake. Here comes James, bringing the James smell to bed.

Three years she could remember, when they were all together still, Daddy and Grandpap and James, before she had to go to work beyond gathering kindling and water and sweeping. Before Grandpap fell dead between rows of beans, before Daddy decided not to take another beating and took the hoe away from Cyrus Boyd. "Why, he never meant to kill old drunk Marster Boyd. Just whapped 'im with that hoe before he knowed what he was doin'. Done it before we could get hold of him. Marster McCutcheon told the judge that very thing. He aimed to run Marster Boyd off first chance he got anyways."

She wiped her eyes, then covered them with her hand and wept. When she looked up again, the shop cat was staring at the window. The leaves of the cedar elm and bodark in the front yard were pale in the moonlight, pale like the undersides of the tender oak and hickory leaves lighted by the cook fires and bonfires of the McCutcheon slaves, when she'd sat on the ground between her father and grandfather and learned the smell of apple brandy and watched bats hunting safely above the flames, before she understood what it meant to be owned.

CHAPTER 18

Joseph had just poured himself another shot of Malachi's whiskey when the Meades' front door opened and Ignatius called from the anteroom, "Hide the bottle, boys, the parson has arrived."

Joseph heard Rachel laugh. Of course she found her husband clever. Never mind that the two Meade girls were supposed to be asleep. She followed Ig into the kitchen where Joseph, Malachi, Pig, and Samuel were sitting around the table.

Joseph failed to draw even a glance from Rachel. "Well, Preacher, you caught us. Drink?"

"Just one," Ig said.

"Back hurting you again, I reckon."

Rosemary set another glass on the table. Malachi filled it.

"Powerful bad." Ig took the glass, pulled a chair away from the table, eased himself down, crossed his legs, and took a sip. "Well."

"Man came down from Sherman today and picked up the two boys," Pig said.

Ig nodded. "We heard. Heard, too, that Brothers Newton and Chambers may not be in jail much longer."

Joseph smiled and shook his head. "Newton. Crazy coot."

Malachi corked the whiskey bottle. "I expect you heard Bill Keller's name, too. 'Bill Keller says this; Bill Keller won't put up with that; old Bill, by God. Bill, Bill, Bill.' He's grown right venerable for man ain't been in town a year."

"He's grown right wealthy is what he's done," Joseph said. "Y'all seen his ad in the *Herald*? 'Engage in Profitable Land Speculation!' Money rarely hurts a man's standing. He spends more on those ads than I make."

"I expect Latimer deals him a generous rate," Malachi said. "I hear those two have become big hog-hunting friends. Out in the river bottom every Saturday night. Them and Pryor. A man could do worse than get in thick with the local newsmen."

"Local propagandists," Rosemary said.

Malachi winked at her.

"Or the local judiciary," Ignatius said. "Word is, Nat Burford's been joining the hunt."

Pig scratched his chin. "How in the hell does Keller shoot?" He glanced around at the corners of the room.

Rosemary said, "Oh! I'm sorry, Pig. It's by the back step." She started through the kitchen toward the back door.

"He's revolting," Rachel said. She was still leaning in the dining room doorway.

Everyone looked at her. "I mean Mr. Keller."

They all laughed. "Accurate in either case," Joseph said.

Rosemary hurried back with a spittoon, which she set in the corner close to Pig, who leaned away from the table and let loose.

Joseph nodded. "That hook."

"No, it's his manner."

"He's watchful," Rosemary said. "Designing."

Malachi laughed. "Unlike Mrs. Meade."

Rosemary waved off the joke. "You know very well what I mean."

They all nodded. Ig said, "Well. Say what you will about Brother Zeph Newton; he's a loyal friend."

Rachel snorted. "Couldn't let Brother Jonah get locked up without him. How would that look?"

Ig shook his head in exasperation. "Rachel."

"Well."

Joseph said, "I think she's right, Ig. You should've been there. Old Newton showed up to get locked up. Sat up front and started in right off. Keller couldn't get in a word edgewise."

"And look at all the good it's done," Rachel said.

Ig took another sip. "I suppose, then, that I'd have to endure incarceration alone."

"We'd send you letters," Malachi said. "From your anonymous former friends and loved ones."

"I'd expect no less. Where's Bekah?"

Samuel sat across the table. He eyed the two-thirds-empty bottle of whiskey. "Shut up in her bedroom, I imagine."

"Have you talked to her yet?" Rachel asked. "Explained things?"

"Not yet," Joseph said. "I'm beginning to think she's a little daft. Anyway, I'm leaving the explaining to her liberator, Mr. Samuel here."

"I don't know what to tell her. She won't even look at me," Samuel said. "She'll probably run off. I wish I'd left her down at Cedar Hill."

Joseph laughed and said, "Oh, telling her she's no longer property will be simple enough."

"The poor woman's world has been upended," Rachel said. "She'll need time to settle in."

"She was just as cross when we first seen her," Samuel said. "I ought to have had better sense."

"Keep the higher purposes in mind, son," Ig said.

Rachel said, "Does she have children?"

"Sold downriver to Louisiana or Mississippi after she run away two or three times from north Alabama, where she's from," Samuel said. "That's what old Montgomery told us. Took off again, and they caught her and sold her to somebody who put up with her for a year before he sold her to somebody else who sold her in Louisiana to the fellow who sold her cheap to Montgomery."

"And you wonder why she's sullen," Rosemary said.

Joseph leaned back and crossed his ankles. "I don't know who cut her fingers off."

Samuel seemed to be studying his glass as he turned it slowly between his thumb and forefinger. "Put her in a coffin and haul her south maybe," he said sullenly.

Ig shrugged. "And what would be wrong with that?"

Joseph said, "That's just not the way old Samuel pictured it."

Rachel pursed her lips. "Hmmm. Well. She's only been here a few days."

"Back to the good preachers," Ig said. "They'll need counsel."

"They've refused it," Malachi said. "McCoy offered."

"I doubt Major McCoy is sympathetic," Rachel said. "I understand he used to own slaves. And look at who his friends are."

Malachi nodded. "But that scene in town the other day tore him up. You could see it. He's probably just standing on principle. That, and he despises everyone in the marshal's office. In any case, Brother Jonah is clearly guilty and has pled such, and crazy Parson Newton seems happy to back him. McCoy knows he can't help either of them, so he's not worried. Just goading Moore, I'd say." He laid his hands on the table, clasped his fingers. "I'd defend them."

Rosemary started to speak but didn't. Ig nodded slightly.

Pig said, "Why, it don't matter who defends 'em or what either man says. Only place they're halfway safe is in jail. If they was to get off, they'd be caught and hung before they could get clear of the courthouse steps." He turned and spat, wiped his mouth with the heel of his hand. "But it wouldn't surprise me a bit if Burford up and let 'em go just to get 'em hung and out of the way. He can't sentence 'em to die for what they're accused of. But if he turned 'em loose he'd at least save the jailhouse door from being knocked in by whichever bunch shows up to haul old Zeph and Jonah off to the closest handy limb."

Joseph eyed Rachel in spite of himself and the grim conversation. Ig was oblivious. Rachel caught his glance and looked away. He sipped his whiskey, studied her some more. It had been over a month, Jonah Chambers or no Jonah Chambers, and Ig had lately said nothing about evangelizing in the hinterlands.

She glanced at him again and furrowed her brow. He looked into his whiskey.

Malachi said to Ig, "You know what Brother Jonah told Burford? Said, yes sir, he was indeed guilty of enticing and abetting runaway slaves, the two he was caught with and a hundred or so others between here and Missouri. Then you know what he said? Asked Burford if he owned any slaves."

Ig leaned forward. "What'd the good judge say to that?"

"He said, 'That is immaterial, sir.' Can't you hear him? Then Brother Jonah said, 'Well if you do, you'd better keep an eye on them.'"

Ig shook his head. "Reckless talk. Not helpful at all. He should have as much prudence as courage."

"Got sand, though," Joseph said. Ig had a point, but he could stand to worry a little more about their abolition work and a little less about his hide. A little more sand wouldn't hurt this bunch. Two years, and so far they'd gotten one freedom seeker south of Horde's Ridge. And who knew where Peter was now? You could fool around and prudently burn up another two years. He glanced again at Rachel. Just once he'd like to catch her looking at him.

A double rap at the back door. Rosemary said, "Who would be calling this close to midnight?" Malachi rose and went with her to the back door.

"Maybe we'd best get started on another coffin," Samuel said.

From the back door Rosemary said, "Alan, what in the world?"

Al Huitt walked into the room, nodded to all. "I got to hurry and get back. I just wanted to tell you. . . ."

"Somebody got 'em," Pig said. "I knowed it."

Huitt said, "Four of 'em. Walked in with shotguns. Bold as brass. Sacks over their heads. Two of 'em was wearing gloves. The two deputies just got out of the way, then got tied up. I'm sure they was expecting it and approved of it."

Rachel touched her temple. "After all I've said." Ig looked pale.

"They're hung by now, for sure," Joseph said. It seemed odd that he felt so little, knowing he could easily be caught. Perhaps coldness and distance were aids in this kind of work. Or maybe courage was nothing more than an inability to imagine your own death.

Al held his hat against his thigh. "I reckon. Maybe."

Pig shifted his chew. "'Maybe,' hell."

Al said, "Queer thing is, the way word got out was when Bill Keller and them showed up to drag the preachers out and hang 'em, they found the two deputies already tied up. Somebody had beat 'em to the jail." He nodded for emphasis. "Now how 'bout that?"

Father's Reminiscence
Transcribed July 27, 1911

L evin McGregor. Your uncle Levin. More uncle to you than any of my brothers by blood.

Let me tell you about . . .

I have to say . . .

No.

I'm sorry.

How can I put this? I'm sorry. I've been thinking about him this morning. He's been on my mind. This has been coming on.

What a ridiculous old man I am.

You've not seen your father this way before, have you? I suppose I'm beyond embarrassment.

Let me gather myself.

I can barely keep my food down whenever I hear about great men. Washington or Jefferson. General Grant. General Pershing, these days. Mr. Rockefeller. Mr. Vanderbilt. Mr. Gould. Men who people our newspapers and history books. Men held up as examples for wormy schoolboys carrying mush buckets.

Sickening. Forgive me for being old and bitter. And ridiculous.

You know most of it, of course. You grew up on it. For the sake of posterity, I'll repeat it—with commentary.

Levin McGregor. Older than me by about three hours, as best we could figure. He liked to claim a full day on me when we were in our prime. Later, he would remind me that I was just as advanced a dotard as he.

We fell in together up in Detroit in the early fifties after we met in Henry Bibb's newspaper office. Working together, we took 117 fugitives out of Detroit into Canada. That's the exact number. Men and women and children. Babies. Old men and women leaning on canes. We kept count. We were young men. The numbers mattered. We knew what everyone else was doing, too. We aimed to outdo them and did.

Levin's move north was more arduous and halting than mine. He ran away from a tobacco plantation in Mason County, Kentucky, in 1846. His mother and father had been worked to death. Both dead before forty. He aimed to swim to Cincinnati. You get ideas like that when you're seventeen and see your older sister cut her own throat with a tobacco knife. He helped drag her out of the field, then had to go back and finish two more rows before dark. You cannot wait with tobacco.

He had never swam before. Said he'd waded the creeks frequently and had floated in some of the deeper holes, but had never been in over his head. Swimming didn't strike him as something he'd have trouble taking up. He found the Ohio broader than he'd expected, and right cold in early October. Just after sunrise, a boatman saw him come up and go down again. He managed to come up again for what might have been his last taste of air when the boatman whapped him with a spare oar and fished him out before he sank. He was nearly halfway across. That'd be ninety yards out or better. I've crossed the river about there—in a rowboat. Yes, I grew up on the Tennessee River, but I would never have tried to swim the Ohio. Too broad. With bad currents. Swim for Ohio and wash up down in New Orleans.

Back at the farm, he was still sick and dizzy from that lick to the head when his foreman tied him to the post and whipped him until he passed out again. He woke up in a tobacco barn, shackled to the wall. Ten days. They gave him a little water and cornbread, unshackled one arm so he could eat. Pissed and shat right where he stood. Flies and gnats and ants deviling those raw stripes on his back. You could find a number of those stout oaken barns in those Kentucky counties that bordered the river, stouter than they needed to be to hold tobacco. But in that country, a man can look across and see the other side, or even if he's not right on the river he can look off in the distance and know that somewhere out near the horizon he might have a chance at a life, if he can avoid the slave catchers. Get up among the free Negroes. Maybe they can hide you for the rest of your life. Or maybe you hope the old man doesn't think enough of you to send slave catchers into a free state or badger a local marshal who probably doesn't want to bother looking for you. Or maybe if you want to breathe free air and never look over your shoulder, never again dread turning a corner or wonder if every stranger or acquaintance, black or white, might be the one who will turn you in for the reward, you can find someone to shepherd you on to Detroit and finally to Chatham. There, you'll be a subject of the crown, but at least you have the same protection under the law as any white man. All of the Republican talk about the Declaration of Independence, the Constitution, freedom, and answering to no king meant nothing to Levin McGregor. Or maybe it did, as he learned of it, and had to live the lies in it. The deceit, the *conceit*, that made proud traitors, willful seditionists, of the two of us. Render unto Caesar? Et tu, Levin?

He went back to work, chain dangling between his feet. Fourteen months later, another slave, a young blacksmith named Matthew, drove the pins from Levin's shackles. They ran, hid along the river for the better part of a week, finally found a rowboat and, under the cover of night, rowed for Ohio. They could see only a few lights. They landed well down-river from Cincinnati. Just before dawn they dragged the boat up the bank on the Ohio side, hid it and themselves in the willows, and waited, bellies rubbing their backbones, for night.

Matthew began to panic when he heard hounds running. Then men and dogs appeared on the far bank. The two lit out in broad daylight, doing their best to keep to cover.

They ran upriver. Matthew sobbed at times, but he knew what waited for him across the river. And if he had doubts, Levin dispelled them by pulling up his shirt to show the boy how captured runaways were treated.

Twice they passed farmers along the road who surely knew what they were. These men nodded and raised a hand. Nevertheless, Levin and Matthew listened for the sound of dogs or shouts because they could imagine no white man who would not turn them in. They made it to Cincinnati at dusk. Finding the Negro section of town proved easy enough. Matthew found work blacksmithing; Levin worked as a stevedore.

They felt safe among the narrow streets and alleys, the little shacks and businesses owned by free blacks and even runaways, this bustling little world where you could go about your business for days without seeing a white man.

Months passed. They shared a room above the blacksmith shop. Levin began to court a free girl, Sue-Ann Ross, a domestic. She read to him from abolitionist newspapers. He listened, amazed. He'd had no inkling that black men could own newspapers or that white men might devote entire publications and most of their lives to freeing Negroes from servitude; in Kentucky he'd been told and had accepted that Negro bondage was as natural and accepted as beasts of burden. He had no sense of geography. One county had been his world, a broad world stretching forever in three directions, fields worked by Negroes and overseen by armed white men on horseback and that's all there was, save for rumors of some slender thread of hope across the river. There was Canada. That place somewhere to the north that stirred imaginations at night while white people slept and Negroes luxuriated in their privacy. Where was it? North. A thousand miles? Like making the trip to town a thousand times. Uncle Fletcher could count to a thousand, and did one night while they listened as raptly as if he were telling an absorbing tale. A thousand. People had done it. There was a white man, a preacher living somewhere along the river on the Ohio side. If you could find him, he could help you. Get you started north. They'd all heard of Ripley, but no one knew its location. Just that it was upriver from Cincinnati.

Now here he was, not in Canada, but living like a free man. He'd done it. No doubt they were talking about him now, Uncle Fletcher who could count to a thousand and June and Thomas and Jane. Wondering where he was and what he might be doing or speculating that he might be dead or caught, then figuring, no, if they'd caught him or killed him, they'd have drug him back as an example to the others who might have thoughts of running.

So a young man who'd been whipped to within an inch of his life and chained to the wall of a barn for ten days, who'd known every kind of indignity, now had a job and money saved and a girl and a growing circle of friends, and then one day in June 1849, after eight months of freedom he looked up from his work to see his old master standing with a white marshal and three other white men, all armed with pistols, save one, who held a set of shackles.

He heard no mention of Matthew, never saw him again. By the end of September, his old wounds, which had been so expertly freshened, were beginning to heal, and he found that the sweat raised by the southern Mississippi sun no longer stung his back.

CHAPTER 19

Samuel had just left the shop on Wednesday morning to pick up a small load of lumber at the sawmill. Joseph was installing hinges on Sarah Cockrell's new armoire when he looked up to see Ebenezer Euler stepping off Polk Street and into the yard. Maybe someone had died over at the commune. Probably not. Most of the original members had given up on the venture and were now working at trades in town. Say what you would about idealistic Europeans, they brought useful skills to the country. Nowadays, at least, you could buy a fresh loaf of wheat bread or get a decent set of stone steps laid or a fence built. Still, he hoped Euler was looking for an undertaker. He didn't know many of the communists personally, and business had been slow. Lately he and Samuel had built cabinets and tables for a few well-off merchants, but he suspected they'd about run through the local furniture budget for a while. If things didn't pick up he'd have to get out and find work framing barns and houses. At least you rarely had to haul and hew logs anymore.

Euler walked into the yard, sweating. As always, he wore a jacket, tie, and hat. Joseph said, "Good morning, Professor. How is it out at the commune?"

Euler stepped under the overhang and shook Joseph's hand. "Dismal. I have only six students left. The rest have deserted me for town." He'd picked up most of his English in Dallas County. Now he spoke with an odd French-accented border state drawl. Joseph enjoyed the mixture and suspected he was one of the few citizens of Dallas County to notice drawl, having spent considerable time north of the Ohio River.

"Hate to hear that. But then I'm sure Mrs. Gray's curriculum is far less rigorous than yours. Ultimately, men tend toward the easier route."

"No logic, no rhetoric, no epics. Just the bare essentials, but then I suppose that's all one really needs in this brutish backwater."

"I don't know about that. You saw the play at the Masons' Hall week before last?

"Absurd. Pitiful. Save for Major McCoy's narration. He has a splendid voice and reads beautifully."

"And Mrs. Clayhill's operatic production?"

"Laughable. You must be able to speak proper German in order to sing proper German."

"I find her first rank."

"Most gentlemen do. It's her singing that offends me."

Joseph laughed. It was always good to see Professor Euler. "How's the corn and bean crop across the river?"

"We'll be provisioning in town this winter assuming the demand for music lessons and stonework continues. Certain realities have forced us to make embarrassing concessions in regard to currency."

"This drought. Everybody's having a hard time of it."

Euler snorted. "Everybody as ill-suited to agriculture as we are. We Fourierists brought stonemasons, musicians, bakers, teachers, but not one farmer. Ridiculous."

"What keeps you there then? Cross the river for good. We could use a little learning in this town."

"My students. I have obligations. Perhaps after I get them through Homer and the rudiments of plane geometry."

"Well then. Old Considerant ain't fell over dead, has he? I hope you're not needing an undertaker."

"Not unless Julie brained him since I left this morning."

"Well, I know you're not looking for a furniture maker. You've got one, and I hope he stays over there."

Euler glanced back at the street and out into the yard. "Perhaps we should step inside."

"Lord, it'll be hot in there."

"I received a letter from some relatives in Castroville earlier this week. My cousin is married to a German fellow. A visitor recently passed through their community. He sends his best."

"I'll open the windows a crack. We get a pretty good draft." He led Euler to his office. His hands trembled as he adjusted the shutters and tried to guess the distance between Castroville and the Rio Grande.

Euler sat down in the spare straight-backed chair, doffed his hat, and used it as a fan. "I smell something good to eat."

"Bekah's busy burning dinner." He stepped across the room and shut the door to the hallway leading to the kitchen.

"Sometimes one accepts whatever help is available."

"She does it on purpose. At least it's ready when I'm ready to eat it." They studied each other for a moment. A bead of sweat dripped from Euler's goatee. Joseph said. "Peter."

Euler nodded.

"How is he?"

"Well as of four and a half weeks ago."

"We talked about asking you folks for help. We suspected you might be sympathetic."

"Sympathetic, yes. But can we afford the potential trouble?"

"Well, that's right. Stir up trouble and everybody might leave the commune."

Euler smiled. "I was surprised to learn that a man who keeps slaves would involve himself in such an altruistic venture."

"Samuel's a friend. He draws a salary."

"I assumed as much. The woman, too?"

"She just moved in. We're not holding her here, but she doesn't know it. For now she has a place to live and plenty to eat."

"You purchased her?"

"We traded some work for her. Samuel's smitten by her."

"I see." Euler fanned himself with his hat. "Interesting."

"So."

"Yes."

"'Yes,' you're here to help, or 'yes,' you're just passing along hopeful news?"

"You're awfully tense."

"Goddamn right. You heard about Winfred Skaggs."

"Along with everyone else in Dallas County. Just as his murderers planned."

Joseph nodded. "Winfred was a friend. We go back a ways. You understand what I'm saying?"

Euler nodded.

Joseph said, "You've learned a lot about me in a few minutes. I can get a lot tenser."

He raised a hand. "Please, I understand your concern, but there's no need for that."

Joseph studied him. Euler had no economic stake in the slavery issue. Why would he trouble himself, if not for ideological reasons? He wondered if Fourierists had an official position on forced servitude. If they opposed it, they'd come to the wrong county.

After a few moments, Euler said, "Will there be more? My sister and her friends prefer to be good hosts. One prefers not to be surprised."

"We hope so. We've been at this for a while. We're finding Texas difficult."

"In every way imaginable. Exhausting and discouraging." Euler pulled a handkerchief from an inside jacket pocket and dabbed his brow. "She's been doing this sort of work for some time, my sister. They have routes worked out. Southward connections. They've shepherded several into Piedras Negras. The Mexicans on the Texas side have proved helpful. Still, it's very dangerous, and the Germans aren't uniformly in favor of manumission. Some keep slaves. Most despise all Mexicans. They're far more tolerant of the various tribes of savages. For my part, I can barely tolerate Germans and their exhausting fastidiousness. As barbaric in their own way as the most rustic Tennessean."

Bekah opened the door and said, "Dinner's about ready. Is that boy back yet? He's fixing to miss it." She noticed Euler. "Who's he?"

Joseph said, "Bekah, this is Professor Euler." The professor stood and bowed slightly.

"I reckon he'll be eatin' here."

"Of course. Professor, I hope you've worked up an appetite."

"Very kind of you," Euler said.

Bekah sighed. "Well then. There's gonna be some little dabs of food on those plates. You've got to tell me how many I'm feedin'."

CHAPTER 20

Joseph often worried that he would have accepted slavery had his mother and father stayed in Lexington, Kentucky, instead of moving the family to Cincinnati when he was eight years old. He could never know for sure, unlike Ig and Rachel, who grew up in slave states—Ig in western Virginia, Rachel in Maryland—yet loathed the institution. Perhaps his character was naturally flawed so that during his formative years he acquired the mores of those around him, however righteous or evil those mores might be. Yes, his parents lived for a time in Kentucky, a slave state, but they had moved there from Pennsylvania where they undoubtedly were influenced by Quakers, though being good Congregationalists, they would never admit it.

He liked to think of himself as a radical, a dissenter, a virtuous traitor, but he worried he had simply absorbed his leanings. After all, he had not been a radical in his community in Cincinnati. He had been a comfortable member and, as best he could remember, a natural conformist who sought the approval of his elders. Even in Kansas, especially in Lawrence, he'd been one free soiler among hundreds. Who could say that he might not have been a self-satisfied member of the planter community had he grown up in Louisiana? Only after Ig and Rachel convinced him to move to the vilest, darkest corner of the South did he feel he could be tested.

Even here there seemed to be no shortage of educated, reasonable people—men and women who seemed no more naturally predisposed to barbarism than abolitionists he'd known in Ohio and Kansas. Yet many of these people owned slaves, and even those who didn't seemed to condone the practice, or at least they didn't openly object to it. Many slaveholders seemed more gentle, patient, and pleasant than he did.

There had always been sadists, of course, and always would be. Most slave owners, however, resorted only to measures they felt were required to ensure discipline among their human property. They viewed their violence toward their fellow men in the same light they viewed the training of a horse or a hound. Yet people were infinitely more willful and complex than hounds and horses. And tougher in their way, with reserves that sometimes drove masters to ghastly measures. You never saw welts, cuts, and burns on horses or hunting dogs. You didn't want to break their spirits, after all. You wanted a lively mount and a dog with fire. But you wanted an obedient slave.

There were few truly independent men and women. Most of what passed for individualism was only aggressive self-interest or eccentricity. Most people—even intelligent, capable people, men born to lead because they were born to certain stations—were followers. Unlike Ig and Rachel who came by their convictions honorably, he sometimes had trouble holding slavers in proper contempt. After all, they might not be so much different than he.

He wanted to be like Levi Coffin, who, as a boy of about seven, formed a lifelong hatred of human bondage the instant he first saw a coffle of slaves being driven along a road in front of his North Carolina home. Had he been born with natural empathy? Others in his Quaker community remained ambivalent, if not indifferent.

Men like Levi Coffin were exceptional, and therein lay Joseph's problem with religion. Everything, it seemed, hinged on chance. He was who he was because he had been born the son of a slavery-hating carpenter and cabinetmaker, who occasionally did contract work for a prominent Cincinnati Quaker merchant named Levi Coffin, who introduced them to the thrill and satisfaction of aiding fugitive slaves, teaching him to hide on the riverbank at night to wait for rowboats or rafts poled in the darkness, or swimmers sent from commercial flatboats. Through this work he'd entered into the wider community of abolitionists, Negro and white, and formed associations and allegiances unknown and out of reach to people born to different circumstances. Those associations led him to Kansas, where he met Rachel and Ig and the Meades and the Van Husses. All talk of God's hand, God's will, God's army, God's wrath, God's judgment, and God's children struck him as productive sophistry, or in its best form, deception for the common good. He believed in belief, conceded the efficacy of belief, yet could not believe. And if he was wrong and wicked, where did the blame lie? With himself? Could he be blamed and condemned for thinking the only way he could? He'd tried self-deception, and it failed. Did Ig do battle with his own unbelief? Could pious slavers be condemned for believing the only way their narrow minds and experiences allowed? Were they guilty of individual evil, or were they victims of hideous, overarching evil to which they had no defense? Perhaps that was the answer. Evil existed. It was there all along to be germinated as a sick economy that bore a sick culture that wrought unspeakable suffering and degradation, and—if Ig and Zeph Newton were right—eternal damnation and torment for the hapless unknowing oppressors in the next.

And given a fecund mix of desire, selfishness, proximity, and denial, evil sprouted and grew and yielded a harvest of betrayed friends and cuckolded husbands, guilt and bitter yearning. Some days, in his desire and powerlessness, this line of thought eased his conscience.

Other days, he considered Levi Coffin, Ig Bodeker, Zeph Newton, and Jonah Chambers, and he cursed his own weakness and wickedness. Perhaps evil was less a seed than a parasite that needed only a willing or unwitting host.

CHAPTER 21

William Still, Chairman
Pennsylvania Anti-Slavery Society
153 North 5th Street
Philadelphia, Pennsylvania

June 14, 1855

Franklin McCutcheon
Decatur, Alabama

Dear Sir:

Please allow me to appeal to your humanity on behalf of James, who left your plantation in September of last year. Of course we are aware of your power to hold as legal property James' sister, the recent widow Rebekah, and her young son, Timothy. However, James, through steady work and thrift, has raised a sum of $750, which he is prepared to offer in exchange for the freedom of his sister and nephew.

Although we understand this sum is less than what Rebekah and Timothy would bring on the slave market, or what they might, through a life of toil, add to your fortune, we trust the satisfaction you will gain from reuniting a family whose happiness you hold in your hands will more than make up the difference.

We eagerly await your reply.

Your obedient servant,
William Still

CHAPTER 22

Bekah had no idea what a casket and burial were worth in dollars, but she doubted her price had gone up.

That boy, Samuel. He hadn't bothered her yet, but he would. No mistaking the signs, the looks. He'd be on her like a grinning, slobbering dog trailing a bitch in heat. He could grin and slobber and pant all he wanted, but she wouldn't be standing for him. Let him sidle up and try to lift a paw. She'd chew him up. Show him some teeth, sure enough. How Joseph had managed to keep from calling him "Sam" was beyond her. She'd call him "Sam" just to see what he'd say. Probably nothing. He'd better not get too sassy with her anyway.

Joseph. "Joe?" Better wait and see. She hadn't called him anything yet. Hadn't addressed him. Just "Here's your plate" or "You like your eggs cooked soft or how?" No need to call him anything unless he got rough about it, and then she'd just do like she did with the Montgomerys and mumble something. Marse. Miz. Missy. Marsjoe. Not Mister Joseph. She wouldn't mumble "Sam." She'd say it where he heard it and knew that she meant it. He looked like a Sam.

Jonah Chambers, now. She'd call him "Reverend." And those two with him, standing up in that wagon, eyes up and staring out over that hateful mob. She'd call them whatever they wanted to be called. They had beatings coming, probably already had the first of them. Their owners might as well go ahead and sell them or kill them because they had some run in them yet. They'd light out first chance. She knew what a runner looked like. She'd been married to one.

CHAPTER 23

Just after two o'clock in the morning, the last Wednesday in September, Ig struggled into his pants and shirt, regretting his unbending philosophy of going through life unarmed, lighted a candle, and answered a knock at his door while Rachel sat up in bed and peered between a gap in the bed curtains just wide enough to reveal most of her nose and one blue eye. Ig eased the door open and held the candle up to light the faces of a young black man and a woman holding a baby of two or three months. A rustle at her dress revealed a small, barefooted girl. Behind them stood another black man of medium height, thick neck and chest. He was balding toward the front.

Ig said, "Well. Good morning, folks. Please come in." He heard much creaking and rustling behind the bed curtains. His visitors nodded and stepped inside. The little girl clung to her mother. The candle lighted the sleeping baby's face. Ig said, "Rachel, we have company." He heard the sound of her brush in her thick hair. No doubt she'd pulled her dress off the chair next to the bed.

The older man closed the door behind him and stepped around the woman. He was powerfully built. His left arm was missing entirely. Not even a stub. He regarded Ig. His eyes showed no apprehension. Sweat darkened his homespun shirt. A single suspender attached to a button on the left side of his woolen breeches crossed his chest like a bandolier. He said, "Brothers Chambers and Newton said you might help these folks on toward Mexico."

The bed curtains parted. Rachel padded barefooted across their one room to light a candle on the kitchen table. The man said, "Miz Bodeker, we're sorry to trouble you at this hour."

Rachel shook the match out. "Nonsense. We're glad to have you. We've been expecting you, actually." She looked pale in the candlelight, the circles under her eyes dark and deep. She'd put her hair up, but unruly strands hung about her face and neck. "Please, come in and sit."

She pulled chairs away from the unfinished table. Ig pulled another one from his desk. Rachel said, "The children are welcome to the bed." The woman looked at the bed but didn't reply. The little girl clung to her even as she sat. The one-armed man said, "Y'all ain't got much room here. I hate we come barging in. I guess Brother Chambers didn't think it all through."

"We've plenty of room," Ig said. He had no idea how they'd accommodate these people for more than a day or two. How would he feed them? Other than Joseph and Samuel, the Meades and Van Husses, he had no idea how much his congregation's generosity might extend to fugitive slaves. Brother Jonah had not been prophesying.

They sat in silence for a moment. The one-armed man started to speak, but Rachel said, "Are the children hungry? Let me gather them a bite."

The young mother looked at Rachel, swallowed, and said. "Oh, no . . ." her voice broke. She swallowed and said, "They ate just a while ago. I thank you, though."

The one-armed man sighed. "That girl needs to eat. The baby ain't weaned. I've got money."

"Please," Ig said. "No talk of that." Rachel took four plates from a cabinet. Ig tried to think of what she might put on them. He'd let her do what she could. The young mother looked over Ig's shoulder at Rachel, who took out her heavy iron skillet. Ig wondered what she planned to do with it. Had she been stashing rations? He felt his visitors' eyes. He felt his own lack of planning.

The one-armed man said, "This is Maxey and Daniel. The girl is Lucille. The baby is William. They come from a plantation south of Bonham. We've had 'em for three weeks, waiting for things to clear out and settle down a little. It's too dangerous to the north. Brother Jonah said you might have something going south. They can't go back now, and we've got more than we can feed. Too much coming and going. Slavers are all every which ways. You can't step out on a road up there."

Ig studied the young man. He guessed nineteen or twenty. Maxey looked even younger. He said to Rachel, "We'll need to alert Joseph and Samuel."

The one-armed man said, "They're busy with company, too."

Rachel turned at the comment, skillet in hand. Her eyes looked huge. Ig said, "You seem to know a great deal about our work here."

"We know about what you've been aiming to do. Mr. Winfred Skaggs was busy before he got caught. Mr. Meade and Mr. Van Huss live too much in town. Too risky. We're hoping they can help some other way. I hear Mr. Meade is a lawyer. We'll give Mr. Pig and Miz Cathlyn a chance to help before long."

Ig nodded. He started to say something about their lack of preparation for this number of fugitives. Then he noticed Daniel studying the room. His eyes were bright, hopeful. There was a brittle crack and something spattering in hot grease. Eggs! He'd forgotten about the eggs Rachel had gathered. Samuel had brought more still. Something had eaten all but two of their hens, but Rachel had found a few eggs about. He'd been anticipating a breakfast of mush and syrup and fried potatoes and Bekah's two-day-old biscuits, scorched on the bottom. You could saw off the burned part.

All eyes, save for the baby's, were on Rachel now. She must've felt them. She turned and smiled. Ig wondered if she might attempt cornbread. Biscuits seemed beyond her, but she often succeeded with cornbread. Now if they just had some meat. He'd recently finished off the last of the canned pig's feet. He smelled coffee and thought with satisfaction of the uproar at Joseph's house.

"How many left with Mister Shaw?" Ig asked.

"A grandpap, a mama and daddy, and a boy about ten."

Ig considered this, then said, "I didn't get your name."

The man thought for a few seconds. Daniel and Maxey watched him. "I go by 'David,'" he said.

From the stove, Rachel said, "Will we be receiving more visitors?"

David said, "I expect so. Last count we had thirty-one in three thickets up on the Red. More coming all the time."

"Thirty-one!" Ig said. "Where on earth are they coming from?"

"All over. A few got loose from the Cherokee and Creek up in the Nations. They ran south. Word gets out. They find us, or they get close enough and we find them. I been in slave cabins all over that river country. The slavers know I'm loose up there, but they can't catch me. Most never lay eyes on me."

"You mentioned thickets," Ig said.

"That word don't do them justice. To some, they're a refuge. To white planters and slave hunters, they're Satan's trap. They know we're in there, but they ain't coming. A few have tried."

Rachel began setting plates and cups on the table. Cold biscuits, hot eggs, syrup, fried potatoes. Ig didn't think the others shared his disappointment over the lack of hot bread. They all ate with little comment. Maxey had nearly finished her plate when she looked up at Rachel and said, "Oh! Y'all not eatin'!"

"A bit early for us," Ig said. Maxey looked unconvinced.

After they finished, David thanked them for the meal and said he'd best get started north before dawn.

Ig said, "That's sixty miles, man! Afoot?"

"Part of the way. I got friends. I'll be back there in five days."

"Anyone we should know?

"In time. It ain't that I don't trust you. But I ain't sure I trust everybody you trust."

Ig nodded. He wondered if David had anyone in mind.

After much protest, Maxey and Daniel lay down in the bed with William, who fussed and had to be fed. Rachel drew the curtains for them. Daniel was already snoring. Lucille lay asleep on a pallet next to the bed.

David thanked them again and wished them luck, then ran northward through the yard and disappeared into the cedars. Ig and Rachel stepped back inside and regarded the sleeping family, then looked at each other. Rachel picked up a potholder, took the coffee boiler off the stove, and jiggled it. Still about half full. Ig eased open the door and carried two kitchen chairs out to the little porch. They took their seats, filled their cups, and set the coffee boiler on the ground between them. It would stay plenty hot until they finished it. They sipped, said nothing. After a few minutes Rachel said, "It's pleasant out tonight. Summer is about over, praise the Lord."

A light breeze kept the mosquitoes away. It was nearly four thirty, but Ig wasn't sleepy. He sipped his coffee and took Rachel's hand. Coyotes howled down toward the river.

—

"Who's gone?" Joseph asked. Things were getting more hysterical by the second. A man couldn't concentrate.

Samuel looked at him with disbelief. "Well, Bekah. Everybody else is still here, ain't they?"

"How do you know?"

"Her window is open, and she ain't in there. What do you think I went outside to check for?"

"I didn't see you go outside. I reckon we should've talked to her."

"I reckon so."

"Hell."

"Hell, nothin'. How many times have I said you ought to talk to her? She's been here almost a month."

"I ought to talk to her. What was wrong with you talking to her?"

"You know very well."

"Now, don't try to feed me that. The only thing I know very well is that you're as scared of her as you are a panther, and you were afraid she'd run off if she knew our arrangement."

"How was I supposed to know she'd be so damn surly?"

"You got a good look at her down in Cedar Hill."

"I had hoped she'd come around a little bit. You did, too, and you know it."

"Oh. 'Come around a little bit.' I don't imagine she was born missing two fingers."

Jere Russell said, "Reckon we ought to go find her before she gets off somewhere and gets caught? We got two hours of dark left." He and his son Alfred, daughter-in-law Beatrice, and grandson Philip had said very little since Zeph Newton showed up with them an hour earlier. They'd been entirely silent since Bekah had realized what was happening and had stormed into her bedroom and latched the door. They were sitting about the kitchen table except for Alfred, who sat on a footstool beside his grandfather.

"No sir!" Joseph said. "You didn't come all the way down here to get caught again, out looking for somebody with no more sense than to run off with no idea of where to go." Then it occurred to him that most fugitives took off with very little idea of their course. He hoped Jere didn't take offense. "I mean, it's a bad time to be throwing a fit and running off."

Jere nodded slightly. The rest of the family seemed to consider his comments.

Just then the back door rattled. Then someone pounded on it. Samuel held his finger to his nose, and they hurried the Russells back into the two bedrooms. Samuel hid them under beds and in closets while Joseph went to answer the door, grateful Samuel had thought to latch it when he came back in after checking Bekah's window. He leaned close to the door. "Who is it?"

"Who you think?"

"Well, goddamn." He opened the door.

Bekah said, "I never thought about you being so glad to see me." She pushed past him, carrying her bag. She met Samuel in the kitchen. He shook his head and turned back down the hall. "Y'all can come on out."

Bekah tossed her bag into a corner, then stood in the middle of the kitchen, arms crossed, alternately glaring at Samuel and Joseph. "You are the sorriest two men that ever lived. Ever. In this world. Lettin' me go on like I was."

By this time the Russells were emerging from the bedrooms. Jere stepped up behind Samuel. "Here, now, Missy. Lord! No way to talk."

Bekah said, "You don't know nothing about it." Jere seemed shocked by her retort. Philip stepped up beside his grandfather and glowered at Bekah. Samuel stepped out of the hallway and into the kitchen. The Russells retook their seats. Samuel leaned back into the doorway and smirked. "Dark out there, ain't it?"

She took two strides across the room and faced him. He said, "Didn't have nowhere to go, did you?"

Joseph sighed. "Come on."

She punched Samuel in the mouth. Beatrice gasped. Alfred and Jere jumped up. "Here! Lord!" Samuel covered his face with his arms and bent away from her while she kicked his legs and rained blows on his head and back. He hollered, "I won't hit a woman, but you better get off me!" The other men pulled her away. Samuel whirled around and glared at her and fingered at his cut lip. "I should've left you at Cedar Hill!"

Bekah flailed and kicked. Beatrice and Philip sat transfixed. Samuel stuck out his tongue and felt it with his forefinger and thumb. "Now look. Like to have bit my tongue off."

Beatrice pulled a pale yellow handkerchief from her skirt pocket and handed it to Samuel.

Bekah relaxed, and the men released her. She turned to Joseph. "You owe me wages!"

Joseph sighed. "Fine. Fine. Hellfire." He looked at Samuel and wagged his head. "We owe her wages." He wondered how much Bekah felt she had coming. He suspected the Russells had decided they'd be better off heading to Mexico on their own.

Samuel nodded, still leaning back into the hallway. "Then why don't you get busy earning your wages instead of sneaking out windows?"

"I reckon I could earn wages in Mexico."

"I reckon you could," Joseph said. "Nobody is keeping you here."

Philip said, "She ain't going with us, is she?"

Beatrice shot him a look and held her finger to her nose. Then she looked at Alfred as if he ought to do a better job of controlling his son. Jere just looked worried.

"Get me on down the road so you don't have to pay me what you owe me," Bekah said. "You think I can't see that?"

Joseph shrugged, held up his palms. "I wonder how things are going over at Ig's. Better than here, I imagine."

Bekah looked at the stove and then at the Russells. "I expect y'all wanting to eat." She walked to the stove, held her hand near it. "No fire built." She shook her head. "Like I expected one to be built. No coffee. No nothing. And a house full of company. With a youngun now." She disappeared into the back room and could be heard digging in the kindling box.

CHAPTER 24

Before dawn Joseph left for Cedar Springs to fetch Pig and Cathlyn. Samuel didn't bother going to the Bodekers. As expected, Ig showed up about breakfast time. By late morning, Ebenezer Euler had been alerted and was working on a letter to his relatives in Castroville about forthcoming shipments of goods.

Although Pig felt sure the Buttses would help again, they needed another station so that his sister and brother-in-law wouldn't be overwhelmed and the passengers put at undue risk. That afternoon he headed down Mountain Road to visit and ask their opinions on other contacts. In the short term they could send the families one at a time, a week or two apart.

Malachi set to work on false papers from false owners in case the freedom seekers were stopped along the way. Samuel started work on a false bottom for the hearse—one that allowed plenty of air. Late that first afternoon, Joseph set about doing the same for the Bodekers' wagon.

All of the women, including Beatrice and Maxey, washed and mended clothing, found extra socks, fashioned knapsacks from scrap material, and treated small injuries. Julie Considerant and Helene Euler came from La Reunion commune to help, but upon seeing the number of people and the tight confines, gathered some sewing and a list of needed items and expanded operations to the Van Huss home. Rachel hurried three pairs of brogans to the cobbler for repair, helped with the wash, and entertained Philip and Lucille. She tried to look after the baby, William, but found she lacked the touch and had to be rescued. Bekah and Cathlyn pulled three bad teeth—one of Daniel's and two of Jere's. Both men groaned and hollered and complained bitterly, but they admitted to feeling much better within a few hours, though they continued to balk at the saltwater rinsing the women insisted on. Jere said he'd always had better luck with a whiskey rinse. Finally, after a round of tortured swishing, Bekah relented and allowed the men a few snorts. Joseph couldn't remember telling her about his whiskey stash.

Nor could he remember when he'd had so much energy—probably way back during those first heady days working with Levi Coffin, and then those night raids from Kansas into Missouri. Texas had been three years of worry and paranoia and hopelessness. At last they'd been forced to act. Why had they waited so long? And why hadn't he and Samuel already fashioned the wagons with false bottoms? Peter had been a start, but here were two families and more sure to come. He pictured the railways forming southward over the coming months and years like snowmelt running down mountains, finding its way through the terrain, forming rivulets and creeks and rivers. There would be the established but secret stations along the way, but the passengers would also find help from fellow slaves. They'd locate the cabins out on the edges of plantations and farms, where they could find a meal and a night's refuge and information about the routes ahead. That's the way it had been wherever he had worked. Why had it taken so long here? Again, he was sure it was because he had always been a follower. Up north, the groundwork had been laid before he arrived. He'd had only to enter the community and do his share of the work. This could have been done all along in Texas. But he and Ig had waited until bolder men—Jonah Chambers, Zeph Newton, Peter, and this one-armed man called David—and the fugitives themselves forced them to act.

There would be setbacks, too. Some who passed through their homes would be recaptured. He couldn't think about that now. Yet he wondered where Peter was.

It was good to see Ig back in form. Joseph always wondered at how such an appallingly fat man could step so lively. He could not remember Ig ever falling into paralysis during a crisis or urgent situation. The preacher talked with the families, keeping their spirits and courage up, told stories from his Kansas days, read them Scripture, and kept watch.

Joseph worried about the traffic between the two homes, but nearly everyone in town knew the Shaw and Bodeker households were close. Hopefully they'd assume church business. The group would have to take more care as the slave traffic grew.

Just after noon on the second day, Pig returned with news that the Buttses would take a family and make arrangements southward, and that another man, Josiah Caulkins, would rendezvous with the second family and take them as far south as Maypearl, where another family would help. *Of course, these people and more like them had been there all along*, Joseph thought. How many fugitives could they have helped in the past three years?

On the third night, after supper, Ig and Rachel visited. The kitchen was crowded. Al Huitt had stopped in, too—to greet the passengers and wish them luck. At first Joseph had wanted as few people as possible to know about the visitors, but after thinking about all the meetings in creek bottoms and cemeteries, he couldn't bear the thought of excluding Al, who had risked as much as anyone. All those furtive meetings, and now here they were piled into his kitchen and living room. He wished Ig and Rachel could've brought Daniel and Maxey and their children. That old paranoia seemed excessive now, but he had only to think of Winfred Skaggs to know that he'd need it again.

He sipped coffee, looked across the table at Rachel, and felt sad, not from longing but from guilt. Here in his kitchen among old and new friends—this was who he was. Not the conniving, frustrated adulterer. He loved Rachel, but at that moment he loved her as Ig's wife. He would fall back into his routine and his desire for her would return, of course, but he could not imagine it now. He felt only guilt and sorrow mixed with thankfulness. He caught her eye and wondered if he could be a better man.

Al Huitt said something while Joseph was lost in his thoughts, and laughter erupted around the table. Joseph thought of the open windows back in his dark office and the other one in Bekah's room at the front of the house. There were advantages to living next to the cemetery. Few people came around after dark.

Joseph glanced at Bekah standing back from the table, leaning against the wall. She didn't laugh or even smile at the joke, but for an instant he thought he saw something, a glint of feeling other than anger or despair.

—

By dusk on the fourth day, the two families were mended and packed for their trip south. The homemade knapsacks were full of cornbread and biscuits and cured meat from the Van Husses' butcher shop. Philip seemed excited. Lucille, perhaps sensing the adults' nervousness, was solemn and clingy. Daniel and Jere paced, while Beatrice fretted over small chores. Bekah helped with final preparations, grim as ever.

Joseph visited the Bodekers' cabin for a quick good-bye to Daniel, Maxey, and the children. Ig and Rachel did the same at Joseph's. As darkness approached, the passengers edged toward the back doors. Rachel teared up, and Ig kept clearing his throat. Cathlyn seemed even gaunter and more exhausted than usual and kept wondering if her boys were driving her cousin crazy.

Ignatius and Pig would leave first with Daniel, Maxey, and their children. Rosemary had procured paregoric from Peak's Drug Store so that William would sleep through the journey. The passengers would lie beneath the false floor of Ig's wagon. Once they were across the Commerce Street bridge and through Hord's Ridge, if the road was clear, they would push the floorboards up so they could breathe more easily. The women were especially worried about William and Lucille in the hot, close space. Joseph and Samuel were careful not to mention that they'd nearly cooked Peter. Pig worried more about hooligans than slave catchers. Mountain Road had a reputation for being dangerous after dark. They expected to deliver their passengers to the Buttses before dawn. Pig would be well armed.

Samuel and Joseph planned to leave an hour later with the Russells. They would head south on the road toward Lisbon and Lancaster, then take a two-track path east to intersect with Mountain Road. Joseph suspected the diversion was unnecessary; they would lose another hour going toward Lisbon and then grinding along the rough road, but Pig insisted. They would draw less attention, and the tactic would minimize the chance of both parties being caught.

At eight o'clock Joseph and Samuel stood in the yard, leaning against the hearse. Joseph said, "They ought to be gone by now." A few minutes later, they heard a wagon clattering west on Columbia Street. Joseph thought of Rachel alone at home. He drummed his fingers on the sideboards. "Stomach's fluttering. Is yours?"

Samuel said, "Fluttering? Like a moth? Naw, mine's not fluttering. No moth in there. I wish it was just a moth."

Bekah kept peering out the back door at them. Samuel said, "I reckon she thinks we aim to just run off. Crazy hen."

Cathlyn came outside. Joseph said, "How are our passengers?"

"Ready to go. I'm afraid Jere's about to wear those new soles off his shoes before he gets started. How much longer?"

"About a quarter of an hour," Samuel said.

Joseph slapped the sideboard. "Hell, let's load up and go." Cathlyn hurried inside and returned with the Russells. The men stepped into the hearse and helped Beatrice in after she'd hugged Cathlyn and Bekah. They lay down with their bundles on their bellies. Beatrice was wedged between them. Samuel said, "That boy will have to just ride up here between us. Nobody will think anything about a boy." Philip looked disappointed.

"Get on up there," Alfred said. Philip climbed into the seat.

Joseph said, "I know it's hot, but we'll have to cover you up until we get across the river. We'll make haste."

"Lay them boards on here," Jere said.

"Bless you, ladies," Beatrice said. Cathlyn wiped her eyes. Bekah nodded and waved. Samuel and Joseph laid the two boards in place. Bekah went inside and left Cathlyn in the yard.

They pulled out and rode north on Lamar. The moon had not risen.

Philip said nothing but kept turning to look back at the bed of the hearse. The brim of his hat rubbed against Joseph's shoulder. They met no one until they turned west on Commerce Street, and then only a few pedestrians or families sitting on their front steps. They waved at everyone they passed. No one seemed to take special notice.

Samuel drove the team onto the bridge, and Joseph felt Philip moving in his seat, trying to look around. "Used to be a big owl lived up there," Samuel said. The hat brim turned again as the boy looked in the darkness at Samuel. "I swear," he said. The air seemed suddenly cool and fresh when they emerged on the west side of the river. "Dark in there, sure enough," Philip said. "I reckon it's dark under them boards, too." Occasionally there was rustling from the back of the wagon. Joseph said, "Everyone doing well?"

"Very well," Jere said.

"Can y'all hear me?" Philip said.

"You hush," Beatrice answered.

Samuel chuckled. "I reckon they can."

They turned southeast toward Lisbon, rode for three miles, then found the turnoff back to the southwest, toward Mountain Road. The more Joseph thought about their diversionary route, the more ridiculous it seemed.

They stopped and pulled the boards away, leaving the three passengers exposed from the waist up. All were sweating but seemed well. Joseph handed Beatrice the water can. They met no one on the rough two-track. Philip was asleep before they reached Mountain Road an hour past midnight. Beatrice dozed. Alfred occasionally snored, but Jere remained awake and talked quietly about his years in Tennessee, Louisiana, and Alabama, and of his children and grandchildren spread all through the South.

They turned south on the main road. At about three in the morning, they met two men on horseback. Samuel heard their voices first and said, deliberately, "Well, I want you to look. What other fools do you reckon are out this time of morning?" The boards scraped slightly as the passengers pulled them into place. Philip never woke. The riders passed in the darkness and said only, "Mornin'," and rode on. Half a mile later, Joseph said, "All clear," and the boards came off again.

Faint pink and orange lined the eastern horizon when Samuel said, "I reckon y'all better cover up from here on. We don't have far to go."

Joseph realized he'd dozed off. "Lord," he rubbed his jaws. "Cup of coffee would go good about now."

"You got to be awake to drink it," Samuel said.

"I didn't need sleep when I was your age. Your time is coming; don't believe it's not."

Samuel said, "Uh-huh." Philip's head rolled back. His mouth was open. "This boy will be raring to go when we get there," Samuel said. "He wouldn't have slept no better on a feather bed."

They passed the turnoff to the Butts farm and continued for three miles, found a trail just past a creek ford, and turned east. Birds were singing. The grass was wet with dew. You could just pick out detail in the trees and brush. They'd gone about half a mile when from the cedars ahead and to the right, someone said, "Whup now." Samuel stopped the team. Joseph said, "Hello."

A horseman rode out of the brush. As he neared, Joseph made out a black man with a shotgun laid across his pommel. The man said, "Joseph Shaw."

"The same."

"Mornin'. I'll take y'all on to the house. Where's your people at?"

Samuel turned and said, "Y'all can sit up now."

The Russells pushed the boards off and sat up, stretching, squinting, looking around. They all stared at the rider, who laughed and said, "Well, just let that boy sleep."

They rode on past small pastures cleared in the cedar and scattered flocks of goats and sheep and a few skinny cattle. Hounds barked just ahead. Over a slight rise they came to a long, single-story cabin set back in the elms. Three other smaller cabins, a few other log buildings, and a barn were scattered among the trees. Another black man stepped out onto the porch of the larger cabin. He carried a Spencer carbine, muzzle up, the butt resting on his thigh, his finger across the trigger guard. Joseph noticed that neither man dressed like a slave. They wore patched white shirts buttoned at the neck, galluses, and breeches tucked into knee-high boots. Both wore short-brimmed straw hats.

The second man stepped off the porch as Samuel stopped the team. He smiled and said, "I want you to look."

Samuel said, "I swear."

The man with the carbine said, "That cadaver made it across the river yet?"

Joseph looked at Samuel, who cocked his head as if to say, "Don't you see?"

A thin white man carried two pails around the corner of the house. He set the pails down and strode toward them, extending a hand. "Before we met you two on the road that day, we'd never seen a dead man blink." He shook Samuel's hand. "Wake that boy up. I imagine he'd eat a bite."

Chapter 25

Over the next two and a half weeks they moved eight more freedom seekers. The Bodekers passed two brothers, a young mother, and an infant onto the Buttses. Samuel, Joseph, and Bekah hid a husband, wife, and twin nine-year-old girls for three days before passing them onto Josiah Caulkins, who had established a relationship with Nehemiah and Dora Haskell four miles to the southeast. More fortunate yet, Dora Haskell's brother, Horace Armstrong—a teamster and freighter and hater of slavery who did a brisk business between Waco and San Antonio. Malachi could draft false paperwork for men who could work for Armstrong on trips south. He, in turn, would deliver them into sympathetic Mexican or free black hands in San Antonio.

David and Zeph Newton brought the fugitives at night as before. Caulkins showed up at the Nucholses' farm just north of Cedar Springs in the middle of the day with a young man who had escaped from a farm near Temple and had ridden with Horace Armstrong to the Haskells, who sent him on to Caulkins. The man, Paul, did not want to go to Mexico. Instead he wanted to try for Detroit or Chatham, Canada, where he believed his mother and uncle had fled after escaping from a farm in Tennessee. That night, Pig put him on a mule and led him cross-country, keeping off the roads, to Silas Hemby, who was astounded when Pig knocked at his door early the next morning and more astounded that Peter had gotten as far south as Castroville.

Hemby thought he could get Paul to Plano or Sherman. Better yet, if Hemby could get word to Zeph or David, perhaps they could take Paul on to the Red River. Word was, two associates of Newton and Chambers, under the guise of slave traders headed for Missouri, had coffled together some fifteen runaways and marched through Indian Territory. But instead of delivering them to Missouri slavers, they unshackled them among free soilers in Kansas, where they were given refuge before heading for Iowa and parts north.

The problem was, you couldn't get word to Chambers, Newton, and David because no one knew where to find them. Yes, they supposedly lived in some hellish thicket up near the Red River. But there were thousands of hellish thickets up there. These men simply appeared, usually with runaway slaves, and didn't ask for permission to leave them. They expected you to take them in. Then they'd disappear again. Since they'd been taken from the Dallas jail, there had been no confirmed Jonah Chambers or Zeph Newton sightings, though their presence was much on the minds of local slave owners. They'd received more than a few inches of print in the *Herald*, which Ig, Joseph, and Samuel read with much pleasure in the knowledge Zeph had recently appeared at their door and taken refreshment at their tables.

Joseph kept Professor Euler informed. Helene and Julie Considerant came by to help with mending and cooking. All three felt it unwise to house fugitives at La Reunion. They couldn't be certain of the sympathies of all of the communists, and it would be difficult to hide a Negro there for any length of time. Furthermore, many in Dallas County regarded the commune with suspicion. There had been no violence so far. Any rumors of abolitionist activity or sympathies would bring trouble, and the settlement was barely hanging on. They would help as they could and make stealthy inquiries.

Joseph and Samuel did three burials, all white children from Lisbon where there had been an outbreak of scarlet fever. They worried about the Nuchols boys and the Meade girls, but so far Dallas had not suffered a deadly outbreak.

Ig reminded himself there were men of physical action and men of mental action. Samuel and Joseph, it seemed, fell into the former category. You could rarely draw either into a debate unless there was some immediate and practical matter at hand—which was fine, except constant doers of small tasks tended to look at men like himself, who grappled with higher concepts, as lazy and of little practical use. No one but Rachel worried about or mentioned the long hours he put into his sermons. Did people think the words just fell out of the sky? Then again, perhaps the words did come as undeserved gifts. Still, it took work to set them down right.

He sometimes felt self-conscious watching other men work and sweat, which was what he was doing while Joseph and Samuel argued about where to dig a hiding place in the shop.

Samuel argued for digging a pit in the back corner where they could

ventilate the space with a stove pipe in the wall and perhaps even ex-
cavate an emergency escape tunnel leading out into the cedar bushes.
Joseph liked the idea of venting through the walls, but he disapproved of
an emergency entrance and exit. The more routes in and out, the higher
the chances of discovery. And with tunnels, you'd end up with rats and
badgers and snakes in your hidey-hole. As it was, they'd have to fashion
some kind of screen over their vent. Could you imagine lying down in the
dark hole trying to be as quiet while things crawled all over you?

Ig had rather not.

The two men agreed on the corner. The shop had a dirt floor, which
they'd been talking about remedying for the past year. They'd dig a chamber big enough for four adults. They'd timber it up to keep it from falling
in. Time allowing, they'd lay in a plank floor. They'd sink the door a couple of inches and cover it with dirt and sawdust. Then they'd pile scrap
lumber over it. The vent would be risky; you could hear movement below—a baby whining, for example. But what if you had to leave them in
there for a few hours? They might smother without an air vent.

They finished talking and waited for Ig's opinion.

"Ingenious."

Both nodded and turned back to their tentative excavation site, no
doubt considering possibilities for a kitchen and guest room. A chimney, perhaps. It was barely 7 a.m.; both men were already sweating and
covered with sawdust. Ig imagined they'd dug a grave and beat together a couple of caskets while they talked through their plan. You never
knew when somebody might die, and you didn't want to find yourself in a
scheduling bind. Ig found their industriousness exhausting or endearing,
depending on his mood. Today he chose the latter.

They stood in silence. The two carpenters mused. Joseph suddenly
turned back to Ig. "You're up and about early." Samuel looked up then.
He'd lately grown a goatee. It was full of sawdust.

"Savoring every second of this day the Lord has made."

They looked at him. He grinned.

"What's the matter?" they asked in near unison.

"We believe Mrs. Bodeker is expecting. The symptoms are promising.
Nearly conclusive, in fact. Dr. Thompson agrees."

"Well!" Samuel said. "That's fine news if ever I've heard fine news."
He offered his hand; Ig shook it.

"Congratulations, sir!" Joseph said. "About how far along?"

"Three months or so, we think. I suppose I'll worry until the signs are
unmistakable."

"Those signs won't be long in coming, if they're coming," Joseph said.

Ig considered the comment. He would have preferred unbridled optimism. "Surely within another month."

Joseph was still shaking Ig's hand—loosely now. "Surely."

"Well, I just wanted my dearest friends to hear the news first."

Joseph let go of his hand at last. "Some kind of celebration seems in order. We could have an early drink, but then Samuel might miss his thumb and hit mine."

"We'll have one soon enough, I suspect," Ig said. "Rachel certainly has told Rosemary by now. A feast can't be long in coming."

They stood a moment, nodding, looking at the planned secret chamber site. Ig said, "Well I have to get on to see Mrs. Maude Samples. She's feeling poorly." He dreaded the visit. Maude's husband, Jonathan, would compete for his attention, ailment for ailment. He turned away toward his wagon. Joseph said, "Wonderful news, Ig. I know you and Rachel have wanted this for a long time."

"Our prayers have been answered." He climbed into the wagon, feeling tired already. The heat. It just beat him down. Suddenly he couldn't think of anything to look forward to the rest of the day. Just heat and Maude and Jon Samples comparing ailments. And his sermon needed attention. Maude would feed him, though.

He pulled out onto Lamar Street, headed toward Commerce and the square. He'd stop by Malachi's house. Rachel would be there. He wanted to see what Rosemary had to say about the news. Then again, the women probably had been speculating for weeks. Should Rachel walk so far? He should have driven her in the wagon. He *had* to start paying more attention to her needs.

—

Samuel watched Ig drive away and said, "Well."

Joseph shrugged. "Well, well." Three months. About the time Ig came out of his last bout with melancholia. He—Joseph—hadn't been with Rachel since. "Great news for a great man."

"Yes, sir," Samuel said. "A fine pair." He looked off in the direction Ig had gone. "I'm anxious to lay eyes on this baby. Ain't you?"

CHAPTER 26

During the wee hours of October 27, David tapped at Ig and Rachel's door. He had with him two young fugitives from the Bonham area, Jacob and Caesar. Just inside the door they exchanged greetings. Rachel, holding a candle, said, "Oh . . . Uh . . . hum." She was looking at Caesar.

Ig said, "Beg your pardon, young man. I believe there's a tick crawling along your neck. He'll dig in directly."

Embarrassed, Caesar found the tick and crushed it between his thumb and forefinger. David opened the door, and Caesar tossed the tick out. "I sure didn't aim to bring that nasty thing in here. Been living in that thicket, though."

Rachel said. "Don't apologize, dear. I was afraid he'd bite you."

Now all three men were feeling their faces and necks. David said, "I swear. No telling what we're carrying with us."

Rachel made a quick meal of cornbread, bacon, honey, and coffee. Caesar and Jacob sat sipping their coffee and nodding, their eyelids drooping. David told Rachel and Ig about nineteen runaways in the thickets up on the Red River. One or two more coming in every week. Word was out. The slaves knew where to come, but the slavers and slave hunters hadn't found them and thus far had not even looked anywhere close. He needed more help or pretty soon the woods would be stuffed with freedom seekers. Rachel got up and fixed pallets for Jacob and Caesar. David said, "What would you do with these two if somebody came huntin' 'em?"

"Unlikely," Ig said.

"I'd say likely. One of these days."

Rachel came back to the table and sat watching David, waiting for his next comment.

"Need a place to hide folks," David said.

Ig said, "I'm next to helpless with hammer and spade."

Rachel said, "Joseph will engineer something."

"Of course. Joseph and Samuel will welcome the task."

"Yes," Rachel said. "Dear Samuel, too."

David nodded and looked about the cabin as if searching for a likely place for a hidden chamber. "Can't just put 'em under the bed. That's the first place somebody'd look. What'd y'all do up in Kansas?"

"We had plenty of help. Typically, we just fed and ministered. Somebody else took them on to their next stop, usually across the line in Iowa. All in all, we had few worries in Lawrence."

"Well, you got worries in Dallas."

"Indeed."

Caesar woke himself with a snore. "Lordy. Beg your pardon, Reverend. Missus. Ain't no way for me to be. Got full and good and warm." He blinked, rubbed his eyes, stretched his arms. Jacob chuckled and sipped his now tepid coffee. Rachel led them to their pallets. They went right to sleep.

David pulled an envelope out of his pocket and handed it to Ig. "Letter from Brother Zeph."

Ig took out his penknife and opened the envelope. It was damp with David's sweat. "I'll have to fetch my reading glasses."

Rachel snatched the letter. "Oh, here." She started to read it, then looked up. "David, would you like me to read it aloud? It's addressed to 'Dallas Brethren.' We're all friends."

David said, "I thank you. Brother Zeph had me read it before he sealed it up, but I could stand to hear it read."

Rachel nodded and leaned back in her chair, then held the letter closer, then farther, squinting. David slid the candle closer to her. She read:

Your humble and faithful servants and apostles of Jesus Christ and our courageous brothers and sisters.

Grace and courage to you our faithful brethren in Dallas. Praise be to God for your steadfastness and courage which so buoys your humble brethren to the north. Even as I write, our Lord provides us further opportunity to serve Him and His children in need.

And yet, as our bounty grows, so does the need to bring other servants into the fold so that they might enjoy the blessing of serving Him. I beseech you, therefore, brothers and sisters, to trust in Him and proceed in the confidence and peace of children of God. For has He not made clear His will? Does not your success thus far demonstrate His desire that you continue in your work and confidently seek others similarly chosen? Do not hesitate in fear and indecision even as He has clearly and lovingly and faithfully revealed His will. For what are our lives if they are not spent in His service?

I write with great joy, full in the knowledge that you, my faithful and beloved brothers and sisters, will go forth with vigor and courage, seeking always to carry out God's plans. Take in His children as you would take in Him. Feed and clothe them and protect them as you would Him, for in doing these things for His beloved, you are doing these things for Him.

Brethren, pray for us all. Pray for our work. Pray for the downtrodden and degraded. Pray even for those who trod and degrade that they might be transformed and redeemed. I charge you by the Lord that this letter be read to all our holy Brethren in Dallas.

The grace of our Lord Jesus Christ be with you.

With much love,
Your Brother in Christ

Rachel handed the letter to Ig, who folded it and put it back in the envelope. "Well," she said.

Ig cleared his throat. David said, "I enjoyed it far more the second time, Mrs. Bodeker."

Rachel said, "David, you mustn't leave now. It's too close to dawn. Please stay and rest. You can leave tonight."

David held up a hand. "I thank you. I'm expected elsewhere shortly. Don't worry over me."

Rachel studied him. "Could you carry a letter back to Brother Newton?"

"Surely."

"I'll be brief." She got up and fetched a sheet of paper, pen, and inkwell from Ig's desk and returned to her seat. Without hesitation she dipped her pen and started to write. She stopped and looked up. "I just want him to know that we've received his letter. Some acknowledgment seems in order—don't you think?"

The two men nodded. She wrote. Ig got up and fetched his reading glasses. David sat politely with his hand in his lap. Ig put on his glasses and glanced at the letter as she returned her quill to the inkwell. Before she could fold the letter, he read,

Dear Brother:

Dallas has received your epistle. I am certain it will be canonized forthwith. . . .

Ig laughed, said, "Darling . . ."

Before he could read further, she folded the sheet and put it in the envelope on which she wrote, "Our Brethren to the North." He handed the envelope to David, who said, "You look a little peaked, Mrs. Bodeker."

"Oh, I think the bacon is disagreeing with me."

Ig said, "I don't believe it's the bacon. I believe it's the time of day. Praise the Lord."

David smiled and said, "Well now."

Rachel got up and started for the door. Ig stood to help her. "Oh—forgive me. At the moment, I'm afraid I can't share in your pleasure," she said.

David jumped up and opened the door for her, then slapped Ig's back as he followed Rachel out.

"Under the bed, perhaps," Rachel said. "Or under the cabinet. No one would think of moving it to look."

Joseph looked at the bed, but he couldn't seem to think about what might go beneath it. He felt numb, shaky. Still, he had to try. He had no idea what she was thinking or what she expected. He'd just have to proceed cautiously and watch for clues. "I'd fix something out in the barn. You can cover the door up with straw or even drive your buggy over it."

She seemed to consider his comment. "But then we'd have to hurry them between the house and barn. I don't want to have to feed them out there. And I couldn't let the little ones sleep out there. It's filthy. And the flies."

"What does Ig say?"

She laughed. "Please."

"We'll find a spot in here. We can start working on it next week, probably. After supper. Five days at the most. But you'll have a mess in here. We'll have to haul the dirt out. It'll stink to high heaven when we pull those boards off. Who knows what's been under there?" He shook his head. "Why don't you let me dig it out in the barn?"

She sighed, pursed her lips.

Joseph said, "You feeling well these days?" He thought the circles under her eyes had darkened. She looked even thinner than usual. Surely she'd be plumping up soon.

"I'm feeling well, according to Rosemary and Cathlyn, who should know."

He nodded, studied her. This was the first private conversation they'd had in nearly three months. "Well. I reckon there's some chance this one will have red hair, or else you'll have some explaining to do."

"Just a chance. It's possible." She smiled. "His confidence has risen lately. He's been in fine spirits."

Joseph forced a smile and tried to clear his mind. "Well, good. So . . ."

"I know."

"Know?"

"The awkwardness."

"No need for awkwardness. We should be happy and go on." He considered the absurdity of his statement.

"Go on."

"I mean—" He wasn't sure what he meant.

She sat down at the kitchen table and propped her chin on her fist. Joseph had never seen her put an elbow on the table before. She looked at him. He shrugged.

She said, "Perhaps we . . ."

Here it came. The end of it. "Yes."

"What?"

"Yes. We know the answer. We both know what to do. Or not do. We have a clear sign. Ig is elated. He's doing better by you—in that way." At least now he'd been the one to say it.

"So that's what you want."

"Of course not. But it's the right and prudent thing. You know it and I know it."

She looked past him. "Well then. We will go on then, as you put it. You're right, of course."

"Don't you think?"

She nodded. Much of her hair had fallen about her cheeks and shoulders. He couldn't imagine her caring for a child. He looked at her long fingers and remembered them on his chest.

He said, "And when you're with Ig, you look so content."

"I love him, after all."

"You never even look at me when you're with him."

"Should I?"

"You know what I mean. You're not even aware of me."

"Oh." She was looking at the table, barely nodding.

Joseph tried to imagine her crying and couldn't. He could imagine her suffering but not crying. He stepped around the table to her. "I'm just trying to think of what's best. What's best for you and Ig and this child." A statement that, of course, fully explained the stirring in his drawers. He caught her scent.

Her chin still rested on her fist. She rolled her eyes up at him. She wasn't smiling.

He looked down at her. Three months. They'd seen each other dozens of times in social settings. They'd faced each other at supper tables. Greeted each other on the street and at Sunday meetings. Yet no sign. Not one furtive glance. Not one acknowledgment. You just never knew. Poor Ig.

CHAPTER 27

From the *Dallas Herald*, November 2, 1859

LATEST NEWS BY TELEGRAPH

Riot and insurrection at Harper's Ferry, Va.

A terrible riot occurred at Harper's Ferry, Va., on the 17th Oct. during which the U.S. arsenal was seized by the mob and all the railroads stopped. The mob at one time is said to number 600 or 700 men. U.S. troops were ordered to the scene, and also troops from Richmond, Martinsburg, and other points in Virginia, who succeeded in recapturing the arsenal. The following are the latest dispatches from the scene of the riot.

Washington, Oct. 18—The number of lives lost in the insurrection at Harper's Ferry was sixteen. The insurrectionary spirit is now believed to be nearly overcome.

From the circumstances that have been brought to light since the insurrection, it would appear that the uprising had been in contemplation for months, and that all the plans were laid deliberately.

The place of the rendezvous was a farm house about four miles distant from Harper's Ferry. The place had been rented for the purpose of the insurrection by one Capt. Brown, formerly of Kansas, who passed under the assumed name of Smith. At this farm house were collected arms, ammunition, and stores of every kind that might be needed in such an affair, and all were purchased and brought there by Brown, who seems to have been the chief plotter and ringleader.

In the attack on the Armory by the troops, most of the outlaws were captured, among whom were Brown, the leader, and his son. Brown had threatened to hang all his prisoners if he was attacked by the troops.

Still Later from Harper's Ferry:

Discovery of Arms and Ammunition—Further Developments of the Plot—

Harper's Ferry, Oct. 19—The Baltimore Grays started in pursuit of Brown and the fugitives under him, on Monday night. On their way, the Grays stopped at the farm which had been hired by Brown as the rendezvous of the traitors, where they discovered several wagons loaded with arms and ammunition, consisting of rifles and pistols bearing the stamp of the Massachusetts manufacturing company of Chicopee. Also a large number of spears and bowie knives attached to poles indicating that a large number of men were to be equipped with arms for their murderous work. It is supposed that these munitions were brought through Pennsylvania.

The insurgents did not attempt to rob the Paymaster's department at the armory, in which there was a considerable amount of money.

Brown, when he was supposed to be dying, declared that his sole object was to free the slaves from bondage. He also declared that no other persons other than those about him were connected with the movement, and that he did not expect aid from the North. He made the above statement in an answer to questions proposed to him. He also indicated that what he had done was right, and that he ought to be treated as a prisoner of war.

CHAPTER 28

Joseph noted the irony in his choice of seat in the Masonic Hall. Without thinking about it, he and Malachi had chosen the same chairs they'd sat in the past three Sundays since Ig had moved his service indoors on account of cool weather. But on this Wednesday evening they'd sat listening to the invective of several local slavers. Currently, attorney Horace Mullins had the floor. Joseph supposed Mullins was worried that his two elderly slaves, a man and woman, would poison his family and run off to Mexico. Mullins stood behind a long table at the front of the room. Several other town leaders sat at the table as well. All were watching and nodding, occasionally adding, "Hear, hear."

Mullins turned and spat a stream of tobacco juice behind him. Ig would be appalled. There were spittoons all along the wall behind the table, but Ig complained there was more tobacco juice on the wall than in the spittoons. "Every chewer should be as accurate as Brother Pig or give up the filthy vice," he often said.

Mullins turned back to his audience, regarding it as if it were a jury. "And is there a man in this room who does not believe that agents of John Brown are among us, plotting their villainy this very instant? Could insurrection succeed here? Let there be no doubt; it would fail as surely as the Prosser uprising failed in Richmond. This is no Haiti. But what would be the cost in pain and disorder, and confusion among our frail-minded servants?"

Mullins stroked his sandy beard. Joseph thought he looked a little flushed. No doubt he'd taken a few shots of tongue oil prior to the meeting. It seemed to be working. On the front row, Charles Pryor bent over his lap desk, nodding as he wrote. Joseph let his mind wander. He'd get the high points of the meeting, with numerous embellishments, in the next issue of the *Herald*:

> The well respected attorney Mr. Horace Mullins made perfectly clear where he stood on the matter of rebellious slaves and designing aboli-

tionist agitators. Not a sound could be heard from the enthralled audience as this faithful and distinguished son of the South eloquently and cogently expounded the principles upon which this great nation and state were founded. . . .

John Brown, that murderous, ridiculous shit-stirrer had set the paranoid slavers aswarm just as he'd done along the Missouri-Kansas border. Let things settle down a bit so you could move a few fugitives without running into a horde of the local vigilance movement at every bend in the road, and "Captain" Brown and his demented sons would dismember somebody—a hapless, misidentified free soiler with a Tennessee accent, for example—or ride through a proslavery stronghold with a wagon load of rusty Sharps rifles and broadswords. Here, things had finally quieted down after the Jonah Chambers and Zeph Newton excitement, and now the Old Man Brown and his collection of lunatics had attacked the Federal Arsenal. For the next year, every slave who endured a preemptive beating from a paranoid master, every fugitive run down by outriders or stuffed indefinitely into some suffocating hidey-hole because it was unsafe to travel, could thank his fiercest advocate.

Mullins was still talking. "And the venerable Whigs, the party of Washington, now devolved into those reprehensible Black Republicans. Surely you know of the mendacity of Chase and Lincoln, . . ."

He—Joseph—might be rightfully accused of being overcautious at times, but he wouldn't be guilty of bringing the Southern abolition movement to a halt with some outrageous stunt. Brown had long gotten away with his puffery in the North and his lawlessness in Kansas, but look what had happened the instant he tried his lunacy in the South. Vigilance, prudence, patience. That's how you got freedom seekers to Mexico and Canada.

Mullins, still: "And Parsons Chambers and Newton, known accomplices of John Brown, operating in our midst, having broken out of our own jail. And do you suppose they accomplished this feat alone? These are grim times, gentlemen. Let me remind you that just this summer, the citizens of this state, in a bout of blindness or naiveté, or somnolence, elected as governor a devout Unionist and pernicious opponent of popular sovereignty, a hypocrite who would keep his own servants while disallowing the same right to our brethren in the Territories. . . ."

And now Ig would be keeping close to home. Rachel would be twice again as big by the time things settled down enough that Ig might feel safe in evangelizing in the hinterlands. Months. Maybe he ought to call on Ann Renner again. Sit with her. Take her around in the hearse. Court her.

He wasn't getting any younger. Rachel would never be his as long as Ig Bodeker was alive. But he had no interest in prim Ann Renner. He wanted Ig to leave town for a few days every week.

Mullins had taken a seat. John McCoy stood up and cleared his throat. "Gentlemen, I applaud this call to vigilance. However, I believe we should keep our fears within scale. Dallas County holds relatively few slaves, unlike the large concentrations found in the plantation south that might be excited into a formidable horde. While we've seen clear evidence of abolitionist treachery, there has been no sign, that I am aware of, pointing to insurrection. It is well to remember that Virginia, with its proximity to Baltimore and other strongholds of abolitionist sentiment, is far more vulnerable to corrosive influences than is Texas, situated as it is, in a far corner of the South."

Near the center of the second row, William Keller stood up. He pointed his hook at McCoy. "August 21, 1831! Major, surely a man of your age and erudition will recall that date."

The room grew very quiet. McCoy looked absently at Keller. "Why yes, Bill. How could I ever forget the sixteenth day after the fifth anniversary of my tenth birthday?"

Everyone laughed. Nat Burford and a few others applauded. Keller looked down at his feet and shook his head, smiling. He looked up again. He'd lowered his hook. "You are nimble, sir. I pity your courtroom opponents."

McCoy took his seat. "The floor is yours, Bill. I've said my piece."

Keller nodded to McCoy and looked about the room. "August 21, 1831. Southampton County, Virginia. Now I see nods of recognition. One deranged yet unusually bright nigger preacher named Nathaniel Turner conceived and led a murderous insurrection against the innocent white men, women, and children of southeastern Virginia. This rebellion, too, was put down in short order. But before Reverend Turner could be hanged, skinned, and his sparse, vile fat rendered, he and his horde murdered with guns, swords, knives, clubs, and any deadly implement at hand thirty-five persons, including infants, small children, and women. Many of these were decapitated and otherwise mutilated."

He paused. There was only the sound of the burning oak popping in the stove, the clearing of throats, and the swish of legs crossed and uncrossed. Joseph had come out of his reverie.

Keller pointed again at McCoy. "Furthermore, in response to Major McCoy's assertion . . ."

"I will thank you to point your hook in another direction, Bill," McCoy said.

"I beg your pardon." Keller lowered his arm. He looked about, addressing the room in general. "Furthermore, it is well to remember that this uprising did not grow out of the vast rice fields or sugarcane plantations of Louisiana, the giant cotton fields of Mississippi or Alabama, or South Carolina where diligent and professional overseers maintain firm discipline over hundreds of slaves at a time. No. This evil and deadly rebellion was fomented on the modest farms and yeoman holdings indigenous to that part of the Commonwealth. Where, according to the confessions of the murderous Reverend Turner, servile property was treated kindly, rarely beaten, and often indulged, not by experienced overseers, but by farmer and tradesman owners."

He paused again and looked out over the room, then back to the front table. "Consider the parallels here in our own beloved home, gentlemen, where our undisciplined and overly familiar Negro population goes about unfettered and little watched, entirely free to mingle and plot with others of their kind, fully vulnerable to the enticements of jealous Northern schemers who resent our way of life. Do not be lulled by gaiety and solicitude. Consider the houndsman. A dog is quite able to wag its tail one instant and bare its teeth the next. But the firm hand is never bitten.

"For those generous, trusting souls who need further convincing, let me remind you that barely three years ago in Colorado County, only a week's ride to the South, some four hundred murderous, traitorous slaves—no doubt incited and assisted by Northern exhorters—were prevented from turning on their masters and community and leaving a bloody wake all the way to Mexico only by the diligence of a few alert citizens.

"Have we forgotten that in this very town, in this very decade, the Elkins woman who poisoned her master, the kindly widower Mr. Wisdom, who had long entrusted her with his household and the care of his children?"

"Organization. Constant and collective vigilance. Firm and fair discipline. These are the essential tools for maintaining our social and economic well-being and the proper and natural order so clearly and eloquently laid down for us by the Almighty through the hands and hearts of the prophets and patriarchs. Take heed, gentlemen. I am not so presumptuous as to claim this wisdom as my own. I simply offer a humble reminder. Our responsibilities are grave. *And if a man smite his servant, or his maid, with a rod, and he die under his hand: he shall surely be punished. Notwithstanding, if he continue a day or two, he shall not be punished: for he is his money.* Our path is certain. Our mandate is clear. I can add nothing to this." He took his seat.

Joseph and Malachi exchanged glances as they stood to join in the applause.

CHAPTER 29

The crazy bitch had ruined supper again. Samuel would fix his own supper from now on. He certainly knew how to do it, and the company would surely be better.

Yes, her cooking had improved, but only after she started taking her meals with Samuel and Joseph. But while the cornbread was no longer scorched on the bottom or the beans cooked to mush or the eggs fried hard as month-old cow flops, the conversation at the kitchen table had gone to hell, which, in Samuel's opinion, ruined a meal as surely as sorry cooking.

She just sat there, chewing, picking at her food, and oozing contempt. She looked good. No getting around that, even if she was mean and crazy. He'd take hold of her if she'd let him. He could put aside his fear and dislike if the chance came along. But she just sat there while he and Joseph talked about work. She didn't even roll her eyes or clear her throat. She made not one comment. Never offered to get up and spoon out a second helping. Never asked if he and Joseph had everything they needed or even if they liked what they had. And her drawing a wage. Part of what had been his wage. Damn overpaid for doing a little laundry, cooking, sitting at the table, and washing dishes. Dust an inch thick in the house. He hadn't looked, but he'd bet her room was perfect as a new dime. He wouldn't think about asking her do anything in his cabin, even though it wouldn't take five minutes to sweep and dust it.

And Joseph. He never seemed to mind the sullenness and the lack of attention to work he had a right to expect. Made you wonder. She was sleeping in his house, just right down the hall from his bed. Didn't seem too far off for a man who would lay with his best friend's wife—the wife of a man of God—to slip down the hall to have little wallow with the comely help, if his first choice happened to be busy with her husband. Bekah never seemed to get on Joseph's nerves, never seemed to hurt his feelings no matter what hateful thing she said. She never even called either one of them by name.

Still, it seemed unlikely she'd submit to any man unwilling to beat the piss out of her. There was comfort in that. If he knew Joseph was snugging his dowel in two holes while he—Samuel—walked around out of his head, he'd be in the next southbound coffin.

Even when he thought about the beating she'd given him that night in the kitchen, he didn't dwell on the taste of blood or the feel of those hard little knuckles smashing his lips. Rather he recalled her scent and the way she'd strode toward him, her thighs against his as he grappled with her, her bosom in his face and her quickened breathing. He could have pounded her right into the planks, and she knew it and knew he wouldn't.

But that goddamn Joseph. He'd never mentioned his fornication, like anybody with any sense wouldn't know that a man didn't go look in on a married woman and then spend half the night fixing whatever needed fixing. Wasn't much needed fixing over there. The Bodekers didn't own anything. Sneaking back in right before time to get up and go to work and then dragging around all day not taking care of his share of the load. A man ought to ask for more wages if he had to do his own job and half of somebody else's. And then having to look poor old Brother Ig in the eye, knowing very well that his pretty little pallid, yellow-headed wife was rolling with his boss, the undertaker. He wasn't getting paid for that.

And he wasn't getting paid to help send everybody who came down the road to Mexico. "Go anytime," Joseph told him. "I want you to stay. I'd miss your help and friendship, but I won't be the one to try to hold a man who wants to go." Well, go where? He didn't speak Spanish, and if he got caught, he might not be hauled back to Joseph. What if he got sold to some cotton plantation owner down at Gonzales or, worse, some sugarcane concern in Louisiana? At least here he drew a wage and got as much as he wanted to eat. He had satisfying work and a nice, tight little cabin. He was learning to read, and he'd surely known sorrier white men than Joseph Shaw.

But the son of a bitch might be just like all the other white sons of bitches and lying with his black woman whether she liked it or not. No wonder she never said anything. What could she do? She was just like him. Owned. Just a fine-looking piece of property. And he'd helped pay for her. Now, how about that? No wonder Joseph went along with his idea even though he needed another slave around like he needed a good case of the clap.

Talk about one lucky-ass slave! Gonna be free for sure one of these days if Joseph had to put him in a coach and drive him to Detroit and put him on a boat for Chatham. Lots of other Negroes up there already. He'd heard about schools and churches and businesses, and there'd be women who'd actually look at him. Surely they could use another carpenter up there. He might resort to undertaking. A man with his skills would never be out of work. He and Joseph stayed busy. No telling how much that miserly bastard made. He could do that, Joseph. Take him north. He could take his property anywhere he pleased. But not yet. No sir. He couldn't leave his business for that long, and besides you couldn't go around turning your slaves loose and expect to come back to Dallas County and carry on with abolition work. He couldn't afford to draw attention to himself or his friends. This work was just too important and the danger too great. There it was. The danger. The work, yes, as long as you could do it without risking your neck or giving up your Negro help. You needed a few appreciative Negroes around to remind you what a fine fellow you were for helping all those poor slaves on to freedom.

"Samuel! Samuel! Good Lord! You're slinging dirt all over the shop." Joseph looked down at him from the edge of the hidey-hole. Samuel stopped and rested on his shovel. He stood shoulder deep, breathing hard, soaked in sweat. The black dirt clung to his forearms and the backs of his hands. The shop door was closed. He smelled the lamp and earth and sawdust and Joseph. He pitched the spade up to Joseph and climbed out of the hole. He dusted off his pants and pulled his sweaty shirt from his chest. "You wanna dig awhile?"

"Why, sure. You just needed to say."

"Well."

"Hell, go clean up and turn in." Joseph seemed to be studying him.

Samuel nodded. "Down another foot or two and then out some. We ain't got to the hard part yet. And it's already crumbling in. We better go ahead and cut some timbers tomorrow. I hope we don't hit water." He opened the shop door and stepped into the cool night.

Samuel loved October and November before the northers started coming down. He stood letting his eyes adjust and his sweat dry. He'd be chilled soon. He looked at his dark cabin and then at Joseph's kitchen lamp through the office window. There'd be a little coffee left and some biscuits. He jiggled the water bucket they kept hanging from a hook near the edge of the awning. About a quarter full. He dipped out a drink. Nice and cool and tasting of sawdust. You couldn't keep it out unless you put a cloth over it, and they never did. Now he was ready for coffee.

He stepped out in the yard and looked at the clear night sky. He'd prop open a window tonight and pile on another blanket. If it got too cold in there, he'd lay his heavy coat on, too. Keep just enough fire going so that it'd blaze right up come morning. Nothing like waking up in the middle of the night with your cap pulled down low and the covers pulled up over your mouth. Everything warm but your nose, knowing you don't have to get up for a while, and you can feel that dark, cold room around you and think about the frost on the grass outside and the night things moving around and then just roll on your side, turn your face into the covers, and let your breath warm your nose.

He could never hold onto his anger. That's where Bekah and others he'd known had him. They kept their outrage where you could see it or hidden just well enough to avoid a whipping or branding most of the time, and it drove them to Mexico or this place called Canada where, Joseph assured him, they'd probably already had a foot of snowfall.

But anger leaked right out of him. For every rotten thing in his life since he'd left the farm and come to work for Joseph, there had been enough pleasure that he could hate only for a while. Then a hard day's work, a satisfying job completed, a meal, bed, and for a few hours he'd be content but denied the pleasure of hating. It was as if he'd been made fully servile now. Practically, he was little freer than the slaves huddled around a fire in the middle of their dirt-floored huts on farms all over Dallas County. Yes, he had a few comforts and good work and, if he came at it with the right frame of mind, the dignity of being paid something for his labor—and though his money was accumulating, as a black man he had little to spend it on. Joseph assured him the money would one day be useful, perhaps when he made his escape; and he could see the reasoning in this. But the price for these gains had been high, for it often seemed they'd come at the cost of the one true, pure pleasure a Negro could enjoy, something he held entirely for himself and out of reach of white people, an ecstasy as sharp and perfect as that brought by a woman's loins. Or so he imagined.

He walked across the yard and stepped through the back door. Bekah met him in the kitchen. He noted the coffeepot still on the stove behind her.

"Y'all about to fall out the bottom of the world yet?"

"Another foot or two."

"You tracking in dirt. Get back out there and kick off them shoes, and I'll broom you off."

He felt her at his back as he walked down the hall toward the door. Outside she went at his pant legs and bottom with the broom. "You want me to sweep that nasty face, too?"

He chuckled.

She said, "I reckon I'll draw you some water if I'm gonna have to look at you." She glanced at the shop. "Still at it, huh?"

"He don't never stop. He gets in too big of a hurry about things, though."

She eyed the shop as she swiped at him with the broom.

Back inside, after he'd washed his face at the basin, he sat at the kitchen table sipping coffee and finishing off a biscuit. He had another one on a saucer. They were still warm and soft. Bekah must have kept the pan along the edge of the stove. That was a new touch.

She sat at the far end of the table with a small sewing box. She sorted some buttons. At her elbow were a pair of Joseph's pants and various heavy socks. He recognized one of his own.

He took a sip and studied her. She looked up at him, pulled off a length of dark thread, and held a needle up to the candlelight.

He said, "Six hundred miles. I can't get it in my head. I think of five miles up to Pig and Cathlyn's, but I can't think about going that far 120 times."

"I know how far two hundred miles is." She pushed the thread through the eye and doubled it up.

Well, she hadn't snorted at his comment. No doubt she knew a lot of things he didn't. He waited. He didn't dare ask.

"Some of it was by river. All through Tennessee. Laying in the bottom of that boat whenever somebody came along. I got my fill of it, but I'd have gone another thousand miles if that's what it took. I never had no idea how many white people there was 'til I tried to run. On old McCutcheon's place there was five of us for every white person. Then you run away and all you see is white people." She shook her head as she held the button along the pant fly. "All over the place. I s'pose you're used to 'em, but I'd never even been to town."

Joseph came in the back door. Bekah said, "I just swept this floor."

"I've shucked off my shoes." He walked into the kitchen, drenched in sweat and covered with black dirt. He eyed the coffeepot and biscuit pan. "Well, you left me two anyway."

"And that's all there's gonna be 'til in the morning. Come on and let me sweep you off a little bit."

A few minutes later they came back in, and Joseph said, "I believe she took off about as much hide as dirt."

They sat at table and talked little as Bekah worked. Samuel's muscles relaxed as he watched her handle the buttons, thread, and needles. He was very sleepy, but he didn't want to drift off. He wanted to sip coffee and watch her work. It was late, but he didn't want to check the time. He'd felt this way the few times he'd gotten mildly drunk. Relaxed, drowsy, but unwilling to waste his contentment sleeping. He closed his eyes and listened to her hands and the soft swishing of material.

She said, "Why don't you two get up and get in the bed?"

Samuel nodded. "I ought to."

Joseph was snoring. Bekah got up and walked around the table and nudged him. He snored on. "Wake up. You need to get in the bed." She nudged his shoulder. "Joseph. You fell asleep in your chair. You ought to go on to bed."

CHAPTER 30

Took off and left your pretty little black ass is what he done. Thought more of his own freedom than he thought of yours. Thought more of it than he thought of you. Or that boy. Your own husband. Then got hisself shot stealing a goose. Your brother up there in Philadelphia sending letters down here, trying to buy you for next-to-nothin', which I reckon is all he thinks you're worth.

Now look at you. Run, if you've a mind to. Hell. Then see what becomes of them younguns when you get caught. Mister McCutcheon told me he's got a mind to sell 'em both anyway, but he knows you're fond of 'em, and neither one of us feels like listening to you squalling over 'em. But you take off now. . . .

She sat in the dark, looking out the bedroom window. The moon lighted Lamar Street, so she could see the ruts and, for a second, a leaf trapped and swirling in a dust devil. To the east the cedar breaks darkened the hills and the taller, scattered cottonwoods, the dark lines of oaks and elms told her of creeks she hadn't seen. The air stirred again, and she smelled rain and smoke from Samuel's chimney.

When you got the chance to run, you ran, if you were made that way, and some weren't. Pious whites never understood, but then they'd never been owned. Timothy had been too big to carry and too young to walk all day, let alone run. He'd have slowed them all down, gotten them caught for sure. Even if she'd known she was pregnant again, she'd have told Robert to go. And he would've. Just like she left Timothy with Uncle Jeff that morning a year and a half later, when Levin and Stephen stepped out of the woods and into her path and said, "James sent us. Come on, if you're coming."

You could travel with a baby, and you wouldn't deny one child a chance at freedom because the other one was too big to carry and too little to run.

Ig sat at the kitchen table watching Rachel brown a skillet full of thinly sliced potatoes. His mouth watered. They were out of bacon for the time being—though not for long, since Pig was killing hogs—but at least the potatoes were frying in bacon grease. He'd always favored fried potatoes for breakfast. "Let's see. Jacob, Joseph, Joshua, Jonah, Jeremiah. I suppose I favor the letter *J*. It has a manly sound to it."

"I don't know," Rachel said. She rested her wooden spoon in the skillet. "What about Jane or Jenny?"

Ig said, "Lovely names. I suppose I just prefer *J*, period."

"Jezebel?"

"My fondness for the letter has limits." He tapped his fork on the table. "Don't you think Joseph would be pleased if we named a son after him? Could there be a more worthy namesake?"

Rachel went at the potatoes again. "I think having two Josephs around would be confusing."

"A middle name then."

"Perhaps."

"It would please him to no end. We could keep it a secret. Surprise him. I can just imagine the look on his face."

"He'd be shocked."

"But pleased."

"Overwhelmed."

"Yes." He smiled, thinking about it. Joseph, the doting uncle, teaching the boy all sorts of tedious, practical skills. "We could name a daughter Josephine."

Rachel shook her head, half sighing, half laughing. "You're reaching." She moved the skillet off the stove and onto a trivet, spooning potatoes onto plates and joining him at the table. They held hands as he said grace over the food.

"Your appetite seems to be returning," he said.

"I should take care. I'll pay for gorging." She looked at him.

"Hmmm?"

"Have you slept at all the past three days?"

"A few hours."

"Ignatius."

"It's the pamphlet. When I lie down, my mind just churns. I'll be able to sleep after I finish it."

"And when will that be?"

"Two more days. I have eight pages done already."

"So five days with no sleep."

"Some sleep. Don't make it worse than it is. What can I do? The Lord provides these periods of energy and clarity. To waste them would be a sin."

"You're haggard and wild-eyed right now. And look at your hands. They're shaking. How can you even write?"

"No, my forearm was resting on the edge of the table. See?" He held up his hand and did his best to relax and hold it steady. He lowered it when he felt the shakes coming.

"We can ill afford another collapse right now, and that's what always happens. Dr. Thompson's diagnosis rings true. Your body balks in order to save itself."

"Rachel."

"I'm sure the druggist could suggest something. You have to sleep."

"It's the baby, too, Rachel. I'll settle down."

"We should go see Mr. Peak this morning. He'll give you something."

"A draught of opium."

"To make you sleep. Dr. Thompson would prescribe it. We could see him first. Then you'd feel better about it."

"A Methodist minister does not resort to opiates."

"Joseph or Malachi could get it for you."

He sighed, smiled. Women were such practical creatures. "Rachel, it's not just public perception I'm concerned about."

She leaned back in her chair and crossed her arms on her chest.

"You're not eating," he said.

"I've lost my appetite."

"Oh—queasy again?"

"Last time you were in bed for almost a week. You're getting worse."

"I . . ." He shrugged and shook his head. She'd been holding this in. Just please don't bring up the weeping. She'd heard him. That's why she'd stayed away. Had she been repulsed, or had she wanted to spare him the humiliation?

"People count on you. Your congregation. Our friends. The Negroes. I count on you."

"So I don't meet my obligations?"

She leaned forward and said, gently, "You are the most gifted minister I have ever known. You are the best man I've known. But you can't perform your duties if you're sick with melancholy. You have an obligation to take care of yourself."

"I do my best work during these frantic periods. I have to make do with what I've been given."

"Perhaps a steadier approach would be more productive in the long term."

He reached across the table and took her hands. She looked pale. There were lines at the corners of her mouth. When had this happened? "Just let me finish this bit of work. Then I'll see Mr. Peak about a sleep agent."

Rachel sighed deep and quick. "No, then you'll collapse in bed. Ig, I don't know what to tell people anymore."

He pulled back his hands. "Now we've gotten to the real matter."

"No! Don't you turn this back on me."

"I've humiliated you."

"Oh, there you go! You always turn it back on me. Go work on your pamphlet. We can't let Brother Zeph outbrazen us."

"Rachel. The pen name. Remember?"

"Have several hundred printed and alert all of Dallas County of our intentions. Pass them out down at the Masonic Hall. Perhaps Mr. Shirek will stock a few dozen copies between his stationery and almanacs."

"Darling." He tried not to smile. So much for his pamphlet. Yet another unfinished manuscript that would become part of his collected papers.

"Oh! We could take out an advertisement in the *Herald*. I'm sure Mr. Pryor would give a fair deal to a man of the cloth." She stood up and threw her napkin on the table and started for the door. "Then the local vigilance committee can come snatch you right out of bed. I'll be a widow, but our fatherless child can draw comfort knowing his father died a martyr. What glory!" She slammed the door behind her.

Ig sat numb. He ought to go out and check on her, but he knew better. She might be on her knees heaving up what little breakfast she'd eaten, but she'd wave him away and say she didn't need his help. Of course, if he didn't go out, she'd blister him for that, too.

He got up and opened the door a crack and peeped out. She was sitting on the back of the wagon, her arms crossed, her back straight, her dangling legs rocking up and down. The breeze felt cold and damp. "Would you like your shawl?"

"No."

He should have just taken it to her. Then she would've had to thank him. He watched her for a moment, then shut the door. He went to his desk. The pages that had so enthralled him now struck him as absurd. *Treatise on the Sin of Slavery* by Anonymous. And who would benefit from this? Who would these pamphlets be distributed to besides those who already sided against slavery? Rachel was right. Quiet, steady work was best. Preach the gospel. Accumulate allies. Draw no attention. He had to think about her safety and now the baby's, not to mention the well-being of the entire Southern abolition effort.

He noticed Rachel's shawl on the back of the chair by the door. He'd humble himself and take it out to her. Apologize and offer to visit the druggist. She'd nod. Things would be chilly the rest of the day, but she'd be back in good spirits by suppertime. Anyway, they were going to the Van Husses. She had to be cheerful there, and sometimes a little forced gaiety melted anger and brought about the real thing. You couldn't be pleasant toward one another all evening and remain mad.

As he stood up to go out, he realized how tired he was. Drained. His thoughts jumbled. Forget the druggist. He felt he could lie down on the floor and sleep for a week.

Father's Reminiscence
Transcribed July 28, 1911

Two years and a few months after Levin McGregor drowned his Irish overseer in a rain barrel, we sat at a table in the meeting room at a hotel in Chatham, Canada, with John Brown and several members of a secret militia. The sight of so many armed and arrogant black men would have frozen a slaver's blood.

Levin had not stopped in Cincinnati after his latest escape. He'd not stopped for anything, for he'd have been hanged and skinned had he been captured. He'd made his journey to Detroit and Chatham in seven months, traveling at night, sleeping in the woods and fields. He'd trusted no one, including other Negroes.

Old Brown and I were the only white men at the table. Conspicuously absent were Mrs. Tubman and Mr. Douglass. There had been much hubbub about their expected attendance, but they'd heard the plans of the subterranean pass through the southern Appalachians, the great insurrection, and the assault on the federal armory. Despite their admiration for the old man's audacity and their affection for him personally, in the end they cast their lots with the sane.

Old Brown read his proposed constitution, gave a rousing estimate of funding from his well-placed allies in New England and New York. We heard again about his exploits in Kansas against the hapless, degenerate slavers. Would we join him and head again for Kansas to drill and gain strength and numbers for his ultimate plan, sanctioned by the Almighty, to bring the harlot Virginia to her knees? To break her and smite with the edge of the sword the men who degrade her?

"God bless you, Captain; we're with you!" We saw his doom, yet we hoped. What if he did know God's will and had been chosen to carry it out? Had there not always been doubters of great men? What harm could he do? So we loved him even as we chose to bleed the South slowly, surgically. No thrust of the sword. Rather, precise use of a million lancets. Bleed her a few slaves at a time. Bleed her and goad her. Taunt her.

We made trips into the South. A white man and his slave can travel freely and draw little attention. Levin knew his lines well. I was the land speculator or carpenter or lawyer, and he was my property. Merely saying this still embarrasses and sickens me.

Sometimes I felt I played the role too easily, and I sensed in Levin an unease or distrust, as if he suspected my racial makeup imbued me with a gift for tyranny. I wondered the same. I've wondered since.

Assignments came from William Still's office in Philadelphia. Escaped slaves came to him with stories of family left behind. Occasionally, they offered money they'd raised by hiring themselves out as laborers or by speaking on the abolitionist lecture circuit. We accepted only enough to cover our own expenses. We were young, had no family, were accountable only to each other, and each held the other accountable.

We went south to bring out those who could travel fast. Young men and women, older children. We gave babies paregoric and carried them in sacks. We traveled afoot or by wagon and boat, a white man and his slaves when it was safe to perform; night skulkers when it wasn't. We always gathered intelligence from the families that sent us. We knew the best routes and where to find shelter and sustenance. Tennessee, Missouri, Mississippi, and Arkansas. In three years, we reunited eleven fugitives with their families in the Northeast, Detroit, and Chatham. We bled the harlot and kept ourselves fed.

Then in January 1856 there came a letter and funds from Mr. Still of the Anti-Slavery society. There had been several attempts to buy the freedom of a young widow and her son from a plantation on the Tennessee River near Decatur, Alabama. Her owner had not responded. Her despairing brother, your Uncle James, had been prepared to try to fetch her himself, but had been dissuaded by Mr. Still who contacted Levin and me. James offered three year's savings—twelve hundred dollars—for our services. He could provide detailed information about terrain and hazards along the way.

We returned half the money along with a letter requesting further details.

CHAPTER 31

The boy, Gideon, died of infection eight days after a pot of hot grease spilled all over his belly and groin. He'd been sweeping the floor around the stove and had somehow gotten the broom handle hung in the pot's bail. His owners, Mr. and Mrs. Raywick, who owned and operated a grocery and a dry goods store a block north of the square, thought the child was about eleven. His mother was their housekeeper, who'd died a few years back, while they still lived in Missouri.

Joseph and Samuel agreed that Gideon seemed awfully small for eleven. Per the Raywicks' wishes, they'd shown up with the smallest coffin they had on hand, drove to the shack behind the grocery where the child lived with an elderly slave named Jacob Isaacson, and, after putting his breeches back on over the swollen wounds, laid him in the casket, nailed the lid shut, and drove on to the slave cemetery on the north edge of town.

Mrs. Raywick, thirtyish, blue-eyed, auburn hair barely showing beneath her winter bonnet, sniffled and dabbed at her eyes as she stood beside her short, slight, bald husband. Their twin girls, auburn-haired like their mother, stood before her with wide, wet eyes as Brother Sid Claggett, a slave owned by Sarah Cockrell, hatless, wearing his work clothes and sawdust from the mill, his Bible held behind his back, recited Psalm 23 and Matthew 15:

> Therefore my beloved brethren, be ye steadfast, unmovable, always abounding in the work of the Lord, forasmuch as ye know that your labor is not in vain in the Lord.

Jacob, in his black breeches, gray vest, and stained white shirt, stood dry-eyed, expressionless, looking northward over the cedars. There were only a few wispy clouds. The early afternoon sun made a heavy coat unnecessary.

The Raywicks were new in town, their slaves little known among the other local Negroes. There would be no wake, no singing, no nighttime burial, no celebration of a life lived.

As Brother Claggett finished his eulogy, Jacob bent and took a handful of soil from the graveside and let it sift through his fingers into his pants pocket.

By two o'clock, Samuel and Joseph were alone at the gravesite, each holding a shovel. A breeze had kicked up, stirring the chimes of twine and glass shards and snuff jars that accompanied the children's graves. On Sunday afternoons, you sometimes saw Negroes walking about their cemetery, scything grass and pulling up weeds and young cedars and repairing or adding to the chimes and filling in badger and gopher holes. There were crosses made of rough timbers, a few engraved headstones, and many limestone rocks marking the graves. The air smelled of cedar, dust, rotting wood, stone, freshly turned soil, and old leather lashings.

Slaves of prosperous families usually were buried in the city cemetery a quarter of a mile south of Joseph's house, just beyond Ig and Rachel's place. White townspeople seemed to assign a special status to the slaves buried among the family members of white owners. Burial services often were presided over by white ministers. Ig had done a few graveside services there. But this two-acre clearing in the cedar, bois d'arc, and elm just north of the intersection of Water Street and Calhoun Street belonged entirely to the people buried there and their decedents. Not even white paupers were buried there; they had their own corner of the city cemetery.

The wind soughed in the cedars, and the varied pitches and timbres of the chimes melded with the brittle *cuk-uk, cuk-uk, cuk-uk* of a crow back in the cedars. He'd been there awhile, flapping and croaking now and again. Clouds had moved in. The wind picked up. Joseph and Samuel talked little. The first few spadefuls of soil thudded on the cedar casket lid and the few handfuls already dropped in by Jacob and the Raywicks. Then there were only the wind-muted sounds of their modest exertions, the occasional stamp of hooves, creaking harness, and the whisper of earth covering earth.

CHAPTER 32

From the Dallas Herald, December 10, 1859

If ever there was the slightest doubt among even the most optimistic citizens of Dallas County that there are among us northern abolitionist agitators ever ready to entice and assist legally owned slaves in fleeing their rightful and benevolent masters and station for the squalid and licentious villages of Mexico, these can now be laid to rest after the capture of Peter, the runaway property of Mr. Alexander Reynolds of McKinney. The scamp was apprehended by a local ranging company along a cattle trail 60 miles southwest of San Antonio. The boy was accompanied by two local Mexicans who claimed he was owned by a nearby Tejano Rancher who had hired him out to assist them in the construction of a stone fence. The two could not, however, satisfactorily account for why they might be out with a Negro on a remote cattle trail at a few minutes shy of midnight. All three were taken to the jail at San Antonio where persistent interrogation of not only the subjects themselves, but of other known Mexican troublemakers and slaves in outlying areas, yielded up the facts as we now have them.

In order to send a message to outlaws bent on theft and insurrection and to those rebellious and less-disciplined members of the servile class, Mr. Reynolds, solid citizen that he is, has arranged, at substantial expense, to have the boy returned instead of accepting the first reasonable offer from businessmen in the vicinity of San Antonio in need of Negro labor and willing to take a chance on this recalcitrant scoundrel.

As satisfying as this outcome may be, the affair raises numerous dark and troubling questions. First, how many pairs of white hands would be required to assist a Negro from Collin County to within a few days' foot travel of the Rio Grande? Dozens? Scores? Hundreds? Have we truly allowed our society to be infiltrated to this grave degree? And is it now a settled fact that the languorous, seditionist Mexican, yet resentful for his race's two crushing defeats at the hands of vastly superior military forces, will abet runaway property at any and every opportunity? From this writer's perspective, that question seems settled. Certainly the economic and social damages from such criminal activities are incalculable.

One can only hope and pray that true Southern men will respond with the stiff spines, vigilance, forbearance, and courage for which their race has so long been renowned, respected, and feared by its enemies.

CHAPTER 33

gnatius woke before dawn, suffocating. Rachel snored softly beside him, consuming part of his precious air. He pulled back the bed curtain, and the coolness of the rest of the cabin poured into his sleeping space. Why did she insist on this ridiculous curtain? Some nesting or burrowing instinct peculiar to women, he supposed. His pillow was soaked with sweat. He turned it over and wiped his temples with the sleeve of his nightshirt.

He turned away from her, but his head was clogged. He couldn't breathe. He rolled onto his aching back again, laced his fingers on his chest, and tried to relax. He ought to just get up, but he couldn't abide the cold, dark cabin, and he didn't want to wake Rachel. Once she woke, she was up for the day, no matter how exhausted she might be. She'd say, "Oh that's fine," but her annoyance would be as obvious as the circles beneath her tired eyes, and of course she'd be sick. Cathlyn and Rosemary assured them the worst of the sickness would pass within the next few weeks. It was testament to a woman's tenderness and capacity for enduring pain—or else amnesia—that she ever gave birth to more than one child. Was there anything more pitiful than a woman on her knees, tears dripping from her cheeks as she heaved up her insides?

Peter would be on his way back to the Reynolds farm. He'd been so close—within a few days of the border. Perhaps he'd grown used to the relative freedom of traveling, dangerous as it was. No master. No toil without recompense. What humiliations awaited him now? Surely Reynolds didn't value him enough as a slave or as a man to pay his way back from South Texas. He'd bet the slaver was gloating before the young woman Peter loved.

Just beatings, if he was lucky.

And did Peter pray for strength from a God who allowed this to befall him and millions of others like him? How did Peter square this? Did he believe reflexively because he had to believe in order to hang on?

Why hadn't he talked to Peter about Job and righteous suffering?

About earthly suffering and heavenly reward? Had it slipped his mind, or was there some other reason? Cowardice? He had not wanted to address the possibility of recapture. Far easier to talk of the courage and strength needed for the journey, the evil of slavery.

Don't discuss likely outcomes. It might appear the Almighty sometimes steps back and lets the odds run their course. If one chose to flee one's master in the South, capture and torture were likely. The odds of escape to Mexico or Canada were slim. When someone made it? Surely this was the hand of God at work. But if an entire family—women and children, too—were recaptured or shot or beset by dogs? Well, then God's will was sometimes terrible and always unknowable, but just. Yes, just. That little boy torn from his wailing mother's arms and sold downriver to some fever-infested swamp in Louisiana or Mississippi—where, if he lived to young manhood, he'd be worked from can-see to can't-see and fed only enough coarse food to keep him working another day—was serving as a cog in the Great Plan.

Perhaps these injustices fueled the righteous outrage that would end slavery. That God allowed these intricate plans to play out to the suffering of innocents instead of simply ending slavery by smiting the slavers—well, best not to ponder those questions. Best not to get into difficult theological points with a fugitive facing a six-hundred-mile journey through the most isolated and dangerous corner of the South. Somehow this was all for the good of mankind which must err, suffer, and strive, just as children mature by climbing Fool's Hill.

So, ultimately, after all the striving and growing and purification through suffering, the world will be obliterated and the faithful and chosen lifted to unending glory and the wicked and unbelieving cast into eternal damnation. One had best trust. One went mad believing that a child's misery was nothing more—or that Peter would be tortured with a lash or branding iron because he had been born a Negro in America, just as one might be born into peonage in Europe.

Here was the injustice. Here were Christ's teachings. Here is what he would do today. Here is what anyone but a beast would do for another human.

Otherwise, why not just put a ball through your brain? Or devote your life to earthly pleasures?

Men had died so they would not bow to an earthly King. Resistance, horror, suffering, and death might lead to justice. Consider the children of Israel.

But if God would favor a certain people, might he then favor a race? But a people could be multiple races. A nation could be multiple races and multiple peoples. But an innocent born to a disfavored people? A born infidel? An innocent infidel? Destined to disfavor by accident of birth? *Cursed be Canaan!* But there are no accidents if God's hand guides all things. So, then, an innocent born to certain damnation, who serves some larger purpose in favor of the chosen?

Suffer in this life, then suffer for eternity should you be born into wickedness or born a Jew or Mohammedan instead of the son of a minister from western Virginia.

Or . . .

Or simply suffer in this life.

The muzzle, cool against his temple. The click of the trigger and hammer, the sharp crack of the igniting cap, the explosion of the charge, Minié ball spinning down the barrel, drilling, boring out the other temple, bone and flesh striking the curtain and dresser like a handful of grit.

Dear Lord.

He jerked the blanket up under his chin and turned away from Rachel. She stopped snoring and cleared her throat. He tried to empty his mind, then fill it with thoughts of his boyhood bed, his father's voice. Rachel. Expectant, slumbering Rachel. Beloved Rachel, warm in her nest, in her flannel gown, long legs drawn up, ankles crossed. He should turn to her. But for the moment, he needed to imagine her.

His breathing slowed. Outside, the wind had laid. He heard his watch ticking on his desk, the hiss and popping of dying coals in the stove, a mouse hunting crumbs under the kitchen table.

Rachel lay quiet. At last, he heard her measured breath and the whisper of her eyelashes as she blinked.

Father's Reminiscence
Transcribed July 29, 1911

I have no more intention of leaving the truth untold than of endangering others by telling it too soon. Others stayed behind. I am certain they told no one. To have done so would have been suicidal, even after all these years.

The letter from Dallas three weeks ago—the one you read to me. Alan Huitt had died. His daughter-in-law honored his request that I be notified. She must have wondered about it. He would have told no one. The risk would have been too great. He was the last, save for me. Rachel Bodeker has been gone for some time now. And Joseph Shaw, the Nucholses, the Meades, and the others. They died with questions. They did what they could, and God bless them.

The Trinity River holds secrets. There were deep holes in those days. Properly weighted, a man would stay down.

CHAPTER 34

December 11, 1859

Rachel finally let go of Ig's arm and walked over to check the cakes, pies, pastries, and candy on the table at the Masonic lodge where, only a few weeks earlier, William Keller addressed the men of Dallas with his hook and soaring invective. She'd gotten through her morning sickness, though she wasn't obviously expecting, especially in the new, full, dark blue dress Cathlyn had made for her from material purchased at Shirek's Grocery & Dry Goods.

Congregants had been more generous lately since the news of her pregnancy had spread about town. She'd gained weight, much to Joseph's satisfaction. He waited for the flock of matrons to clear out, then sidled up beside her.

Merchants and tradesmen and their families packed the room. In the front corner, fiddlers and a local madrigal group were gathering. The following Saturday, the most prominent citizens would be attending a Christmas ball at Sarah Cockrell's new hotel, the St. Nicholas. There would be waltzes and an orchestra. Joseph hadn't received an invitation.

John McCoy would be at next week's ball, yet he'd invited the entire town to this, his annual gala at the Masonic Hall. Though McCoy was arguably the town's most venerable attorney and leader, he often represented citizens of very modest means and allowed them to pay as they could. Mrs. Cockrell's guests would be served by uniformed hotel staff, with desserts compliments of Bell's Bakery. Local women fed Major McCoy's crowd.

"Mrs. Bodeker, expectancy obviously agrees with you," Joseph said.

Rachel smiled at him, then turned back to the desserts. "I intend to have the thickest slice of cake on the table. I hope I'm not being too obvious."

"The glowing mother-to-be admiring the holiday bounty. Fodder of a sonnet." Her cheeks were fuller. Even the circles under her eyes seemed less obvious. "I'm glad to see Ig out tonight."

"He's better. Hopefully we'll manage a few months of peace this time. There's no end to it. I'm reconciled."

Ig seemed haggard and reserved tonight. Normally, he'd be striding around the room interrupting conversations, shaking hands, and slapping backs. Tonight he was quietly chatting with Malachi and occasionally nodding to one of his gaggle of admiring ladies. What was it about preachers that seemed so lacking in undertakers?

Rachel picked up a plate of cake and held it at eye level. "I'd say this one. What do you think?"

"I admire a woman with a precise eye. Probably the carpenter in me." He checked around them. No one seemed to be paying attention. "And long shanks and plenty of ardor."

"I've been even worse than usual lately. Perhaps my condition is to blame."

"Worse?"

"Horrible. Wicked thoughts," she said. "My mind won't let me be. I'd expected maternal thoughts. I suppose there's still time." She seemed to study him.

He heard his pulse above the laughter and clinking china and silverware. Except during their trysts, she'd never mentioned her desires. He reached for a cup of cider with an unsteady hand. He sipped to avoid sloshing and nodded toward empty benches lining the walls. "You should get off your feet." He offered his arm. She took it. "I'll go back and fetch your cider in a moment."

She squeezed his forearm as she sat beneath a window. The panes were fogged and sweating. It was dark outside and near freezing. The room smelled of wool and burning cedar logs, cigar smoke, cider and sweets, rose oil and perfume undoubtedly purchased the previous Christmas season from Peak & Sons. He went to fetch her a cup of cider. By the time he returned, she'd already eaten two or three bites of cake. She took the cup, chewed her cake, and looked up at him. He glanced back at Ig, who took no notice of them. Perhaps he'd better just stand and sip his cider.

He looked at the black window panes and rocked on his heels. He'd never been tongue-tied around her before.

"I've shocked you," she said.

He smiled. Heat rose on his face. "Shocked? No. Moved. Stirred."

Her blue eyes were cool, appraising. The parson's wife, who might be carrying his child. He felt a tremor. Or shiver? And the beginnings of an erection. Wickedness indeed. He didn't know this woman. Nor did Ignatius.

She looked over his shoulder. He turned just as Ig slapped him on the back. "Tell me, sir, have you ever seen a lovelier sight? It's one of those great ineffable injustices that some men are blessed so."

Rachel smiled and looked at her cake. "All this flattery. I should have gotten in this state years ago."

"Flattery? Just speaking the truth, like any honest man of God." He shook Joseph's arm. "Of course this scoundrel has been ogling away while I was occupied with church business."

"You'd hold it against a man?"

"Certainly not."

Two dozen children gathered near the back door shrieked with delight when John McCoy walked in dressed in red felt breeches with little bells sewn along the outer seams, green wool shirt, red cape, and high riding boots. His shaggy white hair spilled from beneath a red nightcap. Little girls tugged and stroked his long, white beard.

"St. Nicholas has arrived!" William Keller announced. He stood near the front of the room, holding a cup of eggnog. He seemed to present the major with a flourish of his hook. The adults applauded.

"Back up, you greedy cubs!" McCoy bellowed as he tried to open a burlap sack. "The good elf can't get his bag open!" The children only shrieked louder and pressed closer, trying to stick their hands in the bag. A small blonde boy howled, red-faced and furious, that his big sister had crowded between him and John McCoy.

"That man," Rachel said, glaring at Keller, "always has to be at the center of attention. And brandishing that ghastly hook. You'd think he'd have more consideration."

McCoy was trying to distribute sticks of hard candy. Several of the smaller children were in the throes of fits as their older siblings snatched the treats. A pair of young mothers moved in to make sure the little ones didn't get left out. Other mothers admonished children not to run with candy in their mouths. Ig brightened. Rachel looked on thoughtfully, her chin resting on two fingers.

"Holiday sweets courtesy of local merchants, no doubt," Joseph said.

"I'm sure they gave the major a rate adjusted to the season," Ig said.

Joseph said, "Speaking of sweets, I had better set aside something for Bekah and Samuel." Bekah had held back one of three cobblers she'd made, but she and Samuel would enjoy sampling some of the cakes. The two had lately been civil. Joseph often found them talking quietly at the kitchen table early in the mornings before work. Bekah still tended toward sullenness, but at least she'd quit burning breakfast and now bothered to bang the coffeepot a few times to settle the grounds. He tried to keep her apprised of the account he'd opened for her, but she always said, "What am I gonna do with it? Build me a house and open a hotel?"

Rachel said, "Are they excited about the Negro gathering?"

"They let me draw out a few dollars for hams and apples," Joseph said. "I'm not sure what all Bekah has in mind. Samuel said Al has a stash of brandy, persimmon beer, and God knows what other kinds of tongue oil. I don't know where he gets it, but nobody who wants to get drunk ever goes away disappointed."

Ig said, "Brother Jonas Suggs has promised them the use of his tent, and of course they'll be using mine. Everyone ought to be in out of the weather, at least. I'm sure they'll have a stove or two."

"And they'll have a big fire to stand by and stare at while they get drunk." Joseph said. "You know Samuel. He'll light half the woods and then have to stand back a mile. I had my shoes by the stove the other morning. By the time I fetched them after breakfast, they were too hot to put on. I had to let them cool on the back step."

The madrigals—Rosemary Meade, Sarah Strong, Joyce Burton, and her teenage daughter April—began "Hark the Herald Angels." A few young men stopped their conversations to listen and to admire the handsome widow Sarah Strong—and April Burton, Joseph suspected. She was a fetching fifteen-year-old. He listened to their lovely, blended voices, studied their earnest expressions. Even plain women seemed softer when they sang. They'd obviously practiced for this night.

He wanted something stronger to drink than the punch and eggnog. Whiskey or brandy or at least hard cider. He wanted to sit on the bench and let the warmth of drink and community and the women's voices wash over him. Despite his closeness to Ig, he was not an especially religious man. He found much of the Old Testament absurd justification for warfare and brutality. And except for the Epistle of James, useful guidance from a simple carpenter, he found little sustenance in the New Testament. Yet he had always been moved by voices raised in unison at Christmas. Earnest song touched him more deeply than the exhortation of the most gifted preachers—even Ig, far and away the most brilliant orator he'd ever heard, including Higginson, Parker, Frederick Douglass, and the demented, murderous, dangerous, irresistible John Brown. Ig, the rotund, melancholic, vainglorious, cuckolded Virginia preacher. Surely, somebody had a flask.

Peace on earth and mercy mild,
God and sinner reconciled.

The singers' eyes were closed. People stood about the crowded room, talking and laughing softly in deference to the performers. Children ran about. Some had taken their shoes off and were sliding sock-footed on the pine boards. Joseph's lust had left him. He simply loved them both again, Ig and Rachel, as Ig and Rachel. And Malachi and Rosemary and Richard and Hilda. He looked about the room. He envied them all: Nat and Anne Durford, arm in arm, chatting with John and Mary McCoy, the major still in his St. Nicholas costume. The absurd but courtly Keller, watching himself as he worked the room. Joseph envied them all and hated himself for the affection he felt for the owners of slaves, while four women sang a Christmas carol. How good must it feel to be able to simply love your own people. How fine it would be to sit on the bench and sip a spiked drink and listen to lovely female voices and luxuriate in the press of community. The flushed children and the swish of wool and taffeta and smell of perfume and lilac and food and drink. Just to look at where and who he was and say, "This is good," and not think of Bekah and Samuel, and Al, who wouldn't dare set foot in the building unless they came to the back door to deliver more food and drink or to carry in more chairs and benches or firewood.

Tonight in Cincinnati and Ripley, and towns all along the north bank of the Ohio, much the same would be happening. Singing and merriment. Fires and torches reflecting off the surface of the river and the townspeople lifting their voices, looking southward across the river at the darkness and misery in Kentucky, knowing that here, 170 yards north, was something good.

Now he felt his separation from the solid Southerners around him. He, the carpenter and undertaker known to most everyone in Dallas County, conspired daily to commit treason. He was not one of these people, yet what was this affection? And could he spend the rest of his life here, breaking the law and engaging in pleasant commerce and conversation with people who would see him hanged if they truly knew him? Slavery would be here his entire lifetime, so entrenched he could see no end to it. He and his few cohorts were aligned against a two-hundred-year-old economy and the culture it spawned. Intelligent, pleasant, kindly, godly people approved of it, believed it to be sanctioned by the Almighty and the Scriptures, or shrugged because the institution did not affect them directly—or so they thought, never mind that the white race was degraded by it as surely as those they knowingly degraded with bondage. But, of course, reasonable men don't speak out or take action against something that lines purses and gives men power even while degrading them and, if Ig was right, condemning them. Speak out in Cincinnati or Ripley or

Syracuse or even Baltimore, but not in Dallas, Texas. Wear your beliefs proudly, righteously, and safely on your sleeve in the North while disdaining ignorant, grubbing, violent Southern yeoman or the planter and all of his affectations and vulgar luxury.

And yet who in this building full of merchants and small farmers and tradesmen quietly despised him—Joseph Shaw—for ostensibly owning human chattel? The efficient, cheerful, self-satisfied undertaker and carpenter. Look at him. Gets a little ahead, and what's the first thing he does? Acquire two slaves. Striving, simple. Just an honest tradesman, he'd tell you. Does he ever face himself, alone, in the dark of night? Does he ever question? Probably not. Better to not think. Thinking gets in the way of a day's work, and there's only so much time, after all. A man had better be practical in this backwater. Leave the philosophizing to the academics across the river at La Reunion. And they'll get practical soon enough, if this drought holds. Half the colony has moved to town and sought honest work anyway. *A slack hand maketh poor.* Fanciful, impractical thoughts maketh poor, too.

He looked around the room. Eighty people, perhaps, talking in groups and laughing, holding cups of coffee, punch, and eggnog, nodding, chewing, and admonishing red-faced, sweaty children. How many slave owners? One in ten? The Raywicks. And he himself in the eyes of most of the room. Who here would stand with their little group if they knew? And which timid souls would stand when it became clear that more than half the town hated slavery and the bullies who supported and enforced it? There were allies in the room. Burford? McCoy? How could he approach them? And if he was wrong?

The madrigals finished the carol to loud applause. Keller started to clap, then threw his head back, laughed, and banged his hook on the table. Women laughed. Nat Burford slapped Keller on the back. The madrigals smiled and curtsied. Sarah Strong fanned herself with her hand. Matrons brought the singers cups of cider. The laughter and talk grew louder; the room felt cozy, but not close. Surely someone had a flask. Joseph thought about slipping out and hurrying home to fill his own flask. A quarter of an hour home and the same to return. But the night was cold and moist. He'd ask around.

Ig was telling a story about a possum under his floor making all sorts of racket at night, directly beneath their bed, and his idea to get Pig to bring his feist down from Cedar Springs and send it under the house after the possum. Rachel listened to him, lovely, with her empty cake plate and cup in her lap, no doubt relieved to see her husband joking with friends.

"We need a cat," Rachel said. "The mice virtually own the place, especially at night. I can't sleep for their scurrying."

"Well, especially since the black snakes have denned for winter," Malachi said.

"I'll take the mice," Rachel said.

"Strychnine works wonders on pests," Rosemary said. "Mr. Peak will sell small amounts to white people. Otherwise, rats would run the town."

"I'm afraid it might work wonders on Bob Boatman's mongrel," Rachel said. "The poor, mangy thing is forever sniffing around the place. It seems friendly but looks so horrid I'm afraid to pet it. Bob loves it, though. Boys can be that way about even the most abject dog."

Joseph caught Rachel's eye, arched his brow in question, and tipped his hand to his mouth in a sipping motion. She raised her empty cup from her lap. "Uh, thank you. Would you mind?"

He took her cup and cake plate. "Delighted." He nudged Ig with his elbow. "I can't abide a man who lets an expectant mother go thirsty." Ig, shaking hands and laughing with Ebenezer Euler and two others from La Reunion, missed the remark.

Joseph worked his way toward the table and punch bowl. A cluster of women blocked his way. He said, "Excuse me, ladies," and they made way without acknowledging him or slowing their conversation. He found the punch bowl empty, but several cups of eggnog remained. As he was selecting the fullest cup, he heard one of the women, Maude Collins, a dark-haired woman he guessed to be in her early thirties—the wife of Angus Collins, one of Dallas's many lawyers—say, "Well the old devil is surely dead by now. I'm sure we'll get it all in the *Herald* any day."

He glanced back at the women. Maude's audience, a covey of younger wives, were all nodding, some solemnly, some fiercely one, a tall, plain, rawboned redhead, a little sadly. "The audacity to think he could take over the federal armory," Maude said. "And for him to believe the niggers would put themselves in peril to go along with his scheme. Pure absurdity."

The madrigals struck up "The First Noel," and the conversation quieted as everyone turned to watch and listen. Joseph made his way back to Rachel, who smiled and thanked him without ever meeting his gaze. She sipped. There. Just a glance. Those blue eyes.

It began like a low hum moving through the room toward the end of the second verse, and by the beginning of the third, Joseph noticed that Major McCoy, Judge Burford, and several of the men were singing. Women joined, and now you could discern the words:

> *To seek for a king was their intent,*
> *And to follow the star wher-ev-er it went.*

Malachi stood beside him, slapped his back, squeezed and shook his arm. Joseph imagined Bekah and Samuel the following night at their Christmas gathering. What mutual sympathy and affection must a gathering of slaves feel, full and fortified, singing around a fire on a December night?

The singers stood in an opening amid Dallas's bourgeoisie. Joseph looked across the room, past the faces of the madrigals. Beards and bristly mustaches and sideburns rose and fell. Men still holding cups, and old Ancil Romack, leaning back into a window, drunk, holding a flask, nodding to the song, his moist eyes closed. Only a few stern patriarchs stood silent. Even the children had joined. The stronger voices began to assert themselves. He heard Rachel's thin voice just behind him, Ig's baritone, and Rosemary's soprano.

No-el, No-el, No-el, No-el.

Joseph sang through the lump in his throat. Then, across the room and to the right, he caught Bill Keller's eye. For an instant they regarded each other, Southerner to Southerner. Solemn and singing, Keller nodded and lifted his hook.

CHAPTER 35

January 1860

I t felt like the grippe. His eyelids were hot, foretelling fever. His legs felt restless. They'd be aching soon. His thoughts came slow. His head hurt. At the kitchen table, Bekah sighed again, hound-eyed, and touched her temple. She felt it, too, but wouldn't admit it. Or if forced to admit it, she wouldn't complain.

She was pulverizing sassafras root for a tea. She'd already tried a rhubarb concoction, but the little boy, Nathan, lay on Bekah's bed, burning up with fever. Martha, his mother, sat in a chair beside the bed, shivering, a quilt wrapped around her legs, a blanket around her shoulders. She'd been dozing on and off all day.

When they showed up with David about ten o'clock the night before, Nathan already felt poorly. His throat hurt so that he could barely croak his name. He woke up in the wee hours crying, unable to talk at all. Bekah made the rhubarb tea, which seemed to loosen his throat a bit. Now nothing worked. He'd been asleep—or unconscious—all afternoon. So far, only Samuel had escaped the sickness.

"If this don't work, then I don't know," Bekah said. "I never felt a child that hot."

Joseph sipped his coffee. It felt good on his throat. Women recommend saltwater and various revolting kinds of smoke and teas, but he'd take coffee for a sore throat—or just about any ailment that didn't attack his stomach. He'd have his with a splash of whiskey right before bedtime. You didn't want to imbibe too early, or else you'd have to maintain a mild drunk all day to forestall a hangover, which could be about as bad as a mild case of grippe.

The little boy, though, was deathly ill. "We can't very well fetch a doctor."

Bekah said, "We'll be fetching the undertaker directly if that fever don't break."

"They'll be fetching the undertaker for us if we let the wrong person in here." He knew Bekah was right, but he couldn't seem to work up any urgency. His mind trundled.

Bekah worked the pestle. "Maybe Cathlyn knows something to try. Samuel could get up there before dark."

Joseph looked out the kitchen window. The weak January sun lighted the bare branches of the oaks, elms, and cottonwoods. The sky was pale blue and cloudless. The water bucket in the shop had been frozen solid that morning. They'd have another hard freeze tonight. Nathan didn't have a coat—just a rough and filthy cotton shirt, wool breeches, and brogans twice too big. Martha wore a work dress that had once been white. She came with her feet wrapped in strips of burlap.

"I'd better go, then," Joseph said. "Samuel can't be caught out on the road tonight. I don't see how these two made it down here."

Word of Martha and Nathan's escape had reached Dallas before they had. Outriders looking for runaways had barged into farmhouses up on White Rock Creek. Pig had run into a little group of riders along the road. They had dogs that Pig allowed couldn't find their food pans. Keller and his vigilance group had been riding the roads at night. Zeph Newton rumors were flying again. Everyone who came in the shop had heard something. More rumors about stolen strychnine. Negroes meeting in secret on the river in the middle of the night. Their Christmas gathering was nothing but a big meeting for the purpose of planning an uprising.

"You'd fall off your horse before you got out of the yard." She stood and dumped the powder into a pan of hot water. The tangy-sweet smell filled the kitchen.

There was a rustle, and Martha appeared in the doorway. Her dress hung on her thin frame. Joseph doubted she weighed ninety pounds. The top of her head wouldn't reach his shoulder. Her torn and abraded foot wrappings trailed her. Her eyes were hollow, her face gaunt. He guessed her to be in her mid-twenties, but already her lips and cheeks sank where teeth should have been. "I can't wake him up." She listed. "He won't pay no attention to me. He ain't movin'." She covered her eyes. "I can't—Marse—I done killed my boy." She leaned against the door frame. "My other one's gone; now I done killed this one."

Bekah went to her and hugged her, then led her down the hall. Joseph followed. Nathan lay beneath the quilts, his arms at his sides, his eyes two-thirds closed. Joseph feared he was dead, but Bekah laid the back of her hand against his cheek. "Lord. I never felt anybody that hot." She looked at Joseph, her eyes still droopy but resolute.

He held out his hands in helplessness.

"Think of a lie," she said. "We can hide Martha." She held his gaze and cocked her head toward Nathan as if to reiterate what she didn't want to say in front of his mother.

They were talking about risking their lives. Maybe it was a blessing that grippe had him thinking like a dotard. He turned and walked back down the hallway, through the kitchen to the back door. He felt the cold through the windows and around the door, and it hit him like a punch in the throat when he opened the door to call Samuel from the shop.

The shop door swung open, and Samuel strode across the yard, dusting off sawdust. "Early supper?"

"Come on in here."

"You look poor as a summer possum." He came in bringing the cold and smelling like cured lumber. Joseph envied him.

"You know Dr. Marion."

Samuel turned solemn and looked down the hall. "Know of him. Young doc."

"I don't have any idea where he stands. We'll hide Martha. Our story is that I've borrowed a pickaninny from a Mr.—uh—Mr. Thompson who was passing through on his way to take care of business in Austin." He looked at Bekah and Samuel. Both nodded. "We'll put Martha in our hidey-hole. Can't we get her to eat something?"

Bekah said, "I'll try to get her to eat some bacon and a biscuit. I expect her throat's too sore. I ought to make a broth, but I ain't had time. She'll need blankets in that hole. That doctor might be here half the night. Maybe she can sleep. Just curl up good and warm in the dark."

"East side of the square?" Samuel asked.

"Frame house. He's got a shingle out. The other three doctors—I know where they stand. Old man Pryor would have the law on us right now." He met their eyes again and held up his hands in question. "That's my plan. That's all I know to do. Speak now if you have reservations."

"I got all kinds of reservations," Bekah said. "But I ain't got no better ideas." She nudged Samuel. "Get on. That child's dying." She turned and headed back toward the bedroom. Samuel hurried out the door into winter sun.

Seconds later, Bekah came back up the hall, steadying Martha, who looked like she'd lost twenty pounds since the night before. "Be all right, honey," Bekah said. "Just hide you away for safekeeping while the doctor's here. You just leave all the worrying to us. Just curl up good and warm and get some sleep. You wanna try to eat somethin'?"

Martha didn't answer, just let Bekah lead her along.

"Well," Bekah said. "We'll be needin' some covers."

Joseph gathered a spare quilt, pulled the blanket off his bed, and hurried out to the kitchen where he found Martha sitting at the table gumming a biscuit. Bekah had poured her a cup of coffee. She said, "We got half an hour, anyway, before he gets down to the square and gets back. And that's if that doctor will get out in this weather to come all the way out here to the edge of town to see a little black boy."

"Oh, he'll come. He's got a wife and three little girls, and he knows I'll pay him." Joseph looked down at Martha, who didn't seem to be hearing any of it. She just chewed the biscuit. He glanced at Bekah, who shook her head slightly and grimly and shivered.

"You're not getting faint on me, are you?"

"Naw." She gripped the back of Martha's chair. "You want another biscuit, darlin'?"

Martha didn't answer but took a drink of coffee. Bekah had wisely filled it only half full. Still, Martha barely kept from sloshing it out. She finished, and they helped her up and out the back door. Halfway across the yard, Martha said, "I reckon I better visit the privy."

"We better hurry, sugar." Bekah looked about. They were standing in an open yard in broad daylight with a fugitive slave.

Joseph said, "Go on with her, and I'll get our hole ready."

Moving the lumber off the entrance took all his strength. He alternately sweated and shivered. He rested a few seconds after moving every two or three boards. He'd nearly finished when the two women came in.

"Well, ain't this something?" Martha said, looking around. She looked like an old woman. David should have seen she wasn't up for a trip to Mexico. He wondered what had prompted her to attempt a six-hundred-mile escape with a little boy. Something horrible, like rape or torture, or just grinding day-to-day degradation. Or had she slapped her mistress and run in fear? She shuffled up to the hidey-hole as Joseph pulled back the door. He wiped his brow, then picked up the lantern to light the entrance.

"It's a bit of a step at first. We'll help you, and then you crawl back away from the door. There'll be plenty of headroom if you're sitting. Fresh air comes in through a vent in the wall. Nothing to worry about." He got in up to his waist and then reached for Martha. She sat on the edge, and then he lifted and eased her in. He climbed back out, and Bekah handed her the blankets. "Honey, just put one underneath you to sit on—here." She got down in the hole while Joseph held the lantern from above.

"Move on back in here," Bekah said. Joseph could just see her feet while she arranged the covers for Martha. He decided the chamber was too small. He and Samuel would need to enlarge it and get more timbers in for support. At least they'd floored it. No need for anyone to sit on cold, damp ground. He should've checked the vent to make sure a cotton rat or something hadn't built a nest in there. He'd better fashion a screen or grill on the two ends. Maybe even fix some sleeping pallets down there.

"Now then," Bekah said. "Sugar, you just lay right here good and warm and take you a little rest. We won't leave you in here long."

She looked up at Joseph as she started to climb out, then staggered. He helped her up and out. "Rest easy now, Martha," he said. As he was easing the heavy door down, he heard Martha say, "Ain't this just the nicest thing y'all got here?"

They piled the lumber over the entrance and went back in the house. About half an hour later, Samuel let the doctor in the front door, then ran around to the back door to let himself in.

The young doctor was blond and balding with blue eyes and side-burns. He set his bag on the kitchen table. "I apologize for the delay in getting here. Half the town's sick. Live on a river and this is what you get." They led him back to Nathan, who, as best as Joseph could tell, hadn't moved.

"What's been done so far?" the doctor asked. He bent over the child, feeling his forehead. He pulled an eyelid open. Nathan didn't move. "Burning up."

"Sassafras and rhubarb tea," Bekah said. "That was this morning."

He shook his head in disgust. "Might as well rely on charms and incantations. This boy needs to be sweated at once." He looked up at Bekah. "Heat as much water as you can. Do you have fruit jars? Also we'll need a bucket of water and hot bricks. Mr. Shaw, you and your girl don't look so good yourselves."

"We better stay away from Miz Rachel for a while," Bekah said.

Dr. Marion said, "It's that wintertime miasma that comes up out of this river bottom. If it makes it to Mrs. Bodeker, she'll get sick. Staying clear of you doesn't have a thing to do with it."

Bekah nodded slightly. "Mmm-hmm." She watched him. "But it seems like to me you breathe in that miasma and it gets all over your insides, and then when you're sick with it you're breathin' it out and you might breathe it in somebody's face and then they breathe it in and it gets all over their insides."

The doctor smiled and winked at Joseph. "Fascinating. Mr. Shaw. I'm sure you have many uses for such a lively mind."

Bekah heated water on the stove while Joseph and Samuel gathered jars and whiskey bottles—whatever containers could be sealed. These they filled with hot water, corked or sealed with lids and, per the doctor's instructions, wrapped with towels, flannel, or linen. They put two in socks.

Dr. Marion pulled back Nathan's covers and placed the vessels between his legs, along his sides, and under his arms, and packed them against his face, using pillows and covers. Then they covered him under a pile of blankets.

Dr. Marion rolled down his sleeves and buttoned them. "Keep water on the stove. As these jars cool, refill them and put them back. Keep at it until he sweats. Let him pour out his impurities for at least an hour, then remove the heat, wash him, and keep him covered. He should improve markedly by morning. If he doesn't, come and get me at once."

In the kitchen, as the doctor put on his coat, Joseph said, "Shall we settle up now or wait and see how he does?"

Marion seemed to consider this for a moment. He laid his hand on his bag. "Oh, let's go ahead and settle up now. I don't think there'll be another visit. Three dollars ought to do it."

Joseph took the money from the cash drawer in his office and paid the doctor, who put on his hat, and, without looking at them, said, "Good evening to you," then stepped into the dark yard and climbed into his buggy. He slapped the reins and drove out onto Polk Street.

They waited a few minutes, then went to the shop to fetch Martha. Joseph staggered as he dragged off the first piece of lumber. Samuel removed the rest and pulled up the hidey-hole door. They held the lantern over the entrance. It lighted Martha's feet. They called to her. After a few seconds, she sat up, squinting in the lantern light.

"Doctor's gone home," Bekah said. "Let's get you out of there." Samuel dropped down into the hole and lifted Martha out. "Like liftin' a youngun," he said.

Nathan wouldn't sweat. They changed water four times. Not long before midnight, Joseph, Bekah, and Samuel sat as close to the stove as they could, dozing. Bekah and Joseph shivered and hugged themselves. They'd piled all of the blankets on the child. They woke to Martha's screams.

———

They prepared the boy while his mother slept. It had taken two shots of whiskey to quiet her screaming, several more to put her to sleep. Joseph had wanted to fetch Ig, but Bekah convinced him Ig would just carry the grippe home to Rachel.

By 3 a.m. they'd dug the grave in a cedar break a half mile south of the town cemetery. They trusted the dense cedar to hide the glow of their lanterns. On the one hand, Joseph hoped Martha would sleep for hours so he could get a few hours of sleep himself. On the other hand, he hoped she would wake before they returned home so that Bekah would have to tell her he and Samuel had buried Nathan's body while she slept. He regretted this cruelty, yet they had already risked their lives by summoning the doctor. In hindsight, it was clear the boy was doomed. People rarely died of the grippe, even children, but Nathan had been too weak from his exertions to fight off the disease.

It was surprisingly warm in the cedars. Joseph had begun to sweat and had taken off his jacket. Now his throat ached and he felt light-headed, but he couldn't leave the digging to Samuel if they had any hope of getting back before sunrise. He leaned on his shovel. Samuel dug on. "You ought to go sit in the wagon and put your coat on," Samuel said. "Else I'll be diggin' a hole for you in a few days."

"Don't get your hopes up." He continued digging. The grave needn't be as deep as normal, just enough that coyotes wouldn't dig it up.

They dug waist-deep, then climbed out and carried the little casket back to the hole, each holding an end, lowered it in place with straps, filled and raked the grave, then covered it with cedar duff, branches, and other debris.

"Not even a headstone for the youngun," Samuel said. "I doubt we could find the place twice if we wanted to bring Martha back."

They tossed their tools into the back of the wagon, snuffed the lanterns, wended their way out of the thicket, and turned north toward town. Joseph caught himself dozing as they skirted the cemetery.

Samuel said, "Dear sweet Jesus, we're caught."

Joseph opened his eyes. Back in town, groups of torches and lanterns moved along the streets like swarms of fireflies.

The wind laid. Samuel said, "Listen!"

Shouts, barking dogs.

There was nothing to do but go home. They couldn't abandon Bekah and Martha. There'd be a patrol on every road leading out of Dallas. Ig and Rachel, the Meades and Van Husses would be implicated by association. The mob's vanguard probably had already busted into the house. Joseph felt oddly numb with the wind striking his feverish forehead. So this was it. Dr. Marion had alerted the local vigilance committee or the marshal. Now everyone in town knew about the fugitives. Samuel and Bekah would be locked up and sold at a bargain to anyone willing to take the chance on Negroes who'd been corrupted by an abolitionist. Not just an abolitionist, but a conniving infiltrator. A title he'd worn with pride among those who shared his belief. A most excellent radical. Now he'd see.

Samuel stopped the wagon. "I don't see no lights over by our place. Just the light in the windows."

"I imagine they're already inside. We've got to just go on in. You know of a good lie?"

Samuel started the team. To their left, weak moonlight shone on head markers of wood and stone. He and Samuel had dug most of those graves. He should be saying something to Samuel. Something about friendship and the good he'd done, about keeping faith. That he'd be thinking of him always. Instead he said nothing as the edge of town loomed. The swarms of lights moved along Water Street and the river and even across the river. Looking for them. Maybe somehow by just driving on into town they'd convince people of their innocence. But of course, the doctor had told of the sick boy. And no telling what Martha, in her grief and delirium and sickness, had said. No doubt Bekah had been slapped around by now. A bad girl from the get-go. People in town knew about her. It wasn't that far to Cedar Hill.

Joseph had always imagined a violent, desperate struggle. Yet now he was only sick and weak and riding back into town to give himself up. He'd rather sit in a warm jail cell than run or fight. He imagined the disappointment and outrage on the faces of his neighbors and fellow businessmen, and now felt vaguely ashamed and traitorous, much to his deeper shame. Surely they wouldn't hurt Rachel. Maybe they'd run her and Ig out of the county.

Samuel drove up Polk Street and into the yard. There were shouts in the distance. They unhitched the horses without speaking. Who was in the house armed and waiting?

No one but Bekah and Martha, both asleep. Bekah had left the coffee-pot on the stove. They filled their cups. Samuel looked out the kitchen window and said, "Somebody's coming."

Joseph started down the hall. "We can hide Martha." But then came a knock on the back door, and now through the window Joseph could see torch and lantern light dancing on the sides of the shop. The neighborhood dogs were raising hell. "Just open it."

Samuel opened the door. Ig and Malachi stood holding lanterns. Other members of the congregation stood behind him. Ebenezer Euler's hat poked around the edge of the jumble of shoulders and heavy coats. They all looked grim.

Joseph said, "Well." Torchlight and cold and the smell of wool and tobacco spilled into the entryway. Samuel looked back at him.

Ig said, "You two would sleep through the Second Coming. We've already been by here once and nearly beat the door down."

They didn't answer.

Malachi said, "Well, they're up now. Wrap up, boys. They'll be dragging the river come first light. Doc Marion went out for a call this afternoon and never made it home."

Mist hung on the river while men in rowboats dragged huge treble hooks along the bottom. Groups hunted along the banks, in barns and stalls, beneath buildings and porches. Pig's hounds and other dogs snuffled in brakes and thickets, causing Joseph and Samuel to worry that they'd find Nathan's grave, but no one looked that far south. Local women and three ministers, including Ig, flocked in and around Mrs. Marion and her girls. Everyone knew the doctor was dead. Indians? There hadn't been an Indian attack in years, and it happened way over near Bird's Fort.

Robbery perhaps. The doc usually had money on him from house calls. Dallas had grown, and you didn't know everyone anymore. And people just let the niggers run loose of a night. They might be jovial enough in the light of day, but you didn't want to meet one after dark when he had the drop on you. And Doc Marion as kindly and indulgent as he was.

Samuel had said the doctor had been alone in his office and had left without telling anyone. It seemed unlikely anyone had been out on such a cold evening to see him en route to his house call.

Joseph and Samuel searched for a while along the riverbank and the fields on their end of town. Joseph wrapped his throat with two scarves—one wool, the other flannel—and pulled up his collar so that he could barely turn his head.

At home, Martha wouldn't eat and said little. After three days the town gave up the search, and Martha went to sleep and never woke up. Joseph, feverish and chilled, dreamed of being buried alive. Sometimes, in his dreams, he was Nathan, sometimes himself. Always it was cold and dark and smelled of decaying wood, dust, and rotten cloth, like the inside of an old shed. Even after he woke, the odors clung to his nostrils.

Five nights after burying Nathan, Samuel and Joseph raked the debris off his grave, dug another one beside it, and laid Martha to rest next to her son.

CHAPTER 36

The last time had been in Tennessee, in a tiny clearing in a cedar thicket just down the hill from an earthen dam. It was warm and pleasant on the thick carpet of duff. The smell of resin mixed with the strange scent of his hair. When he unbuttoned his shirt, the pallor of his chest and freckled arms shocked her.

The baby, Flora, slept a few yards away, close to the fire. Privacy was a luxury for white women who could put their children in bed in another room.

Sorrow drove them together.

The night before, Levin McGregor slipped away from her and Stephen Conklin and swam back across the creek. They crawled out of the water—shivering, gasping, trying not to shout—and clambered up the bank clawing at roots and vines, rocks, anything that might give them purchase. Flora was on her back, still asleep from paregoric. She needed to get Flora out of the knapsack and warm her before wetness and cold put her to sleep for good, but the dogs were closing. She could distinguish their individual bawls now and hear their rustling across the creek, and, farther back, the shouts of the slave catchers.

They topped the steep bank like maniacs. Something left her throat, probably a scream, but she didn't hear it or didn't remember it. Levin had been right there beside her when they started across the stream; she sensed his presence now, thought she heard him and even glimpsed him where moonlight filtered through the tangles.

They started up a gentle hill, through bigger timber. Stephen grabbed her arm. She stopped and steadied herself by wrapping her other arm around the trunk of a tree. The sagging, dripping knapsack pulled at her shoulders. Her lower back burned. Flora felt like dead weight. Maybe they'd given her too much paregoric. Maybe her head had banged against something when they'd clambered out of the creek.

"Listen," Stephen said.

The dogs hadn't crossed the stream. Instead, they continued upstream on the far side. After a moment, when they were no longer desperate for breath, Stephen said, "What the hell?"

"I don't know," she said. "You reckon they're huntin' a crossing?"

"If we crossed, they wouldn't think twice about crossing. We left scent all over that water. Goddamnit, they're running something. Somebody. Where's Levin?"

"He came across. I seen him. Maybe he's on up the hill."

"On up the creek is where he is. Son of a bitch. I should've known." The dogs were close to their quarry now, almost bayed, scent-crazy, their howling echoing off down the draw.

They listened. She sobbed. Stephen cursed. "He was bound and determined to do it," he said, then took her arm.

After a few minutes, they ran out of the timber and into crop fields. The hounds' clamor faded behind them. Farmhouse lanterns shone in the distance.

"I'll carry the child," he said.

"No."

A couple of miles north of the farm, they took shelter in a dilapidated tobacco barn. She eased Flora from the pack and pulled off the child's wet clothes while Stephen stood at the door, looking into the night. She pulled her sodden dress down to her waist and held Flora against her bare breasts, covered her with her arms, and snuggled into a corner.

The baby shivered. Bekah imagined frost on the grass, frozen mud on the creek banks, skim ice around the ponds, and shaggy, luxuriant winter coats on the cattle and horses in the pastures—and then her own thin, wet dress draped about her waist.

She sat in the dust, drew her legs beneath her, and sat Indian-style, hugging Flora. She felt their heat, their life, escaping between unchinked logs.

She looked back over her shoulder at Stephen silhouetted against the moonlit pasture. "She's freezin' to death."

"Bless her heart," he said. "Clear night. It'll warm up early. We'll be thawed by mid-morning."

"No. I mean she's freezin' to death. She won't make it through the night, much less 'til the sun gets up good." She could only whisper.

"Everything's wet, or I'd build us a fire. My tinder is soaked."

They'd left his coat and blanket roll in the boat. His shoes still squished. She turned away from the corner. "You gonna have to come here."

He came to her and knelt. "What can I do for you?"

"For her. Sit down here. Close. Get over top of her. Take your shirt off."

"Take my shirt off. Hell."

"We got to get skin on skin. Your shirt's still drippin'. Unbutton it and pull it back anyway."

He looked around the dark barn. "Maybe there's a tarp or horse blanket or something."

"She'll freeze to death while you're lookin' for it. Sit down right here. Facing me."

He sat down, his knees against hers. He shivered so that he barely managed his shirt buttons.

"Now then. Lean over her."

He did. She leaned toward him. Their foreheads touched. He drew back.

"No," she said. "It'll be all right. Lean over her. We got to get all around her. Hide on hide."

He brought his forehead back to hers. "Put your arms around here," she said. He embraced them. They shivered, but the child warmed them, and they warmed her and each other. After a while, the shivering subsided to an occasional shudder.

Bekah's back ached, but their breath warmed their faces and she imagined the warmth falling on the baby.

"We won't be able to get up from here come morning," he said.

So that white, clammy-looking skin she'd imagined would be like the belly of a fish gave warmth like her own skin. His breath came out hot and strong. The baby slept.

"No need to cry," he said. "We'll make it."

She hadn't realized she was crying. "I get tears on you?"

"I smelled 'em. They smell like new sweat, and I don't imagine you're sweatin'."

She laughed, sobbed. "Be drippin' on the baby."

He drew closer. She pulled her knees in tighter and slid her face to one side, wetting his stubble with her tears. "Oh Lord," she said.

"We'll make it."

"I know it." They would make it through this night. After a while, his breathing steadied. Her feet and legs grew numb, but she felt Flora's warm head and breath on the inside of her arm and on her neck. She checked the tiny feet. The toes curled. There would be no frostbite.

A small rustling woke her. New sunlight spilled through the cracks on the eastern wall. She drew back. Stephen listed forward but righted himself, still snoring. She heard the rustling—or scratching—again, from above. On a beam near the roof, a pair of barn owls peered down at her. They looked awfully warm and satisfied.

Next afternoon he led her along a creek, up a hill through cedars and brambles to a ten-foot dam. The tailrace poured from an eight-inch clay pipe.

They scrambled up the slope and peered over the top. A half-dozen geese flushed near the head of a two-acre pond. Two pintail drakes and a hen flew from the base of the dam. Their beating wings whistled as they climbed, then banked and flew back over the dam. There were no signs of habitation, but the muddy banks were well churned by hogs and cattle. A narrow strip of timber along the inlet creek gave way on both sides to stumpy pastureland.

They retreated into the cedars below the dam, gathered firewood, and unwrapped the cornbread and hardboiled eggs they'd been given by slaves that morning, after they'd risked a visit to three tiny cabins in the woods bordering a huge cornfield. Two elderly women and a little girl seemed unsurprised when the fugitives rapped on the doorframe. Word had preceded them. Stephen had money but hadn't dared travel along the roads or attempt to buy food. Even if he left her in hiding, a strange, bedraggled white man would draw attention. The women gave them a thin, holey quilt and a bundle of grass sacks, then apologized for having no coats to offer. He'd cut open the sacks to make blankets, which they draped about their shoulders.

"Better wait awhile on that fire," he said. "In case somebody comes down when cattle come to water. After dark, nobody'll be out to smell the smoke."

"Well." Flora sat beside her, on the knapsack, quilt draped around her, eating little bits of cornbread. The paregoric had worn off, and she'd been fussy all day. She ate as fast as Bekah could crumble the cornbread for her. Thank God for early teeth. Nine months old and already weaned. She could just imagine running around these woods heavy with milk and Flora on her back. Like she'd let a man carry her baby. He'd probably forget about her back there and rake her off on a tree trunk.

She wouldn't be drinking from the pond, not with cattle wading in it. She'd cut up an egg for Flora, then sneak upstream with her tin cup.

He sat on a log, grass sack draped about his shoulders, making a show of not looking at her. She knew it, because she'd spent most of her life aware of white men's eyes, not wanting them on her.

But now—

She didn't know. In the barn she'd felt mostly relief that her baby would live another night. Mostly.

She didn't know this man. What drove him to take these risks? A sense of justice, or outrage at injustice? Pity? Well, then, pity would do just fine if it got her to James and freedom. How did he feel about Negroes in general? He loved Levin McGregor. The two men got on better than any two brothers she'd known. Still, how could he know a black man fully? Did he think that Levin gave himself up for him? Probably. Had he? Or for her? Or for every runaway slave who had been caught and whipped and burned? Here, you can have me, but you won't get the one you're after. Better teach them dogs to tell one nigger from another. She's gone. And the baby, too. You'll have to get what you can for me. What's left.

Flora fussed while Bekah cut up an egg. Probably thirsty. She'd better get up and go to the creek. Stephen whistled at Flora. "Hey, hey, hey, hey, little girl! Lookee here!" He poured water from a canteen into his cup, then handed it to Bekah. She held it for Flora, who took it with both hands and drank with her mother's help.

Bekah looked in the cup as she handed it back. "Cornbread and baby slobber in there now."

"I don't reckon it'll kill me."

Then again, he might just be a decent man who hadn't been with a woman for a long time, a man who knew he might very well be dead by this time tomorrow, and here sat a woman.

Stringy, light-brown hair plastered beneath his hat. Reddish stubble on his chin, thin sideburns, blue eyes, and freckled hands. He'd come after her, things had gone badly, and now he seemed willing to stay with her. He could have left her and the baby easily enough. Then he'd be relatively safe after he got a little farther north. He'd been kind in the barn. Or at least he'd proven willing to take off his shirt and press up to a young woman's bare bosom. How about that for selflessness and sacrifice?

Still, he hadn't abandoned her. But might he? Could he be just a few thrusts and spasms away from leaving? Or was he fully committed to seeing her and Flora safely northward? Or purely committed to his cause or to finishing the job for which Levin sacrificed his freedom? And how should she judge him? Was he any less decent—less fine, even—if he stayed with her and risked his life for her out of pure principle?

What was he thinking as he looked out the barn door into the brittle, clear night? Surely he considered, if just for an instant, slipping away from this woman and child huddled in the corner. Perhaps those were his exact thoughts when she said, "This child is freezing to death." But he came without hesitation. Because he thought, *My Lord, I have to help them?* or *Well, hell, a man has to live with himself. I know who I am and I ain't a man who cuts and runs from a wet, freezing woman and child. What good would life be if you knew you were that kind of a sorry son of a bitch?*

And then, flesh to flesh, what did he think? *Well shit, ain't this something. Now I've done it. I'm cooked for sure.* Or, *Damn. Ain't this something. Well now. Things ain't ever as dire as man might think. I believe I'll hang with it a little longer.*

Exhausted, footsore, hungry, endangered, exposed, bereaved, with a baby, and this was all she could think of. Shameful. And Robert barely a year dead. Talk about a pitiful, hard-up woman. Like this man would do anything but dump her off on somebody else the first chance he got. Let some other fool risk his neck for her. And Levin brought to bay by a pack of dogs, beaten to his knees, probably branded and hauled south, goaded and degraded worse than the sorriest head of livestock.

The afternoon had grown cloudy; the wind picked up cold and raw, but the cedars sheltered them.

"Won't be as cold tonight," he said.

"Reckon it'll rain?"

He seemed to consider this for a moment, then said, "We've been wet and cold before, ain't we? We'll get by again if it comes to that."

Flora had crawled into her lap, and she realized she was rocking her, stroking her hair and face. Trying to put her to sleep? He was looking at her. "What is it?" she asked.

He drew up his knees and clasped his hands around them. "I don't know of a prettier sight."

She'd heard similar remarks: "Ain't you a pretty thing, now? Well, now, look here at what a pretty little nigger girl." What did he say? How did he say it? "Pretty sight. Pretty girl." She eased Flora to her left arm, prepared to push herself up with her right.

"Mother and child," he said.

"Aw." She relaxed a bit, moved Flora back to her lap, studied her to avoid looking up at him. "She's 'bout asleep."

"I can't recall you ever layin' her down."

"She'll freeze."

"If you want to make a pallet for her, we can cover her with the quilt and these sacks." He pulled the sacks from around his shoulders. "Wrap her up good and warm."

"Then you'll freeze to death."

"Nah. Air ain't stirring in here, and we'll have a fire after dark."

She felt threatened again. Here was a white man trying to separate her from her baby. Get her by herself.

"Me and her keep one another warm," she said.

He smiled. "Anyways, if you was to put her down, you might not be able to keep your feet on the ground."

She laughed but was too busy parsing meaning and intent to enjoy the humor. "Look there. Sound asleep."

"I'll go ahead and build a little fire. Wood's good and dry. Nobody'll come around this late."

He scraped a bed for the fire, then whittled off shavings with his knife.

In a few minutes he had a small cedar fire going. The wind blew away the meager smoke as soon as it cleared the tops of trees.

They moved in close to the fire, facing each other. After a few minutes, he said. "Bekah, you don't need to worry about me."

"Worry about you."

"I mean, I wouldn't lay a hand on you."

They watched the fire. She began to shiver. He said, "Bekah, there ain't no need in you freezing. You remember what I just said."

She didn't answer. He scooted around the fire and said, "We'll just keep warm as we can. That's all." He added one of his sacks to the two already around her shoulders and handed his other one to her, then started to scoot away. She grabbed his forearm; he settled next to her. She pressed her arm against his, enjoying his warmth.

Minutes passed. The sky darkened. He fed the fire and put his arm around her and pulled her close. As she leaned into him, her forehead touched his neck. The fire blazed up, and the warmth felt good on her face. She was sleepy, but she didn't want sleep. She leaned further into him, and he turned his face to hers. Bewhiskered jaws, and those pale eyes. He could be some Irish overseer or bitter tenant farmer, the kind of man who hated Negroes all the more because he could not afford them. Yet there was nothing hateful about him.

"I'll fix her a pallet," Bekah said. "She's got her belly full. She'll sleep right on."

He said, "I'll get us little more fire and try not to burn the whole damn thicket up."

Fine hair on his pale, freckled belly reminded her of the underside of a redbone hound in summer. It would be dark soon. Clouds scudded overhead, and the tops of the cedars whipped, but where they lay, the air was still, and the thick boughs reflected the heat of the fire. It went too quickly, as she had known it would, for he was as nervous as he was needful, and they were new to each other. Perhaps he would stir again before Flora woke. But if not, his weight and warmth were enough.

CHAPTER 37

They never found Doc Marion. Some predicted he'd wash up in spring, when the river flooded. He'd hang up in brush or the roots of the elms and cottonwood, they said. Mrs. Marion and her three girls packed up and left for Waco, where her sister lived. She put the house up for sale through William Keller's Land Company.

Joseph went about his business, always listening and watching for unusual coolness or unusual solicitude from other townspeople. He detected none, just heard the normal complaints about the goddamn Black Republicans, northern abolitionist exhorters, and that nigger-loving traitor Lincoln.

He wondered who and what Marion might have told about Nathan. He wondered, too, if Bekah had killed him. Samuel couldn't have. He'd been away digging Nathan's grave. Ig and Rachel, the Meades and Van Husses had not been involved and had learned of the whole affair only after the fact. Al had not been around and had no reason to suspect Marion was a danger. That left Bekah.

Or perhaps the doctor really was robbed and murdered. That seemed to be the opinion around town. Still, Joseph watched Bekah and wondered. She could have used his shotgun, but no one heard a shot. She could have ambushed him and stabbed him to death. Certainly she was physically capable of the act, even when sick with grippe. But was she a killer? He suspected so. Not a murderer or indiscriminate killer, but someone who might kill you to save herself or those she cared about. She was a hater. He felt that. He'd seen it, and he suspected Susan Reynolds had seen it, too. Mrs. Reynolds probably slept much better since her husband swapped their first and last slave for funerary services.

CHAPTER 38

Samuel'd made headway with Bekah. She'd warmed to him. Lately, sitting at the kitchen table, he'd caught her eye while she worked in the kitchen. At the Christmas gathering she'd danced with him and stayed at his side while the brandy and persimmon beer softened her. She held his hand and laughed with him. Standing around the bonfire, she let him put his arm around her. As they sang, her hip swayed against his, and he looked into the cold darkness behind them, wondering what he could say to coax her away from the warmth, light, and fellowship.

While Samuel schemed, she drank more and shortly went from amorous to sleepy, then weepy and drunk, then sick and embarrassed as he walked her home well after midnight. He'd wanted to see her on to her room, but she wouldn't even let him in the back door. Still, he went to his cabin hopeful. There would be other nights. She'd dropped her guard, and he'd been there.

Joseph didn't wake them the next morning. He grinned and banged the bottom of a bucket with a hammer when Samuel walked out into the cold, clean brightness at mid-morning.

"Well?"

"Well what?"

"Don't give me that."

"She got drunk. Puked twice on the way home. That's all that happened."

"Never even snuck a kiss?"

"Got my arm around her. Then she went from happy to drunk."

"Whiskey?"

"Brandy mostly. Al got it somewhere. I think old man Huitt gives it to him."

"Downed it fast and it backed up on her. Hit her all of a sudden. You'll learn to work a little quicker, my young friend."

"You seen her yet?"

"She came to the back door awhile ago. Didn't say a word. Big crowd?"

"About everybody."

"I had to put the coffee on. I reckon you'll take it out of her wages. Somebody better die in the next week or two or we'll all be out of wages."

"Well." Normally he would have laughed at the comment, but he felt shy, panicked at the thought of facing her. What if she thought—or knew, truthfully—he'd hoped to take advantage of her drunkenness, and then, as if she needed another reason to hold him in contempt, he had failed out of timidity.

He found Bekah sitting at the kitchen table, nursing a cup of coffee, her chin resting in her hand. "Don't be 'specting to come in here and get fed."

"I surely wouldn't, knowing the cook the way I do."

She sipped, glanced up at him, no surlier than usual. "You know you about a ham-handed youngun is what you are."

"Look who come staggerin' in dog-drunk and puking her insides up. You make it to bed or you just slept in the middle of the hall? Joseph said he had to step over you this morning."

She snorted, sipped. Her eyes were puffy but held no contempt. He relaxed. This was just her way of facing him with some dignity.

"You ought to be ashamed of yourself," she said.

"For what? I never done a thing, and then I helped you get home. It's a wonder you didn't stagger off in the river."

She laughed. "Clumsy boy. There ain't no hope for you."

"I don't know what you're talkin' about and neither do you."

"You'll turn eighteen 'fore too long, won't you?"

"Month or two. 'Bout the time you turn sixty." He poured himself a cup. "I got to get to work."

"You better. Draggin' in here almost noon."

"I reckon you 'bout got dinner ready."

"Am I out there tryin' to tell you how to hammer and saw?"

He headed out the back door to work, relieved and hopeful.

Three days after Christmas, Ig and Pig rode up to Breckinridge to hear a sermon by a new minister from Illinois. Word was, he might be an ally. They'd listen and sniff around. Ig would manage to get himself invited to supper so that the two ministers could gingerly probe each other's theology. By late morning, Joseph decided he'd better go and see if Rachel needed anything.

Two coffin orders had come in, one for a very plain, inexpensive box of specified dimensions, the other one was to be stained, carefully fitted, with a felt lining and a hinged lid. Samuel had already cut the large pieces for the rough coffin and was thinking about what trim, if any, might be used. "Rough" meant different things to different people, so he usually erred toward refinement. If a very simple and inexpensive touch could lend a bit of dignity, then why not go ahead with it? He was digging through scrap lengths of ash strips when Bekah came out and said dinner would be ready in a few minutes. He needed to find a good stopping point.

He acknowledged her and went on searching then, sensing her presence, looked up to see her watching him, tracing her finger along the edge of the lid he was thinking of trimming. He arched his brows in question.

"About ready," she said. "Come on."

He washed up and ate at the table with her. They talked little. They rarely ate alone together. After dinner he was dipping a drink from the water bucket when she came out with two pails of ashes from the stove. He offered to take them on to the ash pile. She declined. He watched her walk across the yard and turn right by the barn, holding a bail with only the two fingers of her left hand. Seconds later, she reappeared, the empty pails swinging at her sides. She walked across the yard toward the back door, purposefully focused straight ahead, then she turned and looked at him. Just for an instant. At him—him, not to see what he was doing or not doing. Not looking at him as she might look at Joseph or a chair or the stove or a dog trotting up the street. Her glance was not offhanded or even confident. More like hopeful. She didn't smile, just turned and carried the pails in the back door.

He went back to work, distracted by thoughts of firm thighs.

Then the back door opened and shut. He heard quick steps and swish of legs working under a dress. He took care not to look up until she'd come in and stood there for a second or two.

She said, "You reckon you could help me real quick?"

He laid his awl down in the coffin and took off the heavy canvas apron. "What you got?"

"Somethin' has died. It's behind the bookcase, best I can smell, but I can't move that old big thing by myself."

Sure enough, they found a small rat dead behind the bookcase. As she scooped it up with the ash shovel and broom, she said, "I don't know why we don't keep a cat."

"Every time we've tried to keep one, something comes up out of the river bottom and eats it."

"You'd keep it inside of a night," she said.

He took the spade from her and went outside and slung the rat carcass in the grass and brush across the street. It wouldn't be there long. Not in this hungry country. Back inside he started to ease the cabinet against the wall. It caught on a rough spot in the floorboards and nearly tipped over. He reached up just in time to keep a shelf full of books from falling out. "Lord!" Bekah said.

He pushed again, but it wouldn't budge. He got down on one knee. "I'll push down low and you push up high. Hang on a second." He pulled the case back an inch. "Now then."

They pushed. Bekah grunted, and he felt her taut calf and thigh against his side. The case caught for an instant and then broke free and slid back against the wall. He stood up, but she didn't move; he had her pinned back in the corner formed by the wall and bookcase. She smiled, and for the first time since he'd known her, he saw mirth in her eyes.

"Clumsy, ham-handed pup," she said, shaking her head, rolling her eyes. "I reckon I'll help you this one time. But you better pay attention."

CHAPTER 39

As much as Pig Nuchols liked Richard and Hilda Van Huss, and hoped their meat market earned them a good living, he couldn't understand why anyone other than the aged, infirm, or incompetent (Ig Bodeker, say) would pay for a cut of meat. The creek bottoms were full of it, especially wild hogs, which would fetch you a month's worth of eating for the price of a few ounces of lead and two or three hundred grains of powder. And you could dig your lead out, melt it down, and remold it. You couldn't shoot clean through a young sow, let alone a big old hairy boar, so only a lazy man or a sorry shot lost lead. True, if you fouled up and shot too far forward of the lungs and hit shoulder bone just right, your ball might bust up into five or six pieces, but if you stayed after them, you wouldn't lose much. Better yet, you didn't even have to figure in the expense of feeding your dogs, because they'd stay sleek and happy on whatever rank, gristly cuts Cathlyn or any other woman of quality would refuse to cook, cure, or can. Amazingly, unlike deer, bison, pronghorns, bears, and prairie chickens, you couldn't shoot hogs out. Their number just kept increasing. They tore up everybody's creek-bottom cornfields, spooked horses, broke down pens to breed and half-kill domesticated sows, and generally made a nuisance of themselves. So why not eat as many of them as you could? Pig Nuchols had no intention of ever paying for a bite of meat.

That's why, on a blustery, gray mid-January afternoon, he was saddling his horse and trying to decide which dogs to run, instead of sitting inside tending the fire, talking to the boys, and watching Cathlyn mend various garments. He'd been meaning to get started since just after sunup so he'd have plenty of time to do his butchering before dark, but Cathlyn had started making up stories.

About mid-morning she started a long one about being a little girl and finding a Choctaw canoe covered in brush on the bank of the Tennessee River. Naturally, the Choctaws had stowed paddles inside. He decided he'd start hunting after dinner, which, to his mild guilt, consisted of sweet potatoes and ham sliced much thinner than usual. But by the time she picked up his empty plate, she'd paddled her canoe downriver, though numerous cataracts and streamside Indian and bandit attacks to the confluence with the Mississippi. Harrison asked his mother what she'd been eating during her trip. She stopped and thought for a few seconds, then remembered that in one of the inlet creeks, a beaver dam had burst, letting most of the water out of a pool and trapping hundreds of catfish in ankle-deep water. Of course, she beached the canoe, waded in, and bludgeoned several whoppers with her paddle.

But now, the problem was the cottonmouth that had fallen off a tree branch into her canoe. Or the snake was part of the problem. An equally pressing problem was that in her effort to kill the snake, she'd knocked a huge hole in the bottom of the canoe with her paddle. If Pig wanted to know how she survived a sinking canoe and a water moccasin between her feet, he'd better fetch home some pork.

So he had about half a day, plenty of time, and if it took him longer than usual to find a likely hog, he could just draw it and let it hang overnight to be sure he got in before Cathlyn got too sleepy to finish her story—or at least get through her current predicament. She'd been known to carry a story for a week or more. Usually the boys wanted to go hunting with him, but this time they'd shown no interest. He suspected they'd goad their mother to continue her telling. They could goad on. She wouldn't budge until she had the biggest audience possible.

He was cinching his saddle when he first heard hounds running a few miles to the north. And a sorry-sounding pack it was. Not a decent mouth in the bunch. And even worse, the loudest dog, and current leader, had a hoarse, fast chop that'd make you want to hurry up and shoot whatever he was running just so he'd shut up. It didn't cost one penny more to feed a sweet-sounding hound than one who sounded like a dry axle.

Unfortunately his best hound, and the one with the prettiest voice, a bitch named Margie, was ten days in season; not far enough along that she'd stand for a dog, but he'd locked her up in the toolshed to keep the three dogs, Hank, Zack, and Dan, from killing each other. Now he had to put up with all the whining and panting, and he'd had to line the base of the shed with rocks to keep them from digging and gnawing their way in.

Margie would probably half kill herself trying to break out of the shed when she realized he was leaving with the three dogs. He'd feel bad about her piteous whining and howling, but it wouldn't do to take a bitch in heat out hunting. Pretty soon, you'd collect dogs from every farm in the county.

He'd about given up trying to whistle the three dogs away from the toolshed and was about to resort to cussing when he looked up and saw Tobias Waller riding a mule up the trail to the cabin. There must be news. Tobias made it his business to spread fact and rumor with equal gravity.

Pig stepped out in the lane to meet him. The hounds weren't cooperating anyway. He'd probably end up cutting a switch. They'd be fine as soon as he got them out of smelling range of Margie. Tobias saw him and hurried the mule along, but his kicking looked way out of proportion to the amount of hurrying he achieved. Directly he rode into the yard. The three dogs didn't even bark at him.

Tobias sat his mule. He was slight, with thinning blond hair and wore spectacles. "I reckon you've heard," he said.

"Heard nothing but them dogs running."

"Some boys flushed a nigger just south of Breckinridge. Them dogs are onto him. You aim to get in on it?"

Pig watched his dogs. Zack was gnawing at the corner of the door. The other two were sniffing the walls so hard they might suck Margie through an unchinked gap.

"I just might, now that you mention it," Pig said. "Only problem is, I ain't got but one real nigger dog. The other three will start after one and then take off first time they strike hog scent, and there's a lot more hog scent in these parts than nigger scent."

Tobias eyed the hounds. "Well, I don't reckon it takes but one good one."

"Just what I was thinking, Tobias. I appreciate you coming by. I reckon I can hunt hogs any day. Let me fetch my little gyp."

Pig walked over to the shed. The three dogs realized where he was headed and converged on the door, leaping and pawing, plumes of slobber flying. Margie pawed and growled on the other side. Pig opened the door; the three dogs barreled inside as he grabbed Margie's collar, jerked her out, and closed the door on Dan's ear. "Well shit, boy! I never aimed to mash your ear." He opened the door a crack to check on Dan, who blamed Hank for the pain in his ear, so Pig had to let Margie go snorting around the yard while he waded into the shed and broke up a fine bawling dogfight. Fortunately, the fight didn't spill out of the shed before Pig could kick Dan, Hank, and Zack into different corners. "Goddamn you; don't you move 'til I get back!" he said, slamming the door. All three were sniffing at the door crack before he got out of earshot, but with Margie gone, they'd get along fine. Dan probably had forgotten all about his ear.

Tobias was still on his mule, watching Margie. "Little bitty thing, ain't she?"

"Let's see if she can't pull your ass out of the saddle." Margie would never hurt anyone, but Tobias didn't know that. And he was right about her size. Pig doubted she weighed sixty pounds.

"Well now, Pig, I wasn't slightin' your hound. I was just noticing what a pretty little thing she is."

"She is for a fact, thank you. Me and her best get on if we aim to tree this boy before dark."

"Good huntin' then." Tobias turned his mule back down the trail, but Pig didn't notice. He swung into the saddle and headed northeast, in the general direction of the barking hounds. Margie loped ahead, but he called her in close. He planned to stay out of the creek bottoms as far as possible; he didn't want her jumping pigs or deer or a bear. He'd have to stay clear of farms, too, or else they'd attract a pack of mongrels. When he first moved into this country, you still had to worry about attracting wolves.

He had easy work for her today, though she wouldn't like it.

He suspected the hounds he heard belonged to the slave catcher Ben Thigpen. He'd seen him around, and if he remembered right, Thigpen ran a pack of seven dogs and one gyp.

He rode for three miles, keeping to high ground as much as possible and often reminding Margie to stay close. The hounds drew nearer, and Margie often stopped to perk her ears, cock her head, whine, and listen. He stopped and sat his horse on high ground overlooking Waller Creek. The hounds were working southeast, heading downstream. No doubt their quarry was trying to throw them by crisscrossing the creek, but his ploy wouldn't work—not with such a narrow stream and experienced pack. The gray afternoon had grown colder. Pig smelled rain. They'd have sleet before midnight. He pictured the runaway wet up to his chest and maybe barefooted. Hopefully he'd gotten some guidance about where to go for help. He might even show up at Joseph's or Ig's place. Could David be the quarry?

He watched and listened. The dogs continued along the creek, and though he couldn't see them yet, he could tell they were working both sides. By the fervor of their barking, he guessed the runaway was still half a mile ahead. What the poor old boy didn't understand was how scent clung to the bottoms and in eddies, stuck to the rank streamside brush, and hung on the surface of slow water. He'd do better to forget the creek and head up into the hills, into the shifting breeze and light cover and rocky ground. David would know about that. This was an inexperienced fugitive.

When the hounds were a mile away, Pig whistled to Margie. "Right up here." She reared up on the saddle fender. He grabbed her by the collar and pulled her up across the pommel and rode down into the bottom. He rode down to a wide, gentle bend, into the stillness among oaks, elms, and willows. The creek had been out of its banks back in December, leaving an obvious floodplain of low brush festooned with alluvial debris.

He buckled a twenty-foot rawhide tether to Margie's collar and, while still mounted, led her up and down the bottom, holding the tether high to keep it out of brush, though a few times he had to dismount to disentangle hound and tether or to negotiate trees. They crossed the creek several times, and to his delight she stopped to squat a couple of times. The hounds were drawing near. The ground was trampled by hog, cattle, and horse prints, so no one would be able to track him, and the uplands were rocky. He'd take the long way home.

Here was one advantage of a sweet little gyp. Any one of those three jugheads back in the shed would have jerked him out of the saddle by now or hung him on a limb. Of course they were just what you needed whenever an irate boar decided he'd gone far enough.

He whistled for Margie and pulled her across his saddle again. She was wet and shivering from excitement instead of the cold. She whined and shook her head.

"You'll have me soppin' wet, girl."

Her tail thumped against his leg. They rode up out of the bottom at a trot. It would be dark soon. He kept to a draw so that the pursuers wouldn't spot him. They were close to the bend in the creek and closing on their quarry. The whole pack was at full cry now and sounded even worse close up. If he had a pack like that one, he'd be tempted to shoot the dogs instead of whatever they had treed.

The baying stopped suddenly. Only a few scattered howls and yips. The dogs would be all over that one poor gyp. Now men were yelling. Pig rode for home.

Half a mile from the cabin, he flushed three shoats and a sow from a bois d'arc motte. No need to even put Margie down, though she was about to throw a fit. He'd get his pork home in plenty of time to hear the rest of Cathlyn's story.

CHAPTER 40

"And do what?" Samuel said. She always had to get around to this. The anticipation of it almost ruined what came before. Still, it was usually worth it. She'd be cool toward him for a few days, but she'd warm up again.

"Whatever we wanted to. Or whatever we could afford."

"We wouldn't even understand what people was sayin' to us. Or about us."

"There's other Negroes there."

"So they tell me. You know for sure? You know any of 'em? They might be carrying slop jars for Mexicans." There went her leg. It had felt awfully good across his belly. He sighed and adjusted his pillow. He kept his other arm around her, but now she lay on her back, no longer facing him. "I swear."

"Well."

They lay in silence.

"You think you got it so good here," she said.

"I ain't got it bad and neither do you."

"We ain't free."

"Free as we're likely to be anywhere else and drawin' wages."

"Wages. To spend on what? Who you think owns this little shack we're layin' in? And this bed? Anyways, you're still payin' for that burying he swapped for me. All this talk about good work and abolition. And here we are. I can see it for a while. I'm willing to help for a spell, but I aim to live more than old age a free woman."

"Ain't nobody stopping you from leaving. He'd help get you started." The statement left him cold. He couldn't believe he'd suggested it.

"And as our legal owner, he could load us in a wagon and drive us all the way to Detroit. Or at least to Kansas or Iowa or somewhere where there's such a thing as a free Negro. Why yeah. He could drive us up there and set us free. Sign the papers. If he wanted to. Why even to Mexico."

"And then what?"

"We'd have our wages to get started with. He said anything about that? All I hear about is when it's safer or when things in Texas ain't so dangerous."

"It ain't like you just run off and leave a business for half a year while you take somebody to Canada or Mexico."

"We can pay him. We got wages, remember?"

"We ain't got them kind of wages."

"How long you been working in that shop?"

He didn't answer.

"See there? And who hands the money out? How do you even know yours and mine is set aside? You ever ask to see it?'

"It's in the bank."

"You don't know if you got it or not. How you know he ain't already spent it? He might just hand us a few nickels whenever we need it. Ask him for two hundred dollars and see what he says."

"What would I want with two hundred dollars at one time?"

"It's yours! Tell him you want to see it!"

"Then he'd have to go down to the bank and draw it out and then turn right around and take it back after I looked at it. That's a waste of a man's time."

"'Cause you can't go down there and draw it out yourself. And if you can't, I say it ain't yours. You think it's in your name?"

"It can't be."

"It's his money, then. Or he can say it is and you can't do a thing about it. Tell him you want it. See what he says. You worked for it. Then hide it. Least then you could lay hands on if you had to have it."

"I'll tell him I want it tomorrow, then." He wouldn't, but that was tomorrow's problem. Might as well say, "I don't trust you even though you're risking your life helping fugitive slaves." Tell a man who'd been trustworthy you don't trust him, and he might then assume you don't trust him because you yourself aren't trustworthy.

"That ain't what I'm gettin' at, anyways, and you know it," she said.

"Just arguing, what you doin'."

She sighed, rolled her eyes, and waved off his comment.

He turned toward her and propped himself up on his elbow so that he was looking down at her. "Anyways, don't you think I'd try to get away, go to someplace better if I thought I could find it?"

She looked into his eyes. "What kept you where you were before Joseph bought you?"

He plopped onto his back and slapped the mattress. "I wasn't but eighteen, and I didn't have no idea where to go or who could help me. I never even heard of anybody runnin' off. I wasn't on someplace like you was at, where people run off all the time. I was five years old when I come to Texas. I didn't know nobody and didn't even hardly know where the next farm was or which way Mexico was. I don't believe I ever even heard of Mexico until Joseph told me about it. I bet there ain't more than a dozen slaves in this whole county even heard of Mexico."

"You never came to Texas; you was brought."

"I can't even open my mouth."

"Somebody's hearing about Mexico. How many we moved through here already? And anyways, some people don't need to know where they're going, just that they're going. They won't just keep takin' it and keep takin' it 'til they're too old to do anything about it. Just some poor old nigger waitin' to be planted out with all the others that took it and took it 'til they didn't have to anymore."

"The folks came through here was a lot worse off than us. You seen what kind of shape they was in."

"You don't know nothing." She kicked the covers back and got out of bed and started dressing.

"What?"

She got into her dress, then fumbled with the top two buttons. She came around to his side of the bed and turned her back to him. "Button me up," she said.

CHAPTER 41

On the night of February 16, at about ten o'clock, Joseph answered a knock at his back door. There before him stood one-armed David, briar-scratched, wet to his waist, out of breath, and alone.

He said he'd been on his way to Dallas from a farm in Cedar Hill with a young fugitive named Jack Turner who wanted to take his chances northward. They'd planned to stop at Joseph's for a day or two before continuing to the Red River. After dark, they'd chanced the road. It was bitter cold; no one was likely to be about. And the dense cedar made for nearly impossible going. They rounded a bend and met a dozen riders, all white men from the sound of them. The riders gave chase. David and Jack headed for the brush. He could hear the men pursuing on foot, but he soon lost them in the rough terrain. He also lost Jack and dared not call out to him. If he could stay the night, he'd be on his way come sundown tomorrow. He'd cut across country, and he felt certain no one could track him.

Samuel and Bekah were both asleep. David hung his wet clothes on the backs of the kitchen chairs, put on a pair of Joseph's long handles, and made a pallet on the floor by the desk.

Two hours later, David woke Joseph. "Gotta run. I hear dogs runnin' south of here."

"You didn't say anything about dogs."

"They never had any. They must've went and got some." He'd put his wet clothes back on.

"Maybe they're running a hog."

"Maybe. If they are, that hog is comin' this way."

"Shit."

"I'm gone. You can tell them you heard somebody run through. Tell them whatever. I'm heading for the river."

"You'll freeze to death, man."

"I got a skiff hid. I don't aim to be bayed."

"The dogs will trail you right to the river, and then the banks will be lined with shooters from here to the coast."

"You got a saddle horse?"

Joseph shook his head. "We got a little time. I can get you across the river in the hearse."

"And when you get back, them dogs will be all over it. How you explain that?"

By now Samuel was up and dressed. He said, "I'll run down and get Brother Ig's wagon. Get in it and cover up so there won't be no air scent. Ig can drive you across, then go home. You can run down toward the river to lead the dogs away from here. Ig can pick you up along the way."

David said, "If the parson will head along Water Street, I'll get to him." He clasped their hands and headed out the back door. Samuel ran out the front.

Joseph plopped down in a kitchen chair. From her bedroom, Bekah said, "What in the world?"

Three quarters of an hour later, Joseph heard someone drive into the yard, then heard Ig's voice. Out back, Samuel was helping David out of the wagon. Ig said, "They've got the bridge blocked and a couple dozen men scouring the banks on both sides."

"Well, hell. Speak up, Ig. I doubt they can hear you clear up at the courthouse."

"Beg your pardon. I'm just a bit out of sorts."

"I reckon so."

Samuel said, "Gotta get him in the hidey-hole right now. Brother Ig, you'd best get on home."

David said, "Hidey-hole."

"In the shop," Joseph said. All this palavering and those dogs a half mile away.

"But them dogs will just track him right to our hole. Probably start trying to dig through the lumber pile," Samuel said. They had just stepped into the shop. Joseph was lighting a lantern.

David said, "Wait. Unlatch that window."

Joseph shook his head. "What?"

Samuel unlatched the window. David said, "I'm climbing out. One of you meet me outside."

Joseph said, "We ain't got time for this. You gotta get in the goddamn hole."

"I'll be gettin' in it all right. First I gotta fool them dogs." He pushed up the shutter and climbed out. Samuel started to follow, but David said, "Get back; don't touch me. You don't want my scent on you."

Joseph ran out the door and around to the back of the shop. David said, "I'll lay a trail just a little ways. You stay with me but just a little off to the side. He ran west along Polk Street, swinging out through the brush in the empty lots. Joseph ran along the road. After he'd gone a few hundred yards, he called to Joseph. "Come on in here. You fixin' to have to carry me."

Joseph ran to him, and David piggybacked him. By the time he got back home, Joseph was wondering what a man's arm might weigh. Both men were gasping for breath despite the cold, and Joseph felt heat and sweat through David's sleeve.

He ran into the backyard, thankful that he lived on the undeveloped edge of town. By now Bekah was standing in the backyard holding a lantern. "Good lord!" she said. She walked toward them, wide-eyed, then froze, holding the lantern up to light their faces. Joseph felt David's forearm tighten against his throat, then relax.

David said, "Uh . . . No."

Joseph tried to turn his head to look back at David. "'No' what?"

"Nothin'. I just . . ."

Bekah lowered the lantern.

Samuel yelled from the shop. He'd cleared away the lumber and had the door to the hidey-hole open. "Just dump him in, I reckon," Samuel said. He looked up at David. "Lord, you're peaked. You ain't gettin' sick on us, are you?" The hounds couldn't have been more than ten minutes away.

David said, "You don't reckon there's rats down in there, do you?"

"Rats," Joseph said. "Hell no. You're gettin' damn heavy."

"Fleas or mice or centipedes or spiders or something," David said.

"What? Shit. I'm backing up. Hop off down in there."

David said, "I . . ."

"Come on, come on, come on!" Joseph said.

Bekah held up the lantern. "He's done turned gray. Blood's left his face."

"He's done turned heavy as hell is what he's turned. Jump off." He staggered. "Hell, before I fall off in there and break a leg. Go on! You're stinking the place up. We never will get the goddamn dogs out of here."

David let go and dropped the three feet into the hole. He stood there, up to his waist. He looked down and then back at Joseph and the others. He was sweating. "Please—I thought I could, but I can't. Marster, please?"

Joseph said, "What? What's this 'marster' rubbish?" The stress had finally gotten to David; he was coming apart.

Bekah said, "He's done been in a hole. A bad one, I'd say."

"Well he's fixing to get in another one," Samuel said.

David looked down in the hole. His eyes were wild. Sweat dropped from his goatee. Bekah said, "I know," and ran out of the shop, toward the back door.

"Took off with the lantern," Joseph said. He still hadn't caught his breath and was slightly nauseated from the exertion of carrying a big man a quarter of a mile. They stood in silence for a few seconds. "Gotta get in there," Samuel said. "We'll all be cooked if you don't."

David said, "I got to piss."

"Give him that empty cider jug," Joseph said.

Samuel fetched the jug. David took it but stood rooted, looking at Samuel as if he didn't comprehend. The back door slammed and Bekah burst in, lighting the shop again. She held a nearly full bottle of whiskey. David eyed it.

"Sugar, you be just fine. You gotta hide," she said. "There ain't nothing in there to bother you." She pulled the cork. "Just a sip to get you going."

He took the bottle and took a healthy swig, then tried to catch his breath. Then he took another.

"That's right," Bekah said. "You just keep the bottle now."

"Dogs 'bout to make the edge of town," Samuel said. You could hear the voices of men well behind the dogs. One of the searchers from town could show up anytime. "David, goddamn," Joseph said. "You are going in that hole." Samuel had already read his thoughts and was easing toward the door. He could be back with the shotgun in a few seconds. "Come on now, friend."

David slowly bent his knees, but he kept his eyes on the lantern as if he could not bear to look down into the darkness.

"'Nother little sip, sugar," Bekah said. "You won't be in there long. It's nice and tidy. I watched these two dig it. Come on now."

Only his head protruded. Samuel grabbed the door and lifted it upright. David stopped. "They're almost here, David."

He took another drink, closed his eyes, and disappeared. Samuel eased the door down. "Want to watch his head."

They piled on lumber. Joseph said, "His smell is all over me." He ran into the house and tore off his clothes, bagged them, and stuffed them under his bed while Bekah drew a basin of water. Still in his long johns, he scoured his arms, neck, face, and hands, then changed into fresh clothes. Bekah ran out front and dumped the water in the brush across the street. By the time he stepped back into the yard, the dogs were barking about where Lamar Street petered out into prairie.

Samuel came out of his cabin with his shotgun. "Somebody said there was a nigger loose. Best be ready, I say."

Joseph ran back inside and fetched his own gun. The dogs were coming up Lamar Street. He looked out the window and saw torches and lanterns out on the prairie behind them. He went back outside and waited and listened to the pack.

The first two dogs ran into the backyard, bawling, knowing they were close and closing. Another six followed, a mass of ticking and ears and tongues and various colors of gray, blue, black, and tan hide stretched drum-tight over muscle and sinew.

Joseph didn't try to speak above the din. The dogs converged on the shop, oblivious to the people standing in the yard. They sniffed the foundation and piled on each other, leaping and pawing on the door. One started trying to dig under it.

Hoofbeats. William Keller rode into the yard followed by Marshal Moore, two deputies, and another man dressed in buckskin breeches, moccasins, and buffalo coat—the dog handler.

Joseph pointed his shotgun at the door of the shop. "I believe you've bayed him. We heard something out here and then heard the dogs. We've been trying to get him to come on out, but he ain't budging."

"By god, he'll come out in four or five pieces, then," the dog handler said. "Thug."

A long shadow detached itself from the shadow thrown by the house. A huge, dark-brindled dog, a mix of mastiff and God-only-knew-what other giant, vicious breed padded into the middle of the yard, its small, flop ears perked toward the shop door. Like the other dogs he seemed oblivious to Joseph and the others. The dog weighed 130 pounds if he weighed an ounce.

"Those damn dogs will turn my shop upside down. I've got fine furniture in there," Joseph said.

The handler dismounted and reached into a saddlebag. "Here. Help me tether these hounds." You could barely hear him above the baying. The big dog hadn't made a sound. When a dog really came for you, he never growled or barked. Thug watched, calm, businesslike.

They caught the hounds by their collars, pulled them away, and tethered them to posts and trees and the hearse. A blue-ticked gyp bawled her outrage into Joseph's ear while he tied her up. Then she went straight to work trying to chew through the rawhide tether.

"Open the door," Keller said.

Bekah, who'd been standing quietly just outside the back door, stepped toward the riders and raised her lantern to light Keller's face. A second later, she stepped back and stumbled on the doorstep, barely righting herself. Lantern light flew about the yard and into the trees.

Keller smiled, said, "Damn, girl."

Samuel raised the latch and eased the door open enough to allow a man to leave or a giant dog to enter.

Keller started to speak toward the door, then turned to the handler and said, "Ben, tell them goddamn dogs to shut up. I can't think straight."

Ben growled, "That's enough!" The dogs quieted. There were only a few whines.

Keller turned back to the door. He was still on his horse. "Listen to me, boy. You'd best get your ass out here right now if you ever want to see it in one piece again. We've already got your partner. He had more sense than you. He came looking for us. Turns out those hills are powerful dark and cold." He smiled and winked at Samuel. Ben and the marshal chuckled.

Nothing. Joseph prayed David wouldn't panic down in the hole. He tried to picture him hunkering there. Could he hear what was being said?

Keller turned in his saddle. "Well, go ahead and send that big old mean son of a bitch in after him."

"Thug! Nigger in there! Get 'im."

The dog ran through the door, and everyone followed. Before he could peer in, Joseph heard snuffling and toenails clicking and scratching across slick wood. The dog checked under tables, behind cabinets, sniffed the lumber pile over the hidey-hole entrance, but paid it no particular mind. Dull nose, Joseph thought. Keep those good noses tethered out in the yard.

Samuel said, "Whup," and pointed to the unlatched window.

"Well, goddamn," Keller said. "Usually they'll hole up. This one has some go to him. Ben, let them hounds loose. Get 'em around here to this window."

They untethered the hounds. Five of the six ran through the shop, snorted around and yelped, nosed open the window, and picked up David's old trail. The little blue-tick bitch did the same only after Ben pulled her away from the lumber pile. "What the hell's the matter with you?" he said. The dogs howled off into the night. Samuel and Joseph followed on foot.

There was a stiff breeze from the northwest. The dogs worked a few yards downwind of David's trail. Then, back in the brush, the bawling dropped off into confused yelps. Joseph squeezed Samuel's arm.

One of the dogs emerged from the brush, her head high, snuffing. The breeze lifted her long ears. Joseph recognized the more delicate profile. The bluetick gyp. While the other dogs snuffled about in confusion and Ben cursed, she came toward Joseph and Samuel. She stopped five feet away, nose lifted, inspecting them, then ambled off back toward the house. Joseph heard his pulse. His eyes watered in the breeze. Ben said,

"Somebody picked the bastard up right here."

Keller said, "Horseshit. You see any hoofprints or ruts?"

"We might see something when it's light."

Keller shook his head. "We've lost him."

"Let's go back to the shop," Ben said.

Keller said, "What in hell for? Anyway, there's nigger scent all over the place. These dogs might not even be after our man."

"I done told you, goddamnit, my dogs are after one particular boy."

"I never have believed that."

"You callin' me a liar? Worse than that, you callin' my dogs liars? I might let you get by with callin' me a liar."

"Well, where is he then?

"Somebody picked him up."

The gyp ambled back toward the shop.

Samuel said, "Uh, Mister Ben, one of your dogs 'bout to get off and get lost." Joseph considered Samuel's comment either an act of genius or a display of idiocy.

Ben never looked up. He kept his eyes on the hounds milling around, whining and yelping among the horses' hooves. "Gert! Get over here, you hammer-headed bitch!"

Gert stopped but kept her nose up into the breeze. Ben yelled for her again, and she turned and ambled loose-limbed and houndish back to the pack.

"There goes a dog, now," Samuel whispered.

Ben and the deputies were tethering the hounds together. Thug padded in and out of the lantern light.

Back home, they waited for two hours to be sure the slave hunters weren't returning, then Samuel moved the lumber again, raised the door, and looked into the hole. "He's either dead or dead drunk. I'm bettin' on dead drunk."

CHAPTER 42

March 1860

I t started a month prior, with a letter, addressed to Joseph, from A. Fox of Preston, Texas:

> Mr. A. Fox cordially invites you to his lumber milling establishment at Preston to review his facilities, price list, and inventory. He is certain that you will find his offerings far superior to those found in Dallas County, even allowing for freight costs. He is eager to expand his trade southward through mutually profitable relations with businessmen of honesty, boldness, and goodwill. We understand that a few of our associates have previously called on you, however Mr. Fox wishes to extend a long overdue personal invitation. We beg your prompt reply, as market conditions are especially favorable at this time.
>
> With warmest regards,
> David Singlearm, Manager

Joseph's prompt reply suggested three days in mid-March. Two weeks later there came a letter of gratitude with directions to the business office and lodging recommendations.

After a three-day ride, staying one night with Silas Hemby and camping along the road the second night, Samuel and Joseph arrived in Preston late on the appointed afternoon. They found the livery, then waded in ankle-deep mud along Main Street to the business office of Fox Milling, a windowless, one-story, mud-spattered, whitewashed box. Word of their arrival had proceeded them. Adolphus Fox waited in the doorway. Joseph stepped straight from the mud, through the door, and onto the unfinished board floor. Fox looked up and down the street before allowing Samuel inside. "I beg your pardon, young man. I'm sure you understand."

"Very well," Samuel said.

"I hate to keep my office so far from the mill, but I find conditions there too primitive for conducting civilized business," he said.

He offered straight-backed chairs and sat in another one at his cluttered desk next to a small stove. The only other piece of furniture in the room, a sparsely supplied liquor cabinet, sat within reach to his right. Cold rain pattered on the roof and gusted against the door. The room smelled of paper, ink, drying mud, cigar smoke, and full spittoons.

Fox was tall, heavy, and balding, but his movements suggested energy and physical strength. He had a miller's hands and bushy gray sideburns. He regarded them for a moment, as if deciding how to begin. "Oh. Beg your pardon. I'm sure you gentlemen could use a drink. What's your pleasure?"

Samuel looked at Joseph, who said, "Same as yours, whatever it is."

Fox slapped his thighs, got up, poured three generous shots of whiskey, and retook his seat. "Well, then." He drained his glass and wiped his mouth with the heel of his hand. Joseph doubted this was Fox's first snort of the day. He sipped his whiskey.

Fox said, "My associate, Mr. Singlearm, will be along shortly to show you our current inventory." He smiled. "I regret that it's a trip best made after dark. I'd offer to show you the mill right now but for the sorry weather. Anyway, I trust you're finding prices and quality to your liking in Dallas."

Joseph smiled, nodded, trying to decide how to proceed. Samuel sipped and scooted closer to the stove. Joseph said, "I assume there's something afoot?"

"You'll need to see for yourself. I believe it's important that you do."

"I understand. Where you from?"

"Come from Missouri by way of Tennessee."

"What brought you here?"

"Business took a downturn in Missouri. A certain wild-eyed preacher suggested the economy might be more accommodating here. So far he's been right. I've even made a little profit."

By late afternoon, the rain had slowed to a drizzle. Joseph and Fox walked down the street to a small inn for supper. Samuel stayed behind by the stove with the promise they'd bring him something.

About two hours after dark, David came to the back door of Fox's office. He had three saddle horses. Fox saluted and shut the back door. David led them down a trail that bent westward above the creek. They rode through heavy timber until midnight. Rainwater dripped from the bare limbs and newly budded branches. They talked little. The sure-footed horses seemed to know the route. Joseph's bottom reminded him of how little time he'd spent in the saddle the past six years.

They broke out of the woods and skirted pastures and rail fences. Goats and sheep bleated. The sky cleared. The temperature dropped. A few dogs barked in the distance. Joseph smelled wood smoke. They reentered the woods, then came to a vast draw that fell away into the darkness, beyond the reach of the weak moonlight. The country reminded him of the Kentucky and southern Ohio farmland he'd known as a boy, though it seemed coarser, brushier. After a while, he realized it was the smell as much as the country that reminded him of home. They rode down the draw and into the bottom.

At David's order, Joseph and Samuel dismounted and led their horses along a narrow, gradually ascending trail. David said, "Hitch your horses here. Somebody will be along shortly to look after 'em for you. They'll be here when you leave." In the darkness, Joseph couldn't see anything to tether to. After a moment, David said, "Here." He took their reins, and Joseph listened to him working.

After he tied the horses, David said, "Hold on to your hats. Cover's pretty low for a spell." He led them through the dark timber. The moonlight diminished to occasional shafts through the thickening overstory, then to nothing, yet David lit no torch or lantern. The terrain leveled, and David said, "We'll be crawling for a spell."

Joseph followed close, by sound and touch, yet he occasionally veered into briars and vines and had to stop and feel for his hat. He considered holding it, but since he was on all fours he'd beat it to tatters right off. He felt Samuel behind him doing much the same and cussing softly.

Joseph's back ached, and even his hardened carpenter's hands were getting raw. Already he felt cold, hard ground on his bare knees. Bekah would have some patching to do.

He lost track of the hour although he knew his discomfort made time drag. His body said miles; he suspected they'd crawled only a few hundred yards. North? South? He had no idea. Certainly not in a straight line. Probably a meandering game trail.

After a while they were able to walk in a stoop. That position felt much better, but shortly his back hurt so he was tempted to crawl again. Then David said, "Comin' in."

Someone farther up the trail said, "Come on, if you're comin'." Joseph saw firelight and smelled smoke, heard voices, and then a baby crying. David stood and led them into a half-acre clearing. Firelight flickered against giant black oaks and post oaks. Maybe a dozen Negro men milled about camp, sitting on stumps or blocks of wood by small fires. Other forms lay huddled beneath moldy, smoke-blackened lean-tos and tents. Joseph smelled bodies and wet wool, resin mixed with wood smoke, dead leaves, and rank, fecund forest. Judging from the stumps around the edges, the clearing had been recently enlarged.

Samuel said, "Sweet Jesus."

A child coughed. David said, "Somebody roust the parson." He turned to Joseph and Samuel. "Find you a fire and warm up." He seemed in fine spirits.

They moved to the nearest fire. A middle-aged man sat on a blanket rolled up on a log. He looked up at Joseph. "Mornin', sir." He nodded at Samuel. "Young man."

Joseph said, "I reckon it's morning."

The man chuckled, nodded. "Be light before long." He scooted down the log. "Come in here and warm up. I know y'all 'bout froze. It's a ways in here, ain't it?"

"It's a long way gettin' here. I don't know how far a crow would have to fly," Samuel said.

"Not near as far as it prob'ly felt like to y'all," the man said. "Way it needs to be, though. You better want to get here bad."

Samuel and Joseph introduced themselves. The man wiped his hand on his thigh and shook their hands. "Lamar," he said.

Samuel said, "Lamar, you up early, ain't you?"

He laughed. "About time to change guards. Old men can't sleep no way. You don't know nothin' about that yet. Mister Joseph, now, he'll know it soon enough if he don't already know it." He spat into the fire.

Joseph noticed the slight bulge under Lamar's lip. "Come from around here?"

"A ways north. Other side of the river. Got loose from a Cherokee name of Conley."

Joseph was considering this when someone behind them said, "Well, what did you do with Reverend Bodeker? He ain't laid up again with the black bile is he?"

Joseph turned around to see Zeph Newton striding toward them, coffeepot in hand. He looked to be wearing the same clothes and dirt he wore the day Dallas's most upstanding citizens threw him in jail beside Jonah Chambers. David came with him, carrying four tin coffee cups in the fingers of his one hand.

Joseph stood to shake his hand. "Mrs. Bodeker is expecting. Ig's loath to leave her for more than a few hours."

"Well then, I'm happy they're expecting and disappointed he has such a handy excuse. I've been honing my invective and now it'll rust and dull from disuse."

"He'll find something to sharpen it on," David said. He passed out cups. Newton filled them. "Of course, you see our problem."

Samuel said, "You about to have to clear some more of this thicket if you don't get some of these folks headed south, looks to me like."

"This one and three others like it on the Sulfur Forks," Newton said. "As we speak, Brother Jonah is taking eleven men north across Indian Territory. Just coffled them together and set across the river, just an honest slave trader taking his wares to Missouri. Just ask him. Of course, he'll have a change of heart and bend toward Kansas where our brother and sister free soilers will see the eleven on to Iowa."

Newton sipped and looked about the clearing. "Yet how many crossings can we make before we raise suspicion? Over the past year we've made nine, at various points along the river. Four of those, we've not heard from. There's quite a brisk slave trade among the civilized Indians."

"We'll do what we can," Joseph said. "We haven't heard from you since before Christmas."

"And you won't unless you cast off your timidity and help us develop southward routes."

"I'd say we've progressed. We can't take out an advertisement in the *Herald*. One wrong word and the entire movement could be compromised."

"One wrong word," Newton said. He touched his temple. "Words. Do you know that our brother Silas Hemby is being watched, and has been since they caught our friend Peter down on the border? Do you think we should send him another passenger?"

"Who's watching?"

"Oh, the Dallas vigilance committee has been busy. Such an enterprising group of businessmen. They're doers. It won't do to move passengers along Preston Road or Central Highway, even of a night. Riders are patrolling the roads from the Waxahachie to the Red. But then you knew this."

"I know people are stirred up. David tell you I had a pack of hounds pawing at my shop door a few weeks back?"

"Unnerved you, did they?"

"Not as much as Bill Keller and those deputies."

"Ah, the crown prince of the Knights of the Golden Circle. Brandishing that hook, was he?"

"Knights?"

Newton nodded. "It's a secret organization, you see. They don't aim for you to know."

"How'd you find out?"

"The Knights and the vigilance committees have their eyes and ears; we have ours. Unlike our blind, deaf, and mute Dallas brethren."

"Samuel, you about ready to head back home? I've about had it with the parson's barbs."

"Head back then; we'll get by. Look around before you leave, though."

Joseph slung his dregs toward the fire. "Let me tell you something, Newton. I've been at this work since I was fifteen years old. I've long since lost track of the slaves I've hid, fed, and sent north. Not to mention the ones I fetched right off their master's property."

Newton said, "This is not Cincinnati or Lawrence, Kansas, sir. You cannot retreat to safety among a community of abolitionists; you're among your own people, the same people you left south of the Ohio. Here, you'll share fully the risk with your Negro brothers or you take part in their oppression. There is no middle ground. Risk the fire now or reserve it for yourself for eternity. What revolution has ever been fomented by outsiders? Look around this camp. For the terrible uncertainty of freedom they risk life, dismemberment, torture, separation—all to escape the hellish certainty of bondage.

"The shame is upon your people and therefore upon you. You, sir, born in Kentucky, a slave state. Me, born in North Carolina, moved to Indiana, then Iowa. Do you believe for one instant that our condition was not raised up on the backs of the enslaved, no matter how modest our station? What risk is there in helping a black man after he has already escaped to a free state? What radical has ever been branded or roasted in Ohio? Let the native Northern man do his good work at home. Likewise, let the Southern man do his work on his own cursed and degraded soil."

By now, people were beginning to wake and stir, some undoubtedly roused by Zeph Newton's sermon. Lamar and others began to rise and walk into the woods. In response to the visitors' glances, David said, "Changing guards."

"Unarmed," Samuel said.

"Guns are scarce. We got just 'bout enough for one set of sentries. These will take the guns from them that's comin' in."

The sky had barely lightened. Joseph stood in Newton's gaze. He had no response beyond a nod. Now, even Samuel's eyes seemed accusing. Here stood men committed beyond any he'd known, including Levi Coffin. Safely out of their presence, he might have called them reckless zealots, but in their midst, he saw only his own cowardice. Exhausted, he sensed Newton reloading for another volley.

The changing of the guards was complete. Men came in soaking wet in an assortment of rags. Some had their feet wrapped. A few wore rough brogans. Only two or three out of nearly a dozen had a coat. Most heads were uncovered.

Newton glanced down at the log by the fire. "I reckon Lamar there told you he'd gotten away from the Cherokees."

"He did."

"I suspect he failed to tell you he had a short stay among the Indians. He'd run away from a plantation at Bonham. Headed north and was caught by slave catchers who sold him to a prosperous Cherokee planter. He got loose from there after two years and headed south this time, and being a little lacking in geographic instruction, thought he might make Mexico in a few weeks. Praise the Lord, he broke into Adolphus's mill one night to get out of the weather. One of the boys found him asleep next morning. Only a few here, save for younguns, ain't on their second or third try, and most have the marks and missing digits to show for their trouble." He nodded toward David. "Or missing members."

"We'll do what we can. But everybody can't hide out in a thicket, Parson. We need people in towns and on farms, and that requires prudence."

"Boldness and faith, sir. That's what's needed. While you practice prudence, the oppressed risk everything to be stuck in this dismal forest. Ask yourself what is prudence and what is fear?"

"I will not be called a coward."

"The Lord is my helper. I will not fear what man shall do unto me. Hebrews Chapter thirteen, verse six."

"I'm familiar with the passage." He noticed camp members gathering about. Samuel watched Newton.

The parson raised a finger. "I sought the Lord, and he heard me and delivered me from all my fears."

"Yes, Psalms."

"Chapter thirty-four, verse four. You're familiar with it, but do you know it, sir?"

"Of what help is Winfred Skaggs now?"

"That's not the question, sir. Rather, what good did he accomplish?"

Joseph said, "We've done what we could. Suicide would be of no use to anyone. And we intend to expand our routes. We only ask your patience. . . ."

"'Patience, patience,' sir. I am truly sick of that word. It is the language of cowards! I am out of patience." He strode away toward his tent.

Joseph felt Samuel's silence, the absence of David's arm, and the eyes around him. The skin on his back tightened like scabrous wounds. Images flashed: thick, hard scars, the nubs on Bekah's hand, Martha's spindly legs drawn up in the hidey-hole, and the cold, moldering space inside a buried coffin. "So, we in Dallas are cowards, then. Is that what I'm to understand? We've done no good at all? We were called up here to have our cowardice pointed out to us?"

"I know about fear," David said. "You seen it."

Joseph needed space. He felt the press of bodies. He wanted to run, to crawl back out through the briar and vine tunnel. "I'm not afraid of enemies I know. But if we approach the wrong man, we're finished."

David said, "No. There are others and there'll be others."

"And one more thing!" Newton crawled out of his tent. He'd been listening to the exchange. He seemed restored, back in fine humor. He strode toward them, finger pointed heavenward. "You tell Reverend Bodeker that, although the slavers will dissuade him mightily, they generally won't murder a man of God—at least not on purpose!"

———

They made it back to Dallas in the middle of the afternoon three days later. Samuel walked to the Crutchfield House to collect their mail. He returned with an envelope sent from San Antonio. Inside was a letter dated January 21, 1860, with an accompanying note that said, "We forward this to our associates in Dallas. God bless." Joseph's hands trembled. Samuel was staring at the letter, moving his lips, trying to form the words on the page. Joseph read the letter aloud.

Gentlemen:

I am pleased to report that the cargo you sent last autumn has in large part arrived safely in Piedras Negras and, after being housed for a short period of refurbishment, is being productively employed, much to the satisfaction of all involved. We rejoice in this profitable arrangement and look forward to future shipments. Our partners in this venture all send their gratitude and warmest regards. Much of the shipment will be moved further south as soon as possible as banditry is rife along this section of the border.

Our associates in San Antonio inform us that their storehouses are currently full. However they assure us that border shipments will resume as soon as adequate pecuniary arrangements can be made. At that point they will be prepared to accommodate future shipments from Dallas and from our associates further north.

Regretfully, I must report that, despite your careful preparation in Dallas, one small item did not survive the long and difficult trip and had to be left behind in Fredericksburg. As you might expect, this shortage caused some distress, but after a period of adjustment, encouraging progress has resumed.

Finally, I wish to extend my appreciation for the funds sent along with the cargo. Your gracious support eased the burden for our associates all along the southward route.

Your Faithful Servant,
Luis Vallejo

After much handshaking, embracing, and backslapping, Bekah said, "I didn't know nothin' about funds."

CHAPTER 43

Bekah pulled back. She remained pleasant, but refused Samuel's advances.

"What?"

"I—nothing. I can't."

"Scared of gettin' in a family way?"

"I don't need no more younguns."

"You ain't got none." He caught himself. "I mean no more, you ain't. Not with you."

She shook her head and went back to work.

He no longer took pleasure in careful work, but Joseph failed to notice; spring brought scarlet fever. There were funerals and burials—rituals Joseph could perform in his sleep, right down to earnest condolences.

The relief Samuel gave himself seemed to last only minutes. He'd doze at night or sleep for a while, then wake up to images of stout thighs, and belly, soft on the surface, but firm just beneath, her voice, ". . . uh-huh; that's right. That's right. You just keep right on, mister."

How could you just stop? Had she? Maybe women could do that. Now that he knew, he'd rather be dead than do without.

So he went to see Matilda Suggs. She was thirteen years older than he, but still firm if plump, and pretty. She fed the crews at the sawmill and was known to be cheerfully accommodating to men she liked. She never got pregnant. Men speculated as to whether this made her friendlier because she didn't have to worry or because she remained hopeful.

He'd been joking with her whenever he picked up a load of lumber and sometimes found himself thinking of her on the drive or walk home, before his obsessions turned back to Bekah. The talk became more and more suggestive over the weeks after Bekah began refusing him and the white men at the mill began grinning at him and making jokes. "Sam, you'd best get on back to work now. Ain't nothing here for you. We'll watch out after this girl for you now."

Finally, in late May, after a day in which Bekah had obviously avoided being alone with him—she'd put his meal on the table, then went out in the yard to hang clothes instead of sitting at the table with him—he went to see Matilda. It was well after dark, and his stomach turned as he walked toward her shack on the corner of the Cockrell lot. A feist raced out to meet him, and he held his breath as the door opened and Matilda, barefooted and bareheaded now, said, "Belle, hush!" She grinned at Samuel and said, "What you want?"

He shrugged. "I come to see you."

She pulled the door farther open and stepped back to let him in. "I been wondering when you was gonna come around. I figured you was working up your nerve. I hope you'll get something else worked up before too long."

He already had.

Afterward he lay next to her, disgusted with himself, feeling like a betrayer, listening to her cheerful blather, nodding, "Uh-huh. Well. I swear," adding nothing. But after a few minutes, he'd again feel her flesh against his, feel the heat soaking into his skin and he'd stir and turn to her, and after the third time, he left just to get away, knowing he wasn't finished.

"You better get on back there, 'fore you missed," she said, laughing. "I was about to think I was gonna have to run you off so I could get up and get to Miz Sarah's washing. You go rest up and come on back in a night or two. I kept thinking you was done, but you're a randy gobbler."

Now he understood Joseph's torment, the silence, clenched jaws, raw nerves, the willingness to risk damnation.

There was no moon. The pitch-black streets suited him. It wouldn't do for a Negro to be seen out after midnight. He worried about stumbling on a gaggle of local hooligans out looking for trouble or taking turns with a whore they'd pushed into a dark corner, one they'd refuse to pay or would later rob of what they'd paid. Fortunately, most of the rougher element sought their depletions in Scyene.

Dogs barked at him, but he paid them little mind, other than to whisper "Hush!" which worked often as not. Most recognized his scent and voice. And they barked at coyotes, armadillos, and possums, so their masters rarely bothered to see what the fuss was about.

The muggy night smelled of the river, budding trees and new grass, horses, chicken shit, emptied chamber pots, slop buckets, mud, unpainted lumber, logs in varying states of decay, sunflowers, ragweed and cedar still hot from the day's sun, and here and there, tender growth in kitchen gardens.

Off to the west, beyond Water Street, he heard the hush of the river and the river sounds—crickets and frogs, wild, writhing, desperate, murderous life—down in the bottom. The hum in his ears reminded him of his Christmas brandy and beer buzz and walking home with Bekah staggering against him.

He turned south on Lamar, looked into the darkness, and imagined empty prairie rolling away before him. There were no dwellings for a third of a mile, until he reached home, and then nothing beyond but the Bodekers' place and the cemetery.

When he stepped from Lamar Street into his yard, he realized he'd lost the last quarter of an hour. He remembered not one step, sight, or sound. The scent of Bekah's skin and breath, and remembrance of Matilda Suggs's bosom and bottom and her cot creaking beneath him, left no room for common thoughts and observation. For a second, he wished for old age, death, any relief.

The hours stretched away before him, barren and bleak. He imagined a few hours of fitful sleep, dull headache, dull work while watching for Bekah, hoping, then giving up and heading back down Commerce to see Matilda Suggs.

He walked across the yard to his cabin, opened the door, looked into the blackness, and thought of Bekah in her room. She'd told him she sometimes sat up in the dark listening to the night sounds and remembering. He'd often asked her what she remembered, but she would only say things, like "Old times. Things that don't mean nothing to nobody but me."

Perhaps she was still awake. He didn't dare go to her. She'd run him off for sure and end up waking Joseph, who would shake his head in disgust and ask them to keep it down so a man could sleep, and then there would be the embarrassment the next morning.

He eased his door shut and walked around the house to the front yard. Bekah's window was dark, as he'd expected. The realization that she might be looking at him brought a stab of panic. No, the shade was pulled down. He stared at the window, trying to imagine her on the other side, but couldn't picture her sitting in the chair, in the dark, next to a pulled shade. Surely she was asleep. Odd that she'd have the window shut on such a sultry night. She slept with it open a crack even in winter.

Sadness or sickness, something heavy settled in his stomach and bones. He turned and walked across muddy Lamar to a giant, scabrous bois d'arc, scooted beneath overhanging limbs. Bekah had told him once she liked to sit by the window on Sunday afternoons in summer and watch squirrels carry the horse apples up the trunk to a perch where they grind the hard, green fruit to bits, eating only the tender inner flesh. He checked the trunk for thorns, smoothed the bark a bit with his hands, and sat to watch the window through the limbs and new leaves. The gnats and mosquitoes would find him within a few breaths, but it would be dawn soon.

An hour later, a rooster crowed. He decided to get up. Maybe she'd taken off for good or decided to sleep with the window closed. He was too tired to think it through or feel anymore. At least he wasn't aroused. His eyes hurt. His temples throbbed. The window was still shut. Bug bites covered his face. He'd go start the coffee. No sense even going to bed. Just turn in right after supper. Hell with it. His stomach was sour.

Then she was by the window. He hadn't heard her coming, hadn't seen her until she was there, outlined against the whitewashed siding. Just a soft rustle and the scraping of the window opening. Now he heard his pulse as loud as he'd heard it the night the hounds were coming for David. She looked about, then, seemingly, right at him. She grabbed the window frame, swung a leg up, and disappeared inside. After a few seconds, she lowered the window halfway and pulled the shutter flush with the bottom.

Samuel crouched beneath the bois d'arc limbs. She probably was already heading for the kitchen to build up the fire and start coffee and breakfast. Hell with her. Matilda Suggs would do just fine for now. He stood and stomped the feeling back into his feet. Bitch. He should've known.

———

He watched her window the next two nights, miserable, nodding. Once he woke himself snoring and imagined he heard her coming to the window to look out. He sat barely breathing, feeling exposed, although he knew he'd be impossible to see beneath the heavy, gnarled limbs. The next night, he went to bed before eight o'clock and slept until dawn. When he woke, his covers were barely rumpled.

It had rained during the night, then cleared. The morning was cool, the air scrubbed fresh. He felt like himself again and looked forward to a piece of intricate work on a well-appointed hope chest for a young woman in Lancaster. Bekah wasn't in the kitchen, which suited him. Nor was Joseph. He took his coffee at the table, enjoying the morning quietude. Of course, she'd call them to breakfast pretty soon, but they'd have time to get a little work done and set the day's course. Once you got busy on a piece of satisfying work, the day flew by. Best to get going early. Maybe in a day or two, he'd go down to see Matilda. Probably not, but she was there if he needed to go. Bekah? Hell with her. He had no worry or longing left in him, thank God. Sneaking out and running around town. Samuel didn't suppose he'd say anything to Joseph. No sense worrying him with it, and anyway, he might confront Bekah, and she'd demand to know how Joseph found out about it. Last thing Samuel needed was her thinking he was watching her. She could do what suited her as far as he cared. He did wonder who she'd gone to see, but he wouldn't be losing any more sleep trying to find out. Whoever it was could have her, God take pity on the poor bastard.

He put in a day's work and ignored her during dinner and supper while she and Joseph prattled about weather and local gossip and the armadillo that had burrowed under the house and which boy might have a feist mean enough to go in there and pull him out. But that night, he couldn't sleep. What started as a vague unease, a twitching leg, fluttering thoughts, grew into sweating, miserable, aching insomnia. He dozed, finally, to images of Bekah helping him slide the bookcase away from the wall. Over and over and over.

About one o'clock in the morning, he rose, dressed, and stepped outside into the spring coolness. He walked around the house, across the street, and stooped beneath the limbs of the bois d'arc. He was settling in when he noticed the window was shut tight. He suddenly felt very tired and slightly chilled. After a few minutes he got up and went to bed. He fell asleep at once.

Father's Reminiscence
Transcribed July 30, 1911

Hounds are harmless enough, generally. Once they've brought a man to bay, they'll show teeth and carry on like they aim to eat him alive. They might chew on him some, dart in and grab a pant leg, try to jerk him down—you do need to keep your feet. You don't want a pack pulling you down. You'd be in trouble then. But a man who knows dogs can keep a fair-sized pack buffaloed. It's the catch dog that'll tear him to pieces. Backwoodsmen occasionally called on to run down a slave wouldn't own such an animal. But the real slave catcher would.

They had one that night on the Little Harpeth. Some hellish mix of mastiff and wolfhound or elk hound. I never saw it. I got the story from Levin years down the road.

We were across the creek and up the bank before we missed him and realized what he'd done. He'd wanted to split off and let us cross the stream while he ran up the bank to draw the dogs off. We were all caught otherwise, and he knew it. A white man would have a chance, might get the benefit of a doubt, even traveling with a Negro woman. That's what he said. If they caught us all, then what? It would all be for naught. He'd take his chances. Maybe he could throw the dogs by crossing farther upstream. He knew better. These were real slave dogs. We both jumped all over him. Squashed it. Told him we'd spit on his grave. Hell no, we wouldn't leave him. We couldn't live or go on without him. No sir. So he promised. We'd cross together.

The stream was fast, and the hounds were closing. Levin went about halfway across, then eased back and took off up the bank to draw off the dogs. We didn't dare call to him, and it wouldn't have done any good. He wouldn't have answered us. They brought him to bay under a big rock overhang up on the ridge, five miles or so from where we crossed. He was kicking and hollering, looking to break loose. The slave catchers didn't show themselves right off. From down the ridge, they sent their catch dog. It came without so much as a snarl. Just came out of the dark, and the hounds parted, and that monster was on him. There was nothing he could do but feed the brute his left arm.

CHAPTER 44

I told you, now, goddamn it. He's done sold that little pickaninny of yourn. Had 'im gone two days after you took off. I'd say the little bastard's in South Georgia by now. You wanna keep that other'n, you best keep your little ass close to home. The easy work's over, far as you're concerned. Mr. McCutcheon's leavin' it up to me to learn you how to behave. Well—I got a little lesson works every time. It ain't like I got into this line of work yesterday. I've picked up a few tricks in twenty-three years of drivin'. Don't you worry, though. I'll leave enough fingers for you to grab aholt of a cotton boll or the workin' end of a hoe.

Since the night they hid David from the hounds, Bekah often dreamed of seared flesh. She smelled it in her sleep.

Stephen had blanched and nearly fainted when they branded him, but he didn't scream. The palm was less sensitive than the cheek. She'd lain on her side, her hands and feet bound, watching the iron heating in the coals. She'd seen slaves, always men, branded on the cheek, usually an *R*—for runaway, she'd been told. They all screamed.

They walked back to Nashville at gunpoint. His hand stank. He grew feverish. The wound swelled so that you could barely make out the *A*. She asked him what it meant. He said it was the first letter in "Abolitionist." She'd never heard that word before. Someone who wanted to end slavery, he said.

Abolitionist. She repeated the word over and over to herself as they'd walked to Nashville, and then a thousand times on her way back to Alabama. She thought of the word after Flora died, drowned in her arms, hot as white oak coals—diphtheria, the doctor said—when she ran again, with Mary on her back. And old McCutcheon and Boyd thought they could break her by chopping off two fingers with a kindling ax. Like she was afraid of losing two more. Or her whole hand or her arm. If they wanted to keep her there, they should have chopped off her feet. But then she wouldn't have been much help, and anyway, she'd have found a way to crawl into the back of a wagon or a boat.

She didn't get five miles the second time. There had been no plans. She knew no one, not even one slave on the surrounding plantations. In the middle of a clear, cold October night, she got up off the porch step, went in and gathered a bundle and the baby, walked into the darkness, found the road north, and walked until dawn, listening to the rustling in the frosted roadside weeds.

She rounded a bend and met two slaves pulling a skid loaded with firewood. She greeted them. They nodded and spoke. She continued. She felt none of the fear she'd known during her first escape. She just walked and thought small thoughts. Where would she go? She'd hide in the woods shortly, move only at night. Surely she'd come upon another plantation, and then she'd slip about until she found the slave quarters. Someone there would put her up and give her the lay of the land.

She was looking for a place to turn into the woods when two horsemen, young white men, rode around the bend behind her. One cut off her escape into the woods before she could react. She hadn't even heard them coming. They knew her name. Word had gotten out that quick. She'd become a problem girl.

After she watched dry-eyed as Mary rode away squalling in the arms of another slave woman—the child's reddish hair, green eyes, and freckles had caught the eye of a slave trader passing through on his way to Florida—McCutcheon sold her to some sportsmen headed for Indian Territory to gamble. For three weeks they treated her as well as she'd ever been treated. They left her alone after she'd fed them and done whatever light chores had to be done to maintain five men, two wagons, two span of mules, and two saddle horses. They helped her with the heavy toting. Five young men. All rough and white except one, an Indian who said he was half Choctaw. Nights, by firelight, she leaned back on sacks of potatoes or meal and watched them wager on cards and dice, knives, and marksmanship.

Still in the Louisiana pinelands, the men decided they needed more seed money for gaming among the Indians. The oldest, a tall man with three or four teeth and a few blond wisps plastered across his shiny head, sheepishly told her after breakfast one morning that he'd found a buyer.

Abolitionist. She'd nearly forgotten about the word by the time she was heading for Dallas with a slave trader whose name she couldn't recall now. Two weeks later, at a spot she sensed was within few blocks of where she now sat, she was sold, healthy and in her prime, for four hundred dollars to the Montgomerys, who had never before owned a slave. They were not mean. They were dull, petty, and indecisive. Hilda Montgomery did not approve of her, Bekah suspected, because she did not approve of any other woman on her place.

Bekah grudgingly admitted that at least Hilda Montgomery considered her woman enough to resent.

Rayfield Montgomery had no idea what to do with her and could never think of a chore that wouldn't be carried out with more good cheer by one of his daughters or sons-in-law. She cooked and cleaned, always to Hilda's snipping. She emptied chamber pots, weeded the kitchen garden. She did the wash once, but she didn't get all the lye out of Hilda's undergarments, a small oversight that caused some additional chilliness in the kitchen. After that, her laundry chores consisted of hanging and folding. Hilda Montgomery wouldn't hit her, wouldn't raise her hand. She knew it, and Hilda knew she knew it.

Abolitionist. The word came to her again when they brought Brother Jonah Chambers and the two runaways into Dallas in chains, and again when Jere Russell and his family showed up at the door, and Joseph said, "We'll talk about this. We should've told you right off, but we didn't know how you'd take it. We couldn't have you running off or talking."

Too bad about Samuel. He was a good man; just not the right man. She hadn't meant to lead him on. His confusion hurt her. He'd understand in time.

Abolitionist. She'd never seen it spelled out, but recently she'd heard it whispered about town. There were abolitionists about. Everyone knew it. Churning up trouble. Inciting insurrection. Northern seditionists.

All those years, the word had meant white people who wanted to end slavery, including those willing to help and hide runaway slaves. Why else were captured slaves branded *R* and white men branded *A*? The desire for Mexico or Canada had left her. What could be sweeter than freedom? Helping others achieve it? Or vexing, infuriating the slavers? Killing? Burning? Branding, even? Now there was something sweet to think on. And what could freedom mean for her when her babies were scattered all over the South. If they were still alive, and she'd never know. She'd stay put awhile.

The idea came to her one night, sitting in her room, staring at a candle flame. Just a small brand in a hidden place. Three separate, straight marks, if she could hold steady. A hot nail. Three marks. She couldn't make the wound too serious. She had to be able to work like nothing had happened, like she hadn't burned herself. She chose the inside of her right thigh a few inches above her knee.

The first burn felt clean, purifying, and smelled like his burning palm.

The hiss startled her, then she remembered. She reheated the nail twice, holding it with a folded potholder, and finished the brand.

She pressed a wet hand towel to her burn, rewetted it several times before the pain subsided enough that she unclenched her jaw and drew deep, steady breaths, then she dabed on lard.

Still, the burns kept her from sound sleep, but each time they woke her she felt a satisfaction as sharp as her pain. She'd done this to herself. Tomorrow when she went to him—or the next day or whenever she could get away, she would pull up her dress and show him. A. And if anyone cared to notice, should anyone prepare her for burial, when that time came, assuming she wasn't hanged and burned and fed to the hogs, or weighted down and thrown into the river, they would know what she was—and wasn't.

She stopped dreaming of burning flesh.

CHAPTER 45

In early June, in the middle of the night, David delivered a letter to Ig and Rachel. He had with him two young men he planned to deliver to the Butts family. The letter was an invitation from Rev. Joab Wolford, of Pilot Point, inviting Ig to attend his four-day tent meeting and to preach as many sermons as suited him. The letter went on to say that among the Pilot Point flock were many who would welcome his message. David added that Ig ought to know Joab Wolford and his lay leaders. If Ig would like, he'd deliver a positive reply on his way back north.

Of course he would go. However, Reverend Wolford should know Mrs. Bodeker would be unable to attend for the obvious reasons. Rachel seemed pleased at his opportunity to preach at Pilot Point. David and the three men left in the darkness.

Three weeks later, Ig found Joab's preaching much to his liking, although it bordered on recklessness at times, especially his fixation on the book of Philemon and Paul's exhortation to accept the runaway back not as a servant but as a brother in Christ. Joab made that point several times.

They were sitting under the shade cast by a huge tarp strung from two poles on one side and two cedar elm trees on the other. The congregation sat on benches and on the ground beneath arbors and smaller tarps. Some of the farmers, still in work clothes, squatted on their haunches, and children meandered through. Ig had been introduced to the stern crowd as a righteous, tireless, and fearless warrior for Christ. He sat on a loose straight-backed chair on Wolford's left. The chair listed in all directions so that Ig had to take care to stay centered up, lest he get started in one direction, collapsing the chair beneath him. Once he found the balance point he relaxed, though he had to keep his feet squarely on the ground in front of him.

He was to preach the Sunday night service and then retire to the home of a congregant for a late but lavish supper, or so he'd been promised. He and Pig had arrived just prior to the beginning of Joab's sermon, so he was running on a light breakfast of biscuits and bacon. Interesting as the sermon was, he was having difficulty keeping his mind off of the words "lavish suppers." He tried not to think about the late part and hoped his stomach didn't start rumbling during his own sermon.

He planned to preach on Paul's imprisonment and his exhortations to hold fast in the face of persecution, a thing he could never quite reconcile with Christ's command to render unto Caesar what is Caesar's. Who could say what belonged to Caesar other than Caesar himself? And Caesar could claim anything he wanted, including human property, if it suited him.

He envied men like Zeph Newton and Jonah Chambers but had come to know that he would never achieve their moral clarity. He was a man of uncertainties, but, he hoped, not timidity or cowardice. So many things were hopelessly complex and open to interpretation. Other things—slavery, for instance—felt wrong, though learned men could justify the institution with scripture, phrenology, and other medical and anatomical arts. Yet he could not picture Christ—or his idea of Christ—approving of the practice, despite certain parables, especially his accusation, "Wicked servant!" Admittedly, in his reading of the Holy Bible—and he'd read every word many times—he'd found Jesus and Paul disappointingly uninterested in the issue of bondage, save for a few troubling passages in Paul's epistles to Timothy, Philemon, and the Ephesians. It was hard to rationalize your way around "Servants be obedient to them that are your masters according to the flesh, with fear and trembling. . . ." Never mind the Old Testament.

Then again, you could address only so many issues in a short life on earth—the salvation of the world, for example—even if you were the Son of God. Perhaps he'd gotten the core of his message in place and counted on his followers to sort out the finer points. Wesley said it best: "Who can reconcile this treatment of Negroes, first and last, with either mercy or justice?"

Ig looked out over the crowd. Eighty people, easy, and certainly not all were sympathetic to the cause of abolition. No doubt a few were here to keep an eye on Joab Wolford. Most, he suspected, were simple believers who came to hear a hellfire hot sermon and never even made the connection between the message and the evils of slavery. Still, he wondered.

Suddenly he noticed a few score heads bowed and most eyes closed. He wondered how long he'd been lost in his reverie and hoped no one had been furtively watching him, although surely a few had. He closed his eyes. Brother Wolford prayed for another quarter of an hour. They finished the service with "Rock of Ages," to the accompaniment of a badly tuned piano that was played with aplomb in the shade of a post oak by a graying but still handsome and pleasantly buxom Mrs. H. Raymond Pitt, whom he'd met on his arrival.

The preachers and remaining congregation ate dinner in the shade, sitting on stumps and a few rickety chairs and chuck boxes. A ruddy-faced man with huge hands and a black beard sat on an anvil. Ig and Pig ate with the tall, rawboned, gray-headed Joab Wolford and his almost equally tall, rawboned, gray-headed wife, Emily. Congregants came by frequently during the meal to introduce themselves and exchange news and pleasantries. As some visitors approached, Wolford immediately lowered his voice, regardless of the topic. With others, he talked on at apparent ease.

After the meal, the congregants dozed about the meadow. Others left to go home and take care of chores before the early evening service. Emily Wolford kept glancing at her husband. After a while, he said, "Of course your activities are known to us, Brother."

"I assume so, given who delivered your invitation." They nodded in silence. Ig said, "Us?"

"Me, Emily, and a few trusted soldiers, some trusted more than others."

"Of course. And I suspect many others you would like to approach, but can't quite work up the nerve."

The Wolfords both smiled. Emily smoothed her dress on her lap. "There could be hundreds more just like us. Thousands. But you never know. Currently we're sure of less than a dozen white people. Our Negro colleagues tell us they don't even trust all of their own."

"Fear is our enemy," Ig said.

"Lack of faith," Wolford said.

Ig nodded. "Certainly. Faith mated with prudence."

Pig cleared his throat and looked out over the clearing.

Wolford said, "Yes."

They sat in silence. Ig took off his coat and hung it on a snag. He wanted to unbutton his collar but thought better of it. He looked around. No one seemed to be paying them any attention. After a moment, Emily said, "Brother Jonah wants to send passengers to us. We want to establish another southward route."

"I see. We can take only so many. Too much traffic through Dallas puts us all at risk. A few a month are all we can take right now. We haven't had any for a while."

"Brother Jonah is letting things cool a bit, I'm told," Joab said. "He's been looking north a good bit lately."

"You have history with the movement."

"We helped a bit in Illinois," Joab said.

"Kansas here," Ig said.

Emily looked at Joab, who said, "Your earlier passenger. The one caught south of San Antonio."

"Peter." This couldn't be good.

"We've heard different stories circulating among the Negroes. All the same theme, though the details vary. I've heard once that he was sold off to a planter down near the coast. Most say he's still up here. In any case, you can imagine how it went for him."

"I can imagine, but I cannot know. You have connections with the local Negroes?"

"They're a fount of news. They pick it up in town and from fugitives they harbor. They've sent a hundredfold more on to Mexico than all the white ministers in Texas. They have their own routes, their own secret world. They welcome our help, but they're loathe to trust. Their reach and knowledge far exceeds our own."

"Peter. Do you think they got anything out of him?" The question made him feel filthy.

Emily said, "They've caught a bunch of runaways since we came into this country. You hear rumors all the time about abolitionist instigation, but have you heard of any arrests?"

"Arrests, no. At least one murder."

"Mr. Skaggs. A dear, zealous, and reckless man," Emily said.

"You knew him then."

"Everyone did," she said.

Late that afternoon, Ig stepped up to the makeshift pulpit and looked out over the meadow. If anything, it was more crowded than it had been during Joab's sermon. People had been trickling back all afternoon. Wagons and horses crowded the openings back in the woods. The sun was hot on the side of his face. Perhaps his reputation had preceded him. Perhaps brother Joab's introduction that morning had been spread through the farms and community. Perhaps more people had finished their chores. In any case, a lot more people knew him now than had known him yesterday. His reach was spreading. As had Paul's. That was good. Yes. That was to be sought always. He smiled. Some of the congregation smiled back. Most sat solemn, fanning themselves with hats, shooing flies, expectant. Mrs. H. Raymond Pitt sat on her piano stool, waiting to be called into duty. He reminded himself that many would need to get back home for milking unless they had slaves there to do it for them. Over the next two hours, he stuck to the general theme of his planned sermon, but he chose his words very carefully.

CHAPTER 46

Rachel looked miserable. She sat at her kitchen table, red-faced, sweating, legs carelessly spread, a pillow between her lower back and the chair back. "I just want it over with," she said. "It could be better endured during cooler weather. But then I don't suppose you can plan conception with Ig. You have to ambush him when you can."

"I feel better knowing it's Ig's," Joseph said. He sat at the table with her, his shirtsleeves rolled up, wearing a morning's worth of sawdust furrowed by trickles of sweat. It would have been more pleasant outside, but they didn't want to raise talk. Still, Rachel had opened the windows to catch any draft that might develop.

"I wish you'd stop referring to the baby as *it*," she said. "Surely, you'll call it—him, her, the baby—by name when it arrives."

"I will. But you two still ain't nailed down a name."

"'Ain't nailed down a name.'" She shook her head, rolled her eyes.

"I apologize for my lack of a fancy Maryland education." No wonder Ig went to Pilot Point.

She glared at him.

He said, "Anyway, I reckon you'll be busy with the baby."

"The baby. That's an improvement."

"Well." He leaned forward, as if gathering himself up to leave. "You all fixed up, then? Need anything?"

"Oh, the pathetic, helpless woman." She shook her head bitterly. "Rosemary came by this morning."

He stood over her. He bent to kiss her, aiming for the top of her head. To his surprise, she lifted her face to his. Her lips were soft, her eyes open. "Pathetic, ridiculous, revolting, wicked." She kissed him again. "Wretched, debased, degraded harridan. I'll surely get what I deserve." There was no sorrow in her words, no lust, only resignation. Her lips brushed his as she formed the words. Even in the stifling room, he felt the heat of her breath. She pushed him away. "And old."

"Properly seasoned." His face felt suddenly cool.

"Go home and ask Bekah to broom you off. You smell like a woodpile." She clasped her hands on her belly.

"Be seeing you," he said.

"Ig will be back tonight, you know."

"He'll be glad to see you."

She waved him away. "You're a disgusting opportunist. Go. We'll be thrown together soon enough."

He plucked his hat from the table, smiled, and picked up his tool box on his way out the door. Another month, then a few weeks of recovery, and let the flock of church matrons scatter. Hopefully, motherhood wouldn't bring on a bad case of good sense.

——

Mid-afternoon, two days after his Sunday evening sermon, Ig and Pig crossed Shoat Creek, five miles north of Cedar Springs.

His sermon had gone well; he'd made friends and contacts. Joab Wolford seemed to get on well with the slaves in his area who undoubtedly had knowledge of routes and Negro safe houses well to the south. The movement badly needed a parallel route west of Dallas to carry fugitives south out of the Denton and Gainesville area.

Pig's wagon lurched across the creek, water splashing up to the mules' knees. They rode out of the water and up a narrow trail. At the top, in flat, open woods, they met three riders.

"Whoa!" Pig said, pulling the mules up. Ig noticed two shotguns and a carbine pointed at Pig's chest. Then he noticed the cloth sacks over the men's heads. He shaded his eyes against the afternoon sun and looked into black eyeholes.

Pig said, "Good lord, boys, point them guns somewhere else."

One of the men said, "Pig, how 'bout you throw that cut-down twin bore in your lap over here before I blow your ass right out of your seat." His voice was muffled by the bag. It sounded grotesquely low.

Pig held up both hands. "Strange now, you boys know me, but I don't seem to know you. I can't recall knowing too many folks that go around with sacks over their heads."

"Throw the gun out here, goddamnit. Beg your pardon, Reverend." The others laughed.

Ig felt he should raise his hands, but he lacked the strength. These men knew him. He looked at their clothes, trying to recall any detail from some past encounter in town, at church. His face tingled.

Pig said, "Well now, y'all make a man nervous about reaching for his weapon. Why don't one of you just ease over here and get it."

The man who'd done all the talking looked at one of the others who had one eyehole a little higher than the other and nodded. "Go ahead." He looked back at Pig. "Just one little move, you nigger-stealin' bastard. Just one."

Ig swallowed and found his voice, high and weak. "Gentlemen, I have no idea what this is about. We've just returned from revival."

"Preacher, hell. How long you think you can shepherd people's niggers away and get away with it?"

"I beg your pardon?" He could think of nothing else.

"Boys, this wagon looks a mite dry; don't you reckon it would catch and burn right off? Wouldn't even need coal oil."

Pig said, "You the son of a bitches done it, huh?"

"All old Skaggs had to do was talk to us, but he wouldn't. You two aim to talk to us?"

"Go to hell," Pig said.

"Brother Joab talked to us. It took some doin', but he talked. He sets store by his wife."

"We don't know nothing to tell you," Pig said. Just then, the rider eased the shotgun from Pig's lap.

One of the others said, "We'll have to find a stout limb for the parson, won't we?" More laughter.

Ig noticed the coils of rope hanging from saddles. These weren't cowmen. He wouldn't talk. He was certain, and it brought an unexpected calm. He wasn't sure he could stand, but he'd stand firm. He'd always wondered. Now he knew before he even felt the heat or tasted the smoke. Could you smell yourself burning? Perhaps the smoke would render him unconscious. Maybe they'd just hang him by the neck. He had a sudden image of the flames lighting the dark woods and bull bats hunting above. He would have expected to think of Scripture, to pray for comfort and strength, to express his forgiveness of his killers, but nothing spiritual came to him. Then images of Rachel at home, and of Joseph and Samuel and Bekah, the Meades and Van Husses, their friends, and his congregation. Rachel would bear his child without him. But Joseph would be there, of course. And the others. But what would become of Rachel since he was now implicated? And what did these men expect to learn? Did they already know about Joseph and the others? Would they hurt Rachel? But he hadn't mentioned the names of his colleagues to Joab. Had Newton or Chambers or David?

He heard a wet slap, and two of the riders fell off their saddles and then the crack of gunfire from across the creek. One of the men lay still—the leader. The other was trying to crawl away, cursing and grabbing at his neck and collar bone. The third man heeled his mount and turned, but another round of gunfire spooked the horse. Ig heard balls cutting braches. Bark flew. The horse bucked and reared and threw the rider who landed on his side but scrambled up as Pig leaped from the wagon. The man got to his feet and ran into the woods, downstream. Pig picked up his shotgun and ran after him, disappearing into the shadows of trunks and limbs, but Ig heard their thrashing and footfalls in the tinder-dry woods.

He sat in the wagon. The wounded man moaned and cried and rolled onto his back, said, "Preacher, I'm sorry. I didn't want it. I'm sorry. Help me please. Lord, it hurts. I didn't mean what I said about the limb."

Ig struggled out of the wagon. His legs felt oddly light, but unsteady, as if they might fly away on him. Gunfire off in the woods, but it sounded like a rifle, not Pig's shotgun. He walked across the clearing. The man rolled onto his back. Blood had soaked his shirt so that Ig had no idea where he'd been shot. Now he saw a second wound, lower. He said, "I won't hurt you, son. Just lie still." He ought to say something preacherly. He'd comforted many dying people, but never a murderer. This man may have helped burn Winfred Skaggs. Yet he deserved the same grace as any of God's other children. He wasn't dead. He could repent, find his way to the Lord yet.

He knelt beside the man, took his hand. Maybe he ought to pull off the sack first. But no, it was around his neck. Time was short.

Pig stepped out of the woods. "He's dead, but I didn't kill him. We got some help we didn't know we had." He walked over and looked down at the man beside Pig. "You best walk on down to the creek. I'll take care of this."

"No, Pig. He's about gone, anyway. I can't abide murder."

"Gone, hell. He's hit in the collarbone and it clipped him in the side, looks to me like. Went clear through and missed everything."

The man sobbed. "Pig, now. Please."

Pig said, "I aim to find out who you are, friend."

"Here, I'll show you. It's me." He groped at his mask.

Pig knocked his hand away with his gun barrel. "No sir. Not yet. Brother Ig, get down to the creek. Listen to me. Think of Rachel. Think. I'm thinking of Cathlyn and my boys. Ain't nobody but us fixin' to ride away from here. Now get on or get back."

"Oh, dear God," the man said. "Pig, please, no."

CHAPTER 47

Pig talked as he drove the wagon south along the Preston Road. They'd buried the dead outriders. Ig's hands were blistered. He hadn't used a shovel in years, but he'd felt compelled to spell Pig. They dug the graves back in the woods. Pig had argued for a single grave. Ig had insisted on separate graves. He was already in the wagon and across the creek before he realized he hadn't said a word over the dead men.

"We ought to all be heading north by this time tomorrow," Pig said. "Don't leave together. We'll meet up somewhere in the Nations." He wiped sweat from his nose with a finger stained by the blackland dirt. "If there ain't somebody waitin' on us when we get home."

Ig had been barely listening while Pig talked. "We'll have to alert the Meades and Van Husses. And what do we do about Al?"

"Ain't much to do there," Pig said. "Warn him, I reckon. He might want to head south. At least Samuel and Bekah can leave with Joseph."

"Al might be risking his neck for nothing."

"Nothin'?"

"I mean we don't know how far we've been compromised."

"You think everybody that knows is layin' back there? You think they didn't know nothin' at all 'til they got hold of Brother Joab's wife?"

"How would they know?"

"How'd they know to follow us up there to the meetin'?"

Ig stared at the dusty, rutted road. Just open prairie ahead, broken here and there by plum mottes and cedars. They'd be in Dallas in an hour or so. He wondered if Pig would stop in Cedar Springs to warn Cathlyn before driving him home. He couldn't imagine Rachel in danger any more than he could believe that gentle Pig Nuchols had just executed a young man with his shotgun. Or that he—a man of God—had walked down to the creek and allowed a murder, no matter the reasons.

Murder? Or a man protecting his family?

Murder.

He would not raise his hand to another man. He'd made that commitment, had built a life on that philosophy. So then, how could he have stopped Pig?

He could have stood before the young outrider.

Pig would have beaten him senseless, shoved him aside, and then shot the boy. He'd protect Cathlyn and the boys at any cost.

Still, he should have tried to protect the boy. Let Pig bludgeon away if he would. And he would. Neither Brother Jonah nor Brother Zeph could have backed him down. Pig had killed in the Mexican War. He believed in righteous violence. He was a practical man of the frontier. Why else had he been so agreeable to Pig's company on his ministerial excursions? Why had he tolerated the shotgun? Had he believed Pig wouldn't use it? He had believed it. Or at least he hadn't truly believed anyone would be killed.

"No! No! Pig!" the boy had said. A boy? A young man? "Pig! Lord God!"

Ig imagined the boy facedown, bleeding, trying to shield his head with his arms.

Pig had said, "Might as well be still, son. You don't want me to have to shoot you twice."

The boy wailed, sobbed.

"Should've thought about that before you go around hanging and burning people. I don't reckon you thought about this, did you?"

"I didn't aim . . ."

"Hush now. Be still and show a little sand before I have to tie you up. You can't get away."

"I—Lord."

"Anybody headin' to my place? Brother Ig's?"

"Naw. Nobody ain't—we just . . ."

"I ought to do to you what you done to Winfred."

"I never had nothing to do with that! Pig, you ain't really . . ."

"Shut up." The gun blast. Crows back in the woods. Then the second barrel. "Just stay down there, Ig. I'll take care of it."

They rounded a bend and met a rider leading a piebald mare. Pig said, "Afternoon. Fine-lookin' mare."

The man moved a huge chaw to the other cheek, nodded, and said, "Fellars, I'm right took with her." He rode on.

Pig said, "I tidied everything up. He won't see nothing."

Ig nodded. The site of the murder had been cleaned up. And, to his shame, he hoped it had been cleaned up very well.

"We got some friends we don't know about," Pig said. "Or them boys has some enemies. Or somebody don't want us getting in a bad enough way that we'd talk. A man might get pretty talky about the time the soles of his boots was warmin' up good."

"I cannot imagine." Time to move on indeed. Compared to this treacherous, murderous place, Kansas was Eden.

"Of course, now, they'd just finish cooking you after you told them what they wanted to hear. Still a man hopes. That boy back there did."

"Pig . . ."

"Huh?"

Ig sighed. He could've wept. All the packing and urgency and fear, all the while knowing what had happened. "Do you suppose you'll tell Cathlyn and the others what happened?"

"What you mean?"

"I mean . . . uh . . ." He sighed, dropped his chin to his chest, and rubbed his eyes. The sun sat just above the horizon. His favorite time of day. Meadowlarks flushed along the edge of the road. Up ahead, a roadrunner stopped between the ruts. Just riding along on a lovely, hot, early summer evening, a little faster than normal, but not fast enough to draw attention or kill the mules.

After a moment, Pig said, "I'll have to tell Cathlyn what happened. I don't believe I could go along and not tell her. A man has to unload something like that."

Ig nodded. Perhaps a man did. Here he was, the preacher, being ministered to by someone who'd just sluiced another with two loads of buckshot.

They topped a rise in the trail. Two farms came into view on either side of the road, and just beyond, the cluster of houses that made up Cedar Springs. Pig took a track to the west, toward his place. Dust rose up behind them and grasshoppers and meadowlarks before them.

Pig turned to him. His head bobbed with the rough trail. "If you want to, we can just tell everybody else about being held up, and then somebody shootin' from the woods. We could just say that for now. Except I'll tell Cathlyn the whole story. She'll keep quiet about it, 'til you're ready."

Pig was pushing the mules now. Ig had to raise his voice. "Pig, it's just—I mean I just need some time. This is not my world. You understand that."

Pig's eyes were red and watering in the dust and churned-up pollen. He looked tired, his long face haggard, bewhiskered. "It's the only world there is, Ig. You been in it all along. You just seen a little different piece of it today." He grabbed Ig's forearm and shook it.

When he let go, Ig missed his grip desperately.

They heard the hounds before the Nuchols cabin came into view. They rounded the bend and the dogs charged out to meet them. They drove into the yard at twilight to find Cathlyn standing on an overturned rain barrel, surrounded by her boys, peering into a martin house made from a gourd hung from a line stretched between the eave of the cabin and the lower branch of a cedar elm. Her dress fluttered up when she jumped off, her long, graceful arms and fingers out for balance. As she strode toward them, smiling, the boys clamored to be next on the rain barrel.

Father's Reminiscence
Transcribed July 31, 1911

Except for a brief period during my childhood, I have never been religious or fatalistic. Nothing is meant to be. History, happenstance, and the laws of nature force decisions.

Yet I've been astounded and blessed in ways a long life sometimes allows.

Levin McGregor made his decision on the Little Harpeth River and faced the slave catchers' dogs. A few months later, in Missouri, his captors, unaware that he was wanted for murder, sold him for all they could get—a mere seventy dollars; a one-armed slave wouldn't bring much—to an itinerant logger who was on his way to Honey Grove, Texas. Once across the Red River, the logger, after seeing Levin's one-armed ax work, made the unwise decision to remove the leg irons so that his new slave could move about in the woods without falling.

Within days, Levin found Zephaniah Newton and Jonah Chambers.

After nine months in a Tennessee prison, I returned to Detroit. Waiting for me in Mr. Bibb's newspaper office was a letter from Paris, Texas.

Of course, there were greater surprises to come, the sort of improbabilities that make even a reasonable man wonder.

CHAPTER 48

Samuel found the news heartening and said he'd be ready to go before sunrise. He'd just gather up his tools, quilts, and shotgun. He could stuff his spare garments in his old bedroll. Kansas would suit him very well, seeing as how it was just south of Iowa, which, as best he could glean from Joseph's atlas, was within imagining distance of Detroit, which was a boat ride from Canada. He'd always wanted to ride in something bigger than a rowboat, and he'd never been too worked up about Mexico. There were plenty of freedmen up north, where you could do all of your business in English. And the farther north you got, the less you had to worry about slave catchers. Get far enough north and you could sic the law on a slave catcher. What he couldn't understand was why Bekah sat there looking just as peaked as Rachel, Ig, and Joseph. Worse even.

Joseph said, "We'll have to get another wagon. Hell, I got a house full of furniture. A shop full of tools and lumber."

"Furniture," Samuel said. "And lumber."

Bekah said, "We don't know who knows what."

Samuel shook his head in disbelief. "Now listen at you! Still set on Mexico, are you?"

She massaged her temples. Rachel and Ig just sat. Joseph said, "Hell. It'll take a few days anyway."

Ig said, "Joseph, men died on the road today. Pig and I almost did. Are you hearing me?"

"I'm hearing." He rapped his knuckles on the table. "Pig's heading out first thing, huh?"

"They were in a flurry when I left."

"That don't sound like Pig Nuchols."

"They threatened Emily Wolford."

"*Threatened.*"

"They scared Joab into talking. I judge him a solid man."

"They *said* they did."

Ig sighed and gathered himself. "Joseph, these were hired ruffians, not men of the community. Pig said two were brothers from Scyene."

Joseph leaned back in his chair, looked at the others around the table. "And we still haven't told Malachi and Rosemary and them."

"Or Al," Samuel said.

"Just running. I can't hardly see it," Joseph said.

Ig laid his hand on Rachel's forearm. "I don't see it as cowardice."

Rachel said, "You left Kansas after much good work. You've worked hard here, but now it's time to move on. For now."

"I left Kansas when it suited me."

Ig shrugged, laid out his palms. "We've been together in this forever. I can't imagine heading out alone. But we'll make out somehow. We go to Kansas on our own. We'll get back, Lord willing."

Joseph glared at nothing in particular. He just needed a few minutes to get used to the idea of sneaking off before daylight.

Samuel slapped the table in disgust. "I can't sit here and listen to this. I'm going up to tell Al. It'll go worser on him than anybody. And here we are just sittin' here." He rose and headed for the door.

Joseph smacked Samuel's arm as he passed. "Watch yourself, now."

Someone knocked at the front door. Joseph jabbed a finger at his nose and rolled his eyes toward the half-open window. Then more rapping accompanied by, "Marshal!"

Rachel touched her forehead, then took Ig's hand. He squeezed. They exchanged something with a glance. Samuel leaned back against the wall and crossed his arms on his chest. Joseph got up and opened the door.

James Moore doffed his hat and nodded to Rachel and Ig. "Preacher. Mrs. Bodeker."

Joseph stepped aside and let him in.

Ig stood and extended his hand. "Well, Jim, if you'll just give me a few more days, I'm sure I can turn old Joseph around. Whatever he's done, I'm sure he didn't aim to and has since thought better of it."

Moore laughed and shook Ig's hand. "I leave the truly incorrigible cases to my deputies and the clergy. No sir, I'm afraid I'm in need of an undertaker, hard and desperate as he might be. The Raywicks' old nigger has hung himself."

Samuel said, "Old Jacob? Lord."

"I believe that's his name. Our esteemed coroner is on his way to pronounce the old boy dead. He was hanging from the rafters at the livery."

Bekah touched her throat. "Hung hisself."

"Well, he died from hanging. The Raywicks claim he tried to poison them—may very well have poisoned Mrs. Raywick. Dr. Pryor suspects strychnine. In any case, we'll need to get him in the ground quick. It's hot."

CHAPTER 49

Though it was nearly midnight when Joseph and Samuel arrived at the livery, a dozen or so men milled about, talking, smoking, eyeing Jacob's body. Someone had cut him down. His stiff arms extended beyond the edges of the bales of straw he lay on. The noose—just a bowline with the working end pulled through the loop—and several feet of rope lay in a pile near his head.

Marshal Moore picked up the makeshift noose. "A spur-of-the-moment hanging, I'd say." He pointed upward, toward the beam nearest the edge of the loft. "Just threw her over and tied off up there on one of the poles. Then stepped off, I reckon."

Samuel knelt and touched the rope burns on Jacob's neck. "How could a man keep from grabbin' the rope? Even if he wanted to die? I might want to just fall straight back, but to save my life I couldn't keep from puttin' my hands down to catch myself. And that's just falling back, not walkin' out of a hayloft with a rope around my neck."

"Terrible resolve born of utter despair." Trezevant Hawpe, the county coroner, walked up, his sleeves rolled to his elbows, his cravat still snug, despite the heat. He slapped Joseph on the back. "You can have him. After an exhaustive examination, I've determined that he's dead."

Samuel said, "But if his hands was tied, I could see it."

Hawpe drew a handkerchief from his vest pocket, pushed his hat back, and swabbed his forehead. "Clever boy you've got there, Joe. Sam, is it?"

"Samuel," Joseph said.

"Samuel, he might very well have grabbed at the rope, but if there was any slack at all, it would do him no good. After his failed attempt at murder, he panicked and ran. Ultimately, he saw suicide preferable to justice."

"Beg your pardon, Marster. I don't see no rope burns on his hands," Samuel said. "It'd burn his hands when he hit the end of that rope."

"We found no bindings." He chuckled. "Joe, you're an indulgent man."

Joseph said, "That's right, Samuel. We don't see any bindings, so there couldn't have been any. We're just here to pick up the deceased."

Hawpe smiled and shook his head in exasperation. "Gentlemen, I haven't time for this. It's late; I'm hot and in need of a cool towel and bed." He nodded toward Moore, who, like Samuel, was still eyeing the body. "I'm sure the marshal will take your comments."

Moore glanced at him, nodded, then knelt next to Samuel. Hawpe walked out the door, still shaking his head.

Moore helped them load Jacob's body into a simple cedar coffin. They'd be lucky if the Raywicks paid them for it. If not, the town would pay five dollars for an indigent burial.

As he latched the coffin lid, Joseph realized he'd forgotten all about the ambush and peril and their talk of leaving in mere hours. Work always had that effect on him.

———

Back at the shop, Samuel and Joseph were spreading cedar shavings on the coffin lid and heaping them around the sides. They made indigent coffins of the roughest lumber, and there were gaps despite Samuel's careful work. Joseph guessed the temperature in the high eighties, and it was a quarter past midnight. They'd bury Jacob at first light. You didn't want to be hit by that smell right after breakfast.

The back door opened. Bekah walked out followed by David.

Joseph dusted his hands on his pants. "Well, goddamn."

"Which one of us you so glad to see?" Bekah asked.

Samuel smoothed the shavings on the lid. "What in the world? Joseph, what's got into you?"

"No—I mean I didn't mean it like that. There's been a lot going on is what I mean."

David held out his left hand. "Sure enough." Joseph and Samuel shook his hand.

"Ig and Rachel still here?" Joseph asked.

Bekah laid her hand on the coffin, nestling her fingers into the shavings. "Went home a while ago to get some things together."

"Well, we ain't leaving just yet. What've you been doing?"

She didn't answer, just caressed the coffin lid.

Samuel said to David, "I reckon you heard it all."

"I come to tell you to lay low. We'll tell you if something's comin'."

Joseph exchanged glances with Samuel. Bekah seemed to be out of the conversation, still pondering the casket.

"You'll tell us."

"We will."

"I don't suppose you'd . . ."

"No suh."

Samuel said, "Well."

Joseph walked back toward the shop door, rubbing his palms together. He turned back to David. "You know, it's a little unsettling stumbling around in the dark, trusting people to tell you when something's coming. You see my point?"

David shrugged. "Why sure."

"Two men were held up, threatened with hanging, saved only by gunmen they never saw. You'll have to forgive me for being a little unnerved."

"You all right. For now." He shrugged, cocked his head. "Brother Ig, now, I ain't so sure there. He's doin' right headin' north. I told him out of Miz Rachel's hearing. But you—you leave now, you just as well ride round the square sayin' you break bread with Brother Jonah and Brother Zeph."

Joseph tapped the coffin. "I don't suppose you know anything about this."

"I say he done it."

"Hung hisself," Samuel said.

"That's right."

"Pizoned that woman, too?"

David arched his brows and shrugged.

Joseph said, "Well, I suppose you brought us a dozen runaways."

"Hid two boys from Plano in the woods across the river. Slipped across the bridge after dark. Them boys won't swim. I didn't figure y'all up for company tonight. I get 'em started on toward the Buttses' tomorrow night."

"I don't reckon we'll make you sleep in the woods."

"For sure we won't," Bekah said. Samuel looked at her; she ignored him.

In the kitchen, Joseph rinsed his face at the basin. His head hurt. He needed sleep.

Rachel due in less than a month and Ig hapless and nearly helpless; David, no doubt wanted in every county in North Texas, lying on a pallet in the office; two fugitive slaves hiding just across the river. He should've been alert, terrified. Instead he was only tired. Rachel leaving as soon as Ig could tie down a few provisions. He had to go check on them. He had to check on the others. Maybe Samuel could run down to the square. It was too late to go see Al. It wouldn't do to get caught sneaking around the Huitt place.

"David—does Al know?"

"Al can take care of hisself. No need in worryin' 'bout Al."

Joseph dried himself and put his shirt back on. He was already sweating again. July 8 and already hitting one hundred degrees every day. No rain in five weeks. August would be insufferable. But then he probably wouldn't be in Texas come August. He took his hat from the table and started for the back door. David started to get up from his pallet, but Joseph said, "Be still." He stepped over David and opened the door. "I'll be checking on Rachel and Ig."

"Do that."

He walked through the backyard, by the coffin sitting in the hearse. The stench wouldn't be bad yet, but he breathed through his mouth until he got upwind. He walked down the trail through the brittle weeds. At least there was a little breeze out of the south. The trail crossed Columbia Street, then became a two-track lane down to the Bodekers' cabin. He walked past an abandoned, collapsing cabin and listing barn, down a slight hill. The quarter moon lit their yard. Lantern light shone from the door and propped-open windows.

The wagon was already packed with trunks. The headboard and chairs were tied on top. They wouldn't be sleeping in their bed before leaving. John McCoy owned the lot and buildings. He'd have another renter in less than a week.

Joseph walked toward the lantern light. He'd help them crate their few chickens. Hopefully, there'd be room for the tent. The benches were still in the woods by the creek.

He heard Rachel's voice inside the cabin. Then Ig came out the door carrying something bulky. He shoved it into the back of the wagon, then rested against the sideboards.

Joseph stopped and stood in the road, sixty yards away, watching. Rachel stepped outside and shuffled to the wagon, her swollen belly obvious in the moonlight; she looked into the wagon and said something. Ig, obviously exasperated, said, "Rachel, darling . . ." They stood with their backs to him, arm against arm, fumbling with lashings or repositioning cargo.

Joseph sat down in the dust. How many nights had he walked this lane? All along he'd known that out there, somewhere, a reckoning or painful ending or separation awaited. But he'd pushed it off. Better to think of what they'd just done and said and to anticipate the next tryst. Now he watched a man and wife prepare to leave their home. There would be no chance for a private talk with Rachel. And what would he say to her? That he felt remorse? *I'm sorry. I hope I didn't ruin things for you. I hope you can live your life with your husband and that bearing this child will feel right and untainted, that in your old age you can feel that you and Ig built and lived a good life together, despite what we did.*

He rose, dusted the seat of his pants, and walked down to the cabin. "Well, I was sure if I waited long enough, you'd have the wagon packed.

I see my plan worked."

They both turned around and looked into the darkness. Joseph could tell they hadn't located him. He waved. "Right here."

"Ah!" Ig said. "Now the heavy lifting can begin."

"You must have some stuff hid in the barn then. Looks like everything in the house is accounted for." He walked into the yard. He couldn't see Rachel's expression.

Ig said, "I suppose penury has its advantages."

"Actually, I come to apologize and offer my help. We got tied up with a body. Old Jacob Isaacs hanged himself."

Rachel said, "Oh."

"Dear Lord," Ig said. "I've never believed the Almighty feels anything but sorrow for a man pushed to that point."

"Word is, he poisoned his mistress and panicked. Dr. Pryor and the druggists are looking into it."

Rachel said, "And Mrs. Raywick?"

"She'll make it. In any case, I won't be leaving right away."

"We'll wait, too, then. How long are you thinking?"

"Best go on, Ig. We'll catch up."

Rachel said, "Please tell me someone has alerted Rosemary and Malachi."

"Samuel's headed that way."

They stood in the dark yard. The crickets and tree frogs and heat only made Joseph sadder and sleepier. They needed to leave for their own safety. He needed them to leave because someone had known enough about Ig's leanings to ambush him. Maybe they didn't know about anyone else. Nothing had seemed different at the livery. And yet he felt traitorous for thinking that way.

Rachel said, "Joseph, surely you're not staying for a burial. Leave the casket and let someone else dig the grave."

"We all leave, they'll pick up on it right away. Y'all just slip out tonight. It'll be a few days before anyone will notice."

"You don't think I'll be missed at church tomorrow? I'm afraid I'm a bit underprepared."

Joseph started to make a joke about Pig standing in. "We'll think of something. Just get going."

Ig nodded. Rachel rested her forearms on her belly. Joseph said, "Anything I can help you with?"

Ig extended his hand. "You've done quite enough. We'll be waiting for you in Lawrence." He squeezed Joseph's hand. Then Joseph took Rachel's hand, squeezed and patted it. She wouldn't look, but he heard a sniffle. He could say nothing else. He turned and walked back up the lane.

CHAPTER 50

Joseph got two hours of sleep. Bekah woke him at four o'clock. She looked haggard, too, as if she'd never gone to bed. Samuel was in the kitchen waiting for coffee. David still lay on his pallet, but greeted Joseph as he walked in.

Joseph said, "I ought to have known better than to think you'd sleep through breakfast."

Samuel said, "I stepped over him four or five times and he never moved. But he come awake soon as Bekah patted that first biscuit."

David groaned and sat up. "I expect farmers to get me up in the middle of the night, but not undertakers."

"We'll get a hole dug by daylight and lay poor old Jacob to rest before she hits a hundred."

Bekah said, "I b'lieve I'll ride along with y'all this mornin'."

Joseph nodded, rubbed his eyes. While he wondered if Ig and Rachel had left, someone knocked on the back door. David grabbed his covers and hurried to Joseph's bedroom. Samuel opened to the door. Brother Ig.

Joseph said, "So one farewell wouldn't do it. At least you could've brought Rachel. She's a little easier to take on an empty stomach."

Ig stepped in and doffed his hat. "Rachel's not well." His eyes were bloodshot.

Bekah jiggled the coffeepot. "Whassamatter?"

"She's in pain. Sharp pain. She tells me there's some bleeding."

Joseph said, "Anybody gone to the doc?"

"I thought I'd stop here first."

Samuel said, "I'll fetch Doc Thomas."

Joseph sighed and sat back in his chair. "Ig . . . lord."

"She can't travel."

Bekah said, "She's still got a month to go."

Ig nodded. Samuel was already out the door. Bekah checked the oven. "Biscuits 'bout done. Y'all have to get 'em out yourself. Brother Ig, take me on back to your house."

Another knock at the back door. "Good lord," Joseph said. David, who'd started down the hall toward the kitchen, turned and bounded back to the bedroom.

Bekah opened the door. "Brother Sid."

Rev. Sid Claggett stepped in and nodded to everyone. His shirt was already darkened with sweat. "Young Samuel 'bout ran over me. Mrs. Cockrell said I could 'tend to old Jacob's burial today. I wondered when I ought to get there. I was powerful afraid she'd say no."

Joseph said, "Well, Reverend, despite our best plans, I reckon we'll be digging in the sun today. We'll send for you, come time."

Bekah had already pushed past Reverend Claggett. "Brother Ig, come on!" She headed toward Ig's wagon, mumbling something about preachers and doctors.

Dr. Thomas, backed by Bekah, Rosemary, and Hilda Van Huss, sent Rachel to bed. She didn't resist. With rest, she might carry her baby full term. If she overdid, the baby would come early and might bring deadly complications. If the doctor noticed the full wagon and cabin empty of furniture, except for the bed Ig had hastily reconstructed, he made no comment.

Rachel lay in the hot cabin, pale and sullen, yet obviously grateful and embarrassed at the uproar she'd caused. Samuel and Joseph unloaded the wagon and toted their furniture and kitchenwares back inside, both commenting on the complete lack of tools, save for a poker, shovel, and kindling ax. Here was a man planning to drive his wife across Indian territory. How he'd made it to Kansas from Virginia was a mystery. Samuel suggested Brother Ig did in fact stand in well with the Almighty, a suggestion that Joseph found both comforting and terrifying. You probably oughtn't cuckold a man who stands in well with the Lord.

Joseph couldn't decide if his relief stemmed more from the fact that Rachel wasn't in serious danger from her condition or that she wasn't leaving yet. Maybe this would all blow over yet. Maybe no one would miss a small band of hooligans from Scyene. Yet someone had hired them and would be expecting a report.

Joseph, Samuel, and Bekah were back home by mid-morning. The hearse and casket sat in full sun.

"I knowed we shoulda pulled it in the shed last night," Samuel said.

Joseph said, "I knew I should've stayed in Cincinnati. We better make sure all of our tools are loaded." He sighed. "Workin' on Sunday. Damn."

David was gone. He'd probably left before first light to check on the fugitives across the river. Joseph and Samuel hitched the team. They drove north on Lamar Street, Joseph driving, Bekah beside him, and Samuel sitting on the back, feet dangling, his back against the head of the casket. They crossed Polk, Wood, and Jackson, then turned west on Commerce, heading toward the south side of the square. They said little. Joseph tilted his hat back to protect his neck from the sun. Bekah didn't seem to sweat. They met few people along the streets. Most of the town's citizens were sweating in church or seeking any shade or breeze. The Negroes' night-time church services made sense.

They rode four blocks, past the nearly empty square, then another two, and turned left into a lane just before the intersection of Commerce and Water Streets. Behind Sarah Cockrell's two-story house stood three whitewashed clapboard shacks. Chickens pecked and scratched in the patchy yards and around the unpainted picket fence protecting two small vegetable gardens. Children ran in and out of the open doors.

Brother Sid and his wife, Sally, stood in the shade of a giant cotton-wood, talking with a young black man. The preacher patted the young man's arm, said something, and nodded toward the wagon.

Joseph said, "You won't have to miss dinner. We still have to dig the grave, but you'll be done in plenty of time for service tonight."

Brother Sid walked to them, shaking his head, and said softly, "Them two across the river got flushed early this mornin'. David walked right into it. He run up here." He nodded toward his door. "He's in there. They got men all over that riverbank. Already caught one of the boys. Some-body went after old Thigpen and his dogs." His eyes looked tired, rheumy. "Thigpen gets his dogs down, David's caught and we're caught."

"They'll have a hard time in this heat, them dogs will," Samuel said. He'd gotten down and stood with Sid.

Joseph said, "Remember that one old gyp?"

Shouts came from the direction of the river. Bekah said, "We ought to put him under the wagon boards. Haul him out to the edge of town. They trail him here, he'll get everybody hung."

Joseph considered her comment. There probably wouldn't be anyone at the slave cemetery. Not in this heat. They'd pick another day to pull weeds and tidy graves. Just pull up in the shade and let him set there un-til all was clear. He looked up at the second floor of the Cockrell house. "Anybody likely to be watching from up there?"

"Gone to meetin'," Sid said. "Nobody here but us."

"We'll take him then, if that suits you."

"I know good and well he's got his ear to the door." He turned toward the house. "Get on out here. You headin' to the graveyard."

The door opened and David stepped out. He eyed the wagon.

"Just a short little ride," Bekah said. "Plenty of room under there."

Sweat dripped from David's chin.

Bekah said, "Get you up off the ground where them dogs can't smell you. You leavin' smell all over everything."

David nodded, walked slowly toward the wagon, swallowed. "You gonna have to give me a spell, now."

Samuel dropped the tailgate and pulled loose the board covering the hidden space. It looked awfully cramped, and it was already hot. Joseph thought of Peter suffering in the hot casket. They'd get David to the graveyard and in the shade of the big elms. They should've given more thought to ventilation.

David eased up to the back of the wagon. Sally walked over. "Just crawl right on in there, baby," Sally said. She glanced at Bekah. "Just a little bitty ride up the road where you goin'."

David looked into the chamber. "I ain't goin' in headfirst now."

"We'll help you in feetfirst," Joseph said. "Just take hold here." He held out his hand and forearm for David, who backed up to the wagon. Joseph was already thinking about a new design that would allow a fugitive to enter one way and exit another. Samuel stepped in to help support David as he lifted one leg then the other into the wagon chamber. They shoved him inside. He looked desperate.

Bekah bent to his level and touched his cheek. "I'd give anything if I had a little whiskey for you. It'll be all right, though."

He closed his eyes.

"We gonna fasten you up now," Samuel said. David nodded. Samuel raised the board, then lifted it slightly, so that it caught on two hooks.

They clasped hands with the Cockrell slaves, then turned the team and wagon around in the yard and drove back out onto Commerce Street. Instead of going on to Water Street, Joseph decided to turn back east for four blocks and follow Market Street out to the northern outskirts, then take Calhoun south to the cemetery. Best to avoid the river altogether. Before they made the square, hounds were barking behind them in the river bottom. He didn't dare push the team in the heat. And he didn't want to draw attention. Fortunately there was still little activity along the street, although people sitting in their yards beneath shade trees waved to them as they drove past.

Bekah sat impassive. Samuel greeted a few people from the back of the wagon. Joseph glanced across the square and wondered about the Meades and Van Husses. Samuel had given them the news about Ig and Pig's close scrape. Both families had seemed stunned and indecisive.

Joseph felt better as the houses and businesses thinned as he moved north along Market Street. Most business was still done on the square. Property was cheaper and the houses more modest the farther away you got. Soon they were passing log houses.

Nothing but prairie and cedar breaks lay ahead after they turned west on Calhoun. Joseph pushed the team a little as they rode the three blocks to the Negro cemetery. He whoaed the sweaty mules in the shade of two great elms.

Bekah said, "Lordy."

Two Negro families stood about graves near the center of the cemetery. Samuel said some of them were W. B. Mitchell's slaves. He didn't know them personally. The other slaves belonged to various merchants.

"Nothing to do but get to work," Joseph said. Samuel bent down at the back of the wagon and gave the edges of his shovel a few strokes with a file. "Be through with this shortly," he said. "Nice and cool and shady," he said, then whispered, "We ought to leave her closed, I say."

Joseph glanced at the two families and nodded. Bekah said, "Anybody with any sense woulda brung a bucket of water."

Samuel said, "Anybody with any sense woulda brung three shovels instead of two."

"You just say when you're wore out," Bekah said. "I was a field slave way 'fore I ever saw a white woman's kitchen."

They walked back to the unoccupied part of the cemetery and picked a site in the shade. Gnats swarmed their mouths and nostrils as they worked. Both men cussed. Neither would relinquish his shovel. Bekah went back and sat on the back of the wagon. Occasionally, they heard her humming or talking about the weather or the grave-digging progress, as if talking to herself.

They were waist deep, and the two families still milled about the graveyard, righting wooden grave markers, repairing chimes, and arranging pottery shards.

Samuel stopped and leaned on his shovel. "Brother Sid ain't comin', I say."

"Busy explaining why Thigpen's dogs ran right up in their yard and tried to tear the door off."

Samuel eyed the wagon. "We might have to take him back home."

"We're fixing to have half the county show up at our door." His dread had been growing. Ig and Rachel were trapped in Dallas. The Nucholses probably were already heading north. He couldn't imagine their place empty. Pig kept no stock other than a milk cow. But what would become of his cabin and land? His few crops? With Cathlyn and the boys safe in Kansas, would he come back and try to sell the place?

They heard occasional barks to the south. Thigpen's gyp. The only one in his pack with a decent bawl. The rest sounded like a flock of turkeys.

Joseph checked his watch. A little before one o'clock. Another half hour and they'd be ready to lay Jacob to rest. One of the families had left. The other family, a middle-aged man and woman and a young woman stood in one corner, talking. They'd found a cool spot and would probably be there awhile. What if David just eased out of his chamber? Would the family notice him? Rumors of the one-armed Negro had been growing. Thigpen's dogs had chased David all over the county. People were talking.

Joseph propped his shovel in one corner of the grave. "Let me check on David." He climbed out and walked over to the wagon. Bekah said, "Doin' fine here. Gettin' plenty of air. In bad shape 'fore I opened that door though. Bless his heart."

Joseph knelt. David, on his back, rolled his eyes to look at him. He was sweating profusely. Why hadn't they brought a bucket of water? He'd have thought they'd be better prepared after nearly killing Peter. Joseph looked back at the family. They seemed to be paying him no mind. Just the undertaker checking his wagon. "Have you out of here shortly, my friend."

"Gonna have to be shortly or there ain't gonna be nothin' to let out."

Joseph noticed the woman looking in his direction. He peered beneath the wagon as if examining the axle. Liquid had dripped from gaps beneath the floorboards. There were spots on the dust and brittle tufts of grass and weeds. Sweat? Urine? He smelled only rank weeds, dust, and axle grease. He wouldn't ask. Even the strongest man had his secret terrors. They were taking a risk just by keeping the door open. He stood. "Keep a close watch."

Bekah nodded as if he'd just said the most obvious and childish thing ever uttered.

He went back to his digging. The dogs' barking seemed closer and more regular. The gyp barked every few seconds now. The family left through the far gate and walked down the path toward Water Street. The dogs barked again. Samuel glanced at Joseph as he drove the shovel into the dirt with his foot. Joseph said, "No way in hell I can see. I've been around hounds all my life. This heat. And they're upwind of us." He decided not to mention the sweat or urine dripping from the bottom of the wagon.

Bekah was helping David out of the wagon. He put his arm down, crawled out, then knelt, his head hanging. Bekah felt his forehead. He didn't look like he could run.

Samuel said, "Joseph, I say them dogs are coming up Market Street."

"I don't see how."

"It don't make no difference how. There's fixin' to be people out seein' what's afoot. We're fixin' to have all manner of company."

They had another foot or so to go. "This might be a shallow grave." He climbed out and ran to Bekah and David. "Get him back in the trees. There won't be a breeze but he'll be out of the sun."

"You hear them dogs?"

"Hell yes, I hear the dogs."

David said, "I got to get up from here."

Bekah pulled him to his feet. "And go where? Honey, get back in this thicket. You can't hardly walk." David shuffled beside her as she held his arm.

Joseph closed the tailgate and climbed into the wagon. "We got to move this." He drove it to the graveside. The dogs had gotten closer. "Deep as it's gonna be," he said.

Samuel said, "We got to empty that casket."

"Help me."

Samuel clambered out, and they pulled the coffin out and laid it beside the grave. Joseph fetched the pry bar from the wagon. They looked around. No one else in sight. He pried open the lid.

"Sweet Jesus," Samuel said. He helped Joseph tip the casket toward the grave. The bloated corpse hung. Joseph took the claw end of the pry bar, catching the corpse by the neck and jerking it out into the grave. They threw casket and lid back into the wagon, and Joseph started the team back toward trees and brush near the cemetery entrance. Samuel gagged as he shoveled soil on Jacob's body.

Joseph stopped the team as close to cover as he could, then jumped from the seat, ran into the trees, and hissed for Bekah. She and David stepped out of the cedars. David looked a little better.

"Come on! Come on!" The dogs were coming down Calhoun. That goddamn gyp. He'd never seen anything like her. But she knew David's scent; she'd followed it all over North Texas. Slow but sure, she'd worked it out. A drop here, a drop there. Air scent? Fear scent? She knew where he was that night at the shop. They hadn't fooled her.

Joseph stopped them at the edge of the thicket. He pulled the casket out onto the ground. Samuel was hurrying toward them. Joseph looked into the casket, then caught David's eyes. "It's the only way."

David shook his head, desperation in his eyes. "I can't do this, y'all. I won't be able to breathe in there."

Bekah said, "Only for just a minute. Sweet baby, you got to do it. You can't run from them dogs. Come on now." She touched his arm, urged him toward the casket.

He stepped up and looked into the casket, swayed. "I can't go back to that."

Bekah said, "I know, baby. You done more than any man ought to have to do. You the best man I know. But you can do this. Just this one more time. You done borne worse."

"I smell him," David said. He moved toward the casket, stopped, his legs rigid as a corpse's. The gyp bawled only a few hundred feet away. The other dogs were well behind her. Bekah said, "Come on, sweet baby." She nudged him, but his knees were locked.

"I'll kill ever one of them dogs," he said.

"You can't kill 'em all before this place is overrun with white people," she said.

Samuel pulled the shotgun from beneath the seat, pointed at David. "Get in that box."

David said, "Kill me then."

"I don't aim to kill you. Looks like I caught me a runaway slave. Reckon I'll get me a reward? Or you can get that box and we all get away," Samuel said.

Joseph said, "David."

There were voices and shouts back toward the direction of the hounds. Two black women came through the gate at the far end of the cemetery, saw Samuel and the gun, then hurried away, glancing back over their shoulders.

Bekah was crying, glaring at Samuel. "I'll kill you for this." She knelt and kissed David's hand. "Sweet baby, please. Please get in there. We won't leave you. I won't never leave you again."

Samuel held the gun on David's chest. "Huh?"

David bent toward the box. His breath came in short rasps. Other Negroes, women and men, had gathered at the far end of the cemetery. Joseph recognized Al Huitt's voice.

David put a hand down in the casket. He was breathing like an asthmatic now. Joseph thought he might smother despite the gaps in the box. David swallowed and lay in the box. Tears streamed down his cheeks.

"Be all right," Bekah said. She wiped away her own tears. David didn't respond. He seemed unaware now, in shock.

Samuel shoved the shotgun beneath the seat and grabbed the hammer from the wagon bed. Joseph laid the lid on the casket; Samuel tapped it back down. Several of the bent nails jutted though the casket sides. The three of them loaded the casket back into the wagon. Bekah and Samuel hurried to the grave while Joseph drove the wagon. A dozen or so slaves had gathered at the other end of the cemetery. Sid Claggett came forward, carrying his Bible.

Joseph pulled up alongside the grave. The others stood around it. He stepped down now, casual, nodded to the gathering. Al Huitt came forward. The others stayed back. No doubt their masters had forbidden them from attending the funeral of an alleged murderous slave. The lead hound, the young gyp, ran into the cemetery in full cry. Fifty yards behind came Ben Thigpen and several others, including Charles Pryor on the trail of breaking news.

The hound snuffled around where the wagon had been, then howled off into the brush where David had rested. The rest of the pack poured through the cemetery. Pryor rode into the graveyard and looked toward the gravesite. The hounds howled back in the brush. Thigpen dismounted and urged his dogs on. "Goddamn this heat and dust! A dog can't smell nothin' in it!" Other men and several boys laughed, watching from a distance. Rare entertainment in Dallas.

Pryor rode to the grave. "You people see anything?"

Joseph said, "Charles, we've been up to our eyes in dirt. If a runaway darky came through here, we missed him."

Pryor eased his horse close to the grave, leaving hoofprints in the fresh soil. Brother Sid Claggett stepped toward Pryor and nodded to the prints, then looked back at the casket. "Marster, please."

Pryor backed up his horse. "Oh. Very well. Beg your pardon, Reverend."

"I thank you, Marster."

Pryor looked at the gathering of slaves. "Odd they beat the dogs to the cemetery." He looked again at Brother Claggett. "As it's odd the dogs trailed the boy through your quarters."

"A nigger can't do nothin' 'bout where another one wants to run to," Sid said.

The cedar thicket was boiling with dogs. Joseph and Samuel carried the coffin to the grave and eased it down. It sat surprisingly level. Samuel had gotten in and tamped down the earth over Jacob's body.

The gyp emerged from the thicket while the other hounds snuffled and howled and backtracked. She cast about the cemetery, raising and lowering her nose in search of scent. She swung briefly back to where the wagon had been parked. Her snuffles were audible at graveside, forty yards away. She whined and yipped but didn't break into full cry.

"A right calamitous burying," Brother Sid said.

Sweat ran down Joseph's sides. He didn't see a way out. What would cause the hounds to leave? They'd just bought some time by forcing David into the casket. Unless the dogs got confused and Thigpen grew disgusted and gave up, they'd have to stand here all day. And how long before that gyp caught wind of David in the casket? Here was a hound that trailed him all the way through town, by air scent alone or one drop of sweat and piss at a time. Even Pig would be astounded.

The gyp circled, head bobbing up and down. She swung back toward the thicket then turned abruptly and jogged toward the grave, tongue lolling. She shook her head, wrapping stings of slobber around her muzzle, and came on. Thigpen emerged from the thicket, yelling for his other hounds and started in her direction.

Brother Sid closed his eyes and raised his Bible and said, "Into this earth, and trusting in your sweet mercy, Father, we return your precious son Jacob and we beseech you dear Father to take him gently into your arms. Amen, Lord." He picked up a handful of dirt and let it sift through his fingers onto the casket. The gyp snorted up and gathered herself to jump down on the coffin. Samuel grabbed the shovel and held her back with the handle.

Thigpen strode toward them. "Boy, you touch that dog and I'll kill you."

Joseph said, "We're having a burial here. You touch my boy and you just as well get ready to kill me."

Samuel started shoveling dirt on the grave. Bekah wept. Thigpen said, "Lotta grievin' for a woman-killin' darky."

Brother Sid said, "I reckon Miz Raywick is still with us, praise Jesus."

Thigpen ignored the remark. The gyp snuffled around the tailgate, threw back her head, and bawled.

"Quite a hound you got there, Thigpen," Joseph said. "I might borrow her from you next time I need to locate a grave."

He looked into the grave. Samuel had it almost covered. "It's this goddamn heat. And nigger stink all over the place. Dead ones and live ones and one-armed ones." He peered into the hearse again. Joseph took the other shovel and helped Samuel fill in the grave. All of the dogs were snorting about now. The crowd had moved closer. The slaves glowered while white children ran about the graveyard. One of the men in the crowd grabbed his young daughter and spoke to her sternly.

Joseph covered the casket and counted the seconds, wondering how much air might be in the coffin. They'd thrown a foot of earth on the casket. Might there be some air trapped in the loose dirt? There was no way out. They were burying a beloved friend alive. Bekah stood stone-faced. He could only glance at her. Thigpen watched his dogs. The slaves looked on. Some started to leave. Some of the women were crying.

William Keller rode through the front gate, dismounted, and walked down to the grave.

Thigpen looked at him. "I don't know what it is about this one boy. She never loses anybody else."

Keller said, "It takes a cruel man to run a dog in this heat."

"A cruel man has to eat just like everybody else."

Brother Sid shook his head, his eyes closed. No doubt this was the oddest, most irreverent burial he'd ever presided over.

Joseph felt he might need to step away and vomit.

Keller looked at the grave and said, "Old Jacob." He looked up at the sun. "Keep at it if you will, boys, but I'd rather hunt shade today. Joe, Sam, Bekah." He raised his hook to her, then walked back up the slight hill, mounted his horse, and rode away at a trot.

"Take a rest, Samuel," Joseph said. He leaned on his shovel to keep from tipping over.

Samuel said nothing. Sweat dripped from his chin. He looked at the sun, then up the hill at the dispersing crowd. He leaned his shovel against the wagon and walked over and righted a chime that had been knocked over.

Thigpen said, "Well," and started back up the hill. The gyp worried the tailgate, whining. Thigpen eyed Joseph, the grave, Bekah, Samuel, and Brother Sid. He gave the crowd of slaves a disgusted wave. "Gert! Work in here now! Nigger in here! Right in here!"

Gert snuffled about the grave, but left it after a few snorts and went back to the wagon. Thigpen called her off and yelled at her to get back to the thicket. He stood while she and the dogs cast about for scent. Joseph slowly filled the grave. Thigpen watched them. Gert started back down the hill. Joseph could barely breathe. Sweat stung his eyes, ran into his mouth.

Someone yelled, "Fire!"

To the south, on the square, black smoke rose and billowed toward them, pushed by a stiff southerly breeze.

CHAPTER 51

All along Water Street, men and boys, black and white, had formed bucket lines from the river and were dousing the houses. People with homes and businesses on the square had already retreated and stood dazed, their faces streaked by ash and grime, so that Joseph had to weave his way southward. The heat seared the left side of his face.

More screams as houses and buildings erupted a block north of the square. Women were crying, clutching babies. Joseph could see maybe twenty feet in the smoke. His house probably wouldn't burn. The houses to the north were in serious peril. He felt guilty not helping. People screamed at him as he passed. The bucket line parted to let him by. People stared at him, seemingly uncomprehending. Their mouths moved, but he heard nothing over the roar of flames and hoarse and shrill screams.

Now horses whinnied. Darnell's livery. Surely someone let the horses out. There was Everett Darnell, dazed, his face black. Three horses, one badly burned, its withers still smoking, ran down Commerce Street, crossed Water Street, heading for the river. Joseph smelled burning hair.

An explosion sent people on the street cowering back into the trees. Flames shot up from the roof of Peak & Sons. People covered their mouths with handkerchiefs; others gagged. The chemicals were burning: sulfur, strychnine, quinine, mercury.

Joseph whipped the mules on. He needed to get clear of the smoke. Ahead, on both sides of the street, men were beating something in the weeds and grass with shovels, axes, wrecking bars. Something seemed to detach from the streetside brush. Rats. Rafts of rats. The men were bludgeoning them in a rage. Carcasses lay strewn about the street. Tonight homes would be overrun with them. The riverside brush would be full of them. The owls, foxes, and snakes would feast. Dogs howled.

South of Wood Street the air began to clear. Joseph's throat ached. Beside him, Bekah squinted and covered her nose and mouth with her hand. Samuel rode behind him in the wagonbed.

The square was lost. People had given in to the fire and now concerned themselves with saving their own homes. Men and women lined the streets all the way to Polk. Joseph could not see far to the north. No doubt help had come from Hord's Ridge.

He turned left on Polk and pushed for home. People had thinned out now. The street was nearly empty south of Market Street. Somewhere, Ig was watching it all, maybe trying to help. Malachi's office was gone. All of his papers, his beloved library. Nothing on the square could have survived. Joseph wondered how many bodies and burials he could handle.

He pulled behind the house, whoaed the mules, and braked the wagon. Samuel was already out.

"Wait! Wait!" Joseph said.

Samuel lowered the tailgate. "I'm watching."

He dropped the door to the hidden compartment, revealing David's head. It didn't move. Bekah said, "Baby?"

They pulled him out. His eyelids fluttered. Half an hour in a fetid casket and a good twenty minutes buried alive and then the confines of the wagon and the smoke. Joseph had known men damaged forever from nearly drowning or being trapped in mines.

Bekah kissed David's forehead and hand. He'd clawed his face horribly. Dust clung to his cheeks and nose. She said, "Dear Jesus, he's 'bout clawed off the tips of his fingers." He tried to speak, but nothing came out. They carried him inside, Joseph and Samuel holding his shoulders, Bekah with her arms about his legs. They headed straight for the back door. None of them looked about for others.

They laid him on Joseph's bed and set about opening windows. They pulled off his boots and shirt. Bekah fetched the water bucket. While David sat up, with Samuel's help, and took feeble sips, Bekah fetched towels, which she wetted and held on the back of his neck.

David didn't speak. He drank a cup of water and lay back. There seemed to be no white to his eyes, only dark brown pupil and iris surrounded by blood red.

Bekah washed David's face and chest and arms and stroked his forehead.

Samuel sat in the corner chair and watched. Joseph bent over David and said, "How are you, friend?"

David nodded weakly and pointed to his throat, then shook his head. He clasped Joseph's hand and shook it, then held out his hand for Samuel, who rose and clasped it. Bekah wiped her eyes with the heel of her hand and stroked David's hair. A few blocks north, the roar continued. Occasionally, wagons and men on horseback went by on Polk or Lamar.

A knock at the back door. Joseph got up, eased the bedroom door shut, and answered the door. Rachel stood in the heat, her blond hair disheveled and matted with sweat. Her face was beet red. Sweat had soaked though her dress below her neckline and along the sides of her swollen belly.

"What in the world?" Joseph said. He took Rachel by the arm and led her in to his chair. "You walk all the way up here?"

She nodded but seemed confused. "I insisted that he go help. He wanted to go but wouldn't leave me. I don't know what I was thinking. Have you been up there?"

"Just about rode through it."

"You didn't see him?"

He shook his head. Surely it would all end on this day, in this heat. "Rachel, you can't be—I mean . . ."

"Joseph."

"I'll go find him."

She looked at him. "Please." Her blue eyes looked wild.

"You'd better lie down."

"I want you to find Ig. He has no business up there. He'll end up killing himself."

Bekah came down the hall. She stopped when she saw Rachel. "Carry her on up here." She started back up the hall toward her room, muttering, "Fixin' to fool around and kill this baby." She opened the door to Joseph's bedroom. "Samuel, come help."

———

Ig's vest would have wrapped twice around Mary Alice Bingham, who'd barely gotten out of her house behind Murphy's brickyard. Mrs. Bingham, a petite widow, had been napping when she woke to the smell of smoke. Before she could get on her dress, her roof caught fire. Now she stood in her pantalets and blouse, crying, surrounded by several younger women in the shade of the elms on the west side of Water Street. Ig had thought his vest might save her some embarrassment but decided it only made her look more pathetic. The young women were trying to keep her from view of the men. There was nowhere to take her. Every house within three blocks of the square was in peril. Everyone with horses and wagons was too busy hauling belongings out of homes to worry over a half-dressed widow.

The wind was still up and out of the southwest—unlikely to drive the flames toward Rachel or Joseph, Samuel, and Bekah. The Crutchfield House was in full blaze; flames shot twenty feet above the roof. The

Meades lived behind the hotel. The Van Husses' butcher shop, on the southeast corner of the square, might survive.

He'd already helped empty several houses. Most of the men had given up fighting the fire and had abandoned the square. The heat was too intense. The west side of the square was gone. Peak & Sons Drug Store. Simon and Murphy Brick Yard. The *Herald* office. The Dallas Hotel. Shirek's Grocery. Malachi's office.

People were just watching now, all along Water Street. Men and boys still in their long johns. Women weeping, others blank-faced, most blackened by ash. Wagons loaded with trunks and dishes and chairs and beds lined the street. Piles of belongings lay in yards near the river, upwind of the blaze. Three men dragged and carried a piano down Jackson Street.

By the time he'd arrived, the blaze was too fierce to fight. Ig had helped douse homes and yards and carry away furniture. Fatigue set in. His back ached. His hands were blistered. He'd lost his hat, and no doubt his bald spot was bright red.

He ought to go back to Rachel. She'd be worried. Then he remembered his wagon was full of belongings. He didn't know whose. He remembered silverware and china from a log house, and a young wife, her husband still somewhere in the square with bucket or shovel. She'd been tiny, the young woman, with an oddly husky voice, pert nose, and green eyes. Not frantic, but purposeful. A young woman with plenty of years ahead. No children. They'd rebuild if they had to. "Thank you, Reverend. Could we disassemble the bed now?" She had to look over the pile of quilts in her arms. A strong little girl. With china and silverware already. More than Rachel had. No doubt she knew better than he did the whereabouts of his wagon.

As he carried chairs and Dutch ovens and andirons out of homes, it occurred to him that a man of God ought to be praying. For what? That the fire would cease? He prayed. It burned on. That it wouldn't consume the entire town? He prayed. That the Masons' Hall wouldn't burn? He prayed. Conditions suggested this request would be granted. That no one would die? Might be too late. He prayed anyway, then asked for the safety of those still here and fighting the flames. Somehow this was part of God's plan. He could see no good in it, but it was not for him to sort out. Best to concentrate on the small things he could do. He repeated his prayer over and over, by rote, like he always did in distress. Perhaps the gesture was the important thing, the ritual.

He found himself without a task, walking among the carts and wagons and stunned townspeople. The fire had spread east along Main Street, on the north side of the square. Probably Wester's Barbershop was on fire now, perhaps even the tavern. It would all burn. A black man sat in the weeds, his face in his hands. Ash clung to his hair. His homespun shirt was dark with sweat. He'd propped his shovel against a tree behind him. His shoes lay to one side. Ig went to him and knelt. "May I get you something? Some water." The man raised his head. He was older than Ig, his eyes bloodshot. Ig had seen him around town but didn't know his owner.

The man looked at him, woozy. His eyebrows were singed. He had no lashes. "Marster, my belly has kindly got sour on me. I sit here just a spell, I get up and get busy sure enough." His knuckles were blistered. His face was dry.

"Friend, you need water. Let me get you some."

"I b'lieve I'm feelin' a mite better."

Ig walked away, looking for a bucket. He walked north, toward most of the traffic. A boy of about ten ran by with a bucket in both hands. It banged against his knees.

"Son, is that well water you have there?"

The boy glanced at him but kept going. Ig walked on. Directly he found a bucket sitting on the back of a wagon. It was about a third full. He sniffed; it didn't smell like river water. You didn't want to drink river water this time of year except as a last resort. He looked around, then took it and headed back down the street.

He couldn't find the black man. He thought he'd lost track of the tree he'd been leaning against, but then he found the shoes. The sole on one shoe was nearly melted. The edges of the hole at the toe were burned brittle as dry cane. Ig turned the bucket up and drank. Water spilled onto his chest and tasted of ash.

Flames leaped up on Commerce, west of the square. People pointed and gasped. Women covered their mouths. A man sitting in the dirt along the edge of the road hoisted a jug and said, "Mrs. Cockrell's hotel! Be damn if there ain't a God in heaven after all!"

Ig looked south, down Water Street. Beyond the gathered crowd, the smoke and ash, Joseph strode up the street toward him. No mistaking that bouncing gait. Still wearing his black vest, shirtsleeves rolled up to his elbows. Coming right up the middle of the road like he owned it, arms swinging. Sure enough, he held his course, and bigger men moved aside.

CHAPTER 52

I't started at Willis Peak's drugstore, in the kindling box. Everyone seemed to agree on that. You needed only to consider wind direction to understand the rest. Next, Simon and Murphy's Brickyard, then the *Dallas Herald* office, the Dallas Hotel, and Shirek's Grocery & Dry Goods Store. By the time Joseph had driven home from the cemetery, the flames had jumped Main Street, to the Crutchfield House. "I never saw no fire cross the road," Sid Claggett told him. "The grocery was burnin', then the Crutchfield 'sploded. Got too hot and she just blowed up. That wind's what done it. This whole square was a forge, like the devil was way off somewheres, working his bellows." From there, it spread eastward and burned everything along the north side of the square.

Joseph walked north on Broadway. The wind had laid. The sun nearly touched the horizon. Most who lived a block or more from the square had begun to move their belongings back into their homes. Smoke rose straight up, and even a block away he could still feel the heat from the coals and embers. He turned right on Commerce Street and walked toward the square.

Men with shovels and wrecking bars had gathered just back of Houston Street. They'd wait until morning. Peak's and the *Herald* and the other concerns on the west side were burned to ash. Only thin smoke rose, and occasional gusts made ashen dust devils. But on the north side of the square, heaps still glowed and would glow through the night.

Joseph squinted against the heat. No one could enter the square without bursting into flames like the Crutchfield House. Buildings had burned and collapsed eastward into one other, so that the heaps seemed to grow as you looked down Main Street, toward Jefferson.

He tried to remember where the Tavern Stand had been, and Caruth's old stand, and Carr's Saddlery, but there was no distinguishing the great hotel from the barber shop from the grocery. A gust raised spouts of flame along Main Street and, for a moment, muffled the low roar, popping, and creaking of structure and order consumed and reduced to ash.

There was little talk among the men waiting to sift the remains. They stood sweating beneath their hats, waiting for the chance to ply muscle and iron against helplessness. Behind them, in yards and empty lots, the women were pooling provisions, wrapping burned hands, arranging shelter, preparing to feed their community. Their voices, calm and resigned now, rose above the moaning ruins in the square.

In the center of the square, smoke rose from an open window of the courthouse. From forty yards away, Joseph saw no damage to the roof or doors. The windows remained unbroken. Yet the locust trees on the lawn had been incinerated, the yard burned clean.

The dark red bricks on the west wall of the courthouse seemed afire in the seconds before the sun dropped below the horizon. Nothing inside could have survived. Joseph imagined desks and library and papers burning within a brick kiln. Nothing left but an empty hull.

He left the muttering, dazed men and walked south toward the intersection of Commerce and Houston. In the gloom beneath dusty, ashy cottonwoods, Sarah Cockrell lectured Sid Claggett and a young black woman as they checked over a piano.

"Pure foolishness, Brother Sid," she said. "It's just a piano."

Sid nodded and mumbled something, pulled a handkerchief from his pocket, and began dusting the top of the piano. He bent to wipe one of the legs, but caught himself and straightened up slowly.

"And you've hurt your back," Mrs. Cockrell said.

He wiped his forehead with the handkerchief, said something Joseph couldn't make out. The young woman wiped the keys with her skirt.

"What if the ceiling fell in on you? I can always get another piano." The two slaves seemed far more interested in the piano than in their mistress's complaints.

The young woman fingered a key; middle C, Joseph suspected.

Mrs. Cockrell said, "Well, Myra, I suppose now you'll comfort us all by playing a few hymns."

Brother Sid laughed. Myra smiled. Mrs. Cockrell raised her hands in exasperation. "I appreciate your concern for my property, but for heaven's sake!" She looked at Joseph and shook her head and walked back toward her house, which had survived the fire, though the St. Nicholas, just across Commerce Street, was half burned. Smoke still poured through a huge hole in the roof. She stopped halfway up her walkway and turned, "Thank God, Mr. Shaw, that lovely armoire survived. I came within a hair of moving it to the hotel office no more than a month ago." She turned and strode into the house, no doubt to begin rebuilding plans. What were a few structures when you owned half the Trinity River bottom?

Myra finished wiping the keys, let her skirt fall, dusted her hands together. Joseph stopped. Brother Sid stood watching, his hands clasped behind his sore back. She played three soft chords. They sounded surprisingly sweet coming from a piano that had just been dragged from a burning hotel and set on hardpan. She smiled at the preacher and polished another spot with her fingers.

On Water Street, Joseph found Ig carrying two Dutch ovens, one in each hand. The sun had set, but the street was lighted with lanterns and campfires built on bare ground with ten-foot firebreaks dug and raked around the perimeters. Everywhere were pails of water ready for dousing.

"Ig, your knuckles are about to drag."

"Now I can prod you awake from the pulpit."

Joseph took one of the ovens. "Where to?"

"Down on the riverbank. Several Negro families are camped there. And a few poor whites. This town is generous within limits."

"Where'd you get the ovens? They look new."

"Mr. Shirek's wagon."

"You checked on Rachel?"

"She's resting easy. At your place still."

"No sense moving her."

They turned left, down a trail toward the river. Already, canvas tarps stretched between trees and campfires. Black and white children and dogs splashed in the shallows. Horses had been gathered in rope corrals. The trail turned steep, and Ig shuffled sideways, his huge feet slipping on the worn trail. He was breathing hard, and every few steps he switched the Dutch oven to his other hand. His shirttail hung out, and the mat of dark hair on his great belly showed through his filthy white, sweat-soaked shirt.

It was dark in the woods now, save for the campfires and lanterns. The trail veered upriver. They walked into a camp of what looked to be an extended family of slaves—two elderly men; a gray, toothless woman smoking a pipe, her lower lip bulging with snuff; a middle-aged married couple; and several children of various ages. They looked up from their fire. Joseph saw no bedding. Over the fire, several roasting ears and sweet potatoes cooked on a grill of green elm sticks.

Ig said, "Evening. Perhaps you could use a cooking vessel."

The older woman jumped up and tamped out her pipe. "Lord, Marster, we surely could! Where'd you get it at?"

"We live in a generous town, thank God."

"Thank God, sure enough."

"I'm afraid it's unseasoned," Ig said.

"Best way to season one is to use it," she said.

They were all standing now. "Very kind of you, Marster," the younger man said. "We'll be sure to give it back right off."

"We'll not worry about that now. How are you for provisions?"

They didn't answer.

"Food," Joseph said. "What do you need in the way of food?"

"Oh, we in fine shape on food," the younger man said. "We got away with plenty of meal and corn before our place caught."

"Who're your folks?" Ig asked.

"Marster Stigall and Marster Rogers. They done been down here to check on us," the old man said. "We live just back of the barbershop."

The woman already had set the oven near the coals and was rummaging through some bundles. "I know I got a lard can in here somewhere," she said. "We fixin' to fry something."

Ig and Joseph continued along the dark trail. The river ran low and soft below them. Joseph heard only occasional soft gurgles and splashes. He'd never known the Trinity this low. The air smelled of drying mud. They walked past camps of slaves and poor whites, all familiar faces, but Joseph could name few of them. They spoke as they passed the camps, and men tipped hats, saying "Evening," or "Reverend," or "Mr. Shaw."

Two camps were a mix of black and white families, the women quietly working around the fire while the men talked in the darkness. Joseph imagined their grim nodding and recounting of what they'd seen. Had they been brought together by mutual need? Perhaps one family had meal and the other meat.

Ig said, "Hard times can make for reasonable men."

"Or harder men."

They left the second oven with a young couple. The woman was very shy and spoke only once and too softly for Joseph to hear. Her husband said they'd been living on the second floor of the Tavern Stand and had planned to move out as soon as something became available. He wasn't too worried, he said. They had a small fire, and their horse was picketed back in the trees. Some of the town women had given them some cornbread and beans and a tin of meat.

Ig said, "We'll be getting back up the hill."

The woman said, "Reverend."

Ig didn't hear her and had extended his hand to the young husband. Joseph touched his arm and nodded toward the woman.

Joseph said, "Yes, ma'am?"

She looked down the river trail. "There's a woman down that way a piece. She'd be glad to see you."

Ig said, "And I'll be glad to see her."

They shook hands with the husband and walked on. Ig's breathing sounded more and more labored. The trail bent away from the river, and they saw a fire so small it lit only a man's feet and shins. A woman sat beyond the flame, her face obscured by darkness. They walked through a swarm of gnats; Joseph stepped off the trail and felt a spider web on his face. He spat and cussed. Ig trudged on without comment.

"Hello, the camp," Ig said. He walked in without waiting for a reply, which never came.

Joseph recognized the two, although he hadn't known they were a couple. He'd seen her around doing wash for some of the prosperous merchants. The man he'd seen around loafing, doing odd jobs. Now he barely recognized the woman. She looked emaciated. He hadn't seen her in months. She sat shivering in the heat, yet sweating, hugging herself, her dark eyes feverish and glistening before the flames.

Ig bent near the woman. "Margaret, you look a bit sickly."

"Brother Ig, I'm needful."

"What can we bring you?"

"You can't get her what she needs," the man said. "I could do with a bite, though."

"I'll speak to Dr. Pryor or one of the other physicians," Ig said.

"No need, 'less they can bring her something."

"Reverend, I'm hurtin'," she said. "My bones ache. Way down in the center of my bones."

"I'm not a medical man," Ig said. "I can't say what she needs."

"Hell, I can say just exactly what she needs."

She held her trembling hand to her forehead. Ig covered it with his own, and the trembling seemed to lessen. The man watched without comment.

Ig sighed. "Ah, the poppy."

"Huh?"

Ig shook his head without answering.

"Laudanum is what she needs," the man said. "If a doctor don't bring that or a draught of opium, ain't no need of him coming."

"Perhaps a doctor can soothe her a bit without poisoning her further," Ig said.

"I can't go on like this," she said.

"Only one thing I know gonna soothe her," the man said. "She . . ." He hesitated. "We can get money. But we can't buy what she needs, 'cause both the damn drugstores burnt up."

Ig touched Margaret's cheek with the back of his hand. She seemed to lean into it. He said, "Let's get you off this riverbank. Get you in a clean bed."

"Preacher, I can't get up from here. I'm sick. So sick."

The man knelt close to Ig, but paid no attention to Margaret. "Where to?"

"He ain't talking to you," Joseph said.

"You ain't takin' her nowhere. I can't do without her. Anyways, this ain't the worst of it. She'll tear your house all to pieces."

Margaret drew her knees up beneath her chin, still shivering. Ig squeezed her forearm, then stood up with effort. He teetered. "Legs are about to give out." He looked at Margaret again, then at the man. "I'll do what I can. Will you be here tomorrow?"

"Where would I be goin'?"

"I'll find one of the doctors."

The man shrugged. Margaret shivered.

They walked back up the trail. Ig stopped to inquire about needs. Most said they'd make out fine. Thank God it was summer. A man could abide an empty stomach better in the heat.

Joseph led the way back up the ridge and onto Water Street. He stopped often to let Ig catch his breath.

"Ig, how're you making out?"

"Tolerably well."

"Meaning you're still breathing, I reckon."

"This arm. My left arm. It aches."

"Carrying those ovens."

"I suppose."

By the time they passed the Wood Street intersection, a block north of Joseph's house, Ig was barely shuffling, stopping every few steps to rest. The air smelled of ash and smoke, but less so as they walked southward. They'd talked little since leaving Water Street.

"How're you holding up, boy?" He should've insisted Ig stay behind while he fetched the wagon. It was only a walk of a few blocks. A ten-minute walk at his normal pace, but Ig had exhausted himself along the river.

Ig stopped again. "I . . ." He waved Joseph on. "Almost there. I'll make it."

A few minutes later, Bekah met them at the back door. "Sweet Jesus. Brother Ig, you're pasty."

"My arm, dear. I can't imagine what I've done. I can't lift it. It's useless." He eased into Joseph's office chair. "I'm sorry, Joseph. You seem to be running an infirmary here." He smiled weakly at Bekah. "How are the other two patients?"

"Sound asleep. Just the way I like 'em. Rachel's having to get up every little bit. I believe that baby has dropped. It's getting on that time."

Ig laughed and leaned back in his chair. "Last night this time we were packing. I believe our move will have to wait. And David?"

"Been up some. Ate a bite of supper. He's shook bad. We like to have killed him."

Joseph said, "Samuel turned in?"

"He went off looking for you two. Said something about finding Malachi and them."

"I meant to look for Dr. Thompson."

Joseph shook his head and sighed. "Ig . . ."

"Tomorrow, perhaps."

"I'd say so. If I don't end up fetching the doc for you."

"Nonsense."

All the doors and windows were open. A slight draft cooled them. Joseph noticed fine ash suspended in the air around the lamp. His throat burned. Ig refused Bekah's offer of warmed-up beans and cornbread. She glanced at Joseph, studied Ig for a moment, then said, "Y'all be wanting to wash up." She went outside with the bucket.

Ig grimaced and closed his eyes. "Just a little rest. A little sleep. I'll speak to a doctor first thing."

Joseph slept at the table, his head on his forearms. Sometime during the night he heard Samuel come in and speak to Bekah. He wondered where Samuel had been and what he had to report, but he couldn't open his eyes, let alone move.

CHAPTER 53

Joseph woke to Bekah's breakfast preparations. When he lifted his head, she said, "I was wondering how I was going to get a plate under your face."

His forearms and hands were asleep, but he felt surprisingly refreshed. He worked feeling back into his hands. Despite her lack of sleep, Bekah looked fresh and in fine spirits. Joseph smelled coffee.

Ig was still asleep in the office chair.

Bekah said, "Samuel found the Meades. Their house is still there. So is the Van Husses'. Samuel said Malachi is all tore up about his books burning up at the Crutchfield House."

"His library. His papers. His ledgers. I don't know what he'll do."

"He ain't sleeping down on the river anyways. When you got a bunch of stuff, I reckon it hurts to lose it. Never mind you still got a house to go home to."

David walked in from the bedroom and nodded. He looked thin, weak, and shaken. His single suspender hung at his side. "Come dark, I got to head north."

"You look like running off," Joseph said.

David eyed the coffeepot. Bekah said, "Just about." She took three cups from the shelf.

David said, "I got to go. Hang around here and I'll get everybody hung. And I ain't going back in no box. I can't do that no more. I can't. I'll hang myself first. I got to get busy forgetting. I can't seem to get enough air."

"We should've brained Thigpen and his dogs when we had him alone in the cemetery," Joseph said. "But he didn't stay there long after that fire started. His dogs couldn't smell a thing in all that smoke and heat. Anyway, we needed him gone so we could dig you up."

"You get Jacob reburied?"

"We did." He wouldn't admit that once they got David in the wagon, they dumped the empty coffin back in the hole and refilled the grave.

Bekah poured three cups of coffee. They each took one. Samuel came in, wiping his eyes. "Damn this ash and smoke; I never am gonna quit burning." Bekah took down another cup and filled it, eyed Ig, and handed the cup to Samuel.

"I can't get too upset over that fire," David said.

Joseph said, "A fire." They all sipped and glanced down the hall at the stirring in Rachel's room. Joseph wanted to see her before Ig woke.

"No mystery in it," Ig said. He still hadn't opened his eyes. It appeared he hadn't moved all night.

Joseph said, "Now that's a stretch, even for you. Somebody set it."

"And why?" Ig still hadn't opened his eyes. "Look at it, man. Over a hundred degrees; we're in the middle of a hellish drought; we have a town full of tobacco fiends; a good and indispensable man was in peril; his work isn't finished. Was the fire set? In a manner of speaking."

Joseph shook his head and sipped. "Ig . . ." He wondered if he was more annoyed at the preacher's confidence in divine arson or that the preacher would be awake when Rachel waddled in.

Samuel said, "We still got to figure out what we're gonna do. Pig and Cathlyn are gone, and here we still sit. Like in one day we've forgot all about what happened."

Eyes still shut, Ig said, "I'd say the town will be concerned with other matters. Could it be coincidence that not one person was hurt? And the local grubbers will have the entire square beaten back together in a few weeks. This time next year the whole thing will be remembered as an annoyance, a small irregularity in the town's commerce." He sat up and rubbed his eyes with his right hand. His left arm still hung close to his side.

Bekah said, "Brother Ig, how's your arm this morning?"

"I'll try it out in a moment."

She watched him for a few seconds, then got up and checked the sourdough jar. "I got to get busy before it gets too hot to cook."

Ig said, "Good morning, darling."

Rachel shuffled in, puppy-eyed, and smiled at her husband. She'd brushed her hair. "Bekah, you're a wonderful nurse."

Bekah smiled and sifted flour into her mixing bowl. Rachel brushed past Joseph. He felt the air move and caught her scent. She went to Ig, who started to get up. She motioned for him to keep his seat. "I've been prone or sitting long enough. It feels good to be on my feet." She reached for his hand. "Ignatius, you're filthy." He reached across his body to take her hand, and she moved to his other side and began to smooth his matted hair with her fingers.

Bekah said, "He dropped off before we could clean him up."

"I believe I'll get up and take a look outside," Joseph said. "I'll be back in time for breakfast." She hadn't even looked at him.

"I expect I better stay put 'til tonight," David said.

Joseph made his way past Ig and Rachel and out the back door. It was pleasantly cool after the previous day's heat and fire, but the sky was clear. It would be hot shortly after sunrise. There was a pleasant westerly breeze. Westward, the faint pink shone on the horizon.

He walked out of the yard and turned west on Polk Street. He caught only occasional whiffs of smoke. A rooster crowed a block to the north. Then another to the west. By the time he crossed Jefferson Street he could see morning campfires along the river and lights in the windows of unburned houses, but save for a lone lantern moving along Main Street, there was only a gaping blackness where the square had been. Roosters crowed along the river. He imagined them roosting in trees, food for bobcats and horned owls. He wondered if they'd go back to their burned-out homes. Dozens of campfires shone in the woods and on the prairie. More homes and businesses would burn before the drought broke.

He began to meet people along the street and in their yards, stretching, emptying pots, shushing dogs. Just another morning. The business section of town was gone. He had a fugitive slave in his kitchen. Someone knew of their activities—or at least knew of Ig's. Yet here he stayed. He wouldn't leave until Rachel had her baby. He couldn't. Maybe he ought to urge Samuel and Bekah to leave with David. But then what would the townspeople think? Maybe he could claim the two ran away.

No. Somewhere in this town someone knew. Someone set that fire and someone murdered Dr. Marion. Somebody came to Ig and Pig's aid at the creek crossing.

He had no idea what he'd do the rest of the day. Work in the shop? Why not? He could take Rachel home and then he could help Ig find a doctor and see what needed to be done in town—assuming the preacher was up to it. Ig looked better this morning. Then again, he couldn't stand the thought of Rachel in that hot, unshaded house in the middle of cedar thicket. He'd talk her into staying at his house. Bekah would be there to watch after her. He could sleep on the floor. David would be gone in a few days, if not that night. He ought to go see the Meades and Van Husses.

He stood for a few minutes, watching what remained of Dallas come to life. Ig was right; the town would be rebuilt in no time. People would make money on the disaster. Sarah Cockrell's sawmill would do a booming business. No wonder she seemed so sanguine. Freighters and woodcutters would prosper. Carpenters? He felt a sudden fierce affection for the town he'd soon be leaving.

His stomach growled as he thought of Bekah laying a rasher of bacon in the skillet. He walked along Polk Street, into sunrise. The cedars cast long shadows on the prairie. A coon hurried across the road. He looked southward. A mile or so beyond the town cemetery, black smoke billowed. Someone's house or barn. A lantern, a candle or match. He and Samuel ought to think about digging a fire break. He'd remind Bekah to make sure the ashes were cool before she slung them across the street.

He felt mildly guilty for not sounding an alarm, but by the time the town could respond, the fire would have burned down. There was no saving whatever was burning. One more structure to rebuild. He'd keep an eye in that direction, though. If the prairie caught, the whole southern end of town could burn. He tried to remember if there was a road or creek that could act as a fire break. He'd grown glib, strangely detached, reckless even. Exhausted? Delusional? Paralyzed? He wanted Rachel and breakfast. He could think no further. He watched the smoke. It didn't seem to be spreading. The local farmers had it under control. Nothing would come of it.

By late morning, when Ig and Joseph made it back to the riverbank with Dr. D. B. Thome, whose Main Street office and pharmacy had burned, Margaret and her common-law husband had left. Two young slave women hanging laundry in a nearby camp reported that she'd shrieked and cried and retched through the night but had quieted in the wee hours. By sunup, they were gone.

Dr. Thome said that short of confining the woman so that she couldn't harm herself during withdrawal, there was little he could've done. Relieving her pain with opium, even if he had it, would just be participating in her slow suicide. "Reverend, for this sort of sickness, I believe she needs your counsel more than mine."

The doctor led Ig and Joseph on his rounds through the camps. He had no medicine; all his curatives had burned, but he felt throats, checked for fever, examined blisters and minor contusions, and administered advice and comfort. Joseph liked him at once and regretted not knowing him sooner. Ig continued his questioning and told Joseph to help him remember that the Shepherds needed at least two blankets for their small children and the Hopewell boy needed a shoe. The cobbler's shop hadn't burned. Surely there was a spare brogan lying about. All in all, however, the fire seemed more a serious inconvenience than unmitigated disaster. Other than Margaret, no one seemed to be starving or deathly ill. Men were already clearing the debris from burned-out homesites.

Ig had seemed better and had even started using his left arm a bit, but by the time they'd climbed the ridge and stepped out on the street, he seemed near collapse. Dr. Thome led him to shade, and Joseph fetched a dipper of water from one of the work crews. Ig's arm was aching again, and now his back hurt. He was short of breath and dizzy. The doctor suggested Joseph fetch a wagon and get him home at once. As Joseph turned to go after the wagon, which was parked just down the street, the doctor grabbed his arm and said, out of earshot of Ig, "I'm concerned about his heart. Keep him quiet. I'll stop by before supper. Who has been seeing to Mrs. Bodeker?"

"Dr. Thompson, I believe."

"If I can find him, I'll talk with him before my visit." He looked back at Ig, who was dabbing the back of his neck with a handkerchief. "He's badly overnourished. When I speak to his wife, I'll suggest she rein in his eating."

"You'll have to get on his whole congregation about that."

Dr. Thome smiled. "The beloved minister. Love him right into an early grave."

As Joseph helped Ig into the wagon, he noticed men gathering on the courthouse steps.

Mid-afternoon, David woke up in a fit. By the time Bekah got to him, he'd clawed more furrows on his face and neck.

Ig had been dozing in Joseph's office chair while Samuel and Joseph were gathering tools and supplies to head back to the square to help with the cleanup. Rachel had finally calmed down after Joseph convinced her that Dr. Thome had diagnosed Ig's malady as exhaustion and nerves. He simply needed to rest and recover. No, he didn't need anything to eat. Water would be fine. Joseph moved his easy chair next to Ig so that she could sit beside him.

Bekah yelled out the back door. Joseph and Samuel burst in to find her walking David around in circles, trying to calm him. He was gasping and slapping at his face. "I just can't get no air," he said. "I'm smothering. I got to get outside, out from under this roof. These walls is smothering me."

Samuel said, "He needs a drink of whiskey."

David shook his head, "Y'all got to give me some room. They ain't no air in here."

"Sugar, we got all the windows open," Bekah said. She still had his hand. "You can't go outside in daylight."

Joseph said, "Let's open the doors, too. Get some air moving in here. We'll just have to watch and be quiet."

Ig had woken and now squinted at the scene. Rachel got up, shuffled to the back door, opened it, and slid the scotch under it with her foot.

Joseph couldn't remember what it was like to have his house to himself.

Samuel had fetched the whiskey bottle and was trying to get David's attention when a knock came at the back doorway. Dr. Thome stood looking through the office and into the kitchen at David. He held a medicine bag.

"Pardon me. I thought I had better come ahead. We've received some medical supplies from Lancaster and Cedar Hill."

David was still shaking, gasping. Joseph said, "Come in." He felt oddly numb. No fear. Just fatigue. A desire to know what was coming.

The doctor walked in and glanced at Ig, who nodded and weakly raised a hand in greeting. Rachel stood by her chair. Bekah said, "He's having a fit."

"I have something for him." He set his bag on the kitchen table and opened it. "I have a small amount of laudanum." He took out two bottles and pulled a cork out of one. "Two small swallows." David eyed the bottle. Bekah said, "Come on now, baby. Just a drink or two." She held the bottle to his lips and tipped it. He took a sip, but his lips were trembling and some of the liquid ran down his chin. Bekah caught it with her finger and held it to his lips. He took it from her finger. "One more," she said. The second dose went more smoothly. They helped him into the chair.

Dr. Thome left the bottles on the table. "Go sparingly. I can't leave any more for the time being. What was the trauma?"

"He can't stand tight places," Samuel said.

The doctor studied David. "So he does exist, this one-armed slave-stealer. I had thought him a myth." He looked around the room. "He'd best not be here much longer. Things are turning ugly. A house and barn burned south of here this morning. Carruth and Pryor are up in arms. Word is, the next edition of the McKinney paper will blame the fires on a slave insurrection. Judge Burford has been summoned from Waxahachie. I suggest you spend some time in town to get the mood."

They stood in silence. David was already nodding off.

"It doesn't take long on an empty stomach," Thome said. He turned to Ig and Rachel. "Now, how are the Bodekers this afternoon?"

Father's Reminiscence
Transcribed August 1, 1911

Whip a man long enough—better yet, whip his wife and children—and he'll tell you what you want to hear. "Yes, Marster, we aimed to burn down the town and kill all the white folks and march all the way to Mexico. We burned it down. We done it. We was all in on it. Them preachers talked us into it. Brother Jonah and Brother Zeph."

All but 3 of Dallas County's 1,074 slaves were implicated. It took only a few days to extract confessions.

The toughest ones, those who wouldn't fess up—well, clearly they had something to hide. No doubt these were the ringleaders. All were subject to execution under antisedition and arson laws.

Thank God for bourgeois practicality. The Committee of Vigilance—fifty-two of the best men in Dallas, solid, indispensable mongers of every stripe—could never bring themselves to destroy a million dollars worth of human property. Leave true slaughter to men of ideals.

Gentlemen, let reasonableness prevail! Spread the loss and spread it thin!

The two preachers? Lucky for them, they fell into the hands of Men of Order instead of local rabble. It's one thing to dispose of chattel; quite another to murder innocent white men.

I did what I could, short of suicide.

CHAPTER 54

Six days after the fire, slaves began to disappear. Brother Sid Claggett, Al Huitt, Myra Winn. Others, too, for Samuel noticed and felt an absence along the streets as he and Joseph hauled rubble away from building sites. Money was flowing in the form of area bank loans and notes from the wealthy. Word was, John McCoy, William Keller, Goode, and Latimer were backing new development. Work was plentiful; actual cash was scarce but forthcoming, or so Joseph assured Samuel.

But cash was an abstraction to Samuel, a sum at the bottom of a column of figures under his name in a ledger. He sometimes tried to picture five hundred dollars in bills and coin and couldn't. He doubted he'd ever seen more than five dollars at once.

He'd gone to Mrs. Cockrell's mill to pick up a wagonload of studs, and found Edward Taylor, a gossamer white man who worked odd jobs around town, working in Brother Sid's place. Taylor went hatless; sweat ran down his face and gathered on his upper lip. A yellow paste of sawdust covered his nearly bald head and the few sodden wisps of graying blond hair. When Samuel asked him about Brother Claggett, he only shrugged without meeting Samuel's eyes and started loading the studs. "You aim to help me or just stand there," he said.

"Where's Howard at?"

"It ain't my job to look after him. If he's anything like the preacher, and I 'spect he is, he's hid somewhere sound asleep."

Howard stepped out from behind one of the boilers. Short, slight, middle-aged, he was drenched in sweat and held a large wrench. Samuel arched his brow in question. Howard looked at him, expressionless, shook his head, then walked back behind the boiler.

Samuel and Taylor loaded the wagon. As he drove away, the saw began to whine.

For three days he worked, sometimes alone, sometimes with Joseph, who turned down several cash offers to loan him out. They finished clearing rubble, hauled lumber, and started framing the new livery. Nights, for an hour or two after supper, they laid out work in the shop. On every job in town, he was the only black man.

Early one afternoon, as he walked back to the square after dinner, he met Myra Winn along Commerce Street. She carried a basket of laundry, probably headed down to the river where one of the burned-out slaves or poor whites would boil and hang the garments. Shantytowns had formed on level ground near the river and creeks. The goodwill of the first days after the fire had passed, and now cuttings, fights, and theft were said to be common. The breeze shifted, and Samuel judged a few latrines needed to be filled in and new ones dug.

He doffed his hat and said, "Afternoon, Miss Myra."

Her eyes were puffy. She looked about, started to stop, but went on. As she passed him she whispered, "Watch yourself, Samuel. Don't say nothin'." She glanced back once and headed on to the river.

When he got back to the job site, Joseph, who'd eaten with some of the other workers, met him at the wagon. "Help me take hold of this beam," he said. As Samuel reached over the sideboard to push the beam out, Joseph said softly, without looking up, "Jail's full of slaves. They got a bunch more hid somewhere, trying to beat confessions out of them. That's the word."

"Who is?"

"Committee of Vigilance, they're calling it. Keller, Pryor, Mitchell. You know as well as I do. Rumor is, Judge Burford threw his hands up and left. Just gave up. Moore's going right along with it. He came of a night with deputies and marched a bunch right off to jail."

"Like one of us set fire to the town."

"This thing's heavy. Come on around here and let's take a rest."

Samuel moved to the back of the wagon. The two leaned on the lumber pile. Most of the dozen or so workers had set their pails in the shade and were drifting back to work. The barn was half-framed. They'd finish in another two days. No one seemed within earshot.

Joseph drew his handkerchief and wiped his forehead and the back of his neck. "I say they'll make their way around to you and Bekah. You two do what you think you need to do. I'll help you any way I can. I got to stay for now. Might be a good time for y'all to head north for the thickets."

"We should've left with David."

Joseph sighed, stuffing the handkerchief into his britches pocket. "Yeah."

From up in the rafters, Eli Newcomb, the portly but nimble foreman, yelled, "Joe, hellfire! You and that boy come on with that stick!"

In the center of the square, the courthouse doors were closed. Shouts and laughter wafted out the open windows. A man leaned out a window over the front door and spat a stream of tobacco juice into the tops of the newly planted locust trees.

———

Bekah sat on a stool, watching Samuel tighten his table vise on an eight-foot section of high-grade one-by-twelve oak soon to be part of Mrs. Cockrell's new tabletop. She said, "You been just satisfied as hound in the mash, and now you wanna run. When people are getting locked up and whipped."

"Seems like a good time," Samuel said. "Anyways, you was hot to take off not too long ago. Called me everything but chickenshit for holdin' back. Somethin' holdin' *you*?"

"Get on then."

"I swear." He picked up an awl and eyed the table scale, loosened the vise, adjusted the piece, retightened the vise. "Joseph said he'd help. I don't have no idea how."

"He passed up the chance to load us in a wagon and head north."

"What difference does it make? You're bound and determined to stay. I don't believe you ever had any mind to leave. Just goadin' me all the time."

She stood up suddenly, sending the stool onto its side. "That's the thing about you, Samuel." She pointed at him with the index finger of her three-digit hand. "You! You! You! What can somebody do for you! You never gave anything up. Not a finger, not an arm, not a hand, not a baby, not a bit of hide."

"They fixin' to hear you all the way in town."

"You just work on Miz Cockrell's table. You ain't goin' nowhere." She turned and walked out the shop door.

He stepped away from the table and righted the stool. She was right. He didn't know how to run or where to go. Maybe if David came again, he'd light out with him. Then again, if he tried and they caught him, they'd hang him.

Myra Wynn looked scared. She'd seen something. They'd hurt her. But she was alive.

CHAPTER 55

She'd waited nine nights. She hadn't seen him or heard from him in six. Too dangerous, she supposed. He said he'd come for her. He always had. She'd wait for him.

She'd miss Samuel and Joseph and the others. Brother Ig, especially, and even Rachel. They'd done all they could in Dallas, and now things had turned out bad. Somebody would hang. He'd told her she'd done enough, had endured enough. He'd take her away to the north, beyond the reach of the slave catchers and northern lawmen. Maybe Mr. Still would help find her babies. Maybe his appeals would touch one slaver, if they could find him. Maybe they could raise money. It had been done.

Samuel should leave, but wouldn't until Joseph had enough. Joseph could take him where he pleased, take him far enough north that he could free him without danger to himself. Until he reached Canada, Samuel would always be in danger, even with his legal freedom, of being kidnapped and hauled south to be sold back into bondage. She did not want to stop in Lawrence or Cincinnati or Detroit or Philadelphia or Syracuse or Boston, wherever those places were. All were within reach of the Fugitive Slave Law.

Let others head for Mexico. From the first time she ran, it always had been northward. He knew the way.

CHAPTER 56

They'd nearly finished a late supper when James Moore arrived with two deputies. Joseph answered the door.

Moore seemed sheepish, uneasy. "Uh, Joe, we need to take your people in for a little while. We're talking to all the darkies, you know."

Joseph stood in the doorway. Bekah and Samuel would be listening from the kitchen. "I reckon I can question my own people."

The two deputies stood behind Moore. They avoided Joseph's eyes. He recognized them both, but not by name. Both young men, fair, with sunburned faces. One had a bushy mustache and held a cut-down shotgun. The other appeared unarmed, though he might have had a pistol in his belt, behind his back. Moore said, "I've got to take them in for a spell. Shouldn't have them over a day or two."

The sun was setting. Parts of the yard and the day's work beneath the shop awning were in deep shadow. There was no breeze. Sweat ran into Joseph's eyes. "On whose authority?"

"Mine."

"You don't have that authority. Would you come down here and haul off my horse or my furniture?"

"I wouldn't expect your horse to set fire to the town."

"Bekah and Samuel were with me at the cemetery when the fire started. Thigpen and Pryor will vouch for them."

"They already have."

"Then what's the use in hauling them in?"

"They might know something."

"If they did, then I'd know."

"Nobody thinks his own niggers will put a match to a barn or a house, but everybody thinks somebody else's will. You know that."

"Can't let you have them, Jim."

"Several are talking. Looks like about every darky in the county was in on it."

"What'd you have to do to get that story?"

"Joe, your place didn't burn. People want answers; they want justice."

"Vengeance is what they want, and it's a lot easier to lay it on a tradesman's slaves."

"We got Sarah Cockrell's people and some of W. B. Mitchell's."

"You ain't gettin' mine."

"You want to come in with 'em?"

"I believe we'll be finishing our supper."

"Joe . . ."

"You boys have a good night now." He started to shut the door.

Moore said, "Jack." The smaller of the two deputies kicked the door open. Joseph stumbled backward. Bekah came out of the kitchen with a butcher knife. Samuel caught Joseph before he fell. The larger deputy held the shotgun on Bekah. "Best put it down, girl." She eyed him, held the knife point up, cutting edge out.

Joseph pulled away from Samuel and shoved his finger in Moore's face. "In my damn house. Just knock the goddamn door in. I sure as hell thought you were a better man."

"Just settle down, Joe. This is getting way out of hand. I *will* haul your ass down to the jail. Now tell that girl to put that blade down."

"Soon as your boy puts his gun down."

"Willy."

The deputy lowered the gun. Joseph glanced at Bekah. She lowered the knife to her side. Joseph said, "Who do I need to talk to about this? Pryor? Lattimer? Keller?"

"You can talk to me, but I'm about done listening."

"I thought a man who would stand up to Alex Cockrell would stand up to money. Looks like I was wrong."

Moore said, "That's it. Y'all goin' to town."

Bekah raised the knife. Willy stepped up and hit her on the side of the head with the barrel of the shotgun before she could cut him. She dropped to her knees but held onto the knife.

Samuel said, "Whup!" and stepped in and grabbed the barrels. The other deputy started beating him about the head. Joseph let go a roundhouse and caught the deputy flush in the ear. He dropped like a poleaxed beeve. Moore drew his pistol and shoved in Joseph's face. "You know I'll shoot a man."

"Goddamn you."

Bekah was still on her knees and groggy. Samuel said, "Here now!" and let go of the barrel. The deputy whapped his forehead with the butt. Samuel turned away holding his face, blood pouring between his fingers.

Bekah said, "I'll kill you for that." Willy started to kick her.

Moore said, "Enough!"

Jack tried to get up. Blood spurted from his split ear. He staggered and dropped to one knee. "Christ almighty! My goddamn ear! Son of a bitch!"

Moore said, "You people just accosted two lawmen."

Joseph was breathing hard. He pulled out his handkerchief and held it out for Samuel. "Go to hell." He nodded toward Jack. "Ignorant bastard's bleeding all over my floor."

––––

Next morning, Malachi leaned against the cell bars. "Joseph, there's no one to appeal to. Burford's nowhere to be found. Word is he's gone back to Waxahachie. McCoy has thrown up his hands. We have no legal workings. Pryor, Lattimer, Goode. None of the sorry bastards will even discuss the matter with me. The courthouse steps are sprouting a mob. Negroes not already in here are terrified and won't speak."

Joseph suspected very few slaves were going about their business in town. The half-dozen cells in the jailhouse were crammed full of arrested Negroes, male and female.

At least they'd locked him up with Samuel and Bekah. The cell smelled of sweat and full chamber pots. Several of the men had turned their backs and encircled the women for the sake of their privacy. Bekah had said little. Samuel had tried to talk to Sid Claggett, but the preacher had been taken away and whipped multiple times. His front teeth were broken off at the gum line. Word was, Mrs. Cockrell had made several appeals to no avail. Slave preachers were assumed to be troublemakers, what with their assertions about all men being equal in God's eyes. Dangerous, futile thinking.

Joseph jerked on one of the bars. "You hearing anything?"

"Only hearsay. We know who's running things. The same people who run the town, the men who'll decide what gets rebuilt and where, who gets loans and who doesn't. It's hot, people are living outside, they've been burned out. They want blood. Pryor's editorials have got people seeing John Brown's agents behind every post. We'd be hearing about Brown sightings if he hadn't been hanged last fall. I keep hearing about a weapons cache, but I can't find a soul who's seen a weapon. Now the town is aswirl with Chambers and Newton sightings."

"You get word to Ig?"

"As soon as I leave here. Word may have reached him by now. Half the town saw you three marching at gunpoint."

"Hear anything about charges?"

"Accusations. Formal charges are meaningless."

The door creaked, and Jack the deputy came in wearing a bandage on his ear. Pink blood had soaked through. "Time's up, Meade."

Malachi said, "I'll see you tomorrow."

Jack said, "Maybe you will. You know a man has to wonder why a lawyer would be so damn worried about a jail full of niggers and a black Republican undertaker."

Malachi turned toward the door. "I've been Mr. Shaw's attorney for years. I'm simply doing my job."

Joseph shoved his face between the bars. "How's the ear, Jack?"

The deputy tried to backhand him, but Joseph was too quick. Jack smashed his wrist into a bar. The slaves all watched without expression. Jack cursed and held his wrist against his chest. "Me and you gonna settle up 'fore this is all over with. If they don't string you up first."

———

Just after noon, they brought in Parsons Chambers and Newton and threw them in the cell across from Joseph's. The two were filthy, their faces a scabrous mess. Blood leaked from Newton's right ear. Both were in chains. Willy pushed them into the cell. "I want you to look here what turned up in Hord's Ridge. Couldn't stay away. They had to see their handiwork."

The slaves in their cell helped them to a bench. Newton yelled, "You ought to thank the arsonists. I'd call the town much improved."

Chambers said, "Amen. I hate to see workmen despoiling the prairie again."

The deputy locked the door and studied the two preachers. "Them loudmouths will be shut soon enough." He looked back at Joseph. "They's a big fat preacher outside raising hell to get inside to see you and your boy and girl. We can't run him off, but we ain't lettin' him in. Anyways, I don't believe we got a door broad enough."

"A fine, heartening spectacle, I'd say," Newton said. "I don't believe I've ever seen Brother Ig in so fine a form. Had he that kind of fire all the time, most of the world would have been saved from perdition."

When the deputy turned his back, Joseph put his finger to his nose. Newton and Chambers might be perfectly happy going to the gallows for their beliefs, but life suited Ig very well, at least some of the time, and he was only a couple of weeks from being a father.

As the deputy left, the two parsons smiled and shook their heads. Chambers's lips were so swollen he could barely form his words, but Joseph understood him perfectly: "It's always the same with some men."

———

Samuel judged the time to be an hour or two past midnight when Moore, Willy, and Jack came into the cellblock. The deputies carried chains and leg irons, and wore pistols. Moore carried a shotgun. "Mr. Shaw, the two parsons, Samuel Smith, the girl Bekah, and Reverend Claggett. We're going for a little wagon ride."

Joseph said, "Mr. Shaw? Why the new formality, Jim? It's me—familiar, friendly old Joe, the undertaker. Surely our little misunderstanding about your barging into my home, abusing my people, and shoving a gun in my face hasn't strained our friendship."

Moore didn't answer. He stopped at Chambers and Newton's cell. "Old Jack is fixin' to come in and shackle y'all. I'll lock the door behind him and then let you out when he's done. Anybody raises a hand to him, I'll stick this shotgun between the bars and start blasting nigger parts all over this cell. I've got plenty of shot and powder and all night to take aim."

Samuel had never worn irons. He stumbled going up the steps, and Bekah told him to pick up the slack in the chains between his wrists and ankles. The slaves in their cell had all touched the five discreetly, just a brush with the back of a hand, or a finger or maybe a nod, before they left the cell. At gunpoint, they struggled, chains rattling, into a heavy wagon hitched to a span of mules, probably the same wagon and team Brother Jonah and the two runaways rode into town the summer before. Willy drove while Jack and Moore rode saddle horses to either side.

They rode east on Burleson Street, past the few dark houses and cabins, turned north on Poydarus Street, and rode past the last cabins and sheds. The street petered out into a two-track wending among the cedars and bois d'arc mottes. The prisoners rode in silence against the sideboards. Samuel searched the faces around him, but they were hidden in the darkness. Though the sky was clear and the firmament brilliant, the half moon cast weak light. By the time they left the edge of town, Brother Zeph was snoring beside him. The night air smelled of heat and dust, cedar and grass, and, at times, of hogs or cattle. A few dogs barked in the distance. The coyotes were silent. Crickets chirred.

They rode for a quarter of an hour, crossed a creek so low that there was no audible splash or gurgle, only the scent of shallow, tepid water. They topped the bank, rounded a bend, and Samuel heard laughter and whiffed cigar smoke. Brother Zeph had stopped snoring. The prisoners were all looking down the road, their heads bobbing and weaving with the wagon's movement.

They were nearly at the barn door before Samuel saw the structure, dark save for the weak lantern light inside, and the flicker of a fire nearly burned down to coals in a pit to the left of the door.

Two figures stood up by the fire. A man inside the barn stepped into the doorway. Willy stopped the team and set the brake. Jonah Chambers said, "Good morning, Brother Mitchell. Ain't it a tad early for such a prosperous man of affairs?"

"Morning, Parson," came the answer from the doorway, a voice Samuel had heard nearly every day for a dozen years, confident, avuncular, the voice of the man who'd once owned him. "We figured we'd best get an early start, before the sun comes up and it gets too damn hot to work inside. We got a long day ahead of us." W. B. Mitchell stepped forward, out of the doorway. "I expect we'll knock off for breakfast and dinner, anyway. Y'all come on in. Brother Sid, good to see you again. Joe, Sam, Aunt Bekah." He turned and walked back inside.

They got out of the wagon at gunpoint and followed Moore inside. Samuel again stumbled on his chain. They said nothing. He felt the press of the white men behind them. The barn was lit inside by three lanterns hung on nails driven into posts. This was no pole barn. The walls were of massive oak logs, tightly chinked. Oak beams supported the roof, and all along the walls and on the poles were iron rings. The floor was of hard packed earth covered by a thin layer of dust. There was no loft, no stalls. The barn had not been built to hold four-legged stock.

They all stood just inside the doorway. Samuel's knees trembled.

"Right on in here, now," Mitchell said. He seemed in fine spirits. His sleeves were rolled to his elbows, and he held a newly lighted cigar between his fingers.

Samuel felt the twin barrels of the shotgun in the small of his back. He moved farther inside. The two parsons and Brother Sid looked impassive. Bekah glared, insolent as ever.

Someone shouldered his way through the prisoners and stepped up by Mitchell. Samuel didn't recognize him. Tall and rawboned. Hatless and slick bald on top. Graying brown muttonchops. Probably another hired thug from Scyene.

Mitchell slapped the man's back. "This is Teddy. He'll be asking a few questions. I'm sure y'all want to cooperate, seeing as how our beloved town was burnt to the ground by a horde of treasonous niggers and two or three white agitators." He looked at Joseph. "I swear, Joe, I don't know what to think about you whuppin' on our deputies. And letting your girl threaten officers of the law with a butcher knife. You seem awfully tight with your darkies. Gets a man to wondering. And Samuel." He shook his head. "Samuel, Samuel, Samuel. I thought I raised you better than to grab hold of a lawman's shotgun. But I reckon a boy will about always fall prey to corrosive influences, and we sure as hell seem to have more than our share in this county." He tapped ash from his cigar. "Boys, shut the door.

Let's start with old Samuel here." He pointed to the wall. "Rest of you just have a seat over there. Behave yourself and we won't have to shoot you or chain you to the wall." He looked at Teddy and nodded toward a pole near the center of the barn.

Willy stepped forward and unfastened the irons on Samuel's wrists. The young deputy's hands were trembling, his eyes sorrowful. The chains dropped, and he touched Samuel gently on the shoulder, nudging him toward the pole.

Teddy slapped the pole. "Right here, boy." He seemed resigned. There was no cruelty in his voice. A man about to break a horse or a dog. Get this one done and go to the next one. Dirty business; just get it over with.

Samuel heard his pulse. He knew the stories, knew slaves who'd been whipped but had never thought he'd feel it. Not Samuel, the clever one. He moved toward the pole. Where was the whip?

Teddy kept his hand on the pole. "Put your arms around here."

He did. Willy tied them with rawhide bindings. Samuel turned away from his friends sitting against the wall and felt the smooth post against his cheek.

Sid Claggett said, "Brother Samuel, look right here!" His first words since leaving the jail. "He will not forsake you."

Samuel turned to his friends, their faces barely visible in the gloom, the massive walls behind them, the deputies' guns trained on them.

Teddy looked sharply toward Claggett. Mitchell gave the preacher a dismissive wave, brightening the tip of his cigar.

Teddy walked around Samuel, leaned close, and said, "Now, uh, boy . . . What's his name?"

"Sam," Mitchell said. "Samuel."

"Now, Samuel, I hear tell you're one of the ringleaders in this nigger insurrection. How about that?"

"Nawsir." The absolute truth. He was guilty of breaking the law, yes, but that was not the reason he was tied to the post.

Teddy said, "Beg your pardon, Reverends, but I say he's a goddamn liar."

Mitchell chomped down on his cigar and chuckled. "Teddy."

"Now look here." Teddy leaned a shoulder against the post and looked down at Samuel. "Own up to it, tell us who was in on it with you, who put you up to it, and we won't have to get rough about it."

Samuel shook his head and shrugged. "I don't know nothing about it, Marster."

"Tell us how these two conniving preachers, traitors to their own race, put you and every other nigger in the county to a futile scheme to set fire to the town, poison men of property, have your way with their women, and raise hell between here and the Rio Grande."

"I was at the graveyard when that fire started."

"Is that right?"

"It's the God's truth, Marster." So far no whip.

Mitchell said, "He was, but we're talking about broader treachery here. Any henchman could've set the fire."

"Or any imbecile with a cigar," Jonah Chambers said.

Mitchell laughed. "I suspect I would enjoy your sermons, Parson."

Teddy sighed. Samuel glimpsed movement at his lower back. Searing pain shot through his buttocks, into his legs and groin. His breath left him. His legs convulsed.

Mitchell said, "Mind the kidneys; he can't tell us anything if he's dead." His voice sounded muffled and distant. He looked fuzzy through tears. "Teddy used to earn his keep with his knuckles. He's collected a purse or two with that punch. Give old Sam a minute to get his wind back, Teddy."

Samuel's breath came to him in short gasps, then deep, ragged breaths. Urine ran down his leg and into his shoe.

"Whew. Smell that, will you," Teddy said. "Don't feel too bad about it. I've beat the piss out a good number that wasn't tied up, and had it beat out of me a time or two. It might run a little pink for a day or two." He leaned on his forearm, against the pole. "Now let's get back on track here. Look at me."

Samuel looked up at Teddy. The white man's face was in shadow. Samuel smelled his breath. Strong but no hint of whiskey. As Teddy turned back into the light, Samuel saw scars around his eyes, noticed the crooked nose.

Teddy stood back and crossed his arm. "Who put you up to it, boy?"

Samuel tried to say "Nobody," but nothing came out. He shook his head. Teddy strode around behind him and punched him in the same spot. His legs gave, and he started to slide down the pole.

Zeph Newton yelled, "Pig! Philistine! You'll burn for that!"

Teddy said, "Bill, what we need is a few more preachers around here."

Willy and Jack picked Samuel up, untied the lashings, crossed his forearms, and retied them just below his elbows. Teddy bent and studied Samuel eye to eye, only inches away. "Holding up? We'll move to that other kidney here shortly, if we need to. You think about it for a minute." He backed away, "Boys, I could sure use a little sip of water while old Sam here takes stock."

Mitchell said, "Joe, don't you find this method far superior to the whip? It heals without so much as a mark. Rarely have we had to resort to sterner methods. So far, folks have been very cooperative. Occasionally, though, you'll get a tough one."

Joseph said, "I have nothing to say to you, Mitchell."

Mitchell said, "I suspect you might before we're through here."

Samuel caught his breath again and stood, relieving the strain from his shoulders. He felt like vomiting. Tears dripped from his lips and chin. He'd never known pain like this, could not have imagined it. But the second punch hadn't worsened it. He'd felt the blow, the sharp pulse in his groin and back, but it had not been nearly as searing as the first one. Panic left him.

Joseph and Bekah sat rigid, their hands shackled together, their elbows locked, their fists on their thighs. He could not see their eyes.

Teddy leaned in, said, "Who set that fire at Peak's?"

Samuel didn't answer.

"Who put you up to it? These three?" Without looking back, he swept his hand toward Chambers, Newton, and Joseph.

Samuel shook his head. Teddy punched his other kidney. That same pain. His legs sagged. The burning trickle of piss. But no tears this time.

Teddy's face was red now, his neck swollen. "How about I start breaking ribs one at a time?" He punched Samuel in the right kidney again, but hit him a little high, as he sagged on the post.

Samuel said, "Break 'em."

"Huh?" Teddy rested his hands on his hips. "What in hell did you say?"

"I said, break the ribs then." He waited. Maybe Teddy would just kill him.

"I believe I'd rather break your goddamn thick head."

Mitchell said, "Hold on. This ain't getting us anywhere." He walked over and put his hand on Samuel's back. "Sam, what has got into you? I knew you when you didn't get past your mama's hem. Now you talk to me like you were raised."

"Marster, I don't know."

"Sam."

"I don't have nothing to tell."

"Listen to me, Sam."

He shook his head.

"Get Aunt Bekah up here," Mitchell said.

"I don't know nothing, Marster. I can't tell what I don't know nothing about."

"Get her up here. Come on."

Joseph said, "You're a goddamn animal. How'd you get chosen for this? Or did you choose yourself? Where's Keller and Pryor? This little episode should make a fine editorial."

Mitchell motioned sharply to Jack. "Get her up." He turned to Joseph. "We've all had a turn. Peons and preachers never understand responsibility and duty. Just grub your way to your next meal or let your flock provide. Leave it up to men of property and position to keep order."

The deputies tried to pull Bekah up. She refused to stand. They dragged her to a post ten feet beyond Samuel. She kicked, screeched, and bit Willy's forearm until he punched her twice in the side of the head.

Mitchell said, "Tie her so that she faces Samuel. Let 'em gaze at one another."

The deputies couldn't get her up. She rolled on her side and kicked. Teddy strode over, grabbed her clavicle, and squeezed until she screamed.

"You get your little ass up here." He squeezed with one hand and grabbed her hair with the other and jerked her up. "Wrap your arms around this pole."

She resisted. He squeezed. She screamed and cried and wrapped her arms around the pole. The deputies lashed her forearms together. Teddy said, "Tie her waist so she don't slide down the damn pole. You'd think we'd know how to do this by now."

Mitchell walked to the door, opened it, and called to someone outside. He held the door as a short, dark, wiry man walked in wearing heavy mitts, carrying a two-foot iron rod. The top third was glowing orange. Mitchell shut the door.

"Now then," Teddy said. "Let's find out what the boy's carrying in his drawers. He nodded to Jack, who glanced wide-eyed at Samuel but didn't move.

Teddy started toward Samuel. "Hell, then. I'll do it myself." He ripped loose Samuel's suspenders and jerked down his pants and drawers. Samuel tried to hide himself against the post. Teddy kicked his feet from under him, then kicked him in the ribs so that he hung to one side, in full view. "Give me that mitt." He took the extra mitt and then the glowing rod. "Stand up straight, boy." Samuel felt the heat from the rod near his backside. He tried to stand, but staggered and tried to move behind the pole. Teddy touched Samuel's right hip with the rod. He smelled his own flesh burning before he felt the heat. He yelped and jumped from behind the post, his hands still tied. Bekah hid her eyes.

Mitchell stood silent, grim, watching.

Teddy stepped around the pole and dropped to one knee before Samuel. He looked back at Bekah. "Look right here, girlie. Had ahold of this thing, have you? Spread your feet, boy." He touched Samuel's knee with the rod. Samuel screamed and spread his feet farther apart.

Teddy looked up at the two pale deputies, who seemed to have forgotten all about covering the other prisoners, and said, "Slap her head out from behind the damn post."

They went to her and tried nudge her cheek. She bit Willy's finger. Jack grabbed her hair and jerked her head to one side while Willy cussed and gripped his dented finger.

Teddy shook his head in disgust, then turned back to Samuel. "Now, then, Brother Samuel." He raised the rod to within six inches of Samuel's groin.

Samuel felt his skin shrivel against the heat. Teddy said, "Just think what this hot iron would do to a man's soft parts. It'd keep 'em soft, don't you imagine? Aunt Bekah, you think of something you want to say, why you go right on and say it."

She was breathing hard, ragged, but there were no tears.

Samuel looked at her. Her eyes were slits. She saw him. She wouldn't talk.

Teddy said, "Aunt Bekah, now you remember this thing when it rose stiff and fine. Think of the waste, think of what this hot iron would do to a man. Why, he'd have no reason to live and you'd go on the rest of your days recalling how much you liked this thing, then how you stood right there and watched a fine example of manhood cooked. Think on it." He moved the rod to within a couple of inches. Samuel's breath left him. He imagined his scrotum blistering.

Teddy lowered the rod a bit. "Now, Mr. Shaw, I don't truly believe even the cleverest darky could plan and run an uprising on his own. A white man likely wouldn't hang for his beliefs, however misbegotten they might be. Take responsibility for corrupting one of Bill's favorites, and you'll spare him his pecker and his neck. Why he might even live to plug Aunt Bekah again."

Joseph tried to stand, but Moore pushed him down with the shotgun barrels. "Nobody knows anything! Nobody's done anything. You're beating and burning false confessions out of innocent slaves."

Mitchell said, "Oh, you might be surprised at what's been admitted under little or no duress. Brother Sid here says rightly that the Almighty will not forsake one of his own. The good reverend, on the other hand, forsakes quite readily."

"That is a lie, Marster."

"A man only needs to listen to this insolence to know that we've barely averted an insurrection," Mitchell said.

Samuel said, "Burn me. Stick it up here."

Teddy studied him, tossed the rod aside. "This one's cooled off. Fetch me a fresh one."

Mitchell went to the door again and summoned the man with another glowing rod. Teddy took it and walked over to Bekah. "Boys." Willy came and unbuttoned her dress and pulled it down around to her waist.

Teddy looked her over. "I swear, Samuel, I'd be doing what I could to save my pecker. It might come in awful handy sometime." He held the glowing tip close to her back. She winced.

"What do you say, Samuel, Shaw? You preachers? Be a shame to mark this up. This rod's liable to burn right through her in a second. Just burn clean through before I realized I've gone too far."

Joseph pushed aside Moore's barrels and struggled to his feet. "God-damn you, I don't know anything about anything. Nobody does!"

Chambers and Newton rolled their eyes up at him.

Teddy touched the small of Bekah's back with the rod. She screamed. Smoke rose. Jack turned and vomited. Moore looked away. "Sweet Jesus."

Claggett wept. "God bless you, sister," he said.

Samuel heaved against the lashings, swung his body, raised his feet against the pole, and pulled, screaming.

Bekah shrieked, "Nothing! Don't say nothing! Samuel! Don't! Don't! Don't!"

The hot iron burned her shoulder. She grimaced but didn't scream. Samuel felt blood running hot down his forearms, smelled Bekah's burning flesh.

Teddy said, "Look here now." He lifted her skirt. "Well, I want you to look. Boys, what do you think?" The deputies held her, stone-faced, pale.

"Wait, now, what's this? Spread 'em there, missy. Hold the dress up, Jack." He knelt and touched a spot in the inside of her thigh. "Look here, now. This one's had the iron put to her before. What's it say, Aunt Bekah? It's a little too dim to read down there."

He touched the back of her thigh with the rod. More smoke. No scream but Samuel's. "I done it, Marster! I done it on my own, without no help."

Bekah pulled against her lashings. "No! Burn me again! Burn me!"

He did, this time on her other thigh.

Mitchell said, "Pig shit! Who helped you, Sam? Who put you up to it?"

"Nobody! Bekah ain't got a thing to do with this!" His pants were tangled up in his leg irons.

Mitchell looked at Joseph, brows arched in question.

Samuel said, "No sir! I come up with it all!"

Mitchell said, "Chambers and Newton? They helped you?"

"No sir!"

"If we could incite insurrection, we'd have done it five years ago," Chambers yelled.

"Joe? You'll save his life and maybe the girl's."

"I know nothing about the fire or insurrection! Nothing!"

"Who started the fire, Sam?"

"I done it!"

"You were at the graveyard."

"I set it on the way. It took awhile to get going."

"Liar." He nodded to Teddy, who prodded the center of Bekah's back.

"Just me! That's all! I swear to it, Marster."

"Joe?"

"You've burned and beaten him into delirium. He'll say anything."

"He'll hang."

"Goddamn you. Nobody knows anything."

Mitchell said, "Cut 'em down."

Teddy threw aside the rod and calmly walked out the door. The deputies untied Bekah and Samuel.

As Samuel struggled to pull his britches up, Mitchell said, "Sam, you've just lied your way to the noose." He patted his shoulder. "But I've always known you're a good boy."

They stepped into the early morning coolness. A rooster crowed in the distance. Mitchell said, "Well, I'd call this a day's work."

Samuel started to climb into the wagon, but when he tried to bend and put weight on his arms, he nearly fainted from pain in his back and abdomen. Teddy stepped out of the darkness, said, "Here," and helped him in.

Near the front of the wagon, Moore said, "Good lord, Joe, I didn't have no idea. None. We ain't had nothing like this."

Samuel tried to lean back into the sideboard, but the pain took his breath.

Bekah said, "Lay down here," and eased his head into her lap. He stretched his legs, and she stroked his face and hair as they rode back to jail.

CHAPTER 57

Joseph woke up at home, alone.

A few hours earlier, after a silent wagon ride back to the jail, Moore told him he was free to go. The deputies led the other prisoners inside. Joseph called to Samuel and Bekah, "I'll be back. I'm going to get Malachi."

Bekah and Brother Sid were helping Samuel into the jail. He looked back once, then disappeared into the cellblock.

Instead of going to the Van Husses' to get Malachi, Joseph walked home and fell into bed. He slept fitfully until mid-morning, then rose, washed, put on a clean shirt, and stepped into the backyard half expecting to find Samuel working under the shop awning.

The sun was well off the horizon. No clouds in sight. He heard hammers in the square.

A clatter of hooves. Marshal Moore drove his wagon into the yard. He looked even more shaken than he'd looked during the inquisition.

Joseph stood watching him, too exhausted and empty to work up any anger.

Moore motioned toward the back of the wagon. "Some boys found him in the brush just off the road north of town. Couldn't have been more than half an hour after we passed. He's already getting ripe."

Joseph walked around the side of the wagon and lifted the tarp. At once, two flies found the dried blood on Teddy's shirt collar and slit throat.

CHAPTER 58

Samuel sat in the corner of the cell for most of the next day after his interrogation. The other slaves and the two parsons said little, but treated him with deference. Bekah sat beside him and brought him his meals at feeding time. Late that afternoon, Dr. Thome visited. The men turned their backs while he cleaned and treated her burns.

He asked Samuel, "Passing any blood?"

"Just a little bit. None the last time or two."

"Which pot?"

Samuel nodded to the closest one. Thome rose and checked it. "It's full. I can't tell anything from it." He looked at Bekah. "Check right after he goes. If you see any blood, tell the marshal. Word will get to me."

She nodded.

"I'm feeling better," Samuel said.

Thome patted Samuel's shoulder, squeezed Bekah's hand, then asked if anyone else had ailments that needed his attention. No one spoke up. He looked about the cell, then nodded to Jack, who let him out. He glanced at the other cells. "Might as well check the rest while I'm here."

"Nobody said nothing about letting you into them other cells," the deputy said.

"For heaven's sake, man."

"Can't let you in there."

Zeph Newton leaned against the bars. "No need to worry for now, Doc. We're making out quite well. I suspect you'll be needed yet, though."

"You ever shut your goddamn mouth?" the deputy said.

Newton laughed. Thome glared at the deputy, shook his head in disgust, and started up the stairs.

Bekah sat down next to Samuel. "It'll be all right. Ain't nobody getting hung."

Samuel nodded. She'd said that a dozen times already. His back ached so that he could only doze. He wanted deep sleep. The noose was tomorrow's problem. Right now his back hurt so that he could think of little else but his bed and whiskey and sleep. At times Bekah's lack of complaining about her own wounds annoyed him. Other times, her stoicism shamed him.

Hanging. Mitchell had been pleasant toward him through the interrogation, although he'd been in charge, a man bearing the burden of his position. Bear up in good humor. Sacrifice one of your favorites if that's what's called for. Hate it, yes. Bless Samuel's heart. He'd been good to the boy, but you couldn't save them all. He should've kept him.

A man in charge. Congenial, patient, indulgent even. Terrible when he had to be, but still given to a wink and pat on the back. *I hate it. I hate it. But, hell, what's a man to do? They're hollering for black hide.* He had to give them somebody, else you'd have mobs out hanging thousands of dollars worth of property. Somebody had to run things, had to maintain order. You couldn't leave things to simple-minded grocers and tradesmen. Give them two or three bodies and get back to business.

Joseph, Malachi, and Brother Ig were out there. They'd be trying to get him out, trying to reason with Mitchell and Keller and their ilk.

Joseph could have saved him from hanging, could've admitted that he—Samuel—had been only one black man among several whites. They might spare a slave who'd been instructed and aided by a white man. They probably wouldn't hang a white man even for arson or inciting insurrection, unless he'd committed murder.

But a black man acting on his own . . .

Or one who claimed to have acted on his own, even if every one of his interrogators knew he was lying.

Joseph. He'd protected the movement. Or Ig and Rachel. Or Rachel. Or himself.

He couldn't think that way.

Joseph had made a choice. Did he regret it now? Where would they be if he'd admitted his part? Beaten and run out of Dallas County?

But what was his part? Their part? They hadn't started the fire. They had no idea who, if anyone, had. So Joseph had not denied the truth. He'd not been asked about moving slaves to Mexico or Kansas. He'd been accused of inciting insurrection among Dallas's slaves, and he'd justly denied it.

And he'd saved himself from a beating and ruination and had condemned a man to hang.

And Samuel's own confession? To spare Joseph, the Bodekers, and the others? To preserve a movement that might spring up in another place to help shepherd fugitive slaves on to freedom? To protect people who'd risked their lives for their beliefs?

To protect his friends?

To keep Bekah from being burned again?

So that Teddy would stop?

He couldn't remember. Whatever the reason, noble or not, he wouldn't have to live with it.

Bekah patted her thigh. "You want to lay down here for a while?"

He did. Doc Thome's laudanum came over him. The stone floor felt as soft and warm as his feather tick. He slept.

———

Joseph found the Bodekers' door open. He knocked on the doorframe and helloed the house.

Inside, Rachel said, "I'm afraid I won't be answering the door."

He found her sitting in a straight-backed chair, on a pillow. She closed a book on her index finger and smiled. Mid-morning sun poured through the doors and windows, but she sat in a shady spot close to the bed and looked cool, though haggard. The shadows under her eyes had deepened again. She rested her forearm across her belly.

He stepped in out of the sun. "Never one for an idle mind."

She raised the book. "Balzac. Professor Euler loaned it to me."

Joseph smiled, shrugged. "What'd you do with Ig?"

"He's appealing to Mr. Keller or Mr. Williams or whoever will listen. Have you seen Samuel or Bekah?"

"Nobody's listening. And no, I haven't seen Samuel or Bekah. They won't let me. Doc Thome did say Bekah was holding up. Samuel . . ." He sighed. "He's not dying."

She held the book to her chest and rested her chin on it. "Well then."

"Ig has to try. I know that. I'll try again, too. Malachi's trying." He pulled a chair from the kitchen table and sat down. "Hell, everybody is." A pathetic statement. He ought to be gathering a mob to storm the jail.

"They'll hang him."

"We don't know that."

"We're helpless."

"This thing might just burn out." A ridiculous choice of words. He sighed and ran his hand through his hair. "I mean . . ."

"I know what you mean. We're helpless but still hopeful. Ig's praying. We're praying."

He nodded. "They might settle on someone else. I mean, how many are they going to hang?"

She let go a soft snort of exasperation.

He couldn't meet her sleepy eyes. "I . . . hell then." They sat in silence. There was no breeze through the open windows and doors. Flies buzzed about the room. She fingered the spine of her book.

After a moment, he said, "Well, you don't have long to wait."

"No more than two weeks, probably." She didn't brighten at all.

"Just get through this. Let things settle. We'll all head north."

"Ig could barely climb into the wagon this morning. I'm not sure how he managed. I couldn't watch."

"Been a rough few days. He'll come around. Doc Thome said . . ."

"Joseph."

His throat tightened; he leaned toward her and said, "No matter what happens, I promise you. No matter what." His voice broke. "You understand what I'm saying?"

"I couldn't live."

"You have to."

She opened her book, smoothed the pages, nodded. "I suppose you're right."

He rose. A shaft of sunlit dust blinded him. He bent to kiss her. She didn't turn her face up to his, nor did she resist. Her forehead was cool, but her hair smelled so strongly and purely of her that for an instant his sorrow and shame left him.

CHAPTER 59

"We can't let you in, Preacher. It's a closed meetin'." The young deputy blocked the courthouse door.

Ig recalled that the boy's name was Willy or Billy. "On whose authority, son?"

"On authority of them that's in authority."

"I only want to make a statement as a citizen of Dallas."

"You'll have to talk to Mr. Keller."

"I have."

"Or Mr. Mitchell."

"I have."

"Or Judge Burford."

"I've spoken to the judge."

"What about Major McCoy?"

"I talked with him at length."

"Then you've said your piece." He studied Ig. "How come your arm to hang that way?"

"I overexerted during the fire."

"Well. It won't be that way from now on, will it?"

Ig sighed. Mid-morning and he was already sweating. He held his cane loosely with his bad hand and ran a finger around the inside of his collar. "I expect not. Would you pass a note to those inside?"

"You got one?"

"If you could fetch me some writing materials I'd have one shortly."

"I can't leave this door."

Laughter erupted inside. "Deciding on men's fate with proper gravity," Ig said.

"I reckon so."

"I'll speak to the marshal."

"You know where he's at."

Ig turned and started down the steps. "You keep an eye on that door, son. Watch out for marauding ministers."

"I aim to. That's how we caught them two that's locked up."

Ig eased down the five steps and turned left on Commerce, toward the jail at the intersection with Jackson Street. He'd try again. Moore had refused to let anyone but Dr. Thome visit the prisoners, but he'd make another appeal. No doubt Brothers Chambers and Newton were sitting smugly in their cells, each considering himself Paul and the other Silas.

If arsonists burned the town, then the marshal probably had his two men. No one else could conjure enough reckless, self-righteous outrage. Now men's lives were at stake. If Joseph was right, Samuel was already condemned. And no one could do anything. This was no town, no democracy. This was a regime. Judges were helpless. Men of goodwill spoke only at risk to their lives, families, and property.

Rachel had stopped cautioning him, other than "Be careful. Consider your child." He had to try, or he could not live with himself, could not hold Rachel's respect, and without that he might as well be dead. He'd urged caution, and his urgings had gone unheeded by two ridiculous, vainglorious preachers, and now caution was no longer an option.

Joseph was shaken but not cowed. He couldn't be. But he seemed resigned, sorrowful. He'd seen something. Yes, he'd made appeals to the town leaders. He'd gone with Ig the first couple of times to try to get in and see Samuel. Now he seemed resigned or hopeless enough to wait and see; tempers might simmer down.

But they weren't simmering. They were boiling, thanks in large part to Pryor's editorials, now syndicated and published in papers all over the state. Weapon caches found. Murder plot barely foiled. Strychnine missing. But there were never any firsthand accounts. All hearsay.

Tonight he'd compose rebuttals. Perhaps some of the papers would publish them. Time was short. Maybe someone could courier his editorials up to McKinney or down to Waxahachie. Pig would have done it. Maybe David could help, but who knew when he'd appear again?

Should he use a pen name? He needn't be reckless. A simple appeal for calm and rule of law. Fair, deliberate trials. Methodical law enforcement. *Let's not be hasty, but make sure that we catch and bring the real perpetrators to justice. We cannot risk executing innocent men while the guilty go unpunished.* No reason to bring abolition sympathies into it. No need to endanger Rachel.

He hadn't slept for three days. Yet he felt himself getting stronger as he walked along Commerce. He used his cane, yes, but his left arm felt fine and strong when it took his weight. His stride lengthened, and he imagined the cane marks in the dust growing farther and farther apart as he strode southward.

He'd make his appeal, loudly, so that the prisoners would hear him. They'd know they hadn't been forsaken. The marshal would turn him away again, of course. He'd go home and compose notes for Samuel and Bekah, Brother Claggett, and the two parsons. If the marshal wouldn't allow the notes, then he'd ask Dr. Thome to take them in.

Sweat ran down his back and sides. He began to swing his right arm a bit. He'd fire up Joseph, Malachi, and Richard Van Huss, as he'd done before. Then Professor Euler and the others. The town tyrants would know they couldn't round up innocents, interrogate them in secret, and subject them to unlawful tribunals. Or if they could, there would be dissent, loud and furious. This was not a matter of slavery or abolition, but of Texas law. Judge Burford's failure to maintain order would be known far and wide. Judges and officials would learn to fear the pen.

Several buildings had already been framed on the square. The town would be rebuilt by Christmas. Sarah Cockrell was making a fortune with her sawmill. Meanwhile the poor and black still lived in camps along the river. Already, among the respectable citizens, he'd heard complaints about the smell and the noise and petty theft.

Mitchell and Keller and their ilk would come out richer, with all the desperate laborers willing to work for nothing but a meal.

He greeted people along the street. Women in their yards. Children. Slaves on errands. Most were dull-eyed and offered only a nod. The heat and fear. Despair. And why not? They needed an example, a reminder.

The past Sunday, only Joseph, the Meades, and the Van Husses showed up for his service. He'd saved his sermon; they just sat and talked. He'd try again the coming Sunday. Put the word out. Tack up a few bulletins, handwritten. It'd be awhile before you could get anything printed. Just let things return to normal. Wait. Be patient. Let folks get back to mindless mongering. Then he and his friends could get back to the work they'd come to do. He wouldn't be retreating to Kansas. Hopefully Brothers Newton and Chambers would be run out of town. He hated to admit it, but a community could suffer from a surplus of preachers.

CHAPTER 60

Samuel woke when the heavy door at the top of the steps opened. He sat up, the side of his face still warm from Bekah's lap. He glanced up at the narrow windows. Late afternoon. Moore came down the steps with Willy and William Keller behind.

"Aunt Bekah, Brother Sid," Moore said. "Looks like you've been cleared."

Bekah stood and hurried to the bars. She watched Keller, who said, "We've about got this thing wrapped up. Another few days."

Newton lay on his bench, propped up on his elbow. "Why, Keller, awfully good of you to come down and check on us. You can rest easy. As you can see, we're enjoying the best of care."

Keller chuckled. "Far better than those godforsaken thickets, I'm sure. You got all the ticks plucked off yet?"

"I'll take those bloodsuckers to the ones in this town any day," Jonah Chambers said. "Matter of fact, you look well-fed and happy with the world."

"I came down just so you two could hone your tongues. I wouldn't want them to get dull from disuse." He motioned to Samuel's cell. "Let 'em out of there, Jim."

Moore found the key and stuck it in the lock. Keller turned back to the parsons. "You two will be disappointed, but it appears that your martyrdom will have to wait. It's not looking like you'll be strung up this time. You'll have to work a little harder at it."

"Might as well let us out then," Newton said.

"You ain't wore out your welcome just yet."

Samuel started to get up, but Bekah went to him, knelt and held him, crying. "Don't get up, baby. We won't leave you in here. It'll be all right."

He held her but could say nothing. Now Brother Sid knelt beside him. "Remember what I said in that barn."

Samuel nodded. The cells were silent.

Keller said, "Aunt Bekah."

"I'm comin'." She continued to hold Samuel and kneaded the back of his neck. "Don't you give up. Don't never give up hope."

More silence. Clearing throats. Brother Sid took her arm. She sobbed, drew away from Samuel, and stepped out the cell door. Samuel felt the coldness of the floor and the wall seep into his body, the emptiness in the cell in his chest.

Chambers and Newton were leaning against their cell bars. Chambers said, "Bekah." He held up his right hand, and there was the *A*. He looked to Bekah and then to Samuel. Bekah took his hand with her three fingers and thumb and leaned her forehead against the bars. She was crying still, but silent. Moore and Keller and the deputy watched. Brother Claggett touched her back, then started up the steps. Now Bekah released the parson's hand, turned to Samuel, raised her three-fingered hand in good-bye, then followed Claggett up the stairs.

Moore said, "After you, Bill."

Keller started to leave, then hesitated and looked at Samuel. Footsteps could be heard upstairs. The front door opened. Samuel imagined Bekah stepping out into the street. Joseph would be happy to see her.

Keller held Samuel's gaze, a man who knew what was to come. "Samuel, I'm doing what I can." He slowly raised his hook, as if showing it to Samuel, and touched his forehead in salute.

Samuel didn't answer. He recalled Bekah's good-bye wave. She'd bent her three fingers like a hook.

CHAPTER 61

Bekah hated to leave Joseph this way. He'd nearly wept with relief when he came home and found her in the kitchen. She'd made him a meal of sweet potatoes and cornbread. He looked pale and haggard. She suspected he'd barely eaten since the day of their arrest. He talked hopefully about Samuel. Malachi was still working. Bill Keller had said he was doing what he could.

On the other hand, John McCoy and Nat Burford had washed their hands of the affair.

She didn't tell him she'd already packed her bag.

She watched the street. He'd probably come out of the cedars. They'd hide out for a few days, then Adolphus Fox would meet them a little north of McKinney in his lumber wagon. They'd be up on the Red in less than a week.

She wouldn't be in Dallas for the beatings. Every slave over the age of fourteen. In front of the children. She'd been beaten before, and burned. She'd lost fingers. She would have survived this, too. She would have stayed and taken the lash with the rest, would have preferred it that way, but he'd said no. Get out when you can. You've done enough for now. Who knew what the next few weeks held? He'd done what he could, but he was just one man.

She'd be back, though, sometime, surely, when things calmed down. Brother Jonah and Brother Zeph would take their beatings, then head back to their thickets. Brother Sid and Myra and the others would return to their shacks and back rooms. They'd heal and wait for that soft knock or rustle in the night.

The burns on her back and thigh still hurt, but they were healing. She touched the inside of her thigh and felt the raised scar of her own brand through the thin summer cotton. Sometimes it itched. She always welcomed the reminder.

Poor Samuel. Dear Samuel. Dear Robert. Dear Flora. Dear Mary. Dear Timothy.

A shadow detached from the old bois d'arc across the street. He still moved like a night thing—a cat or a fox—though he canted toward his one arm. You learned to make do.

She took her bag from the bed and swung her leg out the open window.

CHAPTER 62

The jail now held three Negroes, two preachers, two drunks, and a petty thief. Eleven more slaves had been released to their owners that morning. Samuel now had his own bench to lie on. Two middle-aged slaves, Cato Bryant and Patrick Jennings, sat on the other benches.

Cato ran the wheel at Overton's Mill; he poisoned rats with strychnine. He'd admitted under threat of torture he'd given a few crystals to Jacob Isaacson, who'd needed them to kill gophers in his garden. Patrick claimed to have admitted nothing despite Teddy's inducements, but according to his owner, the attorney George Guess, he'd been a troublemaker fifteen years before in Virginia and remained surly and insolent, a sorry slave.

Samuel had known both of his alleged coconspirators casually most of his life, but before being locked up with them he'd never shared more than a greeting or nod with either.

In the opposite cell, the two drunks and Jonah Chambers snored on their benches while the thief—a slight, frail, balding young man named Hickson—badgered Zeph Newton.

"So you're sayin' a man ain't never, under no circumstances at all, right to take what ain't his to begin with."

"A man ought to earn an honest living. You'll find it laid out clear in Exodus. Chapter twenty, verse fifteen.

"The commandments. I learned 'em right off."

"Well then. You got a proper enough raising."

"But say he's trying to feed his wife and starving babies."

"That's where you were headed with Mrs. Ferguson's chickens?"

"No sir, but still . . ."

"I would say the Almighty judges case by case. A man with a starving family and no prospects ought to appeal to the kindness and generosity of his neighbors first."

"And if his neighbors is too stingy or hard up to help?"

"Would he be stealin' from a man as poor as himself?"

"No sir."

"I can't say for certain, but the Lord and the law might judge harsher than I would."

"That don't hardly ease my mind."

"Nor will it shorten your stay."

"Said like a slave-stealin' preacher." One of the drunks, Massy, pale and puffy, spoke with his eyes shut, his head resting on his forearm. "I reckon you would take a soft view on certain kinds of thievery. Seems you bend the commandments to your own needs."

"Now, that wasn't what I was gettin' at," Hickson said. "I reckon the parson ought to sleep very well." He was standing, with one hand on the wall and the other hand in his pants pocket.

Newton said, "I can't be too hard on a man too weak to hold his liquor."

Massy laughed. He kept his eyes closed and his head very still. "Heap them coals, Reverend."

"Warm, are they?"

"A balm to my aching skull."

"I regret every word then."

Jonah Chambers snored, mumbled something in his sleep. Newton glanced at his friend, mirth in his eyes.

Massy said, "How should the Lord and the law judge you, Parson?"

Newton drew up a knee and laced his fingers around it. "I'd say the law has made its opinion well-known. I'm far less worried about the Lord's take on matters."

"Thou shalt not steal?"

Hickson said, "Now hold on . . ."

Jonah Chambers stopped in mid-snore and cleared his throat. "A man might have to suffer the laws of the land, but he needn't obey them if they're in conflict with God's laws." His eyes were still shut tight, but his face was drawn up in irritation.

Newton said, "Amen."

Chambers's face relaxed. His breathing had already become regular, just shy of snoring.

Massy sat up, rubbing his temples. "A rat terrier even in his sleep."

Newton said, "He's snored through his share of my sermons and woke just in time to lead the closing prayer. Then argued several points with me afterward."

Massy looked at the slaves in the opposite cell. His eyes were bloodshot. He still wore a greasy coat. His cravat hung untied around his neck. His gray hair hung on his forehead. He stood and went to the bars. "And what will your maker say about arson?"

Samuel didn't answer. Cato said, "We won't know. He might have something to say 'bout hangin' innocent men. Anyways, I hope we won't find out for a spell."

Massy laughed. "Just three of you left in the cell. Now what do you suppose that means?"

"We never set no fire," Samuel said.

Massy grabbed the bars and shoved his face between them. "I'd say the sacrifices have been chosen. Will they be burnt offerings?"

Hickson pushed himself off the wall and grabbed the bar next to Massy. "Look here, now, goddamn it."

Patrick said, "Don't pay no attention." He sat on his bench, his eyes half closed.

Chambers was awake now, his arms crossed, watching Massy. "You'll be out of here in a day or two, Massy, I reckon."

Massy turned and leaned back on the bars. "Oh, a threat, Reverend? A threat from the legendary Jonah Chambers, intrepid stealer of slaves? I seen you ride into town that day with those two boys. Quite a little spectacle."

Chambers nodded. "Quite a few came out to watch, as I recall."

"Then, be damned, if you didn't get away, the both of you."

Newton said, "We have help here and there."

Massy touched his temple, then clasped his hands behind his back. "Oh, the Almighty. Call on him again, then. Get yourself and these three boys out of here."

"We'll be out soon enough," Newton said. "Keep that in mind whilst you flap your gums."

"Oh, you reckon? What about the three boys here? You know well as I do where they're headed." He looked at Samuel and the others. "What do you think, boys? Reckon these two the ones that done it? Reckon you'll hang in their place? At least you'll meet your maker knowing you was innocent. You can take some comfort in that, I s'pose."

Cato said, "Go to hell."

"I s'pect I will." Massy laughed. "Cussing a white man, now. There's a nigger knows he's fixing to die anyhow."

Hickson looked pale. "They never done nothing. You and me, now, we'll get what's coming, and it probably ain't too much, probably not even what we deserve. But these never done nothing wrong."

The two parsons sat watching Massy. They seemed more curious than angry or sorrowful. Hickson's jaw was set, his blue eyes wide with anger. He watched Massy go back to his bench. The other drunk slept on. Massy sat and looked defiantly at the others, then lay down, crossed his ankles, and clasped his hands behind his head.

—

Late morning the next day, Marshal Moore came into the cell area and stood in front of Samuel's cell. He sighed and looked at each of them. They all stood. He said, "If there's anything in particular you'd like for supper tonight, I'll get it for you if I can."

Hickson said, "You mean like side meat or bacon? Or cornbread?"

"Beer?" Massy said.

Moore didn't turn to look at Hickson. "No, it's beans or mush again for y'all. I'm talking to these three right here."

Chapter 63

All morning a crowd built near the courthouse steps. Joseph watched as he unloaded lumber from wagons for Darnell's new livery. Word was, the Committee of Vigilance would announce its decision today. He wondered how the notion got started. Probably a member of the committee had put the word out to ensure an appreciative audience. The town government and the county judiciary had been usurped by two or three men and a claque of storekeepers, lawyers, physicians, and newspapermen.

The smell of cured oak and cedar reminded him of Samuel. Joseph tried to picture him in his cell, but couldn't. He could only imagine him in the shop or the kitchen. Did Samuel know he hadn't been allowed to visit? Moore had disallowed all visitors and even written correspondence, so great was the fear of escape. They could thank Jonah Chambers and Zeph Newton for that.

Bekah would be well on her way to the Red River by now. No doubt David came for her. He couldn't blame her.

He sat in the shade of a pile of studs and ate his dinner of hard-boiled eggs and scorched cornbread. He'd gotten out of practice after the months of Bekah's cooking. As he was finishing, he saw Ig limp onto the courthouse lawn, look around, then ease into a sliver of shade thrown by the west side of the building.

Other workmen sat about, eating and talking. Though most were friendly, or at least polite, they all avoided Joseph's eyes and company. They'd stopped asking about Samuel. Joseph did hear a piece of conversation that morning: ". . . a damn shame. He's a right good carpenter," someone said.

He needed to get back to work. Work, when his closest friend was locked away for arson he couldn't have committed because he was busy burying a fugitive slave. Just go to work. Or speak up and get a dozen other innocent people hanged or beaten or burned. They'd probably hang Samuel anyway, just for his association with white abolitionists. The thought sickened him. He spat, then got up and walked over to see Ig.

Even in the early afternoon heat, the preacher looked pale. He'd clearly lost weight. He seemed relieved to see Joseph. He leaned on his cane with his right hand, and barely lifted his left hand to clasp Joseph's. The gesture felt more like an embrace than a handshake.

Ig said, "How you holding up?"

"Doing all I know to do."

Ig smiled weakly, sadly. "Working. I envy you for that. I couldn't write a sermon to save the world."

"How's Rachel?"

"Miserable. More than ready to deliver. She's not talking, barely eating. And of course she won't cry, though it would do her some good, I think."

Joseph said, "You're leaning on that cane awful hard."

"This heat. Hellish. More than any Virginian is bred for."

"Or Kentuckian."

More people had gathered.

"Probably in there arguing about who gets to come out and make the pronouncement," Joseph said. "I say we just stand here in the shade and see what happens." He looked back toward the livery site. Dinner was finished, and the others were going back to work. He turned his back on them.

"Ig, you ought to sit. Let me see what I can find you to sit on."

"No thank you. I'm doing very well." He teetered on his cane.

"Let me get you a drink of water." He started back to the work site to fetch his water jar.

"I thank you," Ig said.

Before he got off the courthouse lawn, a commotion on the steps stopped him. The doors were open, and above the heads of the crowd he saw W. B. Mitchell. Joseph hurried back to Ig, who'd started toward the door. They crowded onto the bottom step, then backed away to better see and hear Mitchell.

"It's about high, goddamn time," somebody yelled.

Workmen all over the square dropped their tools and hurried to the lawn. Mitchell watched and waited while other members of the committee gathered behind him. He wore no coat, and his sleeves were rolled to his elbows. He held an unlit cigar between his fingers.

Men jostled and laughed. Others leveled angry shouts and demands. Women and children came out of houses and stood in their backyards, watching the courthouse. A few slaves stood quietly in the street, shading their eyes with their hands.

Joseph's mouth was dry; his arms felt numb and heavy. Perhaps it had all blown over. Maybe Mitchell and the committee would be satisfied with a whipping and jail time or expulsion or mandatory selling to someone outside the county.

Ig dabbed his forehead with a handkerchief. People kept coming. Joseph spotted Malachi and Richard crossing Jefferson Street. He waved, but they didn't see him. He started to yell, but no one would hear him above the clamor. Mitchell was smiling and talking to someone on the top step, nodding, probably joking about something, very much in charge, a man you could count on to take care of things.

The courthouse lawn was full, and people filled Commerce Street. Mitchell raised his arms, and the crowd quieted.

After a moment, he said, "I will make this announcement as brief as possible, for it brings me no pleasure whatsoever." His pleasant demeanor was gone. He looked out over the crowd. "It is especially painful to be betrayed in the most egregious manner by those whom we've loved and trusted for many years. But as has been the case in so many similar instances of servile treachery, the principal scoundrels have been those who had ingratiated themselves so as to gain freedom and trust in order to carry out their designs.

"We have carefully and fairly interrogated most of the Negro population in the county. We have questioned witnesses and disentangled conflicting accounts. We've heard every lie imaginable and every claim of remorse, true and false. No doubt, guilty men will go unpunished, or insufficiently punished, but in matters of life and death one must be completely sure."

Somebody yelled, "Get on with it, for godsake."

Another said, "Brief, my ass. It's damn hot out here."

Mitchell nodded and raised his hand in acknowledgment. The sun washed the redbrick courthouse pale and dull. There was no shade anywhere on the square. Joseph could hear Ig breathing.

Mitchell said, "Well, then. Tomorrow morning, just after sunrise, three Negroes whose guilt has been determined beyond any shadow of doubt—Patrick Jennings, owned by George Guess; Samuel Smith, owned by Joseph Shaw; and Uncle Cato Bryant, owned by Mrs. Aaron Overton—will be escorted to the riverbank and hanged by their necks until dead."

The crowd murmured. There were angry shouts.

"Is that all the hell y'all could come up with?"

"What about them damn preachers?"

"We've acted with the greatest care and restraint," Mitchell said. "Better to spare the guilty than to hang an innocent man."

Tom Overton, Aaron Overton's nephew, said, "Who's gonna pay for old Cato? I knew damn good and well whose niggers wouldn't be strung up. I don't reckon none of your people fessed up, huh, Bill?"

A few people looked back at Joseph. He felt rooted, nauseated. He realized Ig was yelling. "Confession, by what means, sir?" Ig hobbled toward the steps. His face and neck were flushed. He raised his cane. "A complete abdication of justice! You offer only sacrifices! You will own up to this!"

A few people looked at Ig in horror. Most, including Mitchell, ignored him or didn't hear him. Mitchell raised his arms again, and the crowd quieted.

"And the two preachers, Parsons Newton and Chambers, having been found guilty . . ."

"In a court of law?" Ig shouted. "Or by a depraved mob?"

Now people turned to look. Someone said, "Shut it, preacher!" Others shouted their agreement.

Mitchell held out his hands, "Brother Ig . . ."

Ig pointed his cane at Mitchell. "Tell these people how you gained your confessions. Tell them what you did to Bekah!"

Willis Peak said, "Somebody better shut him up for his own good."

Mitchell said, "I do not doubt that rumors abound, but I assure you . . ." He looked at Joseph.

"Burned her with a rod," Ig heard himself say. "Burned her and Samuel both. Do you want to hear where?"

"And who gives a good goddamn," came the answer from the crowd.

Mitchell turned and nodded to Marshal Moore, who eased off the steps.

Mitchell continued, "At a time yet to be determined by the committee, Reverends Chambers and Newton . . ."

"Men of God!" Ig shouted.

". . . will be publicly whipped and expelled from the county."

More shouts. People from the streets and courthouse lawn converged on the steps. "I know another one needs it, too!" Some in the crowd were pointing and shaking fists and fingers at Ig, who shouted and thrust with his cane. A man stepped out and swiped off Ig's hat, but Moore stepped between them. Dr. Thome stepped out of the mob, picked up Ig's hat, and handed it to him.

Ig put on his hat and directed his cane back at Mitchell and the committee. "There will be a reckoning, gentlemen!"

Moore said to Joseph, "Joe, get him out of here." Malachi and Richard hurried up. They took Ig's arm and tried to lead him away, but he fought them. His voice had left him; tears and sweat streamed down his face.

His eyes were wild, bulbous. Joseph grabbed his sweat-slick wrist, but he jerked free.

The crowd on the steps began to clear. Others gathered around to watch the struggle with Ig, who turned to point his cane at Mitchell and swiped Willy across the temple. The deputy said, "Hellfire!"

Moore jerked the cane from Ig's hand. "Hold him. Willy, help."

Joseph wrapped Ig up from behind. The others grabbed his arms. Moore got in Ig's face. "Reverend! Reverend! Stop! I'll lock you up!"

Joseph said in Ig's ear, "Ig, listen. *Listen.*"

Ig began to relax. He glared at Moore, who handed the cane to Willy.

Moore said, "You've just got a little overexcited." He seemed to have said this as much to the onlookers as to Ig. Joseph began to relax has grip.

Dr. Thorne gripped Ig's forearm. "Reverend. Remember what we talked about," he said gently. He looked at Joseph. "You've got to get him out of this sun."

Moore said, "Where's your wagon at, Preacher?"

Ig didn't answer. Moore said, "Willy, go find the parson's wagon and get up here with it." Willy headed toward Commerce Street, rubbing his temple.

Joseph released Ig and said, "You hearing me, Ig?"

Ig nodded weakly.

"I'll drive you on home," Joseph said.

Ig didn't respond. People had started to clear out.

Joseph said, "Can I see Samuel?"

"I'm sorry, Joe," Moore said. "There ain't gonna be another escape."

"For godsake," Malachi said.

"I'm sorry. Nobody gets in. You can thank Brothers Chambers and Newton. I like to have never lived that down." He walked away toward Commerce Street.

Mitchell stepped off the courthouse steps, out into the lawn. He regarded Ig with bemusement, then reached back and struck a match on the bottom step and lighted his cigar. He shook the match out as he stepped into the lawn, then tossed it over his shoulder.

Chapter 64

For once, Joseph sat, unable to allow himself the succor of work. Nor the comfort of whiskey. Samuel had neither. For now, he would have neither. He slouched at the kitchen table, listening to the settling of the house and the tiny, soft scurryings he normally didn't hear. He eyed the shotgun over the mantel. No. Samuel wouldn't have that, either.

After the announcement on the courthouse steps, he'd driven Ig home. The Meades and the Van Husses arrived at the same time. Rachel teared up but said little. She hardly met Joseph's eyes, and when she did, he saw only sorrow. She tried to fuss over Ig, but he refused her attention and insisted she lie down. He'd lost his voice; he exhorted in harsh whispers.

They all sat in the heat of the cabin, but there was little to discuss. Malachi said he'd appeal again to Burford and McCoy to intervene. Yet further appeals would be useless. A few well-placed small-town businessmen had subverted the law. A district judge had been helpless. Someone had to hang. They picked three. Take care of business. Keep things running.

Ig said, "I'll wait outside the jail and walk with them as far as I can."

They all nodded. The women dabbed their eyes.

Joseph drew little comfort from his friends. Their presence made him miss Al and Samuel, Pig and Cathlyn more sharply. He wanted them all there.

He rose and said he needed to head home. Rachel waved her hand before her face, shooing a fly. Their eyes met for an instant. Malachi and Richard slapped him on the back. From his chair, Ig said, "Will you be . . . ?" His arm hung against his side.

"I won't be going. No."

Ig nodded, exhausted, sorrowful.

Joseph stepped outside, then turned in the doorway. "There's something else I have to do. You know?"

"Of course."

But so far, he hadn't started. He'd been sitting at the table for over two hours. The mantel clock ticked. Sweat trickled in his sideburns. Finally, he rose and drank a dipper of water, then stepped out into the early-evening stillness.

He carried his lantern into the shop, lighted another, and hung them both on posts. He stood for a moment, looking at Samuel's footprints in the sawdust, his neatly racked mallets, his three-drawer toolbox, his cut marks and figuring scratched here and there on pieces of scrap lumber, his fingerprints in the dust on a new rolltop desk.

Joseph went back to the kitchen, lighted the stove, and filled the coffee boiler. He'd need a good strong pot tonight. Maybe he'd sleep tomorrow night or the next.

He went back to the shop, took a lantern from its peg, and held it over a pile of high-grade oak he'd picked out for Mrs. Cockrell's new hotel dinner table. He imagined Samuel, sweating and well-dusted in his work apron, running a hard fingertip over the grain.

He rehung the lantern, pulled on his apron, and rolled up his sleeves. At some point, you just had to do what you could. Samuel would understand. He'd approve.

He went back to the lumber pile and picked out the best pieces. Things were beginning to take shape in his mind. He figured Samuel to be an inch or two short of six feet, but he'd make it a little long just to be sure. He had several sets of good brass hinges he'd saved for pie safes and desktops.

He whisked off the top of his work table, opened all the windows, and scotched the doors open. Outside, the crickets and cicadas were starting up. The grass and trees soughed. A draft cooled him, and for an instant he could imagine autumn.

CHAPTER 65

To his mild surprise, Samuel dozed on and off through most of the night. During wakeful spells, he mused that by this time tomorrow he would be hanged and several hours dead. At other times he refused to believe it. He felt more dread than fear. Mostly he was tired and sad and wanted it to be finished, although he knew that come tomorrow morning, his life would be dear to him. Sunrise would look very different than it ever had. He'd lived through his last sunset; his sadness in that knowledge settled in like a deep ache. Supper had been biscuits, bacon, and fried potatoes. He regretted now that he'd hardly tasted them.

He sat on his bench, leaning back against the wall. At times he drew in one leg or the other and held his knees with interlaced fingers. Across the way, the preachers, drunks, and thieves snored and groaned and scratched. Old Cato lay on his side, facing the wall; his lack of snoring or steady breathing made Samuel suspect he wasn't sleeping. Patrick paced.

During his first days in jail, Samuel had felt like an outsider, a semi-free tradesman among slaves. He'd not discussed his arrangement with Patrick and Cato, but they seemed to sense he'd lived differently. As time passed the difference melted. He was another innocent black man about to be executed, sacrificed to the white public's need for revenge and the town leaders' desire for order.

But for the past few hours, since supper, each man had kept to his own thoughts, save for an occasional meeting of the eyes, a shrug, arching of brows, acknowledgments of their shared fate.

Samuel guessed the time to be around four in the morning. He was awake for good now. His stomach began to flutter. He dreaded the crowds more than the noose. They'd be out, lining the streets, throwing horse turds and hedge apples. Moore's deputies would dutifully keep them alive for the hanging. Just because you were hanging three innocent men didn't mean you ought to give in to a mob. Leave legal murder to men of position. Here was a town of order, thrift, propriety, respectability.

A breeze stirred outside the narrow barred window. He rose and went to it, stood on his toes to look out. It was pitch black save for two lamps in the distance, along Jackson Street. He smelled dust, cedar, and summer grass, heard the rustle of parched elm and post oak leaves. He stood and breathed it in and regretted that he hadn't done so more often, instead of sitting and brooding in the stink of chamber pots and sour rock and drying wood and sweat.

Moore had told him Joseph was asking after him, pleading to see him, that Malachi and Ig had spoken in his favor at great risk to themselves. Of course they had. Since Joseph's release, Samuel had swung between resentment and sorrow for his friend. He imagined Joseph and Bekah sitting at the kitchen table. What could they say? Or would Joseph be seeking solace in the shop? Would they come tomorrow?

Bekah's touch. Now that was something to remember, to get a man to the end of his life. After the interrogation, her touch had been one of affection and respect and caring, nothing more. She loved him that way, the way she'd long loved David and might one day love Joseph. She'd tried to love him differently and had for a while. But someone had come back. He knew the very day.

A rooster crowed in the distance. His stomach churned. He breathed deeply, and the night smells calmed him. He felt a presence at his back. Patrick, a head taller than he, closed his eyes and drew a breath through his nostrils. "Smells awful good, don't it?"

Samuel nodded; his throat tightened. Patrick laughed and grabbed Samuel's shoulders and shook them, then slapped him on the back. "We don't have to put up with this much longer. Nawsir. Be done with this shit right off."

From his bench, still lying on his side, facing the wall, Cato said, "Y'all just wake me up come time. Be the latest I've slept since I was a baby."

"Let somebody else turn that damn wheel," Patrick said.

"Yessir."

Samuel could think of nothing he'd rather do than handle his tools and a fine piece of oak or cedar, watch the shavings or sawdust fall away as something fine took shape, and smell stains that brought the grains up so dark and fine you could feel them. He hoped his tools would be used. He doubted Joseph would be too sentimental about such things.

He turned to see Jonah Chambers leaning against the bars, studying him. Parson Newton sat on a bench against the wall. Their faces betrayed no sadness, only a knowing concern. Samuel nodded, said, "I be all right."

A hint of a smile came to Chambers's eyes. "Think on what you got done in this life. It'll stand you in good stead in the next one, I'll say."

There was movement outside the cell area. The front door opened. Probably Moore coming to work. Outside the window, southward, the sky was still dark, but Samuel felt the deep pink lining the eastern horizon. Two dogs barked. People were stirring. Most of the milking was done already.

The drunks and thief were up now, sitting and milling about the cell. Samuel caught only furtive, remorseful glances.

Voices outside. Cheerful, workaday. Jobs had to be done. Materials were being hauled to the square. But he felt something else. A gathering. People would be standing out in the street. He felt the press against the jail walls. Forty yards distant, through the window, he saw the flick of a match and the glow of pipes and cigars. Men watching the cell window.

The sky lightened. They paced.

A rattle of chains and the door opened. Moore came in, followed by his pale deputies carrying leg irons. There were no threats. The irons were passed between the bars. "Boys, put these on," he said.

Samuel closed the irons around his ankles, and the others did the same without protests or comment. He bent and gathered the wrist irons. They were cold, and he tasted the metal in the air.

Patrick said, "I'd like to empty out good before . . ."

Moore said, "Sure thing. Go ahead. Hell, let 'em wait. All of you might want to. You know . . ."

They finished up. The deputies opened the cell door and motioned for the prisoners to come out. Chambers and Newton, the drunks and thieves were silent, but all were standing, leaning against the bars.

They started toward the cellblock door, dragging their chains. Samuel's back still ached from Teddy's blows. He stooped under the weight of the chains. Jonah Chambers said, "Look right here. Look here." They stopped. The lawmen stood silent, uneasy. Chambers reached through the bars and slapped at the prisoners' backs and arms. "Can't nothing hurt you." He grabbed the back of Samuel's hand. Samuel felt the branding scar. "Go right on," he said. "Walk right on out there."

Ig was waiting for them just outside, leaning on his cane. People lined the streets, silent, watching. They wouldn't be quiet for long.

Ig said, "I'll walk with you."

The morning was still fresh, but already horses and people had churned dust and ash into the air. Samuel looked south, toward home and then north toward the Red River. Already, construction on the square blocked most of his view, but still he glimpsed grassy hills and cedar mottes.

The crowd pressed in, and Moore moved the prisoners close together and started them down Jackson Street toward Commerce. Samuel tried to straighten his back, but couldn't. Ig walked beside them, silent for once, struggling to keep up. The crowd began to murmur and then shout. Boys ran out to taunt them. Ig was talking now, but Samuel heard him no more than he heard the oaths and vulgarities of the people he'd walked among for the past fourteen years. Women were fanning themselves. Some looked shaken. Some looked on in disgust. The town leaders said these men were guilty, so they were.

The lawmen slowed to allow Ig to catch up. They turned on Commerce Street and headed for the river, down toward the sawmill where Samuel had picked up so many wagonloads of lumber.

Ig was saying something about Joseph, but Samuel couldn't make it out above the shouts of the townspeople. Something about Joseph not being there. Samuel looked at Ig and nodded. Of course Joseph wouldn't be there. He had work to do, and he'd be hard at it. A man could take comfort in that.

Father's Reminiscence
Transcribed August 2, 1911

The fire. Of course you want to know about that. The reason three innocent men were murdered. The reason your mother at last gave up on Dallas and accompanied Levin northward. The reason every Negro in Dallas County was rounded up and beaten to within a lick of death.

In the end it comes down to this: I would not abandon Levin McGregor again. He'd given an arm for your mother and me. I gave only a hand—you couldn't meld into the darkest, vilest pit in all of the South with an *A* branded on your palm. The loss was minor. No more serious than your mother's loss of two fingers. With practice, a hook serves about as well as a hand, better for certain tasks.

But the fire. Levin McGregor lay smothering, buried in a coffin. Time was short; the slave catcher and his hounds and the onlookers wouldn't leave the graveyard. I failed to consider that southwesterly wind. I should've set the fire on the northwest corner of the square, but I found Willis Peak's kindling box first, and no one paid me the slightest mind, though I feared for some time afterward that someone had seen me.

At times, I've told myself that I struck the match then kept my secret out of loyalty to a cause, or for your mother, or, at the worst times, to save my own hide. I've not had those arguments with myself for some years now.

I set a fire that condemned Samuel Smith, Patrick Jennings, and Cato Bryant to the noose in order to save Levin McGregor's life. Of course I couldn't foresee that outcome. But, had I foreseen it, would I have let Levin McGregor smother in a coffin?

I expect not.

AFTERWORD
Father's Reminiscence
Transcribed August 5, 1911

Anyone who knew Ig and Rachel Bodeker would be astonished that they made it to Kansas with an infant daughter before cold weather set in. Levin got them across the Red River. They were in Cincinnati shortly after Fort Sumter fell.

A few weeks before the secession vote, I quietly found a buyer for Joseph Shaw's place, and he slipped away by night. He barely looked at me when he came to my office for the required signatures. He never knew. The risk was too great for those who stayed behind. The fewer people who knew everything, the better. By early fall, he'd joined the Bodekers in Cincinnati. With funds from the sale of his house, he bought his way out of service in the Union Army. He was an abolitionist, not a soldier, and he vexed slave hunters along the Ohio River until the end of the war.

Brother Jonah Chambers made his way back to the North, where he received a commission and eventually served with occupation forces in Mississippi after the war. His humane nature kept him from enjoying the humiliation of his countrymen. He left the army at first opportunity and returned to the ministry in Iowa.

Zeph Newton worked in the thickets through the end of the war, then disappeared. There were murderous grudges in that country, and many of the deserters who hid out were nothing but criminals. I hope Brother Zeph slipped away to agitate under another name for another cause.

Dear Alan Huitt, beloved friend, so trusted by the townspeople, found employment with his former master and married well. His letters, written by his wife, and later by his oldest daughter, kept us informed of births and deaths. So faithful a servant was he that the Huitts buried him in their family's section of the cemetery.

The Nucholses, the Van Husses, the Meades. People who risked their lives for the cause. We've never heard from them. I last saw Malachi Meade walking along Water Street a few days after the hangings.

Who would've imagined that old Ig Bodeker would have outlived his Rachel by six years, and Joseph by two? The Bodekers' daughter—Bekah Jo, they called her—still lives in Cincinnati. Al reported in one of his letters that she's said to be the mirror image of her mother. She must have been a comfort to the men after Rachel died, and especially to Ig after Joseph slumped over in his workshop.

I wish you could have seen your mother's face when I rode into Joseph's yard that night with Ben Thigpen, the slave catcher, and all those dogs. The only time I ever saw her at a loss. Those years apart, when I had no hope of seeing her again, I tried to remember her face. Then, under the direst of circumstances, with no idea that the dogs were tracking Levin, I could barely keep from laughing at her expression. Yet I prayed that she wouldn't startle and give me—*us*—away. I shouldn't have worried.

The clever false trails and the hiding place beneath the workshop floor didn't save Levin, for he wouldn't have been taken. They saved old Thigpen's life. In those days, I kept unsavory company and worked my way into grim predicaments to keep Levin and the parsons appraised.

After she left Dallas, your mother served in the thickets for a spell, but when war broke out, Levin brought her here. You've long known this. I add it for completeness. Levin reclaimed his name, though I'm certain his spirit haunted the woods and back roads of North Texas until the end of the war.

I had planned to stay in Dallas until Al felt he'd done all he could and was ready to head north, but he declined to go, and the tide of the war shifted so that even a man with a hook for a hand began to look like a conscript.

Like Joseph Shaw, I hated slavery, not my own people. I would not wage war against them nor participate in their humiliation. I wanted to free slaves. Had the Confederacy prevailed, I would have returned to Texas.

I left it to Colonel Higginson and other vindictive Northern puritans, who never saw the inside of a prison or thicket, to burn through the South with Negro soldiers who wouldn't be staying among white Southerners with long memories and a retributive honor code.

I fear another two generations could pass before the hatred dies.

About the Author

Henry Chappell is the author of two novels, *Blood Kin* and *The Callings* (TTUP, 2002 and 2004), four non-fiction books, and dozens of articles. He lives with his family in Parker, Texas. www.byhenrychappell.com